Dante's War

SANDRA SABATINI

Dante's War

A NOVEL

KEY PORTER BOOKS

Copyright © 2009 by Sandra Sabatini

All rights reserved. No part of this work covered by the copyrights hereon may be reproduced or used in any form or by any means—graphic, electronic or mechanical, including photocopying, recording, taping or information storage and retrieval systems—without the prior written permission of the publisher, or, in case of photocopying or other reprographic copying, a licence from Access Copyright, the Canadian Copyright Licensing Agency, One Yonge Street, Suite 1900, Toronto, Ontario, M6B 3A9.

Library and Archives Canada Cataloguing in Publication

Sabatini, Sandra, 1959-
 Dante's war / Sandra Sabatini.

ISBN 978-1-55470-113-1

 I. Title.
PS8587.A2117D62 2009   C813'.6   C2008-906677-4

The publisher gratefully acknowledges the support of the Canada Council for the Arts and the Ontario Arts Council for its publishing program. We acknowledge the support of the Government of Ontario through the Ontario Media Development Corporation's Ontario Book Initiative.

We acknowledge the financial support of the Government of Canada through the Book Publishing Industry Development Program (BPIDP) for our publishing activities.

Key Porter Books Limited
Six Adelaide Street East, Tenth Floor
Toronto, Ontario
Canada M5C 1H6

www.keyporter.com

Text design and electronic formatting: Martin Gould

Printed and bound in Canada

09 10 11 12 13 5 4 3 2 1

For Bruno

Prologue

Dante De Angelis coped with the streams of sand snaking across the desert road the way he coped with hairpin turns in the ancient streets of Spoleto. He pressed his foot on the accelerator and steered the rattling truck into the skid until the thin rubber found the road. He was driving the colonel's booty away from El Alamein as fast as he could to meet the western retreat. He was driving along the Via Balbia laid by Il Duce's hard-working infantry to facilitate the transport of supplies to his army and air force. Dante had to keep the windshield down to avoid any reflection of the sun that might pinpoint his position to the Allies and bombers. His goggles caked with fine silt sand. He could not keep them clear of the thick layer of desert collecting in front of his eyes, and he had to slow down every few hundred metres and steer blindly until he could scrape off enough sand to see the road in front of him. Stopping the truck altogether was too risky. It might not start again or the heat from the ground might blow what was left of the rubber on the tires if he stopped for too long.

The wind had finally died down so that the sand for once lay barely waving, almost still. The road was clear and the evening was fine. The six-tonner, nursed along since it came off the ship at Tunis, was holding together though the tires were bald and patched. It was nearly at its maximum speed of forty-five kilometres an hour with, for once, all five cylinders firing. Nothing short of miraculous. Dante kept his eyes focused in front of him. The sun was setting behind him and he would have to make camp.

To the south, he could see smoke rising from behind a hill of sand. In the pink early evening, it was difficult to see at first, difficult to distinguish between the sand and the sky, but the smoke was black and rising in the stillness. Dante pulled carefully off to the road's edge as though he were parking on a busy street in Rome waiting to meet *la bella* Angelina. He sat for a minute watching the horizon before he opened the door. He knew he was not in Rome. There was no mirage. When he first arrived in the desert, under the influence of fatigue and thirst, he had seen the light bend before his eyes and produce sights of wonder. He had drunk his water ration too hastily and pissed it away. He had marched without a helmet against orders in order to try to catch some kind of breeze. In the high heat he believed he could see fresh water flowing and fronds of palms beckoning like dancing girls toward a stream, the splash of which it seemed his own ears could hear. He had seen such phantom cities rise in stippled layers above the sand, in rich colours with all the sounds of a thriving market town.

But this was no mirage. Only smoke rising behind a hill. He got out of the truck.

The hill, like everything else in this damned wilderness, was further away than it seemed and his boots were filling again with the everlasting sand. He walked and walked and cursed himself for the fool that he was, but if one of their boys was in trouble, he could not drive past the possibility. One of their boys, one of the Signor Churchill's boys. What difference did it make? He could not move past the wounded. It might cost him his own life. He was worried about getting lost. He looked ahead of him to sand that was shifting like a sea, a landscape in motion and never still. He would need a compass always with him to navigate here. There were no landmarks, no real land. In the expanse before him, he could not fathom what it was that any of them sought to conquer. He looked back over his shoulder toward his truck and forward to the diesel smoke.

When he crested the hill, he saw the RAF insignia on the charred back end of the Spitfire. The plane was broken in half against the desert with a black and broken man at the fulcrum. His torso spilled onto the sand and Dante could see, when he got close, that the pilot's legs must be crushed under the upturned nose of the fighter.

He stopped, dropped his head. Another enemy defeated.

He had spent months, years, putting planes in the air, keeping them there. Planes whose purpose was to accomplish just this: a smoking rival aircraft; a broken burnt man.

"It was a bad idea, you see. Defying reason and instinct, and here is the proof—as if you needed more."

He crossed himself in the presence of the awesome dead. He stood silently in the silent evening.

The pilot moaned.

He moaned and moved.

Enough time had passed, time like light, illuminating all that came behind, but to utter useless effect. Dante had come to war, he had met Angelina whose shape wooed him as much as her calmness had done. He wished only to see her again. He wished to claim and reclaim the territory of her skin, to see himself in the wide regard of her grey-green eyes. He spent every day looking back or trying not to look back, tamping down his longing, banking it as a man might a smokeless fire in the desert, trying not to give away his position. As though he himself had no body, not one capable of bliss. Enough time had passed for Dante to understand where he was and how he had got there, but the future was brilliant black. A hole, into which he could see nothing, imagine nothing, least of all his own escape from this waste. His release into green love and desire fulfilled. And now this boy.

"So, you see, you get out of your truck and find that the situation here is even worse than you thought."

He wished to stop wasting air, to stop speaking to himself. He thought the heat was finally ruining him. He had a headache.

"Here is the situation. Soon the sun will drop behind the far ridge of sand and you will be here with your nearly dead enemy in the black darkness because your feet will not carry you away."

He paused as though he were listening to himself and preparing in his mind a counter claim.

"*Si, capito.* I understand, but I cannot leave this dying man alone."

"You know how cold it gets in these nights. If the wind picks up, the sand will hit you."

"Yes, stinging and cruel. It will remind me of my father."

"This plane crashed and this boy should have died. Quickly. Instantly. It is not your fault, nor your responsibility. In fact, he is your enemy. It is your duty to make sure he dies."

Dante was at least sensible enough to know he could not win an argument against himself. He walked around the plane. How could the pilot have survived? Dante moved closer to the smoking fuselage, worried that the fellow might have enough life to reach for his pistol. But when he saw what was left of the man's hands, he knew he was safe.

"*Signor?*"

He bent down and touched the pilot's arm.

"*Signor?*"

The pilot's lips moved before his eyes did. Dante bent closer. The pilot was whispering. The smell of burnt and burning skin, of burning diesel, oily and thick, slid up Dante's nose. He kept swallowing, gulping against his own gag reflex. He bent nearer and looked in the pilot's eyes. He was young, this man. Perhaps even younger than poor Marseille, who had flown so fast and high.

"*Non parlo inglese.*" I do not speak English.

The boy said, "Please. Please." He said, "Please, are you an angel?"

"*Sono italiano.*" Dante pointed to the insignia on his own uniform. I am your enemy.

The young man smiled. He smiled and his lips cracked and bled. The skin on his cheeks cracked. "I am not dead."

Dante concentrated, looked for clues in the sounds of the foreign words.

The boy could not bring his hands together. He could not gesture. He looked at the sky.

He said, "*Deo*."

"*Deo*."

The dying warmth of the sand was suddenly burning through the thin leather of Dante's soles, as though hell itself were seeking escape, a breath of fresh air. The pilot tried to move his arm toward Dante, now on his knees beside the wreckage. Dante took his canteen from his neck and moved to lift the boy's head. To put his hand on the young man, even to offer assistance, took some deep breaths. He lifted him and tilted some drops of water onto his lips.

"Gently, fellow. Take your time."

He laid him down against the skeleton of the plane.

Dante scanned the horizon. To the east, his friend Marseille had smashed into the desert. To the northwest, his friend Sabino was buried in a grave that Dante himself had dug, unmarked but not unmourned. Dante himself, like a ghost awkward on the earth, thin and dried up, a man without a shadow under the arcing sun.

This boy beside him would join Dante's friends in oblivion soon, if Dante were any judge of breaths and their last measures.

Dante put his hands on the top of the boy's head where there was no blood and no scorched flesh. He was so close to his enemy. Dante had served in the Regia Aeronautica with pride because it was the best air force in the world. In the Royal Italian Air Force since before the beginning of the war, he had put his hand to whatever job was required. He fixed the planes, he had flown them, had dropped bombs, listening to the navigator, factoring the coordinates, concentrating on the moment of push and pull, a strictly clean, mathematical moment, exact and composed of quadrants and degrees, sine and cosine. He had seen structures far below him disappear in fire and smoke and felt pleased with the accuracy of his work. Until El Alamein, he had never had to see effect after cause. He had almost never been in proximity to the viscera of the dead and nearly dead with their voices in his ears. Even Marseille when he died was still beautiful. *Corpus intactus.*

Dante could not turn his eyes from the boy. He understood, of course, the request. *Deo.* He understood what the boy asked of him. He ran his finger through the sand, drawing parallel lines. Hesitating.

Dante finally crossed himself again and said on bent knee the Our Father.

> *Pater noster qui es in caelis,*
> *sanctificetur nomen tuum;*
> *adveniat regnum tuum,*
> *fiat voluntas tua,*
> *sicut in caelo et in terra*

Hallowed be Thy name.

Thy kingdom come, Thy will be done on Earth, as it is in heaven.

The boy breathed deeply and a strong smell of diesel came off his breath. His face seemed smooth. Beneath the black skin, Dante suspected that he was too young for whiskers, that he most probably had that British red complexion, the isosceles red imprints of boys who kick footballs around outside in cold, damp weather for hours at a time. Dante probably had several years on this fellow, who must have been a precocious student to get into a fighter plane at such a young age. He must have been an excellent pilot to bring a burning plane to the sand without exploding it. An unfortunate excellence, Dante thought. There would be no pyramid raised in the desert for this boy to mark his life. He would only return to dust.

He said, as one would to a visiting child, slowly, "*Io sono Dante.*" He put his hand on his chest. Every movement, slow. "Dante," he said again, and then he touched the boy's shoulder softly and nodded. "*Dante, é?*"

"George."

"*Ah,* Giorgio, *si. Buona sera,* Giorgio. *Comé va?*"

A stupid question. It was clear how things were going for Giorgio. Crystal clear. He was afraid that *povero* Giorgio might attempt another terrible smile. He kept his hand on the uncomplaining pilot, a man he and his gunner would have cheerfully shot down out of the sky, as someone had clearly done. He thought how one of his comrades would have kept this score, notched his wing beneath the sign of the green mice, the Sorci Verde squadron.

Direct hit.

Dante's enemy was dying and he himself was so thirsty. He said the Our Father instead of the prayer he wanted to say, which was nothing more than *God, God damn you*. How did he come to this place? And how was he going to get out?

Beside the broken young man, Dante kneeled as he had not done since he was a child. As he bent to the earth, he saw the drops in the sand. He thought oil must be leaking behind the boy's helmet, then finally, stupidly, he saw the clean wet tracks down the sides of the boy's face, and he understood.

Dangerous. Foolish to cry in the desert. Water as precious as air here. But the pilot would presently need neither. Perhaps Dante himself would soon join the hosts of the dead, of friends and enemies excised from the memory of the earth, the gold braid of their uniforms left to rust in the desert.

The boy whispered, broken lips moving. Dante leaned close to hear.

"Thank you."

They were very far from home, both he and his dying companion. He had come such a long way to be thanked by his adversary. Dante waited with the pilot as the space between breaths grew longer. He waited in the chilling air until the boy died. Dante lay down in the ground beside him, coughing in sand, with no tears to offer to the dust.

Dante

His mother, Maria Pia, used to tell him the story of his birth, as though he were an exceptional baby born for a certain purpose. How she dropped the clay bowl on the floor that afternoon and had to bend over the kitchen chair.

"Those pains," she said, "they came no matter what. I lay down, I stood up. I bit your father's good Sunday belt. You were coming, my Dante, and with some fury."

She tickled him as she spoke, as though to show him that she did not mind. Whatever pain she endured had given her this baby boy.

She took his child's hand.

"Here," she said, "just a small tight circle of pain."

She circled his hand in the air in front of her middle.

"This is the pain getting bigger and bigger and still you kicked out with your heels and pressed against the sides of me as though you were not sure of the way out! I would have laughed, honestly, if I could have."

"Here, in Spoleto. Not Rome, where there might have been a doctor, but on this back street in the old city. That old midwife and my mother-in-law, your *nonna*, worse than useless. They wanted to get the priest. They thought I was screaming at the devil, sending him back to hell. But it was only you. Listen, Dante. There are times when a woman has to scream. Do not try to stop her. Eleven pounds! Dante, a calf that size would keep us in meat for the winter!"

Dante did not enjoy this story. He twisted in his mother's embrace. He did not like to think of having been the cause of so much pain. He especially did not like to be compared to a calf.

When he got older, his mother, told him, "I thought I would die, of course. Like my sister, like my aunt, trying to make myself big enough to have you, bigger than the pain. You should thank me, my son, every day. I kept repeating to myself, *va bene, va bene*. It will be all right. And it was. It is. *Guarda!*

"This is what I did. When you were coming and the pain was bad, I pretended to be in my mother's kitchen looking out into the garden. I was not in pain. I was a girl washing dishes in a sink as old as Michelangelo's mother, waiting to be invited by my friends to play outside. I could see the sun on the path in high summer, drawing out the blooms until they blushed and fell and the branches made fruit. Fragrance and bees. This is what you do, my Dante, when it hurts, when you are in trouble with your father. Listen as you can and then look out the window. Listen for the bees. See the dew. The pain will fade, I promise."

She told him it had been a beautiful day. He knew it had taken his mother weeks to recover and that he would have neither brothers nor any silly sisters because of his difficult birth. He would be her only child, her only son.

"The women, they held you, cleaned you up a little and rocked you, but still you waved your fists at all of us.

"Your *nonna* said, 'He is a fighter already, Maria Pia.' *Allora, piccolino*, are you ready to take on the world?"

His mother looked out the window toward the city hall where his father worked.

"A fighter, you would need to be, *mio figlio*."

Then she would snatch him against her at this story of his birth, of her lonely day, which prickled her eyes every time she thought of it.

Dante came into breath with clenched fists, in a fury, as though he knew Giuseppe was waiting for him. Giuseppe and all the others against whom, as a young man, he would lift his fists in rage.

For his mother the story was nothing short of miraculous. From his earliest days, Dante remembered his skin coloured, patched by bruises. Tender spots of amber, indigo, and puce. He climbed on chairs and low walls, pushing stools over to tables to climb onto counters and shelves. He fell often. He learned not to cry. His patient mother would pick him up and soothe him with a soft song about the *piccola testa dura*, the little hard head, who rammed his way, head first, into places he did not belong. As he became calm, the song began to involve bouncing and tickling and Dante would forget the harm of climbing and be driven only by the thrilling necessity to get higher and farther, as high as he could once his father, whose large hands sometimes knocked him down, had gone to work.

Some bruises looked as though storm clouds had marked his body. Not all of them came from falling on the floor from height. As his legs strengthened and his curiosity grew, he moved away from the kitchen. He found his way to the tunnels below the house, built in the days when the house itself was a cloister and the hidden passageways permitted the nuns and monks to meet in secret. He prowled the tunnels out of sight of his mother and father. He learned not to mind the closeness of the space. It was only dank and dim. He made himself stay where he was, feeling his way in places where the light did not penetrate. His eyes would discern enough of the wall and the floor to navigate the turns to the places in the corridors where the few bulbs cast a sad light in the murk. There were no monsters of any kind and the tunnels themselves were good hiding places on the days when his father came home from work angry about papers on his desk and conversations on his telephone or in his office, things that Dante could not understand, but that usually resulted in a beating for him. If he could get away from the sound of his father's voice, from the smack of his hands, Dante did. There were enough passageways to keep him busy in the evening and often out of harm's way.

Years later, when Dante curled into foxholes, laughable dents in the ground meant to conceal a grown man from harm, when he fought with men and against men from all the wide world, he would close his eyes and imagine a homecoming, perhaps driving along the turning road to Spoleto, seeing its ancient walls and towers, brown and strong straight lines against the curves and green trees of the city. He would see the gardens there with pink flowers and red tomatoes, with tall beans growing sweet in the drenching sun. With his greatcoat pulled tight around him and curled in his hole against the chill of the desert, Dante would sometimes take himself again to Sabino's garden door or to the hermit's cave. He would recite the names of the streets whispering against the wind. Slipping easily out of his memory and conjuring themselves in the African desert before him. The streets of his home made a place for him, a firm place to which he might anchor himself as they had never done when he walked them every day. If he could take Angelina there. If he could live long enough and get out of the war with a complete skin, he would take her there. He would be fastened, secured to some earth. He would drive a car, heading out from Rome along the via Flaminia, passing Magliano and Otricoli, Narni and Terni.

That drive is not long past the aqueducts and bridges, across streams of cool water where the stones are broad and smooth. He imagined showing Angelina, Angelina in a car beside him, her calm gaze taking in everything.

Our house is there, on the edge of the ancient town, still within the medieval walls, strong and old. That thick wood of the door was hand-carved and it has stood firm for generations. Thick walls kept the rooms cool in the hot dry summers and the small casement windows looked out onto a town you could hardly believe you were seeing with your own eyes.

He would take them both home in his mind. He imagined her beside him and himself replete. In the trenches, such thoughts could only do for so long. The stones in his boots, the sand in his mouth, the weakness in every joint and muscle forced him to pay careful attention to the present.

But there were some events he would not revisit. He had never spoken to her of his father.

When he was four, he took two pears from the tree in the garden. He took them before supper, dragging out a chair and climbing on it, balancing on the chair-back as it leaned against the trunk. He reached and grabbed the pinkest fruit he could claim. Biting into it, juice running and eyes closed, he did not see his father come into the garden. He did not realize that Giuseppe was home from work. He heard the belt buckle just before the slap across his shoulders.

Dante choked on the fruit.

"Where do you think you are? What are you doing?"

His father's rage was, as usual, huge. He was fast with that belt. It scalded Dante's short legs and streaked his back before he could get away, retching and breathless to the other side of the tree.

"Your mother is in the house cooking the supper and here you are taking food as if you were a prince and not an ungrateful boy! Get out of my sight and don't let me catch you stealing pears again."

He walked away, threading leather through loops and dusting off his hands.

Dante looked up. The tree was bending with fruit. Bending branches made the pickings easy for a small boy, even though he might need a chair. Dante ran to the subterranean passageways of the house and pushed his aching hot back against the cold stone of the wall until he could stop crying.

When he went in for supper, his father, as a form of punishment, told him again about the bridge and the fortress. He said if Dante continued to be a bad boy, he might find himself thrown over the bridge with no one to save him, just like the poor woman. Dante might cover his ears, but nothing would prevent his father from telling the story again.

"The bridge runs between the people and the fortress. The Ponte delle Torri. The man was once so angry with his wife that he dragged her out to the middle by the hair, in full view of the inmates in the fortress. She was screaming and crying and begging for her life and the inmates were banging their tin cups against the bars and crying out for the guards to help. She was spitting blood in her fear, tearing at her own throat with her fingernails, begging for her life.

She loved him; she was the mother of his sons. He was crazy to think she would go with anyone else.

"'Do not be crazy,' she implored him.

"Can you imagine, Dante? That woman begging for her life?"

Dante would move the pasta around on his plate. It was a terrible story. He had to listen to it though he had heard it before. Perhaps this time his father would change it so the woman would be saved. He had to listen, but he could not eat. If he put one more bite in his mouth, he would vomit. He could feel the burning tickle in his throat.

"Probably that was the wrong thing to say. That man, he punched her in the face with a closed fist so that her teeth rattled on the stone of the Roman bridge and he picked her up off the ground and hauled her to the edge. I have seen those teeth myself. Her mother embedded them in the stone with a little concrete. I'll take you and show you. The inmates, doomed and hardened men, shouted to the guards about the lunatic on the bridge and the poor, poor woman bleeding and crying, her feet and legs planted like a mule, but too weak to prevent anything while the man dragged her and punched her, not resisting, not holding up her hands which he had crushed, both in one fist so he could hold her and drag her and still punch her, this man who was short and strong, this husband. He was screaming obscene and terrible accusations so that she no doubt would have crossed herself if she'd had a free hand to do it; she would have said a quick prayer for her husband's damned soul. But he was screaming and gathering his strength to lift her and throw her through the circle cut into the wall of the bridge right into the sky. Her dress, caught by the wind, flipped over her head and muffled her last crying words as she spiralled through three hundred feet of space, shocked into silence by the rocks below."

Giuseppe would strike the table for effect, jarring the crockery so that it banged and cracked, *fortissimo,* against the ears. If Dante cried, his father would laugh, satisfied that the story's lesson had been understood. He seemed to think that if Dante were frightened enough, he would surely behave. If Dante did not cry, his father would offer details on the viscera and brain matter that the searching men of Spoleto found when they climbed down the gorge to retrieve something worth burying. He talked until he got what he wanted.

Finally, Dante's head would bend as though he could hide the tears his father sought. His head bent to the table and his neck ached. One day, he thought, I will lift my head and I will not bend it any more. The wrath inside him, small as he was, flared. For now, Dante kept his head down so as not to let his large father see his red face.

Why did his mother not help him? To his child's eyes, she looked as large to him as his father did, but she stayed quiet and only folded her arms across her burdened chest.

The sudden, inexplicable misery, the injustice both of the actions of the man and the insistence of Dante's father that he listen to every detail again and again, disturbed his childhood dreams.

"Listen, Dante. That bridge is a thousand feet long and I am telling you, it is a marvel of line and design. Only we could have built it."

"Did you build it, Papa?"

"Only the Italians, do you hear? Engineers of brilliance. Artists and artisans. Look at it next time. It's been there since the fourteenth century, for God's sake. You can walk across, even a baby like you, and be safe. You can see the whole river valley. I used to take your mother there."

This news frightened Dante. There was a woman in the story whose mean husband threw her over the edge. Dante looked at Maria Pia, imagined her pale flowered dress flying up over her face. He looked away.

"You can look through the circle and see the entire vista to the north that spreads the gem of central Italy before you. You are lucky to be born here. You see the green and the hills stretching in one direction and the town in another. You take visitors there and then you can tell them the terrible story of the jealous husband and the desperate wife and the minutes that the prisoners in the fortress above the bridge spent hollering themselves hoarse trying to draw the guards' attention and aid to the woman below and finally succeeding, but too late. The small uniformed figures arriving only in time to see the skirt fly up over the woman's face as she turned in the air below the bridge."

Giuseppe filled his mouth with the steaming chicken.

"Only the Italians," he said again through the meat in his mouth.

In rare better moods, Dante's father would compel him to listen again to the illustrious history of the bridge.

"Listen, boy, and learn something for once."

Dante's father would recite, as though from a textbook of local history. Across the Tessino gorge, toward the mountains of Castelmonte, the Ponte delle Torri stretches between the hermit's cave and the town below. There is a walkway along the south side that has conveyed water and supplies from Monteluco to Spoleto. It has conveyed Popes, most notably Julius II and Nicholas V. Even Pius II. It has conveyed some members of the Medici family, the Barbarossas and Borgias. The Aldobandinis and the Viscontis, to and from the Rocca embedded in the hill. This bridge you see right outside the window. And the fortress, look at it, boy. Those sheer walls have protected the privileged for almost seven hundred years. The walls are cold, thick, and tall, protecting the first and second courtyard behind arched passages with patchy frescoes still evident in the stone. I will take you to see the frescoes. You can see Spoleto with the long stretch of the Ponte in the picture. You can see Orvieto and Perugia.

"What year was it built, Dante? Come on. You should know by now."

To remember and answer correctly his father's question would keep his father's mood pleasant. But at first, he could not recall. His father would raise his hand, ready to rattle the boy's feeble brain and bring the year, 1362, to utterance. Only a few ringing slaps in his young life and he never forgot again.

"Matteo Gattaponi finished it in 1362."

Dante looked out the window across the table. This one opened on the valley, on his father's vines, on the streets below. The bitter green leaves of the garden curled against the cool evening air and Dante imagined he could smell them and could curl himself, too, against his father's anger.

Dante kept clear of the fortress. It was nothing to him. Not beautiful. Not interesting. Just a place for bad men that his mother had warned him about. A prison for political dissidents, whatever they were, would-be assassins. It was in his backyard, looming, and if he crossed the bridge at all, it was to see the hermit for whom he would leave gifts of his mother's *pannettone*. He preferred the bridge, which for him was a way out of Spoleto, into the forest and around the mountain. The *ponte* was frightening to him, but he made himself step out, so squeamish at first and then finally, with Sabino beside him, more confident. It was square, like his father. All Roman straightness supported by arches that stretched down to the valley below, symmetrical and precise. It was cold to look at, but warm and rough to cross. Close up, he knew, the lines were less than perfect and the stone, its crumbled surface, was still so solid beneath the imperfections. There was a rail and a steep drop to the river almost two hundred and fifty feet below. In his dreams as a child, Dante was blind and falling. He walked close against the wall, to and from the caves and he did not listen to the convicts shouting at him and blowing him kisses from the windows far above and behind him in the fortress.

Down the street from the amphitheatre and around the corner from the fortress and the giant bridge, Dante ran with a stick that struck and bounced off what was left of the medieval walls. He ran through the streets as though something was chasing him. He ran until the Spanish flu caught up with him. All around their house, the doctors were marking the doors. He had heard his parents speaking low and late at night, as though by whispering they might avoid notice, the disease might pass over them.

Dante was in his room when his mother came home from the church. She had gone to light candles, to ask the saints for protection. He heard her ask his father, "What is this new curse?"

His father was displeased about the candles. The superstition of it. He had told her before that he was a man of standing in the Fascist Party whose wife ought not to spend so much time in the church. "It is not a curse. There is nothing supernatural about it. It is an infection, an influenza and it is spreading like a common cold."

Dante's mother did not understand.

"It passes from person to person. It's coming from the war. The soldiers got it in the Great War and then they went home and took it as a little gift of death with them wherever they stopped. No more visitors, Maria Pia. Keep the doors and windows closed. We will be all right."

Dante closed the heavy wooden shutters on his window.

The next day, he sat in the grass behind the kitchen, digging with a spoon he had stolen when his mother was not looking. He could smell the pears, sweet on the breeze. At first, he thought he could probably get away with pinching a couple of them before his father, with his thick leather belt, got home from work. He looked at the tree and it seemed to look back. Leaves turning to look at him. The branches bending to encompass him. The sweet fragrance grew heavier until it seemed he would choke on it. The back of his neck prickled, hot and cold.

His mother turned to him when he said, "I closed my window, but I think something came in."

He leaned left, dropped the spoon as his head hit the ground.

The fever burned through his body. He was so hot that the skin inside his mouth seemed to be boiling. Hot, wet, and dry, all at once. His mother changed sheets as the flu forced the fluids from his body. The fabric seared his skin. His eyes closed hot and when they opened, he felt the weight of something on him. His mother was keeping cool cloths on his face, neck, and groin. The weight he felt was the weight of her own body as she laid herself on him to keep him still when the seizures took him. He felt his head lift—his mother's hand behind his head—and water, undrinkable, dank and scorching cold, slipped across his lips and down the side of his neck. The doctor came and washed his hands, splashing at Dante's bedside. The water hit Dante's body and hurt him. Dante saw the doctor shake out a pressed towel and dry his hands, first one hand, all the fingers and in between, and then the other, with the formality of the priest when he holds the Host. The doctor lifted his wrist, plump pink hands pressed on his pulse. He shook his head.

Do not shake your head, Dante wished to say. Do not shake your head.

The doctor's brows pulled together and met across the centre of his nose. Dante saw his mother cover her mouth.

Do they think I am not alive?

The doctor looked at his watch.

"Prepare for the worst," he said.

Dante's hands became pale, cold, and still. Maria Pia stroked them, would not stay out of the room though the doctor had quarantined him, as well as the whole house, now quiet and dark and only ever soup cooking on the woodstove that Giuseppe must have served himself while Dante's mother stayed with him. Dante only knew some of this. If he opened his eyes, she was there and smiling. He thought things must not be too bad.

He wondered where his father was. Perhaps he had already died of the influenza. Perhaps Dante would get better and he and his mother would be dutifully clad in bright black. Dante looked to the doorway of his room. His eyes were hot, but it seemed to him that he saw his father standing on the threshold with a plate of peeled pears, as if Dante could eat. That Giuseppe was speaking, asking for forgiveness from God and from his own son. Dante wished to say something, but his voice would not work. He was dreaming, he thought. The bruises from the last beating faded during the course of his fever.

The doctor told his parents that Dante would die. He was four years old and would remain both thin and hungry the rest of his life. Nevertheless, he did not die.

When the fever left him and he was able to sit up, his father put Dante on his lap, pressed him into the angle of his own strong arm, and spooned thin broth into Dante's mouth.

Giuseppe said, "No one knows why you are alive, my son. Maybe it was the candles. I shall say nothing more about them, whatever the Party thinks."

Maria Pia cried whenever she looked at him.

"*Poverino*, look at you."

Her tears made Dante anxious. He felt all right. His skin was not aching. He was hungry and yet unable to eat. He did not look in a glass. He did not see his own thin body or his own hollow eyes. He did not know himself to be an armful of bones no matter how much *gnocchi* she scooped into his open mouth. He just kept eating until he could stand on his own feet.

He woke up one morning, thinking he could smell bacon. When he went downstairs, there were new books on the table beside his breakfast and a shirt and tie ready for him.

"You go to school today, my son."

His mother turned back to the stove with her hand over her mouth.

One day, Dante thought, I will ask her why she is always crying.

"I thought I had to be five years old."

"Your father says you are ready."

For once, his mean papa was right.

"I will come with you."

He wished his mother would dry her tears.

"I know the way."

He did not want a weeping woman taking him to school in front of all the other boys, perhaps kissing him or rubbing his cheek.

"I know the way," he said once more.

He could not wait. He pushed his legs into new short pants and tucked in his shirt. He smoothed his hair and pulled up his socks. He knew the way and he would go to school. He could not wait.

In his hurry, Dante tripped and fell to his knees on the stone path to the main street. He would not cry on his first day of school. He would not run home. He sat on the ground looking at his leg and then looking around him for something he could use to patch himself up. He would tie some leaves against the cut, or put some good dirt on it to stop the bleeding.

"You need help?"

A boy stood beside him unfolding a handkerchief.

"Are you going to the school?"

"This is my first day."

"You are bleeding."

Dante looked at the boy. He was as round and squat as Dante was lean. Even his head was round.

"Who are you?"

"Sabino. You are Dante. I've seen you before. I live over there." He pointed to a house up the hill from Dante's

"We are going to be late maybe."

"No, we will not be late. We are almost there."

"I am bigger than you." Dante wondered if he would have to fight this boy, who was not so big as his father. He thought he could knock him down.

"Taller, maybe."

"That's bigger."

"Bigger goes both ways." Sabino stood straight and showed his wingspan.

"You look like a vulture."

"*Grazie, amico.*"

Sabino stood before him undisturbed. Perhaps Dante would not knock the boy down yet.

Dante took his shoelace out and tied the makeshift bandage around his leg.

"*Grazie,*" he said.

"*Andiamo.*" The boys moved down the street with their arms across each other's shoulders.

Signora Cannone, the teacher, was a monumental lady whose husband had succumbed to the Spanish flu and who, as a result, turned herself into a punctuation mark, a woman who clothed herself in black, dress, stockings, and even her apron, sharp black in the green garden where the class was held in nice weather.

Dante stared at her while she spoke in her gentle voice. He listened to the stories she made up about the letters of the alphabet to help the students remember the sequence. He learned to write his name on the slate in his lap. He left his house early in the morning by the side door used long ago by the nuns. He threaded his way through the passages of the narrow streets along the ancient wall, past the large stones that Sabino told him were laid in place by giants who had only one eye each, the former inhabitants of Spoleto. There were dark doorways to pass, and old, bent women whose noses curled to meet their chins, sweeping steps with palsied hands. He and Sabino walked together, one tall, one short. Once Dante could see the black-clad Signora, he felt safe. From everything.

Angelina

It seemed to Angelina that parents loved to tell children the stories of their birth. In the church, she heard the story of Moses, whose mother passed on the details of his miraculous birth and rescue. And Mother Mary, of course, must have, from the safety of Egypt, told Jesus stories he might have found difficult to believe about shepherds conversing with angels, blind prophets and quickened wombs and wise men coming with a little nest egg to see them through the lean years in Cairo. Mothers tell their children how they came to be, Angelina thought. She had heard enough of these stories around the kitchen tables and the washing well in San Placido. As though one's means of arrival might foreshadow one's way of being in the world. Angelina's parents were not different. She knew she came peacefully into a world in which she lived peacefully through days and nights. She came easily, Graziela told her.

"I had been feeling this, *io non so*, I don't know, a tickling, in rhythm, a sudden clamp all around my middle that made me giggle as I did at my own confirmation and I could not hold the laughter in. Oh, my mamma was so angry with me. But there you were. You were coming and all I could do was laugh.

"I wondered if your papa would be back early."

She told Angelina about the long afternoon, the sun stretching across the kitchen window, how the clamp grew firmer and then suddenly urgent. Her mother had time only to call for the next-door neighbour. Graziela did not make the climb up the stairs to her bed before Angelina's head was crowning. Ever practical, she stopped where she was. She reached for a tablecloth and spread it as best she could beneath her. Angelina eased her way into air with the Signora Pambianco to catch her and wrap her in a blanket that the woman had had the foresight to snatch from the back of her own chair. The baby Angelina mewed and stretched, fastened on to Graziela's breast and was peaceful. The women laughed together in the middle of the afternoon.

"Signora Pambianco said, 'Now, Graziela, *come va?*'

"And I said, '*Molto bene*, Gisele.'

"Gisele said, 'I have never seen or heard of a baby coming like that, Graziela. Look at her, already calm, already feeding. She will indeed lead a blessed life. *Que bella bambina.*'

"I did not like such talk with a baby only a handful of breaths into her measured life, into her mother's arms. Perhaps the angels would take you away. Perhaps you were too peaceful for this earth.

"But Gisele thought I was ridiculous. I saw her frown.

"She said, 'Listen, Graziela, *senti*, the angels will not steal this one for heaven. Do not fill your mind with such worries. Never mind how I know what you are thinking. You forget, I grew up with your mother. I know the things she used to say. She is a beautiful baby with a peaceful soul. Already you can see that. You just rest and enjoy that little one.'

"So, Signora Pambianco stroked my hair and my cheek and helped me to bed. Then she sent her grandson to get your papa and tell him that there was a very important package waiting for him."

She was named Angelina, perhaps in deference to those angels, hungry for beauty, so that they did not take her to heaven too soon. Never sick, never fretting, she waited with watching eyes for her mother, Graziela, or her proud father, Alfonso, to attend to her.

Graziela told her that the priest at her baptism, not Father Paolo, the bad one before him, stumbled over the blessing, so disconcerted he was by her mild gaze as he spilled water over her head in the name of the Father and the Son and the Holy Spirit. *In nome del Padre e del Figlio e dello Spirito Santo.* She looked like she understood. Like she believed him. The water dripped into the font and Angelina sighed as if to say, *Finally. Finalmente,* I shall ascend if my big father drops me on the tile floor.

Angelina was doubly cursed, or blessed. The eldest and a girl. She lived in thin air and moved with her parents through the cadence of their days and seasons according to when she must plant, prune, and water. When to feed the animals, when to start the bread, how long to cook the pasta, when to change the baby. First baby Nico, then baby Berto, the two brothers who came after her. "Like this, Angelina," her father would say. "You space the seeds like this."

Or he would say, "You pull and squeeze the teats. Pull and squeeze at the same time. Start with your thumb and your forefinger. Roll your fingers down so the milk comes out. Look, you are so small, you don't even have to bend. Be gentle, *mia figlia.* This old girl is patient, so take your time."

Angelina's head fit right under the warm belly of the cow. She reached with small fingers to milk and learned to squirt a stream at the waiting cats.

"Not too often," her father would say. "There is nothing more useless than an overfed cat."

Her father built the first house they lived in beside the garden. He had collected scrap iron, melted it down and made rough hinges and nails. He chopped and planed the beams to support the roof and walls, and moved his wife and daughter in. When that house burned down, the family moved a few doors away to the house of Angelina's *nonna.* Not many San Placido families ever changed their address before dying, so the move was unusual. Angelina was still a small child when it happened. Her father built new beds and a new table and chairs. The credenza had been Graziela's and she had brought it with her to San Placido on her wedding day. It came with antique linens and solid crockery and these, along with some oil lamps, blankets, and pots composed the extent of Angelina's family's estate on the earth. If some object of luxury was missing, she did not know it. When her brothers came along, Nico and Berto, she fought with them, as anyone would do to put sense into such livestock. They fought quietly, with stealth, so as not to disturb their parents or their parents' neighbours. They went out to the fields to settle disputes and they landed punches and tackled each other among the cows.

San Placido had neither cars nor any electricity in the few houses that lined the road going up. The modern world did business below in the valley. There were guns in San Placido, of course, to shoot game for stew. Rifles mostly, and mostly of a vintage that required constant care to avoid misfires and accidents. Nothing in the village prepared her for the violence that she later found in others and, finally, in herself. Perhaps the murderous glances of Zia Anselmina, but even she seemed as inevitable as the early bitter snows that sometimes scorched the harvest. Until then, however, Angelina could look up the road and down it and, if she chose to, she could tell any visitor what was going on in each and every ancient habitation. She knew the whole small village and all its inhabitants.

In San Placido, the sun shone on the good and the evil. By eight in the morning the stones of the houses in the village were washed in bright light. The lane through the village marked a white trail toward the sky, sitting blue and still above the trees and the garden. The air was new in San Placido, new and cold every morning, drifting down from the white mountain snow. Angelina sank deep under her covers, up to her nose in cotton and wool to keep warm in the early dawn.

In the summer, after her chores were finished, Angelina went down to the shallow brook that frothed and rolled underneath the stone bridge on the way into the village. With the other children, she could step from one bank to the other on the smooth, cold rocks, and they would laugh and gasp when their feet slipped on the stones and were plunged into the ticklish cold. They could do this without their mothers telling them to be careful, since there was, in the shallow water, no fear of drowning. Though everyone still talked about the Franceschini girl who had slipped backwards onto the sharp rocks at the shore. She had lifted herself right back up, laughing and chilled with her wet dress pasted against her backside. She went home for lunch and died before the sun set, of what the doctor called a brain hemorrhage.

If Angelina stepped outside after lunch she saw the houses bleached in the high hot afternoon and it was hard for her to open her eyes, so neither she nor any of the other inhabitants made the effort very often. They went to ground, low to the ground on low beds that their grandfathers had built. They dampened flannel with cold water from the cistern and lay low with wet cloths over their faces. Even the restless children in the house next door ceased their mischief and were still.

Angelina knew all the houses and all of their histories.

At the first house on the corner, after the left turn off the mountain road, the *famiglia* Martinelli baked loaves of bread and sold to the ones who could not make their own. Angelina often fetched the loaves for her neighbours. The *vecchietti*, the old men, sat on the bench between the garden and the cistern, watching the children play, surrounded by the scent of yeast and heat, the warm flour worked by warm hands, the dough rising. These were the ones whose wives had died of hard work or childbirth or the cancer and whose daughters had run off to the town to find an easier life. For these the Martinellis made bread, sour, brown, and hard. For the new mothers and for the priest they saved the tender *panini* and sold it at a loss.

The small church across the road was built into the side of the mountain, its stone steps leading down to the entrance. Angelina knew her village was a small one, but when she stepped inside the church, she felt that she could be anywhere in Italy, anywhere on earth, and not see anything as beautiful. Outside, the church was low and snug against the earth. Inside, the ceiling was high, the blue and gold painted arches drew her eye up to heaven, to the seraphim and cherubim, to the blessed Lady and her Baby painted above, suspended just below heaven. Angelina felt that she and everyone else in that humble congregation were only a breath away from joining them, that they would be gilded instead of drab, splendid and spectacular. It was hard to listen to the priest and not stare instead open-mouthed at heaven.

To the right of the door, the stained glass windows concealed the view down the valley of the cemetery where all of her relatives found their rest. The crosses that marked the graves were stone or iron. The cemetery was one of her favourite places. It was well cared for and often, on a Sunday after Mass, quite busy, as the living came to tend the real estate of the dead and the stories of the dead. This was where Angelina found out about wars and plagues and illnesses and age. She was both curious and alarmed by the various detailed stories of loss, and also reassured by her neighbours. Their casual talk and tender weeding of plots. They talked about where they might like to be buried.

"Not in the sun, put me under the tree where the branches hang over. That way only the morning sun will shine in my face."

"What nonsense you speak. You will hardly know the difference once you're gone."

"Still."

Angelina worked with her parents and neighbours as they pulled the dandelions out and transplanted wild roses from the sunny side of the valley. She helped pick flowering branches from the almond and crabapple trees and place them in containers with water at the head and feet of the plots, marking paths through the small, quiet space. They tended the graves like private gardens in which were planted all the treasures of the past. They did not linger, but there was enough to do, keeping the weeds under control, picking up stray branches and leaves from the trees that grew on the outside of the old stone walls. They bent and straightened more often than even the Mass required and their work reminded her of prayer. Their fingertips lingered on the markers and traced the path of names carved into them. They prayed for their dead, those to whose lives they were infinitely and intimately tied. They taught the *bambini* to care for their *nonni* and *zii*, their grandparents and uncles and aunts. They told Angelina and the other children stories of Zio Giacomo's goitre, burgeoning out of the side of his neck, how in spite of the pain it must have caused him, he would sometimes paint funny faces on it and terrify and delight the children.

"And here is Nonno Filodoro, who planted beans in the garden high on the mountain that grew overnight into a stalk the size of three tree trunks." Antonio, a friend of Angelina's father, pointed to the grave in the corner.

"Of course, he climbed into the sky and came down with a chicken, stolen from the giant in the castle at the top of the stalk, a chicken whose eggs were flavourful beyond compare and who could only lay when Nonno Filodoro played his violin. Look, look up behind Signor Rendimonti's house to that low cloud and you can see the castle dangling above the mountain, see the giant hanging out of the topmost window in the clouds up there and when the lightning zigs and zags toward little San Placido and the thunder rattles the coffee cups on the shelf, you can here the giant roaring for his long dead chicken."

And the children, holding tight to their small pails and trowels, would look up to the sky on the left of the village and certainly see the cloud castle and the terribly unhappy giant.

Angelina had asked, "What happened to the beanstalk?"

She liked beans. A stalk that size must surely have yielded a sweet and overflowing crop.

"Well, it had to be cut down, did it not? You see that fellow up there? The size of him? You would not want him stomping around town searching under your bed in case you were the one who stole his chicken."

Antonio pulled her braid as her father had never done, and laughed softly. This gesture of his, of the hand of her father's good friend reaching out to her, was something she thought about in quiet moments. In the night, her room was silent. The old, thick walls of the house insulated her from the sounds of her parents settling into sleep. She could not hear her mother shifting in the creaking bed across the hall, adjusting her nightgown down around her legs. She did not hear her father let himself drop onto his side of the small bed and fall into a sleep that was deep and immediate. Most often, Angelina herself slept like the departed. But having spent a good part of the Sunday afternoon with the dead, she was curious about them, and about the living. Nonno Filodoro had got himself a magical hen and had cooked the most delicious eggs and baked the most delicious breads and sweets for visitors. First, he had to play his violin and all the village knew that soon after they heard the beautiful sound of Filodoro's violin, *le dolce* would be coming, warm from the oven for everyone to share. Antonio had told her a story that could not be true and had tugged on her hair for no reason. Not to twist it into its usual plaits as her mother did, not to dip it in ink at the school as her wretched cousin had done. Just to make her smile and believe something about San Placido and about Nonno Filodoro that was fantastic and nice. Hours after the congenial cemetery and the funny story and Antonio's kindly touch, she smiled in the darkness.

The walnut tree outside Angelina's house was large, so large that it took her two brothers and three of her grown cousins standing around it with their arms stretched out as wide as they could stretch, and their faces pressed against the bark, to embrace its girth. It shaded them through the long heat of the summer and kept the worst of the snow off in the winter. When she was small, Angelina climbed into the thick branches and surveyed her mountainside. Up above her sat Folignano, a village she could almost touch from her seat above San Placido, but that took two hours to walk to because of the switchbacks on the road up. There was no reason to go there. Only unpleasant people lived there, bundled against the weather and sour to strangers. Everyone in San Placido knew that the people in the village above, few as they were, suffered from constipation and sties. She might climb the tree to get away from Anselmina or to watch for her father below coming up the road with the donkey, but she did not dream of leaving, she did not look with any sort of longing toward the horizon. She would climb back down and land solidly in front of her own front door.

Up the street from Angelina's father's house lived Zia Anselmina, who loved the terrible inert heat, the stillness of the summer afternoon where even droning insects were stupefied into silence. Angelina could see her sitting with her cardigan on through the worst of the summer. Until the Germans came to San Placido, until they brought the blunt ends of guns, guttural shouts, cold threats, and stink of cooked cabbage with them, the only menace in the village resided in the *malocchio*, the evil eye, of Zia Anselmina.

Angelina had heard her say that she was the only woman in San Placido who had not sinned for twelve years. At any social event presented to the villagers, wedding or funeral or baptism, Angelina would see Zia Anselmina sipping many toasts to the poor young couple (or the dear departed, or the heaven-bound infant). It was supposed to be happy, a wedding, Angelina thought. At the celebration afterward, Zia Anselmina would speak of the boy who had waited at the altar, who had promised to lead his wife to judgment day. That girl he married would, according to Zia Anselmina—who was really nobody's aunt, nor anybody's mother either—soon die from the long agonies of childbirth, or from the hardship of life on the mountainside, or from the beatings provided by the fresh-faced child beside her in the clothes of a man (the suit creased and shiny, borrowed from a cousin in Rome, the white collar gaping at his neck, cinched as well as possible by the tie twisted into a knot at the top). It was terrible to listen to her.

Zia Anselmina would explain that she had not sinned since the day her husband walked under the ladder against the side of the house where she balanced, propped four feet above him and she had, in her astonishment at his reckless invitation to limitless bad luck, cursed at him, profaned the name of the Holy Family and dropped by accident her brimming wash bucket off its perch, off the ladder and onto the soft back of his bent head. She had not, fearing her own power, cursed since. She remained sanctified in black, as far from sin as the sky from the water. Her barrel chest clad in starched black, pulled and pulling across her body, small legs in black stockings below her skirt, jammed into her husband's shoes ("good leather yet," she said to anyone who looked askance, and "he did not need them anymore"), swollen ankles and insteps surging, wave-cresting flesh above the laces.

Angelina thought she was like a terrible clown. One you should not laugh at, for fear of your soul. Anselmina grabbed her when she was nearly twelve years old and on her way to the brook. She had

Angelina's arm clamped in one hand while with the other she waved a bent finger.

"You watch your step, little girl. I watch you and I know. These others know nothing, but I see the evil in you."

Anselmina's fetid breath came at her in waves. The stench of new wine and vomit. Angelina wondered if her mother would come and save her before she died.

"Don't think that priest will help you. The evil is in your heart. Remission of sins! As if such a thing were possible for such a one as you. I, I have taken the body and blood of Christ this morning. This morning and every morning."

Anselmina laughed, a sound came out like the sound of Angelina's father's hacksaw.

"Every morning, every afternoon, every evening. The blood of Christ in my tumbler. My demi-john keeps me in a blessed state of grace. Don't you forget it."

Angelina wondered how she could get away before Anselmina thought to curse her outright. Might her mother be coming to work in the garden? Perhaps her father would have forgotten something in the house for which he would need to return. She begged the skies for such a change in the order of the day to come along and save her. She looked into the face of the old woman and saw her eyes turn to the left and right, unfocused, suddenly. The grip on her arm slipped and when Angelina pulled away, she saw Anselmina stagger. She stepped back toward her and took the old witch's arm to help her back to her own kitchen before she fell over. Anselmina was much heavier than the girl thought she would be, and it took some force to get her to the bench outside the front door.

"I will not curse you, girl. I have not cursed anyone since my Tino died. Suddenly, I tell you. Of a sharp and accidental blow to the head!"

She laughed again that sawblade laugh, rusted iron on green wood. Angelina wanted to cover her ears, but she sat the woman down and said "*Ciao, zia*," and moved away down the hill to the stream.

The old woman was inescapable. She would sit on the bench in front of her small house, the stair and walk swept clean, morning, noon, and night. The village widows would go mad with the sound of the husk broom on the flat stones, swishing back and forth beyond the capacity of ears to bear. Then she would sit perfectly still on the bench watching the *ragazzi* play in the street. She would warn them:

Don't throw the ball too high. You will break the windows.
If the ball goes in my garden, you rascals, I am keeping it.
Watch out! The priest is coming!

She kept all the balls, even the India rubber one that would bounce all the way to Rome, the boys thought, if they could slam it hard enough. Berto and Nico took turns, each outbouncing the other's effort until one of Zia Anselmina's windows was smashed and the flying shards blinded her ugly cat, Thomas.

Angelina and her brothers set aside their small feuds for the walk home from school or from the brook, from any errand or chance that took them past Anselmina's house. They held hands and Angelina put the boys on her right, on the safe side. She and the other children stepped as lightly as they could when they went from the small schoolroom behind the church, around to the road and passed Anselmina's house. How old she was, nobody knew, but they had been raised on stories of crones and gypsies eating children or taking them away for some unknown purpose and Anselmina, with her bent back and her twisted fingers, which all the children had seen, seemed like the local embodiment of a terrible possibility. And she could speak German.

None of the children believed that Anselmina had not sinned. Unless sin was something very narrowly defined by God. Or unless sin could be wiped out by Anselmina's broad backside that polished and smoothed the ancient wood of the pew in the small church in San Placido. The bowed members of the small parish winced together as they listened to the now concave kneeler as it creaked beneath the weight of her wide knees. The children leaned close to their parents while Anselmina ground out the prayers of the rosary, her whiskers moving up and down as she told her beads.

She glared at Angelina when the girl walked past her house.

A terse *Buon giorno*, a catarrhal greeting, forced from her throat.

Anselmina took her turn cooking for the priest, who, she announced to any who would listen, ate inhuman amounts of her *carciofi*, her artichokes and warm bread. Angelina admired the Father's courage. For herself, she believed that anything Anselmina prepared was most likely poisoned. Or, at least composed of wrinkled or rotting vegetables from last year's root cellar. Father Paolo did not even pinch his nose. He greeted Anselmina, everyone could hear him, he greeted her as warmly as though she were his own sweet auntie as he stepped across the threshold. Angelina wished he would notice the scattering of rubber balls and painted sticks that the children had lost to Anselmina's custody, to notice and perhaps ask for them back. Though sometimes, as though by accident, his foot might kick one across the path so that a child might scoot and reclaim what was lost before the old woman noticed.

When she was a young girl, Angelina was one of the troupe of children who followed the Father on his circuits of the town. Father Paolo was a tall man in a loose white collar. That was obvious. Angelina's mother had offered to let down the hem of his cassock. In fact, all the few single ladies of the parish had each in turn stood ready with needle and thread to perform the same service. Angelina had heard them, and heard, as well, the Father's polite refusal. He would bow his head humbly, but he always said no. Angelina wondered if he just liked to see the shine on his boots. She admired it herself. There were not many in San Placido who took such trouble unless they were going somewhere special. She was sure that even if he was vain about his boots, even if his too short robe gave him a nice view of them as he walked, head slightly bent in all meekness, and even if every single citizen of San Placido knew or suspected the vanity, the handful of God's people there would not have minded. Angelina knew that they would think it a small price to pay for the presence of their tall and gentle priest. He was all a man should be, they said. He was courteous and warm, proper with their young sons and daughters who clustered around him for the sweets he kept in his ample pockets on his loping walks around and through the town. Though Angelina had not heard anyone talk about it for a long time, she knew that everyone remembered the last priest and the private lessons he invited some of the boys to and what the men of the village had done to him behind God's back.

This one bent low in the small doorways and smiled when he sat in the kitchens watching the *signore* stir sugar into the espresso that burned his lips. He ate, but not too much. He ate seconds, that was only common courtesy, but he refused thirds, which Angelina's mother and all the ladies appreciated and spoke about. He admired the men's wine, commented on its good strong flavour, an honest wine to make a man's face shine with the goodness of God, good for the stomach and the heart. But they never saw him weave or stumble. Only his cheeks reddened like a boy's after a glass or two. He was gentle with their children and could make his eyes bug out at them if they were restless during the Ave, so that they smiled into stillness against their mothers' sober sides.

Angelina had seen the women of the village wish him a warm good day as he passed.

Buon giorno, Father Paolo.

Ah, *certamente, signori, buon giorno*, indeed!

Youthful, tall, fit, and able, he was regarded on his walks by the ladies, their arms folded under heavy breasts and shaking their heads, who nodded in the Father's direction and said to Angelina, as she came into her womanhood, *what a waste*.

From the pulpit, he invited them to come to God, to meet him in the confessional.

"Remember, my children, if we confess our sins, He is faithful and just to forgive us and to cleanse us of all unrighteousness."

Father Paolo had extended to everyone the same invitation to repentance, but not everyone felt the need. Angelina's eyes and the eyes of the congregation turned to Zia Anselmina who, as she had not sinned since well before his arrival, shook her head at his ignorance. Anselmina took offence. Her mouth pinched even more tightly and she seemed to draw all the darkness in the room toward her. The black of her dress, flat even in the sunlight that beamed through the tall, narrow windows of San Placido's small church. Angelina knew that the old woman would leave the mass and go home to do some vigorous sweeping at the front door. She would complain as she swept, reverting to her father tongue, which no one in the village could understand. The meaning, nevertheless, was clear.

When she peeled her carrots, she again spoke Italian. From the yard beside her house, Angelina could hear.

"That priest is arrogant. Self-righteous. Ought to be looking at the tree in his own eye before he went with tweezers and a magnification glass at the splinter in mine. There is something wrong with a good-looking priest. It goes against God. They will see. It will come to no good."

Anselmina, the vicious guardian of San Placido, watched the good father like a hawk.

Angelina gave her as wide a berth as was possible. That woman would cause as much trouble as she could on this earth.

Angelina had never seen the old woman near the brook. Sometimes the mothers shocked the children by joining them, splashing and laughing, as though these solemn, scrubbing women knew how to have fun. Even her own mother, before the pain came, took off her sturdy shoes and rolled down her cotton hose. She lifted her skirt and smacked the water so that Angelina was suddenly drenched. The shock of the water, the shock of seeing her own mother's white knees, her good working mother, laughing and not minding, made her gasp. She splashed back and then Graziela, her arms like windmills, drenched her daughter before she fell back in the water, cold and breathless. Even Signora Pambianco and her grandson were soaked and shouting. Anselmina must have been able to hear them, but such noises seemed only to aggravate the old woman more. She stayed inside her house where she sat watching the Father exclaim over the scalding heat of her coffee and sharp crunch of her exemplary biscotti, recalling this priest at the altar saying out loud to all the hard workers of San Placido that there is more joy in heaven over one sinner who repents than over ninety-nine righteous persons who need no repentance.

The whole village could hear her argue with the priest. The ones in the brook stopped splashing to listen.

"What kind of absurdity is this now coming from the Church?

Why would heaven not rejoice over the righteous?"

The Father responded gently, too gently to be overheard.

As she grew to maturity in the house next to such acrimony, Angelina wondered what, if anything, Anselmina had ever known of joy. Joy in heaven, joy anywhere. She seemed to have no expectation of this and no path to it. She was the woman in San Placido who had not sinned and was therefore safe from repentance and from joy, from the slippery stones and the sharp crack on the skull that followed.

Dante

Where his *kindergarten teacher* was a woman who would speak softly to him and ease the lessons of authority into him with sweets and gentle emollient words, every teacher after Signora Cannone preferred to give orders that Dante preferred not to follow.

"Dan-te!" the teacher would shout from the back of the class, so prolonging the distance between the two syllables that Dante at first thought there was some unknown pupil in the class with the strange name of *Dan*. The *te* took so long to utter that Dante did not in his head make the connection.

Even Sabino understood first and tried to save his friend a thrashing.

"It is you, Dante."

"Me?"

"De Angelis! Are you deaf?"

The teacher would be at his side with the thick ruler, the weapon that he lifted and snapped in a tight sweep. Dante would duck, and Sabino would duck as well, but always a bit too late, so that the edge of the teacher's ruler would cuff the innocent one on the ear or the side of the head, sometimes drawing blood.

Dante was sure it was not his fault. He could not sit still. The letters would not remain calm on the page he was asked to read. He stared at them and they moved, rearranged themselves too quickly to be grasped and pronounced. The teacher first banged the ruler on the desk before aiming at Dante's hand or arm.

"To the corner with you, De Angelis. You will learn to comport yourself properly in this classroom."

Dante moved to the corner and waited. Sooner or later, for some transgression Dante could not see as he was facing the wall, Sabino would be beside him.

One afternoon Dante got hold of a piece of chalk. He wanted to see if he could roll it all the way to the front of the class. He practised his aim and gauged the force he needed so that the chalk would land, with luck, near to where the teacher paced in his daily rants against capitalism. He tapped Sabino's shoulder to point out the chalk on the floor. He did not want him to miss the trick.

"For the fascist, the state is all and all serve the state. There is none of this weakness, this seeking after profit for the sake of the self. We must believe, obey, and fight!"

The teacher's black shoe smashed the chalk in the silent and waiting and serious classroom. The chalk cracked and crunched and the children giggled. Dante tried to slip his dusty hands in his pockets, but he was not quick enough.

"De Angelis!"

The teacher leaned above him, all the force of his lunchtime garlic *panini* smothering Dante.

The teacher saw the white chalk dust on Sabino's shoulder.

"And you, Sabino. I should not be surprised. The two of you to the wall, immediately."

Sabino smiled and rose, bowed his head to the young girl in the seat in front of him and moved to stand by Dante, facing the wall.

Dante said, "*Mi dispiace*, Sabino, so sorry."

Sabino said "*Niente*. It's nothing. I think they painted the wall since we were here last. Can you smell it?"

The teacher would scream "Silence!"

Sabino kept Dante calm, but he did not keep him out of trouble. Dante bent his head at the wall. He tamped down his fury until it could find a satisfying outlet. As he moved through levels at school, he found ways to pay back his teachers for their injustices. He planted his mother's pincushion on the teacher's chair. Not a sophisticated trick, but the teacher's screech was superb. The beads of blood that formed on the backside of his wool trousers were captivating. Unfortunately, Dante's mother had embroidered her name on the underside of the cushion and so Dante was lashed by the teacher at school and then by his father at home.

He filled one teacher's galoshes with manure. For this, he did not get caught red-handed. However, when he stole the teacher's briefcase to place in it rotting tomatoes, his hands were quite red and smelled of mould.

The teacher called him incorrigible. He was useless, worse than useless, and would no doubt end up with the hard-boiled criminals in the Rocca. Dante longed to grow stronger. Stronger and bigger. He would make his mark. He would show these teachers and his own father.

The boys went often to the gorge after school. They collected rocks to throw over the Ponte. Dante named targets on the other side. At each throw, he raced against Sabino, lifting his arm, arcing it and throwing with all his strength. Sabino's always went faster and farther. They rarely hit the target. Instead, Dante listened for the splash so far below.

Dante wanted to see the hermit's cave, just across the bridge.

"Let's go. We will just have a look and see what it's like."

"I don't think it's a good idea. The hermit, he is a holy man and should not be bothered."

"He's probably lonely. He needs visitors. Anyway, look. He's not even around. At least, I can't see him. He hasn't got much room to hide in there. Maybe he's gone to do a little shopping in the market."

"I don't think hermits shop, do they? We should think about this. Not just bang on a rock and say 'hello.'"

Sabino had to think all the time. His father died when he was six. He had three younger sisters and his mother. He thought about everything, whether what he did would please his mother or help or hurt his family. Dante sometimes lost patience with him. His friend would miss the whole world if he didn't learn to act.

"Come on."

They crossed the bridge and climbed up the side of the gorge to the hermit's cave, which was empty. There was a plate of food set on a rock just inside the cave. Someone had left warm bread and *cannelloni* for the hermit's supper. Dante was, as usual, starving. He gripped the rock ledge to finish the climb into the cave when he felt Sabino's hand on his arm. When Dante looked back, he found Sabino staring right back at him, the corners of his mouth for once curled down.

Dante stopped of course. The cave, the hermit, the stations of the cross painted in old ochre and russet on the cave walls, the sacrifice of food waiting for a man so old and slow and devout that even Dante understood the transgression of taking the offering away for his young, hungry stomach.

"*Allora, andiamo.* Let's go home. Your mother will have something for us."

Dante had never seen Sabino's mother outside of the kitchen unless she was in the market bargaining for the food she was about to cook. She would certainly set a plate of some good thing before them.

"Sabin, do you think you eat as many kilos as you weigh?"

"*Sì.*"

"That is a lot of food."

The boys climbed down the steep path to the bridge looking back over their shoulders to see if the hermit came to get his dinner. They went home to their own kitchens for supper, but Dante wanted to go back.

A few days later after school was out in the afternoon, Dante had waited long enough.

"Sabin, let's go see the hermit."

"We went before."

"I know, but this time, let's go see him. Actually see him."

"What will we do with the hermit?"

"We will ask him about God."

"Dante, what about God? What do you want to know?"

"Does he see God? Does God talk to him? I do not know, but it will be more interesting than throwing stones over the *ponte*."

"What will you do when you find out about God?"

"I'll be a hermit too. I'll live in the cave and all the *signorine* will come with food and love and all of them will want to marry me and I will have a very difficult time staying a hermit."

"Why don't you be a priest instead?"

"Then you have to live in a house and sleep in a bed with sheets. Just like at home. You have to bathe and put on clean clothes and it is always the same."

"*Allora*, the hermit is really more like a gypsy."

"Yes. But he is not a traveller. He stays in one place, that hermit. He is really his own man. He does not go to school to be scolded, he does not have to do chores. That's the life for us."

"Aren't you afraid?" Sabino asked. "Do you think he will be nice, or mad?"

"Maybe both."

"We could go and find out. We could bring some good rocks to throw. In case he tried to kill us. Or curse us."

"What? Do you think he's kept himself alive eating children or something?"

"Well. Not really. But why is he a hermit?"

"Maybe his wife died."

"Maybe he killed her."

"Maybe we should bring him something."

"We haven't got anything."

"What about the marble you won?"

"Yes. I have that."

Dante had watched Sabino work for that marble, practise rolling and hitting rocks so that his aim was deadly accurate. When that ugly Giacomelli started bragging about his skill at marbles, about how he never lost and he could take anybody, Sabino, with a borrowed marble in his pocket, said quietly from the edge of the circle of children on the playground, "I'll give it a try."

Perhaps it wasn't fair to suggest that Sabino should give up his treasure.

"Never mind," said Dante. "What would a hermit do with a marble?"

Dante talked Sabino into climbing the gorge, slipping and ripping his shins. He showed him again where the shallow fingerholds and toeholds were in the side of the rock wall. They held fast to outcroppings of moss and used the sturdier branches for leverage. He wanted to be careful not to kill his friend.

"Sabin, *piano, piano*. Go carefully. Look where you are putting your hands and make sure your feet are safe."

Sabino did not answer.

Dante kept talking to Sabino, foot here, hand there. Take a rest now. The last part is steep. The gorge would not forgive a mistake and a loose shrub would rob Sabino's mother of her son. Dante was not afraid for himself. He was used to climbing. But Sabino had a red face.

Just short of the precipice, they wedged themselves in a thicket of acacia near the top and spied on the old man who moved feebly and bent in the shadowed space afforded by the cave. Dante pushed Sabino's shoulder down out of view behind the bushes so that they could watch as the hermit walked along the path, past his place of residence, to the dark trees behind to relieve himself. Dante watched and waited, but he was not really certain why they were there. He had begun to feel uncomfortable. Not cramped in his limbs, but a bit ashamed, as though he ought not to be spying on the movements of such a simple life. Sabino, pushed up against the rock with his grip on the bushes and his head against his arm, looked as though he might fall asleep soon if something did not happen. Dante began to believe that the hermit was most likely deaf and perhaps rather blind when the old man suddenly turned and came straight out of his cave to the edge of the gorge. The hermit looked over the valley as though to spit. Both boys froze, startled by the voice above them. The man they had been watching had not sung a song or even hummed while his body formed the postures of prayer. Dante had not heard his voice and believed that not even God himself had heard his creature utter a single sound.

When the old man said, "Good afternoon" to the bushes at the cliff's edge, Dante almost jumped out of his skin. He held on to Sabino whose foot slipped out of its hold for a terrible moment. Dante stared at his friend's face, inches from his own, both sets of eyes wide and white-rimmed.

"*Buon giorno, signori.*"

Dante's brows went up. Sabino's shoulders lifted and dropped, resigned.

"*Buon giorno, mio padre.*"

"Arise, my sons. Come here and let me have a look at the ones who have been climbing up my gorge and watching me as though I was in the zoo and I was the monkey and not them. Will you not join me? My house is plain, but my company is rich."

Dante hoisted himself onto the path in front of the cave and leaned over to help Sabino.

Sabino asked, "What does that mean?"

"It means he is going to talk our heads off."

The hermit's cave curved into the wall of the escarpment. There were two rough rock chambers, half circles separating one space from the other. One escaped wind and rain in the outer chamber and, with the fire burning low to the ground, the inner chamber was dully lit and comfortable for Dante and Sabino, whose muscles had cramped and stiffened on the cliff side. There were two seats of rock and a long bench set against the inside wall. Farther in, on the other side of the fire, there were old blankets folded neatly across a pallet.

Dante looked around, surprised to see the cave so tidy, warm, and colourful. He put his hand across his mouth to hide his grin. He was sure that the hermit lived in the best of possible worlds. Everything he saw made him more certain. The old man brewed some tea out of hot water and herbs.

He handed them steaming cups, delicate and floral. He went into the other chamber and Dante could see him searching in a box for something. The hermit came back with a linen handkerchief and a bowl of water. He stooped before Dante's knees and rinsed off the blood.

"One good thing about short pants is that when you climb the gorge, you do not have to worry about tearing fabric that your good mother will have to mend as she scolds you."

"Scolding, that doesn't hurt," Dante said. He had not even noticed that his knees were scraped. Sabino had come up the gorge without a scratch.

The hermit met his eye. "But other things do, I think."

Dante looked away at the frescoes on the rock wall.

"Drink this up while it's hot, *ragazzi*. It will strengthen your climbing muscles."

Sabino looked at his scuffed worn shoes, but Dante grinned. This was better and better. The hermit sat peacefully before them while the boys tried to drink the infusion they were given before it was cool enough to taste. The smell of earth and mustard and months-old cheese was rising in the steam and Dante scalded his tongue drinking too quickly.

"Do you like it here?" he finally asked.

"Here? Could you be more specific?"

"Specific? You know. Here." Dante looked around. Perhaps the hermit was mad.

"Well, if you mean Earth, then I would say, yes. With a visitor's sense that the place is quaint and pleasant, by and large. If you mean *la bella Italia*, then I would have to confess I have not been anywhere else, and if by 'here' you mean Spoleto, I would say yes again, for although I have been to other cities, none soothes my rough soul so well as this one. And if you mean this cave overlooking this gorge, then, again, I must say yes, for it holds me and comforts me without making me feel so comfortable that I forget my true home."

Dante was trying to understand. He looked at Sabino, who had his eye on the covered dish by the entrance.

"Do you not wish to be comfortable?"

"It took me a long time to discover that I am a stranger and an alien, that the lovely world is not my home, nor yours either, young man, however far you wander. The cave reminds me. So beautiful."

"*Sì*." Dante could not agree more. He looked around. If he put his arm straight up from where he was sitting, his fingertips would graze the ceiling. He looked at the old man and realized for the first time how very small he was. Even Sabino might nearly be as tall and Dante himself was probably taller.

"Why do you live in a cave? May I ask you this?"

"What a good boy you are. You may ask and I will tell you the truth!"

No adult had ever spoken to Dante this way. The hermit sounded so pleased with him and curious about what Dante might ask next. Always he had been told what to do. Indeed, his father spent many of the few hours between supper and bedtime telling Dante loudly of his uselessness and ineptitude. He had been scolded by his teachers and his mother, his aunts and uncles who might slap him or press money into his palms and he could not predict which it would be or why, but never had anyone spoken to him as though he were anything more than an object to be directed or corrected, a child without will or design. A bad child or one who might at any moment slip into an abyss of misbehaviour. This dusty hermit told Dante he was a good boy. He said plain and clear what Dante had felt his whole young life, that he was a stranger on the earth with one stubborn friend who stayed beside him. That he had not found his place. The Via Monterozze was not his home. He had no home. He sat straight up at the thought of being told the truth by someone.

"Why do I live in a cave? But look at my cave. Is it not commodious and comfortable? No taxes, no washing, no cleaning, no dusting, or fretting. And the *belle signore* from the edges of Spoleto bring me some supper almost every day. They bring candles and say prayers and I sit quiet and agree with them and add my thoughts to those being lifted to the saints and angels and to the highest throne of heaven itself. You cannot get all that in a house in the valley!

"But let me ask you. Why do you live in a house? Do you like it?"

Dante looked at Sabino who was smiling as though the hermit was telling the best jokes he had ever heard, but Dante was serious.

"I have always lived in a house. I am not very holy—"

"Yes, you are. Completely."

"My mother says that you are a holy man and we must respect you and your privacy." Here, Dante had the wit to pause, embarrassed.

"She says that we should only approach you if we need special prayers. I think she is one of the women who bring supper here. But I don't think she would let me live in a cave."

"Why not? Your parents don't say anything to me about living in a cave."

"But you are holy—well, special."

"As are you. I can prove this."

"How can you prove it?" Dante had a sudden vision of himself in gilded robes, rich purple and scarlet with golden thread, making the sign of the cross over the body of his vicious father.

"Stand here." Both boys stood. The hermit turned them with their backs to the cave opening. He placed them side by side, facing the inner wall while he himself remained by the opening, hands folded and still as he faced the sky.

"I'm sorry, father. Your paintings are colourful, they're really something, but I don't see how they prove that Sabino and I are holy."

"*Patienza*, my boy. Can you count? Have you learned your numbers at school?"

"*Certo*, father. Of course."

"Can you count backwards, say, from a hundred?"

"*Si, senti*. Cento, quaranta dicianove, quaranta diciotto, quaranta diciesette. Allora, papa, veramente? Truly, you want me to count backward? But what will that prove?"

"*Aspetta, aspetta*. Hold onto your trousers, fellow. One more. What is the next number down?"

"*Quaranta dicisei!*"

"*Guarda!* Look now, my sons."

At that moment, the afternoon sun came full blaze around the cloud that the elderly man had been watching. Dante could feel the sudden sun hot on his back, see it hit Sabino between the shoulders, and the angle, low in the late afternoon, illuminated the hermit's cave. As they faced the wall, they saw their own silhouettes in relief against the cave wall and around the shadow of their shoulders and heads glittered beautiful blue and gold haloes, a blinding brilliance around each rumpled child's shadow.

The turning from dark to light made Dante's eyes water. The hermit passed each of them a fine white handkerchief.

"'And he shall wipe every tear from their eyes; and there shall no longer be any death; there shall no longer be any mourning or crying or pain. Behold, I am making all things new.'"

Sabino stood, the shorter and stockier trace, bemused and smiling at his beatified outline. Dante stepped away, unconvinced and strangely chilled. This talk of tears, mourning, and pain on a sunny day was unconvincing, although perhaps the hermit had met Dante's father.

"Now *ragazzi*, have some cookies, made by *le belle signore della città*. The lovely housewives of the city."

The hermit winked and passed them a tin of *pizzelle*, which they ate gratefully. They eased themselves over the precipice as the hermit made the sign of the cross.

"God bless and keep you in his love and peace."

The boys slipped swiftly down the ravine.

When the Fascists came to Dante's school with cookies and framed portraits of Mussolini, one for each classroom, the children had to be hushed and scolded to stillness. The teachers gave them certificates with swirling Latin letters, certificates of membership in the Fascist Party and the education officers passed out pencils and flags to the children in Dante's class. Dante forgot about the hermit in the excitement of his introduction to Fascism. He ran home with his gifts to his father who, for once, was pleased with something Dante did.

"Look, Giuseppe," his mother would say. "Dante is a member of the Party, too."

Angelina

There was an artesian well in the centre of San Placido's garden. The water ran freely from between the rocks at the side of the mountain until someone thought to attach a spigot in the shape of a lion's head. In later years, the stonemason built an elaborate trough with an angled ledge inside it to use as a scrub board. Over the decades, the stonework had worn smooth on the inside, but the detailed edges of the carving on the outside, the doves and the laurel leaves, were as distinct as ever. The water had been flowing for as long as anyone could remember and in the mornings the women of the village would lift up their baskets of sheets and shirts, underdrawers and socks, with their bars of laundry soap and halved lemons for pressing into oily stains, they would knuckle the dirt out of the clothes, folding and rubbing the fabric between their thumbs and the heels of their hands under the cold water until everything was citrus fragrant and white.

While the women of the village worked, Angelina, when she was very young, picked field flowers for her mother. Sometimes she would be allowed to help and then her own hands would grow raw under the water with her mother's, working the soap into the clothes, rinsing them under the mouth of the lion and then twisting and squeezing them out.

In the absence of Anselmina, she felt lucky to live in such a place. Around the well, there were the women of her life and, young as she was, she could see they were strong, strong and fun, women who would splash water at one another on hot days and help one another lift heavy, wet sheets and twist them to dampness. To Angelina, it seemed like a game. Her own wrists grew strong in such play as she begged for a turn to wind the linens with her mother.

Around the pooling water there grew wild cherry trees, almonds and pines, wild rose and hyacinths low to the ground and making all the air around the working women fragrant and heavy in the hot summer. They laughed, these women. The bed linens they scrubbed told them everything about each other; they knew when Aldo had eaten too many cherries or when the young daughters started their bleeding. Some of the ladies had to wash their sheets more often than others. They talked, these women, and from them Angelina learned about marriage. Some had husbands, they said, who were insatiable, though Angelina was not sure at first what that meant. Hungry? Thirsty? No.

"He lies there, I tell you, like he is on hot coals, waiting for me every night. I finish in the kitchen, and bathe myself. All lovely and fresh, skin still damp, and there he is with a baton at full salute."

Here, the ladies gasp and cover their mouths, laughing and nodding, most of them.

"I see him, staring at the ceiling, trying to dream up the words to say. You know, the kind ones that he has not said through all the long day, the words that might unlock my nice thighs, even, magically, make me moist and willing. Which, truth be told, I am anyway, though it doesn't do to let him know it!"

About men and women, Angelina learned what she knew at the well. The women, so practical, dealt with the sheets. Sometimes one would smile quietly, as though the marks she rinsed reminded her of something lovely. Angelina grew more curious. She thought of the few boys in the village and wondered if she would one day be washing linens upon which she had lain with one of her schoolmates. The idea sent her to the ground in an unusual fit of giggles.

Even if it meant she would be a spinster, looking after only her brothers' children and her aging parents, she could not think about a single boy in San Placido as someone whose sheets she would consent to scrub. Perhaps when she was older, her papa would take her to Visso where there were many more young men. Perhaps one there would seem to be worthy of curiosity.

Angelina tried not to look at Anselmina, whose wattled neck shook as she turned away from the sheets. The old woman looked disgusted by the stains on the linen. Yellowed and crisp, those linens were. Anselmina spat into the dirt beside the cistern. She was usually at the well earlier than everyone else, as though she must finish her work before those young wives, and some not so young, got up to the well. As though she did not want to wash her clothes with theirs.

Francesca, whose husband Antonio had recently died, finished quickly with her own small basket of linens. Angelina was one of the few in the village who could recall that Francesca was Anselmina's sister. Since they were as different as the bright day from the sooty night and since they seldom spoke and never embraced, Angelina's neighbours in San Placido did not often think to put two and two together. When her own washing was done Francesca would offer to help, especially the young brides, showing them, without saying anything, what the best way was to get their sheets white as snow, how to use the rocks around the cistern and without damaging the fabric, erase the traces of love, as she liked to speak of them.

All was washed out in the cistern at the top of the village, and while the women smiled and chatted and looked the other way, nothing went unnoticed.

Angelina could not get to the poor beast quickly enough. Anselmina had seen him first, the black dog trotting up the path, and threw stones at him, stones which he dodged lightly, as though he understood her malice to be a grand game. Angelina ran down to place herself between the rocks and the thin dog before Anselmina could blind the creature. He did not seem put off at all by his reception.

He trotted to Angelina and sniffed her hand, licked it before she could pull it away to have a better look at him.

She asked her neighbours if they knew of the dog, whose it was or where it might have come from. As she went from house to house, the dog followed her and sat apparently patient and certainly panting while she made inquiries. She did not want to be encumbered by the care of this fellow, no matter how polite he seemed to be. No one in San Placido knew where he had come from.

"So, dog, you come up the mountain in the black night with no explanation? You look a little hungry, but not too bad off. What is your story, I wonder. Do you live in Visso?"

Each of the people Angelina spoke to came out to have a look at her new attendant. They patted him and brought him small treats. The boy next door, Carlo, put out a bowl of water. The dog stuck by Angelina as though she were a walking fragrant roast beef whose aroma compelled him to accompany her.

He was peaceful apart from the days that the *postino* rode his bicycle up the mountain with the mail. On those days, the dog would have to be restrained. Angelina tried to hide him behind the house, but the bicycle bell drove him wild. The only mark of difference between the *postino* and the rest of the villagers was the fellow's black uniform, the epaulets, brass buttons, squared hat. As the dog had never so much as growled at anyone in the village, not even Anselmina, Angelina concluded that the beast must hate uniforms. He seemed to need to kill them. The terrible clanging bell announcing the postman's arrival drove the mild dog to distraction and murder and within one month, each of the villagers had shared in assisting both dog and postman to continue living. If the postman was killed by the dog, the poor thing would know only a few days of rejoicing before some government lackey, perhaps on another bicycle, perhaps even in a car, would drive up the mountain with some kind of stamped paper that would result in the creature's being hauled away to certain swift death. Italy was mustering for war, they knew, and there would be enough destruction in the world without adding one single dog to the lists of the dead.

But for his hatred of uniforms, the dog was a patient companion, playful with the children, stepping gingerly around the old women, solemn, still and quiet during the mass, and alert and smiling as he accompanied Angelina back and forth in her daily duty to her family.

The dog followed Angelina on her walk from the house to the field to get her father and brothers for lunch and then again, when she went to call them for supper. Back and forth, some feet behind, it trotted with its nose sometimes up in the air and sometimes pressed to the dusty hedge along the path's north side where the forest climbed higher on the right side of San Placido. It followed her, snapping at every fly and frog and racing at every gesture of Angelina's hand.

"What is it, dog," she bent to ask him. "Can you smell those chickens on my hands? Do you like them raw or roasted?"

The dog barked and tried to lick her face. She pushed him away and he jumped back as though he must be closer.

Angelina talked to him, or, she talked about him to the air in front of her.

"*Questo cane*," she said, "this dog has not got the sense God gave a turtle, walking around in the heat of the day as though the village belonged to him, as though I needed a guard in this place where nothing happens. Perhaps *questo cane* thinks Zia Anselmina will attack me with her broom, or that I shall fall off my own feet on the mountain and require assistance."

A lick on the face or a wet nudge against her thigh with his muddy nose. He would be some help, certainly. She looked at the dog, stern.

"What help would you be, dog?"

The dog, who had come to recognize his name as Questo, tilted his head and cocked his ears. Angelina burst out laughing.

Still, she smiled when she saw him waiting faithfully in the morning by her door.

"This one, *questo cane*, he is hungry again," she said to her mother.

And Questo would prick his ears, ready to eat or play or walk, depending on where and how Angelina and her lovely fragrance proceeded.

Angelina was finished with school. She had not been to the classroom for over a year, but she knew what was going on in the world. She knew that the German leader, Hitler, had come for a visit to Italy. The papers all reported on the cordiality of the visit, how much Hitler enjoyed meeting his mentor, the Duce. He came on the train, the punctual train, and the King and Mussolini met him at the station. The photographs printed in the paper showed the Duce saluting the train and the King, so much shorter than anyone on the platform, standing to one side. Angelina remembered that the King was armed with a sword. A sword.

They went on a tour of the city of Rome in an open car. To the Palazzo del Quirinale, to the Porto San Paolo, the Porta Capena, and the National Monument to Victor Emanuel. At the national monument the three men left the car. The King and Mussolini stood and observed as the guest of honour laid a garland at the Tomb of the Unknown Soldier.

He was in Italy for a week that time. She read about German arms, about the cities and countries that Germany had entered in order to assist with governments. How they had united with Austria, occupied Rhineland, and taken over Czechoslovakia. How Mussolini had sent Italians to Ethiopia to make for himself the start of a new empire.

Everywhere in the news that came up to the village, she read about tanks, planes, guns, bombs, mines, and peace. All this for the sake of peace. And the King had waited at the station with a sword.

She did not know what to think. Angelina wondered if the Duce's friendship with Hitler would mean that Germans would come to San Placido to help with the harvest. This was ridiculous. She could not picture the streets of Visso blocked with heavy armaments. She looked at the black dog sitting beside her, his back resting warm against her leg.

"If the Germans come, dog, you had better learn to mind your manners. We all had."

Nico came out of the house. "Don't worry. I'll protect us."

He waved his father's hunting rifle. The dog looked up at him, yawned and walked to the sunny side of the wall.

"Don't hurt yourself with that thing."

"You know I am a splendid shot, Angelina."

"I don't think you know what splendid means, do you?"

"I bet I could hit a rabbit at a hundred yards."

"There would not be much left of the rabbit. And it would be full of shot. A rabbit would be nice, Nico, but you've got to think before you shoot, okay?"

"Women do not understand anything."

Dante

At school, Dante noticed that some of the teachers were gone—all those who had not talked loudly about the benefits of Fascism and the glories of Italy under Mussolini. Dante was required with other students to dust the large photographs of the Duce on the classroom walls. Dante's teachers talked about the importance of war to Italy.

He took the damp cloth and wiped it along the gilded frame. He cleaned the Duce's face with a show of reverence. He listened during the school day to the teachers tell him that fighting was natural and beneficial. Good for the state and good for its citizens, especially its boys, especially Dante who would grow up to be a good soldier, who would fight for the glory of Italy.

He had to join the Black Shirts at fourteen. His father was a city official and a member of the Party and Giuseppe told Dante that he was now old enough to start attending meetings two afternoons a week. Meetings where he would learn to recite the tenets of Fascism, where he would learn to march as young men all over Italy were doing. Dante went, but he had a hard time keeping his shirt tucked into his short pants, and he could never keep it clean. Dante sat restively. He had been in his seat for too long, listening to another man telling him in a loud and abrasive voice how his life would unfold. The pain in his fingers from too many strokes of that rod kept him fixed in his spot in spite of himself. The Duce glowered down at him from the wall.

His mother washed and pressed his black shirt, but every time he put it on, he broke out in hives. Red welts puckered his face so that the other *Balilla* his age, members of his nationalist youth group, called him *buffo* and offered him cherry tomatoes to stick on the end of his nose. To go to the youth night, to learn about the glories of Italy and empire, to learn to stand straight and still and march sharply and in unison with the other boys was torture enough, but the black shirt and tie chafing the red welts on his neck was terrible and he would moan before the meetings and complain about his sore stomach or sore leg or sore head and beg his soft mother not to make him go. He was not interested in the toy guns they were given. The creed, "I believe in Rome, the Eternal, the mother of my country, I believe in the genius of Mussolini and in the resurrection of the Empire" made him squirm with an itch and a shame that felt as red as the hives under his shirt.

He asked his father, "Why is the Duce always on horseback? Why is he always standing in the balcony looking down?"

His father reached easily across the table and boxed his ears.

The week of his sixteenth birthday, his parents took him to Rome to hear Primo Ministro Mussolini speak. Dante stepped on the train and swaggered down the aisle to a seat. In a tie and long pants, he was going to Rome. But he could not escape his mother's oversight. She watched him so as not to lose him, no matter how much he might yearn to be lost. They walked past vendors and soldiers and girls in the highest heels Dante had ever seen. He could not comprehend their ability to balance and he turned, staring, to watch them walk away. He lagged behind his parents. They waited, at first quietly and then with beckoning gestures.

"Come along, Dante. Hurry up."

He could see people glancing and smiling. Other boys on the piazza, laughing at him, the big boy pulled along behind his mother. Maria Pia, unnerved by the noise and the people, squeezed the blood out of his hand with her grip. He walked down the Via dei Fori Imperiali, across to the piazza where Mussolini stepped out on the balcony and greeted the multitude waiting to hear everything he would say. Dante had read the papers. He knew that Italy had invaded Abyssinia. He said the name out loud and slowly. A sinuous sound and seductive. Abyssinia. Perhaps he might get there some time. Addis Ababa. Perhaps Mussolini was right to invite such places to his table. Dante looked up at the balcony to the man on whom every eye rested. Whose broadcast speeches went out to the world. Whom heads of state visited and who would be, the papers said, the salvation of Europe. Dante looked at him and almost believed. He was such a small man, but his stature was without match on the earth. Dante's parents stood sombre and rapt, and he watched them, their gaze fixed on the man at the distant balustrade, and wondered at Mussolini's command.

"He is so short."

Again, his father's blasting slap, the vermilion print against his cheek.

Dante grew to have firm convictions, clear notions about the parameters of justice and how he and others stood in relation to them. When he left Rome on the train after the speech, after his mother did a little shopping and his father smoked some cigarettes with the men at the coffee bar, Dante was confused. Abyssinia would have to be the furthest he could get from his father. Perhaps Mussolini would provide the means for him to get there.

He went to the *ponte* and threw rocks with Sabino when they got back from Rome.

"Listen, Sabino, everybody, my father, my boss, his boss, the priest, all of them with any scrap of authority, can barely keep their feet on the ground because the hot air of their own pronouncements would lift them off the earth, their shirts swelling under their necks so that the belts on their trousers are necessary to keep them from exploding, from filling up each trouser leg with the hot air that would turn them into complete buffoons."

Sabino's rock hit the other side of the gorge. He said, "I don't know what you are talking about.

Dante pushed him.

Sabino pushed back and Dante fell. He refused the hand up.

"And they can tell us every minute of every day what to do, even how to sit in a chair as though we had been dropped on our heads and addled our brains, they can tell us, *senti*—when to piss and when to pray—it is outrageous."

"Sometimes it is nice to be told what to do."

Dante pushed him again, hard. Sabino barely moved.

"Can you not see it? Can you not see that we are wolves among sheep? That we have a destiny that men with moustaches decide we may not fulfill?"

"I see, Dante."

Dante stepped back a few paces, ran at his friend to knock him down. Sabino moved out of the way. Dante nearly went over the precipice. Sabino caught him.

"If you tell me I should look where I am going, I will punch your nose."

Sabino laid his finger against his lips.

"I did not say anything about how you are always falling."

Dante flung his fist and missed Sabino's nose.

"One day you will be the one dusty and bleeding, you *masso*!"

"*Si, certo.*"

The boys prowled down to the bottom of the gorge and sat, throwing rocks at the birds that perched on the high ground jutting into the middle of the river.

Dante said, "I have to tell you something. I am telling you so that you can be ready, but if you spill the beans to anyone, I'm sorry, we've known each other all our lives, and your parents will grieve and hate me and perhaps hunt me down, but if you tell anyone, I will kill you."

Sabino smiled.

"I am leaving this town. I am packing my rucksack, I am taking what money I can find, and I am leaving home for good."

Sabino nodded. "When will you leave?"

"As soon as I can. I cannot stand too much more of this. My mother wants me to be a baby forever. She would like to push the pasta right into my mouth and then wipe it for me. My father orders me around, tells me I eat too much of his food, break too many of his shabby tools, drink too much of his water, sleep too much in his house. As if everything were his. All that his eye falls on. I cannot stand too much more."

Sabino again nodded.

"Leaving is a good idea. I get away from my father and make my fortune somewhere. Maybe the north. Milan or Bologna or somewhere where things are happening."

"I will come with you."

"Ai, *basta*, *Sabin*. You cannot come with me. You would not survive on your own and besides, your family needs you."

Sabino looked at Dante, thin and pale, and thought he knew which of them would survive best on his own.

"I will come with you. *Verrò con voi.*"

Dante did not want company. In the vision he had of a courageous and pioneering journey to a future, he saw himself alone and heading to all the possibilities of the north. To industry and wealth. Italy was at war. If he did not become a soldier, he could at least get a job. But he could not accomplish anything if he had to look after Sabino.

"You cannot come with me."

However, Sabino had decided.

"I will come with you."

Dante would just keep quiet. He would leave on his own and that was that. Sabino did not seem able to grasp the consequences of such a decision, the thought that must be put into it. One must consider the future, the possibilities of deprivation and loneliness. Sabino had slept in his mother's house every night of his life. He was not used to such things, Dante thought, ignoring the facts of his own life. A fellow like Sabino could not pack up and leave the dear familiar on a whim. His family, the mother so gentle, three sisters, all depending on their quiet brother. Dante would not allow him to make such a foolish mistake.

He left. He scrounged his father's old military tent, one of the tents from the terrible war, made of four pieces that four soldiers would carry in their packs and then attach when it was time to set up camp. Dante carried all four, plus blankets and oil and food. He would cut through the mountain to the next valley so as not to be spotted on the roads leading into Spoleto. He went to his father's bank to withdraw ten thousand lire but the teller would only allow him to take three hundred. One lire for every kilometre that he hoped to travel.

He took also money from his mother's purse, the thin, pinched bag she kept between the mattress and the bed boards in her room, the black leather worn along the edges and cracked in a solid strip down the centre where the purse was pressed against the creaking wood. He took her housekeeping money, meant to feed his father for the coming month, including the money she had skimmed off the top to give something in the house, in her closet, in her garden, some colour. A fabric end or a handkerchief from the market, tulip bulbs. He took all of it, leaving behind the only note he would write to her in her lifetime.

My mother, I am gone. I have taken your money and I will pay you back, every penny, as soon as I can. I hate my father, but I love you.

He left it under his pillow so she would find it when she made his bed.

He would be free and there would be no one to tell him what to do.

He went in the morning down the city street, past the church and the train station, past the small hospital, the barber's, the dry goods store, the bakery, without raising one eyebrow. While his mother washed the dishes, while his father went to the city hall where the hot small offices of the central administration of the Provincia del Umbria were housed, Dante walked out of what had been his life. If his back ached from the last belt-thrashing his father had administered, he ignored it. He walked past the ruins of the aqueduct and along the black road to Rome. He was cheerful and light, as though he had climbed the thousand steps to the top of a high and holy shrine and stood suddenly upright, healed of all that had bent him lower to the ground. He would get to a city in the north, find a factory and work his way up. He would get an apartment. He could fix things, all kinds of things. That would be useful. He would be fine.

He walked on the side of the road.

He was nearly to Terni before he unwrapped the cheese he had packed, also his mother's. He ate some of the hard bread as he sat by the waterfall at Marmore. His clothes were getting wet from the mist thrown up by the cascade behind him. He did not mind it. He sat with his back against a tree and imagined his mother finding the note, perhaps clutching her chest and screaming for his father. Maybe even collapsing. The neighbours would run right into the house. They would fan and pat her and wonder about the doctor and whether they should go to the expense of fetching him. He imagined his father's fury. Dante sat, drinking free water, free of crockery, free of sound. He did not hear his father's loud voice, abrasive, accusing, asking if he was not perhaps a camel from the deserts of Africa that he should drink so much at one sitting without any consideration for anyone else at the table. All this he could hear while the cold water ran past him. He bent and scooped, lifted and spilled. There was no table, no floor. The front of his shirt was soaked through and it would dry in the sun. He gave up trying to keep dry at all and stomped into the middle of the stream as if he were an infant, splashing and falling down.

Dante's mother had sometimes taken him to see his father at his office, at work, to get a sense of his importance. Once, Dante had spun on the chair and knocked over the ink. His father could not beat him at work, so the punishment came later in the afternoon, after lunch and his father's nap. Before he put his belt back on, he came into Dante's room and warmed it over the boy's backside.

He was free of that now.

Giuseppe would be at his office at his desk, stamps on the right, pens and pencils in the centre, calendar of important events slightly to the left. The black telephone, prominent on the corner of the desk ready to sound the portents of the emerging Fascist authorities under whom he laboured. One of the ladies of the street would come for him with the terrible news of his wife's collapse and his son's disappearance.

He was out. He was free. He spread himself out on the bank, taking up as much breadth as he could on the earth.

He wondered what Sabino would think and whether he would keep quiet about the direction in which Dante had chosen to travel.

His clothes dried in the sun the next morning, but he had spent the night in a wet tent and the damp and the lack of food and the weariness that burdened his every footfall rendered him vulnerable. Just outside of Narni, he sat down on a rock. It was midmorning and the bees murmured drunkenly around the poppies by the side of the road. Just down the hill, he could see a man at work in his field, scything the new hay. The torpid air weighed on Dante's limbs and when he braced himself to rise, his head emptied of blood and he fell between the waving red flowers. He did not think the August heat sufficient to account for the vast heat of his body. He waited for something. For his head to clear, for his legs to regain their strength.

After some time passed, he pushed himself upright. He used the rock to lever himself onto his feet and he managed some steps toward the man in the field. He tried shouting, but his voice, which he had not used since speaking at length with himself in Terni, only cracked and stalled. He tried waving, but could barely lift his arm. He stepped off the road and went to the fence. Using it for support, he managed to walk far enough to draw the man's attention. He lifted his hand and fell finally down.

After his flight from home and his adventures on the delirious border between life and death, rolling and writhing on the straw pallet that the farmer had seen fit to lay him on at some distance from the livestock, the precious pigs and cattle whom Dante might contaminate if he were housed too close to them, after his dreadful father found him there and wept at his side and then rose to beat the farmer with his own staff out of frustration and fear for his only son, after the bumping, turning road that rose and fell with his fever, the road that finally took him home to his clean bed and the soothing ministrations of his mother, Dante recovered once more, this time from typhus, and once more, against all odds.

Back in his room in Spoleto, he sat for long mornings looking out the window at the garden below and at the town as it stretched beneath his window. He followed the street to the ancient Roman wall that divided the old town from the new and then followed that to a vision of the Ponte and beyond it, to the Rocca itself.

He had been to Rome. He had heard Mussolini with his own ears, and though he had grown out of his black shirt and was, for the moment, too weak to be his own man and chart his own course, he felt that he must go. Not to enlist would be cowardly, Dante thought. To wait until one was called up, to be the only young man in a city of old and infirm who could recall the battles of their own youth would be too shameful. Perhaps the Duce was, in his exhortation toward glory and war, fundamentally correct. Dante had time to think. Dante's father and his parents' friends, dressing up and saluting the portrait of Mussolini that now hung in all the buildings of the town, were playing at something that had already passed them by. Dante would be the one to leave, to put his feet on the path to glory. He would be a man. He would not run away any more. He would give up the childish games that so amused Sabino and him. No more raw eggs on the Professore's chair at school. Perhaps no more school at all.

First, he must eat more soup, as his mother commanded. He must grow strong again. Beneath his nightshirt, he could count his own ribs. He was thinner than he'd ever been and, as he got stronger and was able to move slowly down the street, the young children began calling him Pinocchio, his stick arms and legs, even under his clothes, resembling nothing so much as a wooden marionette.

He lay most days as the waxing and waning panes of the sun arced across his room. He was surprised at each day's finish, at the ease with which time, normally so full of motion and talk, exchanges and activities more or less significant, ceased for the most part, but afternoons and evenings followed on the heels of mornings with relentless consistency while Dante, weak and quiet, slept or gazed into space, his head held to his pillow like steel to a magnet. His father, having rescued him from the brink of death, now stood outside the room. He stepped across the threshold with a new awkwardness, dodging in to place a book or fix a shutter, suddenly shy around his son. Dante wanted to ask what was wrong. He never thought he would miss the threat of a slap on the face, but this new father, quiet and clumsy, was too strange to him. He acted with reverence toward Dante whose life had been spared twice. Did Giuseppe believe perhaps that God above had spared Dante for some crucial purpose of his own and that he, as a good father, had better not interfere?

Whatever the cause, his behaviour made the days peaceful, these days of no choice. No decisions, no exertion, no real visitors, except the quiet Sabino whose blue eyes closed on tears and who shook his head when he saw his friend so gaunt and frail. Dante lay still as a swaddled infant. He had listened to the radio, to Mussolini talking about justice for the Italian people and glory for the empire. Outside his garden, the *vecchietti* in Spoleto discussed their pleasure with the Duce because he had cleaned up the streets and given them all government pensions for their long years of service to the state. As everyone noticed with approval, the trains arrived on time, the criminals were sent to jail, and the roads and sewers and municipal water supplies were in tiptop shape. Weak as he was, these were not Dante's concerns, however. The breeze moved the leaves; the leaves turned this way and that. Perhaps Fascism would make him good and strong. It would be like his mother's soup and he would be fortified and rise up once and for all.

When his father brought him back to Spoleto, weak and skeletal thin, Sabino was the first one at his door. His eyes downcast, dark lashes over blue irises. Sabino sat in the chair brought into Dante's room for visiting and hung his head, his shoulders sloped, hands curled one into the other, perfectly still. There was no fight in the lines of his friend's posture, no possibility of throttling any sort of sense into someone as stupid as Dante. Dante knew he must be a shocking sight.

Sabino said, "*ciao,*" and "*come va?*" as though Dante might have just paused, suddenly supine, in the middle of a commonplace day. Sabino came day after day to sit in the chair in the corner. He brought cookies and cakes that his mother sent for Dante. He brought crossword puzzles at first. As Dante got stronger, he brought checkers and chess. They moved to the back garden and Sabino passed his time throwing rocks at cans set up on the ancient wall. The recovery was slow and steady. The passage from broth to eggs to meat took months and there was not one day that passed without the stolid presence of Sabino, for whom even Dante's father developed a grudging attachment. He showed the boy his wine press and his personal signed photograph of the Duce.

"That Sabino," he said from his post at the threshold of Dante's door, "he's not as stupid as he looks."

High praise.

Angelina

Angelina *was just eighteen* when her cousins from Rome invited her to stay.

"They want you to work in the store."

"*Si, mamma.*"

"A store, Angelina. On your feet all day."

What did her mother think? Angelina was on her feet most days. Up the mountain, down the mountain. And not strolling either, as she had seen the wife of the teacher do. That woman, flushed and floral, brushing her hand along the needles of the pines and the soft leaves of the cypress, as though God put them there for her pleasure. Angelina stopped herself.

I sound like Anselmina.

"Roma?"

"*Si*, Roma, but it is still store work. You would have to dust. To stand and be courteous to all kinds of snobby Romans. Convince them to buy things that nobody needs. Would you like that?"

"Our cousins are Romans."

"Yes, but they know where they come from."

"Why do they want me?"

"Zia Maria is sick and Stefania cannot be trusted to work alone.

Your uncle is barely managing. You go to Rome for a few months and then come back."

Angelina had been to Rome only once. When she was eleven, her mother had taken her down the mountain on the donkey to the train station in Visso. The station was near the main square where her father sold produce and what scrap iron he could find. On that trip, Angelina had been able to smell the bakery before she saw it. They walked past the window with fat hard bread on display and dainty pink pastries topped with cherries of an unlikely red. She had seen them before, but this time she was in the town more or less on a holiday. She was not helping her father set up his stall. She was dressed in the best clothes her closet provided. A pressed dress of thin cotton with a bow tied at the back. Her mother had borrowed the neighbour's daughter's shoes and shined them to a high gloss.

They were going to Rome, she said, and they could not look like bumpkins.

Angelina could not have cared less about her clothes. She was going to Rome.

Angelina remembered getting off the train at the Roma Termini in such noise as she had never heard. Crying infants and shouting porters, hawkers selling trinkets, people shouting into telephones. She would have liked to cover her ears, but she did not wish to embarrass her mother who walked easily, as though nothing were more natural than stepping off a train in what must be the biggest city in the world. Her formidable small mother passed through a crowd that seemed to part before her. She was rigid and as tall as her spine would permit her to be. Angelina straightened up and walked beside her past the taxis and buses and through the streets of Rome. They walked and walked and walked down street after street until Angelina thought perhaps the entire population of the world had decided to move to Rome.

They made their way turning left and going straight, and then left and then straight, then up the stairs to a street that came out behind the Coliseum. They found the steps that took them down to the street. They walked along with the Forum on their left. They crossed the Piazza Venezia and turned left again toward the Tiber. Angelina noticed that at every left turn, her mother said a prayer, barely whispered. *Sinistre.* Too much turning to the left was dangerous to the soul and one had to guard against it. She was glad herself to square her shoulders on the street that would take them to the Città del Vaticano.

They went for the Easter blessing, down the dark corridor of the Via della Conciliazione. The street was dark and fragrant with the smells of the onions and eggplant melting against tomatoes and hard cheese in the small apartments down the long street's corridor.

"*Guarda*, Angelina," said her mother. "The Duce will tear all of these buildings down soon. You will not see them the next time you come to Roma."

"Tear them down?"

Even Angelina could tell that the buildings were as old as some in San Placido.

"Hundreds of years old and that man is coming with his machines to make an avenue, a broad avenue, as though we were Parisians, or worse, Americans."

Angelina could not imagine such a change. She looked all around her at the flowers hanging out of ancient windows. In spite of the April warmth, Angelina shivered as she and her mother walked in the shadows of the ancient buildings.

When they came to the end of the street, Angelina's eyes blurred with the brilliance of the sun on St. Peter's Square. She had stepped, as Father Paolo often said, out of darkness and into marvellous light. In the wavering heat, Angelina's mother pulled the girl's arm through her own as they walked across the square toward the Basilica. She could feel her mother breathing deeply. Nuns crossed their path, clusters of them, dark or white-clad, sombre, pale, and clean. One walked with a limp and two sisters accompanied her on either side, bearing as much of her weight as she would permit. There were tourists with cameras, held against their chests with long leather straps. They posed their wives and children and framed photos, squinting against the light.

Angelina's mother crossed herself, lifted a tender finger to her forehead and heart and crossed her two shoulders, ending with a kiss. Her head bowed. Angelina did the same. They were climbing the stairs to the Basilica, passing the Swiss Guard and the stern Fathers and humble monks and the families of pilgrims and unbelievers. They entered St. Peter's and Angelina stopped.

The air was cool and shadowed inside the church. The whispering lisp of tourists around her speaking softly before the Pietà, or the statue of St. Peter, or the reliquary, or the candles, all within a circumference of marble and gold, struck an echo in the vast hall. She looked up at the dome, at the paintings of the apostles, at the inscription that she could not understand. Light, and more light, columns of it, solid and defined, as though there was a heaven and bits of it were escaping, as though there was such a thing as magnificence, a separate thing, uncommon and immanent, this light penetrated from the very arc of the dome to the marble of the floor beneath Angelina's borrowed shoes. Her head was back as she regarded the light. The days were bright in San Placido, but she had never seen anything like this. At home, her eyes were mostly down. With a knife to cut meat, you had to watch what you did. When you plant a vegetable or milk a cow, you should pay some attention. In this place, she could not bend her head. She lifted her face to the dome as though it housed the radiant sun itself.

She could not take it in. After some minutes, Angelina looked around, expecting to see others like her, dumbstruck and fixed in one spot, but there were none—only people milling about, pointing at this or that object. She began to feel that she too should move on and look at the sculpture and paintings and memorials to the dead Popes and heavenbound saints. She followed her mother. Her eyes blurred.

The rest of the day, the mass at the Basilica, the choirs, the long day of prayer and waiting and walking, she did not call to mind. Only the crossing into the threshold of a place of both tenebrous darkness and hallowed light. Those complicated words of the Latin mass, which she had said so often in San Placido, were realized here.

Dante

Once Dante recovered from typhus, he and Sabino got jobs working for Signor Giallo, who owned a garage at the edge of the city. Signor Giallo was a friend of Dante's family and Dante knew how it would have humbled his father to go with his hat in his hand to see his more prosperous friend and ask him for a favour. He was a good Fascist and believed by many to be on his way to great things, city council or the mayor's office even. Dante worked first on small engines before turning to larger car and tractor motors. Signor Giallo told Dante he would not be paid for the first year, that he should consider the work his apprenticeship and that in the second year, as he proved more useful, he would start to make good money. Sabino was paid in cash just few lire a week for cleaning up the shop. He seemed pleased with his wages and, if he had not the promise of better things to come, Dante envied his friend even so little pocket money.

Dante learned to weld, to wire, and against all odds, to keep his mouth shut. He used the wrench and the drill. He was filthy every day under the engines of cars and tractors. He was on top of them, working, sometimes in them. His bread had the taste of diesel.

On the first anniversary of Dante's employment, he approached

Signor Giallo to ask him about wages. Smiling behind his desk in another new wool suit, he told Dante that because he had proved himself he would now be paid six lire a week.

"*Sei lire?*"

Dante's face reddened. It was enough to purchase a package of cigarettes, no more. He thought his fist would slide off the cheek of Signor Giallo, so slick it looked. Oiled.

"*Si, si!* Dante, boy, no need to thank me. You have done very well and you will continue. I see a bright future for you here. You and your friend. I would hate to lose you both."

Dante understood. Any trouble he caused would land on Sabino's head as well. And on Sabino's family for whom even *sei lire* would make a difference. And on his father's head, his proud father who went so boastingly to the meetings of the Fascist Party, who tipped his hat as though a clerk's job in the city hall of a city outside Rome placed him in Mussolini's antechamber.

He did not know how long he would be able to work for Giallo. For his father's pride, he cared less and less, but he would have to warn Sabino so that his friend could try to find another job before Signor Giallo expelled him from this one. Sabino would be able to find something. He was quiet and followed instructions to the letter. He would be fine.

When the military school opened in Spoleto, Dante saw his chance to get out from under his father and his boss. He would enroll in officer training. He would get out of this town, finally, out of the country. The sibilant *Abyssinia* rang in his memory. He would perhaps be stationed there and see things not one person in Spoleto had ever seen. He would go away and not come back. Not until he could wave a fistful of lire under his father's nose and buy a golden bracelet for his mother, one without charms or medallions. No Holy Mother, no Saint dangling from it. Something that would distract her when she rolled dough, that would get in her way. Something utterly without use. He would decide on his own behaviour. He would read and speak and people would listen. He was eighteen and these were the things he could predict.

This time he did not run away. He told his weeping mother and silent father that he was leaving. He got to the bottom of the stairs and closed the door on the ancient house of his father.

He proceeded left on the Via Monterozze. His boots rung on the cobblestones in the quiet evening, but the echo alone could not account for the strange sense he had of being followed. He turned the corner at the bottom of the hill, keeping his eyes front. He would not look over his shoulder. He would not. Still, his neck began to ache with the conviction that someone, enemy or friend, was following him in lock step. He walked easily up to the gates of the school with a light duffel bag over his shoulder, a hand in his pocket, sizing things up. Looking them up and down, these buildings on the outskirts of town that would open his future to him. He could have giggled like a girl. He was leaving everything familiar behind.

He reached to open the gate and a figure ran in front and pulled the handle for him.

"Ai, Sabin, what are you doing here?"

"I think the military school is a good idea. So does my mother. They will have to feed me there."

His friend also carried a duffel bag. It was not properly fastened and it appeared that socks were escaping from the back end. He stepped back from Dante, still holding the gate so that it swung wide open. He bowed and ushered his friend into the courtyard of the school. Dante looked back at the traffic, at the bell tower of the *chiesa* in the distance, at the Rocca squatting behind it. Sabino would not listen to reason. And in truth, removing his appetite from the family table would leave considerable surplus for his mother's younger children.

"All right. However, we cannot both be *motoristas*. You have to aim for something else. How about a cook? You're brilliant in the kitchen."

"I was thinking."

Dante waited.

"I was thinking I would see about being a pilot."

"But you can't see past the end of your nose."

"The end of my nose is quite far away from its beginning."

Dante hung his head. "Come on, then. No point in following behind me if I am going to have to keep your plane in the air."

They registered together at the academy. They would be trained as paratroopers, gunners, and mechanics to serve the empire. They were handed cards to sign, swearing an oath of allegiance to the Fascist Party. They were given uniforms and assigned bunks and told in fierce tones what would happen to them if their kit was not maintained to perfection. This did not seem to Dante as though it would be a difficult task. He was finally a man on his own. With Sabino.

The orders, however, constant, staccato assaults, were relentless.

Lieutenant Alessio spat into the air, onto their faces. Dante had signed up to join the victory parade. To augment the glory of his country. To escape his father's house. He did not think he would be worse off. Here he was made to understand that in spite of what he had managed in his life to date, at the military school he could neither stand nor sit nor chew his food with any facility. He was worse than retarded.

"To call you sons of whores is to insult the whores, hardworking women who know how to make a bed at least, which is more than I could say of you. You are without doubt the poorest collection of recruits to insult the eyes of proper soldiers! I call on all the saints of heaven to regard the current misassemblage of so-called men. I have never seen such a hopeless crew."

The lieutenant took out his handkerchief and mopped his brow. The new soldiers stood before him, still in the sun. To sway would be to draw his attention from the general to the unpleasant specific. It did not matter. He turned his back on them as they grunted and heaved through another and another punishment of fruitless pushups. He turned his back on them and called to the heavens for help, to St. Jude, the patron saint of lost causes to assist him in burning off the dross and turn such execrable creatures into Italian soldiers. He said these prayers loudly, and without hope.

Dante pulled the sheet sharply across the bunk so that the end pulled suddenly and he fell on his backside on the concrete floor of the dormitory and smacked the back of his head against the steel rim of Sabino's flawless bed.

"*Merde*, Sabino. Why is your bed so close to mine? How do you get those sheets to stay in one place? This is a bed. I would climb in it very soon and not care one bit whether it was tucked or not. I came to learn about planes. I am heading for the Regia Aeronautica, not the Hotel Venezia."

It was outrageous. A waste of a man's time, he thought, to pull and tuck as a woman might. But he had been threatened with jail by the *tenente* and so he stood up, bent, pulled the bedding taut, tucked for inspection.

Sabino moved to the other side to pull the fraying blanket across.

Dante went out to stand in the grand *piazalle* of the Scuola Allievi Ufficiali. The lieutenant paraded in front of the soldiers, squinting at each of them, up and down. He brushed off invisible lint from the uniforms of those unfortunates who stood within reach. He moved down the rank and scrutinized each soldier in turn. He came to Dante. He opened his mouth wide and let the spit fly.

"Signor De Angelis, what do you mean by this?"

"*Quello?*"

"This blood on your collar! I would concede that you might have cut yourself shaving except that you are bleeding from the back of your head. *Allora, signor,* how is that you are standing on parade and bleeding all over the proud uniform of your beloved country?"

"If we were directed, sir, to do the work of soldiers and not of housemaids, then perhaps these wounds would be more glorious than they are."

Dante's fists were clenched and ready to fly. Why should this man have power over him? He pictured the *tenente's* nose flattened, bent sideways, and pouring with blood.

The men beside Dante remained at attention, completely still. Sabino held his breath.

"Ah, *signor*," the lieutenant said, his voice gentle, "You are perhaps not finding the quarters measure up to your standards. Perhaps the facilities fall short of those at your mother's palazzo on the Monterozze?"

The lieutenant turned to Sabino.

"Soldier, how did this man come to be bleeding from the head? Is his brain too big?"

Sabino stood quietly. The lieutenant's nose almost touching Sabino's, though the fellow had to bend a bit to accomplish this.

"Soldier, you will answer."

"Sir, no sir. The soldier was making his bed when he fell back and hit his head on the metal of the next bunk."

The lieutenant turned his back on the men. Sabino's chest sank as he exhaled a long breath. Perhaps that was it.

"Corporal, dismiss the men. Except De Angelis."

Once the men had dispersed, the lieutenant turned.

"I have a job for you, De Angelis. One that will keep you occupied and out of trouble. One that will help you to develop the discipline of an officer, should you live long enough to become one. We're having a terrible time with the light bulbs around here. They disappear into the homes of the mothers of the men who go on weekends to be with their families. From now until Christmas, you will proceed to each of the barracks and the recreational rooms and remove and store each and every light bulb. There are about one hundred. Then you will rise at four in the morning, reverse your weary steps and screw in every light bulb that you have previously removed. You will guard these light bulbs and assume personal responsibility for them. You will guard them as a mother falcon guards her eggs and I expect you to peck out the eyes of anyone who comes between you and your light bulbs.

"This will keep you out of prison for now. Perhaps it will train you to be a perfect soldier for the glory of Italy."

Dante met the officer's eyes, unblinking. He might as well have been uttering prayers for the dead, for all the notice Dante gave to him. His palms relaxed at his sides. He would not punch the man yet. He had to get out of Spoleto. Therefore he had to stay in the school.

"*Capisci*, De Angelis?"

Dante waited just a breath.

"*Si. Tenente. Capito.*"

Dante saluted, barely waited for the return gesture before

turning his back on the laughter of the officers smoking nearby.

Within the first month, in spite of his careful attention to the light bulbs, Dante was thrown in the brig not once or twice, but three times. Wherever his mistake occurred, always Lieutenant Alessio was there to see it. Dante did not know if the lieutenant watched the other cadets as scrupulously as he watched him, but he bore the brunt of such close observation and nearly got himself drummed out of the school. Alessio watched him like a falcon watches a mouse. Always with precision, always from a distance until it was too late and the falcon dropped on its victim. Dante felt sorry for himself.

To Sabino he said, "If only I were the enemy, a pink British soldier. Then Alessio might hope to gain some reward, some medal for his signal devotion. As it is, I am sure he is only getting for himself a headache."

Sabino was shining his boots. "Perhaps he is pleased with your progress."

"Yes, he speaks regularly about his pleasure when I am in jail."

Dante had slept in through trumpets and reported to roll call in his pyjamas. Dante had stood before the flag, which hung limp in the languid air, and joked about the officer's flaccid appurtenance. Alessio, who may or may not have been having trouble with his wife—depending on whom Dante listened to—heard this and had the military police put Dante in the hole for forty-eight hours. The light bulbs had to look after themselves for days at a time while Dante learned the discipline of confinement.

Alessio's orders haunted Dante from the moment he woke until the moment he laid his head down. If he was not in the brig, the lieutenant's face was pressed close to his own. Dante thought he had escaped such daily condemnation when he left the house of his father. Here it was again. Would it be everywhere? In the farthest reaches of the campaign, would he continue to find these men?

"Tuck in your shirt, *ragazzo!*"

To be called a boy by this man was blood boiling. Dante raised his arm high as though to salute the lieutenant, which had the effect of stretching his shirttail further away from its proper place. For this, Dante was sent to the kitchen to peel wet potatoes until his hands pruned and cracked. He had not known that there were so many potatoes in all of Italy. He had peeled every last one of them, he believed.

He walked slowly from the kitchen, filthy and hot. Alessio was waiting for him to upbraid him again for his appearance.

"You will not amount to anything, boy. You will not get out of this school unless you are thrown out face first. You will be sent to your mother's home in shame to put on an apron and peel potatoes for the rest of your life. It is all you are fit for. You are a shame and disgrace to your father, to me, to the Duce and to Italy. Get out of my sight."

Dante had no strength to respond and no inclination to see another potato while he lived on earth. He hung his head in agreement and went to the barracks where he fell dead asleep.

After a month of light bulbs, guarded preciously underneath his bunk and behind his kit, after a month of listening to the serenading tenors of his company sing to him, "Electrician, technician, *vieni qui perche le luce non fare adesso*," he was promoted by the *Tenente* Alessio to reservoir manager. His job then was to start the pumps in the dark morning so that the reservoir contained enough water for the students when they woke up at 6 a.m. The work kept him exhausted and resentful, but it kept him out of jail as well.

Finally, the soldiers had permission, after three months of training and the rough company of men, to leave the compound after lunch. Dante was anxious to escape. Anxious enough to skip lunch altogether, but since a failure to show up at lunch might result in more trouble than that hour was worth, he compromised. He came into the mess promptly and headed to the table with the rest of his company. His posture, excellent, his stride, measured and confident. Heads turned all around him as he passed. He saw Sabino shake his head. Dante was wearing his best, indeed his only, suit. He would not have to return to his quarters to change and he imagined that in less than hour he would be downtown at a bar having a drink or seeing a film without having to elbow his way through crowds of soldiers that would explode from the school's exit onto the quiet town.

He strode through the mess doors to his place at one of the long tables. Among the uniformed men he sat, distracted by the afternoon's amusement. When he looked down the table he lost his appetite. Shirt after shirt along the whole table and across the whole room all identical, pressed, more or less decorated, but all the same. And Dante sat with his double-breasted suit on, a solid mass of flesh and wool, unable to evaporate. He kept his head down, dipping his bread into the sauce and eating low to the plate. His lieutenant, at the officers' end of the table, rose and came toward him. Dante rose as well. He would not let a pig farmer look down on him, no matter what his rank. He met the man's glare and smiled.

"De Angelis. Stand up straight, man."

Dante was standing straight.

"Look at me, you disgusting excuse for a soldier. What is your business coming into the hall with your clothes on? We feed soldiers here, not fancy city men. Which are you, *bambino*, a child of the city who has lost his way? Or a soldier and a man. You had better make up your feeble mind!"

With each sentence, the lieutenant's voice rose in pitch and volume as Dante held himself still only inches in front of his face and waited for the man to finish. There was spit on Dante's face from which he did not flinch and worse, breath from the man's mouth that would have curled nose hair. When it seemed the man would never run out of wind, Dante turned and left. He crossed the courtyard to the open gate, leaving behind him the open mouths of his comrades. He hopped on a passing bus before the lieutenant could have him arrested.

In the centre of Spoleto, Dante leaned at the bar drinking espresso and listening to the radio. Sitting like this in a bar in the city of his birth, he could easily believe himself a visitor, a man who might be on business, a man who might look at the ladies in skirts and seamed stockings walking by, who might speak to one and buy her a drink. Those skirts smoothed across hips and buttoning at narrow waists. Clusters of such women walked everywhere in the piazza and he could not take his eyes off them.

He ordered a *panino* and sat outside watching the *nonni* and the sweet young girls moving across the square among the cars and shops. *Carabinieri*, lounging on duty, glanced at him and pulled their shoulders back, adjusted their uniforms. Dante thought they might come toward him, that they had, by some miracle of communication, already heard that he had turned on his heel before a superior officer and walked out of a military school in civilian clothes and without permission. He did not think they would arrest him, but he was not sure. He had never been arrested until he went to the military academy. He used to think it would be shameful, but now the brig seemed as unavoidable as kitchen duty. He only hoped to avoid doing something that would leave him facing court martial. Really, he had impressed himself with his own restraint. The lieutenant's nose was intact. Lovely, aquiline, unharmed in spite of severe provocation. Perhaps Dante had learned something about self-control. He still felt a rage inside himself, a choking fury that made his breath feel tight in his throat. But he had not taken a swing at anything more vulnerable than his own flimsy pillow.

Dante took a brief inventory. He sat at the bar, perfectly clean and presentable. He had enough money to pay for his food. He had not kicked a priest or propositioned a woman. He watched the *carabinieri* cross toward him, but for once, he did not meet their eyes. This business of looking at some people in the eye, especially Lieutenant Alessio, did seem to provoke them. Such people, so easily aggravated, Dante thought had an inflated sense of their significance on earth. He did not want to be arrested by the civilian police. Dante put some cash on the bar.

He stopped at the lavatory and rinsed off his face and hands. Good strong hands, honest face. Dashing moustache, he thought. It was a puzzler. He had performed all of his tasks and without complaint. He played cards, sometimes winning, sometimes losing. He had not been punched in the face by his fellow cadets, or worse, ignored. He had friends among the men, not only Sabino, but others as well shared a joke or a cigarette. All should have been well.

He wandered around Spoleto, up toward the cemetery and around to the oldest part of the town, to the curling steep alleyways of shops and dark doorways. He turned right into the courtyard of the Duomo. It looked cold to him, stone blues and greens, spires reaching upward. But reaching for what? He did not go in or light a candle or bend the knee. The old ladies went in and out. The nuns lifted their heads from their prayers, looked at him and looked away. What had God given him that he could not claim as having fought for himself? And why should he return thanks? He did not.

In the park, he sat alone. Up here, he could not see a single one of his fellow soldiers from the school. They must be down in the main square where the food and drink and girls were all handy. He should go back and join them, he thought, but he sat still. He would be back in the brig soon, putting in time until he graduated and made himself useful to the imminent war effort of the Duce. The wind blew through the leaves and it was cool in the shade. And so quiet. He looked at his hands and then bent to see his shoelaces. Properly tied and resting on the high shine of shoes. The grass beneath them looked strange. There was no grass at the military academy. He laughed quietly, thinking for a moment how grass had become unrecognizable. This is what his life had come to.

He walked until he came to the Torre. He paused at the edge and looked across. The hermit's cave was lit by the waning afternoon sun. He almost thought he could see movement in the shadow of the cave and he stepped onto the bridge. It could not be the hermit, who must surely have gone to his eternal reward by now. He had not seen him for more than ten years, not since he was a curious boy, drawn to the cave and to the hermit and not only because he could smell food. Dante walked across, careful about the edge. When he got to the other side, he found the path to the cave overgrown, the bushes and trees grown close together. The silence, more profound. He pushed his way onto the trail and followed its turns to the cool entrance of the cave. In the sudden dimness, he could not quite see. Dante heard the old man speak before he saw him. The sound of the voice startled him.

"Dante, you have grown into a man. Time has done its usual

trick, I see. What are you up to? It has been a long time since your feet found their way across the *ponte*. I do not suppose you still enjoy cookies?"

Dante bowed his head, words clustered on his tongue, cumulating against his lips. He did not wish to speak them. Words of complaint, injustice, whinging words of the hardships of his new life. The dam burst. His mouth opened. He told the ancient man, bent before him, paper blue skin and glistening eyes. The hermit sat composed, intent.

"The worst of it is that in the house of my father, I was ordered about every morning and night. One angry person commanded every waking moment and I thought that was like hell. Now I am in a dormitory with a dozen men, it seems, telling me what to do, when to do it. When to shit—excuse me, father—when to breathe, when to eat and when to sleep. Today, I have walked out of the gate in spite of orders to remain and when I return, it will be to the brig."

The old man was so quiet. He tossed some crumbs he held in his hand to the lighting sparrows. He took his time. When the hermit did speak, he pronounced each word with care, as though each one were holy in itself, nodding in between, as though sorting through language to find wisdom he would consent to pass on.

"I agree, young fellow, that is a trial for you. This business of taking orders from angry men may always be your test. One finds them everywhere in peace and in war."

"I will not last."

"You know that the Eternal One takes the long view. This you do not need me to tell you. He will cultivate your character and your gifts, perhaps through the most frustrating and banal of events."

"Character. Now you sound like Il Duce."

The hermit smiled. He was slow about shaking his head.

"I am not like the honoured Duce because I am going to tell you that it is not the state, but God who holds you, my son. For his glory and for your joy. Why not see what he has to teach you?"

"Father, all my life, I have gone to the church. Every person of my acquaintance, every relative, every soldier—all the good people and all the mean people—wear a golden cross or make the sign of the cross. I look all around and I see churches and crosses and statues and frescoes, but inside I am barren of God. I am so angry that if you, even you, my father, commanded me to take one more breath, I would expire out of spite standing where I am."

"I think that one cannot judge one's life—all the things one will do or think or believe, by how one feels in any given moment."

Dante kept quiet. Though the hermit had led an interesting life, it was likely circumscribed, no doubt, by the confines of his faith.

"I am glad you are well, father. I should return to the school and face my punishment."

The older man laid his warm hands on Dante's. The hermit's light touch startled Dante and his head bent of its own accord. When the man spoke, his voice was vibrant, percussive, as though the heart within his chest might be missing beats.

"Some wandered in desert wastes, finding no city to dwell in, hungry and thirsty, their soul fainted within them. Then they cried to the Lord in their trouble and he delivered them from their distress and led them by a straight way until they reached a city to dwell in.

"May the Lord bless and keep you, my son, and lead you to the river of his delight."

"Amen," Dante said. Inside his hard head he asked, what is the use of this prayer?

On his return to the school, he changed into his uniform and approached the lieutenant. Alessio signalled the military police outside the door and had Dante escorted to the brig. He did not say a word. Dante served his time in confinement with the mosquitoes. He covered his head with a blanket and went to sleep. When they released him the next day, it was to kitchen duty where he spent the remaining weeks before graduation with wet potatoes until his fingers rippled and roughened against the mottled skins he peeled.

Against the expectations of the lieutenant, Dante made it to graduation. After the ceremony, Alessio approached him.

"Well, De Angelis, here you are. Out of the prison and into the fire."

"*Si, Tenente.*"

"You will be all right, fellow. Having survived my tender attentions, not much that the British can direct your way will discourage you."

"*Si, Tenente.*"

The lieutenant laughed and made to offer Dante a kiss of friendship. Dante stepped back.

"Still, you would like to kill me, I think."

Dante paused. Kept his eyes forward.

"*Si, Tenente.*"

Dante was assigned with Sabino to the north to Ciampino, just outside Rome. They worked along side one another as bomber mechanics. They were there with a crowd of other soldiers standing still before the wireless when Mussolini declared war.

The men listened while just a few miles away in the Piazza Venezia in Rome, Il Duce had called one of only four general assemblies of all of his uniformed supporters. Sirens sounded throughout Rome and every soldier or guardsman in the city stopped what he was doing, donned the uniform of his rank and station and ran to the piazza.

Dante said, "There must be thousands there."

They could hear the waves of cheers through the radio. Dante could picture the scene, having been to the place in front of the balcony. Mussolini would be standing there, a small man looking out over a stone balustrade. All the men would be wearing black beneath him. People would be crowding onto the streets and balconies of all the surrounding buildings. The Monument to Victor Emmanuel would be dappled with black. People would hang off statues, waiting for what proclamations would come. Every square foot of standing space would be occupied in those minutes before six o'clock. Dante turned away from the radio. Outside on the airstrip, the flags and banners moved sluggishly. Finally, they could hear Mussolini at the microphones.

> *Fighters of the land, the sea and the air, Black Shirts of the revolutions and of the legions, men and women of Italy, of the Empire, and of the Kingdom of Albania.*

Listen - the hour marked out by destiny is sounding in the sky of our country. This is the hour of irrevocable decision. The declaration of war has already been handed to the Ambassadors of Britain and France.

We are going to war against the plutocratic and reactionary democracies of the West, who have hindered the advance and often threatened the existence even of the Italian people.

The events of quite recent history can be summarized in these words — half-promises, constant threats, blackmail, and finally, as the crown of this ignoble edifice, sanctions. Our conscience is absolutely tranquil. With you the whole world is witness that Italy has done what was humanly possible to avoid the hurricane that is overwhelming Europe, but all was in vain.

It would have been enough to revise the treaties to adapt them to the vital demands of the life of nations, and not to regard them as infrangible throughout eternity.

It would have been enough not to have persisted in the policy of guarantees which have shown themselves to have been above all fatal for those who accepted them. It would have been enough not to have rejected the proposal which the Führer made last October when the Polish campaign came to an end.

But all that belongs to the past. We are today decided to face all the risks and sacrifices of war. A nation is not really great if it does not regard its undertakings as sacred, and if it recoils them those supreme trials which decide the course of history.

We are taking up arms after having solved the problem of our land frontiers. We want to break off the territorial and military chains which are strangling us in our sea for a country of 45,000,000 inhabitants is not truly free if it has no free passage over the ocean. The gigantic struggle is only a phase of the logical development of our revolution. It is the struggle of peoples that are poor, but rich in workers against the exploiters who fiercely hold on to all the wealth and all the gold of the earth. It is the struggle of the fruitful and young nations against the sterile nations on the threshold of their decline. It is the struggle between two centuries and two ideas.

At that memorable meeting in Berlin I said that according to the law of Fascist morality when one has a friend one stands by him to the end.

We have done that and we shall do it with Germany, with her people, and her victorious armed forces. On the eve of this event of historic importance we address our thoughts to his Majesty the King emperor and we salute equally the head of an allied Greater Germany.

Through the radio broadcast at Ciampino, Dante and Sabino could hear the bells across Rome ring out the news of war. They could hear the applause that accompanied each punctuated pause in the Duce's declaration of war. They could hear Mussolini explain. The call to war was a call to a higher morality.

"Did you hear that, Sabin?"

"*Quello?*"

"The higher morality. I wonder what the hermit would say about that?"

Sabino had no reply. The Duce's broadcast concluded with the national anthem. The soldiers unbent themselves to stand and salute the flag behind them, each man's face shaded by his right hand. They had heard their fathers' stories of war. Now they would get a chance to find out for themselves, to make history for themselves. Dante wondered how they would fare, with what courage or despair he and his brothers would meet the looming future. He returned with Sabino to their quarters.

By noon the next day, the lieutenant informed the squadron that they would be deployed within the month. The men went on three weeks' furlough to say goodbye to relations, get drunk, find a girl. Sabino went to see his family, but Dante did not wish to revisit old wounds. He would see his parents in the last few days before he shipped out. He did not think he could endure three weeks under his father's roof. Spoleto itself seemed in his mind too small for a soldier, a man about to be launched into the world. He wanted a big city, to find a place, to strut in uniform down wide avenues, to see women he had never seen before, who were neither friends of his mother, nor related to him, nor had any claim on him. Dante went on his own to Rome.

Angelina

Her mother's voice brought her back to the kitchen in San Placido.

"You will go to Rome and help out at the store until your aunt is better again."

"*Si, mamma.*"

"Tomorrow, Papa will take you again to the train. Remember, you do not get off until the last stop. Stefania will meet you and then take you home."

Angelina packed the family's suitcase and left early with her father. Her mother had given her some lire to spend in Rome, as well as her own old purse to carry it in.

"Hold it close against you, like this."

Her mother pressed the leather against her bosom.

"Remember there are thieves all over the city, especially now. The war is on. There will be soldiers and these are not always the heroes of Italy. I don't care what anybody says. You can put a thief or a rogue in a uniform and he is still a thief or a rogue. Perhaps both at once."

Her mother's instructions continued.

"Remember to get off at the last stop. Do you know what Stefania even looks like any more?"

Her mother looked in the credenza for a photograph. There was not one.

"Don't worry. They all look the same, your father's family. She looks like your father, only much younger and shorter."

Angelina nodded.

"And wider. Much wider through the hips."

Angelina did not think she would be looking at the hips.

"I will look for the nose. It turns left at the end, I think."

Her mother laughed. "Turning toward the food, I think."

"*Certo.*"

"And watch out for the men. I told you there will be soldiers there. The worst kind. Here today and gone tomorrow. They will not be like your brothers or your cousins. Nor your neighbours. Keep your eyes forward and walk quickly. Understand?"

"*Si, mamma, capisco tutto.*"

Angelina went to her room to sort a few things to take with her to Roma. It would be so strange to leave her mother and father. She would not have to cook for her ravenous brothers, at least, and work in a store could not be as demanding as that. She sat on her bed and looked out the small window over the valley. The dog, that dog, was chasing something, a rabbit or a mouse down the side of the mountain and she wondered that he did not break his neck. Angelina would have to speak to her mother about slipping some food to Questo while she was away. If she asked Carlo to look after him, that boy would certainly do it.

Away. Angelina tried to imagine the mountainside covered with roads and cars and fashionable people, sounds of music, engines, perhaps the arguments of neighbours who lived too close to one another to ignore. It might be fun to live in such a place for a while. Over the next few days, she said goodbye to the cows and to her friend, the widow Francesca. She slipped passed Zia Anselmina without having to say anything. No doubt the woman already knew of her trip. Father Paolo stopped by the house to wish her well. He shook her hand and gave her small kisses on her cheeks as well as some lire for her to spend in Rome.

"Perhaps you will need a new rosary," the Father said.

"*Grazie, Papa,*" Angelina said.

"Or some *gelato*. It will be hot in the city."

"*Gelato*, Father?"

"*Senti*, Angelina. Listen. We bless the Father of our Lord Jesus Christ who blesses us richly with all things to enjoy. Including *gelato*."

Father Paolo raised his hand. "The Lord bless and keep you and draw you ever closer to him."

Her father took her to the Visso station, kissed her on both cheeks and went off to fix the wrought iron fence of one of his rich clients. When he had turned the corner, Angelina picked up her suitcase and left the station. She crossed the square, passed the same leather goods store and went into the *pasticceria* where a loud bell announced her arrival.

A woman came out from the back and without looking up, said, "*Signorina?*"

When the old woman saw who was before her, she said, "Ah, Angelina! At last you have come into the shop for a treat, eh?"

Angelina smiled.

"*Si, signora.* Please may I have this one?" She pointed at a tall pink pastry with cherries on top.

"You don't waste any time, I see. You know what you want when you see it, that is certain. Had your eye on this one? It is a beauty and my personal favourite. This will melt in your mouth, child, like a dream you never knew you had. Just heavenly. You have an eye for what is delicious in life, do you not?"

Angelina did not know what the woman meant. The sale was sure. She did not have to be persuaded.

The *signora* lifted the pastry from its place and reverently placed it within a silver box. Around the box, she tied silver ribbon into a bow before with gentleness she handed it over the counter to her customer.

Angelina had the money in her hand ready to pay. The *signora* waved her away.

"Tell your good father to save me a kilo of beans this summer. Okay?"

Such a request would be too difficult to explain to her father. Angelina was sure that no one in her family had eaten such a confection as she was about to enjoy. She would pick the beans and bring them herself when she got back from Rome.

"Certainly, I will. *Mille grazie, signora.*"

"*Buon appetito, signorina!*"

Angelina returned to the station in time to take her seat facing west on the train into Rome. She held the pastry box in her lap. A child leaned back from the opposite row in front of her and stared at the silver ribbon, at Angelina's fingers gripping it. Perhaps he thought she would drop it. Perhaps the moon would fall on his head, she thought, looking at him. The box was the most uselessly pretty object she had ever held. She was going to Rome by herself on a train with spending money that she had almost already used to purchase this indulgence. She pressed her other hand against the train window to cool her palm and to hold herself still.

È pericoloso sporgersi.

It is dangerous to lean out.

She had to decide about the pastry. If she ate it on the train, she could hardly enjoy it in full view of the giant brown eyes yearning toward her. If she waited until she arrived in Rome, there was a good chance that Stefania, or several of her family members, would be at the station to meet her. Then she would have to make a gift of it to Stefania's mother. They would criticize her for being so extravagant as to purchase such a luxury and at the same time for not bringing enough for everyone. Now the silver box in her lap seemed a bad omen. A poor decision. She could not recall the fragrance of the cherries that had teased her so much so that she would be willing to spend some of her parents' hard-saved money on what could benefit no one but herself. The train heaved and Angelina's shoulder hit the window pain. The box slipped, but she caught it again.

When she got off the train in Rome, she walked over to the boy and his mother.

"*Per lei, signor,*" she said to the small child.

She kept walking before his mother could refuse or thank her.

The streets were busier, more crowded than she remembered.

She waited in the terminal for Stefania some thirty minutes before venturing outside. There was no one that she recognized. On market day, Visso was busy, especially in good weather, but this train station was crowded, as though every train from every place were arriving at the same time. People speaking so many different kinds of Italian that Angelina did not recognize parted around her as she stood still on the platform. Angelina waited. She could have eaten her pastry, she thought. She clutched her mother's purse a little closer to her body as though there was some danger that the lire inside might escape as fruitlessly as they would have in Visso, if not for the promise of her father's beans. She could imagine that young boy, his mouth covered with cream, saving the maraschino for last.

"Angelina!"

Finally, there was her cousin, short and squat with her nose veering left. Laughing.

"Stefania, where have you been?"

"Have you been waiting? Waiting long? Ah, don't think about that now. Look at you in Rome. We are going to have so much fun."

Stefania embraced her and pushed her arm through hers.

"Come on, the walk is not far. Look at this place. It is teeming with lovely young soldiers. It's as though the whole city is having a party for young people, don't you think?"

"*Piccola ragazza*, you never change. I am surprised your father has not married you off to the first young man to come within your grasp."

Stefania laughed as though she had never heard a better joke.

"Marriage!"

"*Si*, marriage. Is that not what you are after? You look at every boy we pass."

"Angelina, *cara mia*, looking is not buying!"

They walked past shops and cafés. In the open doors to one restaurant, the men were speaking loudly about Churchill. It was Angelina's first time to hear the strange name that she had read in the newspapers pronounced. So abrupt the English name sounded to her, abbreviated, like the bark of a small dog. Angelina and her cousin stopped in front of the mural that Mussolini had had painted at the Ministero della Cultura Popolare of the Mare Nostrum, the grand display of his intentions to dominate all the shores of the Mediterranean. Rome, with him, was conquering the world again. For Stefania, Mussolini was making a party to which he had invited all the young men of Italy.

The mural was for Angelina one more thing to catch her eye. Out of her small village and beyond the gaze of the aunties and neighbours whose approbation she had not known herself to seek, Angelina lengthened her stride. Around them were shops of all kinds. Shoes, dresses, hats, pastry shops with pink and blue confections stacked in lofty tiers, butcher shops with prize pigs hanging for the women of the neighbourhood to pinch and choose. The cars streaming by along the avenues and narrow streets and Stefania, as Angelina recalled, the same chatterbox as she had been before.

Around corner after corner, they passed soldiers. Young men in uniform, smoking cigarettes and admiring the skirts that swayed past them. Angelina felt she had never been so far away from home. Her father, Nico, and Berto would be coming in from the field for a lunch that she had not prepared. Her mother would wash the dishes by herself. Angelina walked, looking into the faces of the boys they passed. She wondered how long it would take before her ragamuffin brothers joined one of the legions of the new Rome. They would be old enough soon for the war. She could not imagine either Nico or Berto assembling weapons and putting them to any good use. When the cows were stuck in the creek bed, it was Angelina they called to coax the beasts out, to slap their backsides and pull on their ears. She kept them going when the work in the fields had to be done. It was Angelina who could tell about the weather and how much time they had to plant. These were not things over which she had to pause and wonder. Her brothers, they did not seem lucky enough for war, not bright enough to find a way to survive. She was tougher, she knew, than they were and if they went to war, if they signed up for service, she did not believe they would make it home again. These boys in Rome did not appear frightened. Not at all. She could not understand. It was as though they were charging like true youngsters into something about which they had given only the most shallow attention. The young soldiers looked right back at Angelina, flushed with life. They shouted to her and to her cousin,

"*Signorini, aspettate!*" Young ladies, wait!

They held out their arms for the women, waving them back.

"Wait for what?" Angelina asked, turning. "Wait for you? To grow whiskers?"

The boys had been sitting on the rail beside the Forum. When Angelina spoke, the friends knocked each other forward so that they each fell staggering to the ground.

She shocked herself, speaking as though she were standing on one of San Placido's three dusty lanes talking back to Berto and Nico and the other *ragazzi* in the field below instead of on one of the busiest streets in Rome, where anything might happen and she, not knowing even which direction they were going.

The wind blew up around them. Angelina caught hold of her hairpins while Stefania's skirt lifted and twirled above her knees and the soldiers whistled and cheered. Stefania turned and curtsied, her eyes bright. Angelina grabbed hold of the girl lest she permit herself to be propelled right into a scandal. The wind swept against them so that they had to lean forward on a day that had, just moments ago, been one of perfect calm.

The faces of the boys stayed with Angelina. Eyes curling and keen in the bright sun. Faces flushed and shadowless. They looked well-rested, those boys. Their elbows bent and resting on each other's shoulders, choking on cigarettes they must have felt obliged to smoke. The soldiers were pressed and starched in their uniforms. Caps over clipped hair, sheared from their heads by enlisted barbers. They would go to some theatre of war, whatever that meant. In San Placido, she had heard even the farmers and widows speaking of war as though they knew what it was.

Alfonso, Angelina's father, had a gun that he used to shoot a deer or two in the fall. She had loaded it herself and even fired it above the San Placido garden, hurting both her ears and her shoulder. She shot at nothing. Broken jars, good for nothing but target practice. She had tried for rabbits, but the gun ruined them for cooking, even if she was lucky enough to hit one. The pelt exploded, the meat flew, centripetal, obliterated like the glass of the jars.

Her brothers might hold such weapons and aim them at English people. Angelina could not imagine any reason good enough to justify that. And here were the soldiers in Rome, each one a boy really and not grown much beyond the thrill of stealing warm bread from his mother's kitchen. Smiling and smoking, they were the heroes of Italy, caught, she thought, in a strong wind, though not of their own choosing. Not a breeze that would make them laugh and give them a glimpse of a girl's thigh, but one to toss them like the chaff from the field, tossed high in the air to separate it from the wheat, to watch it blow across the mountains until it disappeared. These boys whistled and called out, but they did not interest her. She walked past them, leading Stefania as though she knew the way.

Dante

He *sat in uniform* on the train. The fields were coming at him and sliding past. He crossed one leg over the other. In his pocket was his train ticket. His identity papers, his orders, and a few thousand lire. He had a satchel in the rack above him. No one beside him to speak to. He was quiet. He would write a letter to his mother, explaining the urgency of his orders. She might see Sabino in town, but that would be all right. Dante could not go back. He would write her such a nice letter that she would be glad to read it, to know her son well without having to endure the inevitable friction that Dante and his father provoked. He did not want to feel that old rage again. He was, he thought, probably as large as the old man, but he did not think he could lift a hand to strike him in recompense for all that he had had to endure. In Rome Dante would find a cheap place to stay, and walk the city alone. Perhaps go to a dance hall and see some of the lovely Roman girls, high-heeled and chic. He watched as the outskirts of Rome, rough apartments and clotheslines with bright, fixed shirts, flew past as the train came on to meet them.

When Dante walked past the Coliseum and in front of the Forum, he saw the poor fellow standing in the heat in mail and draped by a woollen cloak, posing stern-faced under his helmet for the purposes of completing a photograph. Discreetly, and to his left, was a dusty fedora upturned and sitting on the asphalt, with a few lire bright against the dark felt.

Dante lifted his hand in a salute to the centurion as he passed. He was curious and wished to talk to the man, but he had no lire to spare for the hat. Dante's eyes moved from the hat back to the man, who stood stock still on one of his own legs and one wooden leg, clearly visible under the skirt of his costume. He remained at attention before Dante and said, sotto voce, "Monte Bianco."

"Piccolo Saint Bernard Pass?"

The centurion nodded.

Dante whistled. "Frostbite?"

"*Si.*" He held out his hands, both missing fingers, for a swift moment before hiding them in a fist around his sword and his staff.

"Photograph?"

"*Come?*" Pardon?

"If you want to chat with me, you must take a photograph."

"I do not want to chat with you."

"Yes, yes you do. I can see it. You have nothing else. You are on leave. You are strolling. I saw you."

"I don't have a camera. *Mi dispiace.*" I am sorry.

"Pretend."

He formed his hands in front of his chest in the shape of a camera and shaded an invisible viewfinder from the afternoon sun. He clicked his tongue and turned the crank and smiled at the centurion who looked straight ahead.

"How did you come to be in such a costume?"

"The Duce has seen fit to amuse the wealthy German tourists and upper echelon officers that you see around you in the cafés, those officers who are here to make sure that we sustain the Axis agreement in Rome. Herr Kessler, you know him? He asked Mussolini to post some ex-soldiers—those whose injuries were not so serious as to nauseate the tourists—to stand in costume in front of the entrances to the Coliseum, or the Forum, or the prison of St. Peter and St. Paul. *Allora*, here I am in front of the Forum and dressed as a centurion. Impressive, don't you think? Please, take another photograph."

The man wore replicas of the leather corselet, the mail, and the ornamented belt. Below, his skirt was double-pleated and on his shins he wore thin metal greaves. Off his left shoulder hung a fine red cloak and in his right hand he held the twisted vine stick that signalled his office. He was a sight to behold and Dante stood aside every few minutes as passersby photographed the fellow and dropped a few coins on their tour around the monuments of ancient industry and war.

"I signed up the day the Germans invaded France. Signor Mussolini wanted the Italian people to share in the glory of conquest, you know how it was. I couldn't wait to bite my thumb at the disgusting French in their own front yard."

"Your company went north?"

"How did you know? It was not in the papers. Nothing was. *Piacere*, move to my left and frame another shot, *signor*. There are German officers on the street over there and I must be seen to be earning my keep."

"*Certo.*"

Dante stepped to the right and molded his hands again.

"You know how news travels," he said. "We hear things. The commanders cannot live in tents and barracks, speak to one another and think we carry turnips between our ears. We heard about the glorious march in to France. How could one plan such a campaign? Did you even have rations? Were you outfitted for the mountains?" Dante moved again and seemed to frame another shot from the side. The officers across the way moved on from whatever had held their interest.

Dante said, "When you are a soldier, for a while you can keep your eyes closed and your mouth open, but eventually, you run out of words and you start to find out what is going on."

"And what is that?"

"You, *signor*, know better than I what is the state of things. Our friends, the Germans, invade France, and the brave Duce sends troops for the Champs Elysées parade."

"Brave, yes. Maybe. But, *dio mio*, to send us through the mountains? In short pants and old farming boots? Not even enough pots and pans to feed us, never mind food to put in them. And not any mountain. The wise leaders took us over that Mount Bianco. The highest point in Italy. Everybody missed the parade."

Dante knew there was more at stake than a parade. He had graduated from the military school. He had listened to the Duce's speeches, the exhortations to glory and manhood that made Dante feel proud and also sick. He understood the drive to recover dignity after the first war. He knew, he believed he knew, what Mussolini wanted—a piece of the action for the father of Fascism. They had to get back what was lost.

"You are lucky to be alive, my friend."

Dante looked at the man's prosthesis.

"Do you still feel the old one?"

"Right down to the bunions. *Otto cento mort*. Three thousand, more, in what they called a hospital. Eight hundred dead and the only enemy was the snow."

"That is a pretty good leg." Dante bent to admire the hinge where the wooden foot met the wooden ankle.

"*Grazie, signor*. I made it myself. Mountain spruce from my father's back garden. Light and sturdy. I have been thinking about painting it."

"No, leave it be. It is an honour to you, *signor*."

"We were imbeciles. We still are. But we are breathing and the sun shines on our faces today and not on our bones. *Allora, adesso*, it is time for you to take other photographs of my city. *Arrivederci*."

Such futility and bravado that had cost this good man his leg, and many others all the breaths they would ever take, was chilling to Dante. He knew that his training as airplane mechanic would keep him safe behind friendly lines. He would not, like the army, march on the enemy to meet them in direct combat. He looked at the space where the centurion's leg should have met the earth. He did not think he would be brave enough to do what this man did.

The centurion looked at him, his face composed to peace.

"Do you know," he said to Dante, "I believe it's true, what the English poet says. That they also serve who only stand and wait."

Dante saluted the man and walked away on his private tour of Rome.

Angelina

At the deli of her uncle, Angelina worked ten- or twelve-hour days. She cut the meat and cheese and cleaned and kept the floors and counters glossy. It was a small space. With her aunt sick and Stefania so easily distracted, the place had been sadly neglected. They were lucky no inspectors had come by to cause trouble. Each day the blades were bleached and scorched in hot water. Angelina liked the work, so simple and defined. Occasionally, a couple of German soldiers would come in and demand samples of the meats. They always came in pairs, never alone. They would try to flirt with her at first.

"Ciao, *signora*. Aren't you a lovely thing?"

Angelina would ask them what they wanted to order.

"Are you available, miss?" One would nudge the other. "May we have six slices of your best feature?"

Angelina waited in silence.

"Ah, so sorry, miss. You are a deaf mute, yes? We find these everywhere in Italy, don't we?"

Some would mock; some stood stern and fierce, pointing at the meat or the cheese and making signs for inches. She imagined as best she could that they were cattle ready for slaughter to whom she must extend decency before they were killed. Dressed in black uniforms, leather and ribbons polished to gleaming, they lounged against the tall counter leaving fingerprints on the glass. They had pistols with them. They were Italy's allies, Angelina knew. They were possibly not very dangerous, but she wished to turn and leave when they came in, as though a bad smell came in with them, a fragrance of cologne on thin warm skin, a smothering aroma that made a fight with the aromatic spiciness of the meats and cheeses she served. They were not like the Italian soldiers who whistled and chatted, bold as they could be. These Germans sometimes looked pleasant, but they were not. They teased her as though she were theirs, a pet they might indulge for a while before taking a switch to its hindquarters. They seldom paid, especially if they were officers.

When she got back to the apartment after mopping up and locking the doors, her aunt each day summoned enough energy to have the table laid for supper, the red cloth spread out for her, the china brilliant.

"Sit, sit, child. You have had a long day."

"*Zia*, you need to be in your bed. I can make my own supper."

"*Carissima*, I have been in bed all day while you have been on your feet. Sit and eat now."

"I had a long day, too, mamma."

"Stefania, while Angelina is working hard in the deli, you stand outside the store and pretend to sweep so that the young men may admire your waist and arms. You would sweep one of those boys right to the church and marry him if you could."

"Nothing wrong with getting married, is there, mamma?"

"Just see that you do, careless girl, and don't bring home any surprises."

Stefania pinched her mother's cheek and laughed.

"Ah, my poor mother!"

Angelina had not heard mothers and daughters speak to one another in this way. She held her breath, waiting for one of them to lose her temper, but they only laughed at one another and handed around the food. Angelina sat. There was nothing for her to do even to feed herself.

Soon, Zio Franco forced her to accept a wage. Only a few hundred lire a day, but it was money now that she held in her own hand. She did not know what to do with it. She sent some home to her mother, but with the rest, she was uneasy. She walked past shops in those brown shoes that she wore on the train from San Placido, shoes that had been handed down to her, still thickly soled. It was not necessary to replace them or add to the burden of things she would have to carry home.

Stefania said, "You are so lucky, Angelina. All that money. What will you do?" She would point out pretty things on their walks through the city. Not one sensible thing caught her eye. Shoes with heels too high for a reasonable woman to take ten steps in. Dresses in impractical shades of blue or white.

"Come on, Angelina. Buy something. There must be something you need."

"What about something you will need in San Placido? A sun hat, perhaps."

When she returned to San Placido, Angelina supposed her mother would need the purse back, but she did not want Stefania with her when she made a decision. On a Saturday afternoon when the shutters were still closed against the late afternoon sun, she went out to find something useful while Stefania was still asleep.

Angelina stepped into the shop and chose the plainest and least expensive purse on offer. Dull and black, it had a strong clasp and a good solid strap. It would last a long time. She touched the leather, feeling for flaws. Snapped it opened and then closed. Angelina did what she had seen her mother do on the few occasions when she had to buy produce from the *alimentari* in Visso. She turned the purse toward the sun at the window as though it were a turnip in the late stages of blue mold and listened, frowning, to the sales clerk.

"I can assure you, *signorina*, that this purse is of the first quality."

Angelina would decide for herself.

"*Grazie, signora*. I see that the leather has been scratched here. Perhaps some other customer was not careful with it. I do not think you can sell it as first quality now."

She bargained with the woman until they agreed upon a price. It was her own and first possession. She would keep Zio Franco's lire in it for a while until she could find a better hiding place.

Even over such a plain thing, Stefania rejoiced when Angelina brought the purse home.

The Roman spring was warm, already humid and noisy with the engines of empire. Angelina walked near the razing of the ancient buildings next to the Piazza Venezia where Mussolini was going to build a monument to King Victor Emmanuel II. In Rome, Angelina had taken on the habit of all Romans, reading the papers to find out what was going on. She read the point and counterpoint editorials for and against the monument. The lavish expense, the further ruin of historical landmarks, and the Duce's intention to make his mark on the architecture of the Eternal City. She did not know if only old things could be magnificent. Some ancient things, she thought, were perhaps past their prime. She endured the noise on her quick walks along the building site, as well as the stares and clamouring flattery of the men working on the footings.

Early on a Saturday morning, Angelina leaned over her cousin's bed, sprinkling icy water on the foolish girl's pretty face.

"*Andiamo*, lazy girl. You know your mother wants us to go to the market for her. Hurry up or all the good things will be gone."

Stefania pulled the sheet over her head and rolled over.

"Angelina, go back to sleep, can't you? It is too early."

"You sound like my brother. Soon you will grow a patchy beard like him, sleeping the day way."

Lying prone, with her arm stretched out over her head in complete repose, Stefania's purple bruise was plain to see. She had banged her shoulder on the corner of the cupboard door the day before and now the mark was dark. Angelina leaned forward and pressed on the bruise while the girl tried to sleep. It was cruel, but rather pleasant to take this lazy lump and inflict some pain on it.

Stefania groaned, but she did not move. Angelina smiled at the still form beneath the quilt. She wished she could lie like that far into the morning the way Stefania longed to do. To lie and stretch, open her warm eyes and close them again without a whisper of a thought, never mind a responsibility. For her, the mattress seemed to have its own ideas; it seemed to push her out of bed in the morning. If she held still too long, her legs would twitch and her feet get itchy. She had to get herself up and now she had to get Stefania up. The problem with Romans was that they were too soft. Too civilized. They needed to feed some chickens, or wring their necks for supper. At the crack of dawn. That would straighten them out. The day was waiting and Angelina did not want Stefania's mother to wait with it.

"You liked those drops, *piccolina*? Maybe you like the whole bucket?"

Stefania pulled the sheet down to see Angelina looming over her with her mother's wash bucket, brimming with water.

"*Va bene, va bene.* I am up, you see? I am up. Here we go once more to the market on a lovely Saturday when we could be sleeping. What do you think is going to happen today, *cugina mia*? What do you think will be so exciting that it will not wait one more hour?"

"The radicchio will grow brown and dry, waiting on the shelf. Just like you! The fish will stink, also like you. The chickens will rot, more like your teeth than you. Hurry yourself. Wash for once!"

"So cruel, you are! Do they teach you that in the mountains?"

Angelina nodded. "Yes, I have a neighbour who gives me lessons."

Stefania smiled.

"I will get up if you promise me to talk to a soldier today."

Stefania held her arm and stroked it, light and smooth.

"I am so sorry to disappoint you, my sleepy cousin, but I will not speak to a soldier today or any day. My mother warned me about them before I left San Placido. They are not like my brothers, good solid young men! They are whistlers, talkers, looking for a dance or a kiss before they go off to war."

"So? What is the harm in a dance or a kiss? Poor things. We may be the last Italian women they see. Imagine if they had only Russian peasants or African women to dance with. We owe them something for their heroism. They whistle and call, Angelina. It is so dull that you never speak to them when you know they might be sent off to their death at any moment. I would die to talk to a soldier."

"Then you better not open your rosy mouth."

Stefania leaned up on her elbows to admire herself in the mirror across the room.

"You think I have a rosy mouth? That sounds nice."

"Stefania! Hurry up, child."

"Don't call me a child. I'm just as old as you are. Much friendlier though." She looked at her cousin. "But not as pretty. I don't get half the whistles that you do."

"I will wait for you downstairs."

As she left the apartment, Angelina could hear her cousin shouting, "Promise you'll talk to a soldier today!" The laughter echoed along the tile floors and down the hall. Angelina had to laugh as well at the silly girl. Talk to a soldier, indeed. What for?

Angelina had already braided and pinned her brown hair. The dress she washed the night before had already been ironed and was back on her again. Tonight she would wash her other one. What did she think would happen today? They would have a little break from the store, perhaps visit some shops and have a *gelato* at the place near the market. Sit by the fountain. She thought about tossing a coin over her shoulder into the frothing water, but what would she wish for? What did she expect? What would a kiss feel like?

Finally, Stefania came down the stairs to the front of the apartment.

"Don't you shake your head at me, *signorina*. You are worse than mamma for getting me out of bed. At least she leaves me alone for a few minutes. A girl needs rest you know. You will be wrinkled before your time, Angelina, if you do not take proper care of your skin."

Angelina walked ahead of the prattling Stefania. Not quite out of earshot. They caught the bus at the corner of the Via Garibaldi and sat in blessed silence until it was time to get off. The women walked past shining windows, Stefania looked in each one and offered her opinions about the goods within. What she would buy when her father paid her a proper wage, how she would wear that blue dress or tilt the matching hat.

"Look, Angelina. See? It would sit over my hips just like that."

Angelina turned to look in the window. The dress had buttons and sleeves, a fitted bodice and a fuller skirt. One of the buttons looked like it would fall off without much effort. She was about to say so when something in the window's reflection caught her eye.

She saw a soldier, alone, cross from the opposite side of the street and come toward them. He was smiling and not watching for traffic, as far as she could tell. She turned away from the reflection and toward the flesh. Dark hair he had, and a face lined at the corners of his mouth. There he was just a few paces behind them.

"Come on, Stefania. At this rate, we will never get to the market."

"But the dress. I could at least try it on."

Angelina was already moving down the street.

The soldier was following behind, barely gaining ground.

"It is a beautiful day, *signorini*."

Stefania, of course, turned.

"*Buon giorno, signor. Come va?*"

"*Molto bene, signorina, grazie, e lei?*

"Very very well, thank you."

"*E lei, signorina?*"

Angelina would not answer. She waved her hand and pulled at Stefania to keep the girl moving. Even though she and Stefania had not known any real difficulty with them, Angelina would not be stopped by a soldier in the middle of the street in Rome. He was not one of the Germans, just an ordinary Italian boy dressed up in a uniform. No menace at all. Besides, she was her mother's daughter. He would be here today and gone tomorrow. Who knew what he would like to accomplish within those few hours. She had errands to run for her aunt and the day was wasting.

"Pardon, *signorina*? I did not quite hear you."

Stefania, amused, repeated to Angelina, as though she had not heard, what the young man had said.

"*Signorina*? The gentleman is asking how you are on this fine day? Can you not understand Italian any more?"

"I understand," she said.

Angelina kept a steady pace. There were thousands of men in

Rome. Desperate, they seemed to her, especially the soldiers. Desperate and shameless. She was not amused by this one. Not worried about him, either. He was quiet and smiling, stretching his legs out to keep up with her and still lagging behind.

"I saw a centurion the other day. Have you seen that fellow?"

Angelina could feel Stefania looking at her. The girl half skipped to keep up. She grabbed Angelina's arm to slow her down.

"Angelina, did you see a centurion?"

The soldier laughed. "Not an actual centurion, of course. A fellow in costume, hired to entertain the passersby. He only had one leg, but he had interesting stories to tell."

"Would you like to hear one?"

Stefania slowed down. "I would."

Angelina stopped finally and turned. The soldier had been following so closely that when she stopped, he stumbled into her. She lost her balance and grasped his arm for a quick moment. She stepped back. She was almost as tall as he was.

Rome was full of men. Full of soldiers. They would come on leave before shipping out to Africa or Yugoslavia or Greece. Anywhere Mussolini decided. Here was one more, wanting her to see him, talk to him. She had seen the girls of her village grow up and find men around whom to act foolishly. The next thing that happened was that they would be at the well washing the blood and seed out of their sheets until the baby came very shortly afterward. Or there was no blood. Sometimes a girl would take an over ripe tomato to stain the sheet on the first night. Everyone could tell except the groom. In any case, Angelina was too practical. She had enough work to do without taking on more. First the work of feeding a man and then added to it, the work of a baby.

When the men whistled at her, called out to her, "*Ciao, bella, bellissima,* come here to me and marry me now before I die, kiss me, *innamorata,* sweetheart, don't walk away" she laughed at them. They might have been cattle bawling for feed. They could not touch her or hold her. She would not let them. She was in Rome. She was doing easy work at her uncle's deli and he was paying her money for it. She missed San Placido, she missed her family, but not so badly that she was not happy to be in the city. And here was a soldier, standing before her with warm blue eyes. Another one, but she did not shake him.

He was not as young as she at first thought. There was nothing heedless about him. He did not seem like a man who would find a way just to kiss a girl before running off to Africa.

He stood still with his hands in his pockets.

"It is a beautiful day. I think we are going in the same direction," he said. "*Signorina?*"

"What do you want?"

"I think, to go for a walk with you. What do you think of that?"

She had seen his reflection in the window. Even cloaked in light, his face had pleased her. In the flesh, the angles and creases of that face caught her. Her gaze was caught like burr on a wind-filled sheet and nothing would budge it.

For the soldiers in Rome, she knew she was a distraction, a skirt to look at before they went to the war. But this soldier looked at her and she thought that maybe for years she had walked the earth as a ghost might walk. Peaceful or contentious, barely touching the surfaces she crossed. This young man smiled and she slipped into herself. Felt her feet on the ground tingle as though new blood looped through her veins. There she was in his eyes. Herself. Angelina. Tall and slim, lips full and only just frowning, arms folded across a small waist. Plain blue buttoned dress. This woman, new and strange to herself. His blue eyes making her into something she had not before felt herself to be.

From a simple glance. It was ridiculous.

"A walk. With you?"

"*Sì.*"

Stefania was already pulling the market basket from Angelina's hands.

"I'll go on without you. I know what my mother wants." She tapped her head and turned back up the hill. "I'll meet up with you later," she called back over her shoulder.

The two strangers watched Stefania walk away.

"*Mi chiamo* Dante. Dante De Angelis."

"I am Angelina."

"Angels are everywhere today, I think."

"*Come?*"

"I am De Angelis and you are Angelina. That must be a strange coincidence."

Angelina did not think so. "Where would you like to walk?"

"Angelina, let's walk a little further to the garden, the Villa Borghese. We will find some shade and get acquainted. Do you like *gelato?*"

"*Non adesso.*" Not now.

"Of course not now. After lunch!"

He kept his promise, first taking her to a long lunch on the Via del Mattonato. The Lucia, just opened the year before. He ordered the cuttlefish, a thing she had never heard of, with snow peas, funny things, to lie so flat.

"The pea stays in the shell," she finally said.

"*Sì*, you eat the whole thing."

She sipped the wine and pushed the strange food around the plate. The sun was too warm and the food too different from what she was used to. Angelina had difficulty making it go down. She could not think of anything to say. Dante talked into her silence.

"The food here is very good, don't you think? It is a bit difficult to find."

"I am afraid it seems expensive."

"They give discounts to soldiers."

"Really?"

"I don't know, Angelina. But it will be all right. Soon I will be deployed to some godforsaken place where the only food for miles may be what I can dig up with my own hands. Who knows?"

Who knows, indeed. She did not know what she was doing or what her aunt might think of her. What Stefania would say or whether they would be upset. Angelina was sure she should go.

"Don't worry," Dante said.

"Worry about what?"

"You looked like you were about to jump on the next bus. Don't worry, Angelina. Your aunt will not mind. I will meet her and then she will be charmed. All will be well, you'll see. Besides, you haven't had your *gelato* yet. And the shop around the corner is famous. You must try it."

"All right."

She didn't know if there was something corrupting about the city, about the shops where you could buy anything or the restaurants where one could sit and be served food that someone else had prepared. She would normally feel a bit ashamed of such ease, but Dante leaned back in his chair and appeared as innocent and peaceful as a child discovering something astonishing. She was conquered by the painful hope that it was her. She felt her muscles ease and she turned her head to look at her neighbours and at the passersby. What a rush they seemed to be in and how pleasant to be still. She listened to his story about the centurion. She laughed when he told her that he himself was really a saint who had not yet been beatified. He had this on good authority from the saintly hermit of Spoleto.

"That's enough nonsense, at least for five minutes. *Andiamo*, dear Angelina. Do you know, I like your name very much? Let us go and find something refreshing."

They walked around the corner to the *gelateria*. Dante ordered her the *limone*, which she loved, and she moved with him among the shoppers and hawkers, unaware of the rising heat of the afternoon or the passing of time.

She was, however, aware of the ice and her tongue against it. The lemon was delicious, but instead of cooling her, she could feel the heat in her face. Angelina kept turning away from Dante to look in shop windows. She tried to scold herself. She would think of the farm, of the cattle, of her parents, her chores, her brothers, the pleasure of throttling them, but then the gelato would melt and she would slip her tongue around it and Dante would seem not to watch.

Angelina walked alongside Dante, listening to him speak, words in a stream coming out of his mouth, underneath his moustache. She watched the ground move under her feet. She listened to the stories he had heard from the poor old soldier who had found a job dressing up for German tourists. His friend, Sabino, was also on leave, but was visiting his family. No, Dante did not want to visit his family. His mother cried too much and fussed about his absence. His father, well.

"I was born in Spoleto. I am from there. Not too far away."

She spoke quietly. "I am from San Placido. It's small, but it's not far from Spoleto."

"San Placido," he said. "*Bella* San Placido."

"I think Spoleto is very famous. I have never been."

"We have the giant bridge there. And we have the hermit, too. Our very own."

He put his hand out to assist her on the last high step into the villa grounds. She looked at his hand in front of her and wondered if he meant to stop her.

"*Signorina*. May I take your hand?"

She could feel her face reddening, warmth upon warmth encroaching.

She placed her hand in his palm and took the last step, breathless. He smiled again and turned her hand over. Her open palm was warm from the climb. Dante stroked the skin, none too soft, that he held in his own fine hand, stirring the blood underneath to quickness. He kissed the white inside of her wrist, quick and light, and held her hand for a few minutes more as they walked through the shaded gardens.

Dante

In Ciampino, Dante worked on the engines and instrumentation for the Savoia-Marchetti 79 Sparrowhawk.

"Listen, Sabin," he said from inside the cockpit. "I'm going to tell you about this beauty."

"Dante, I have heard your father speak and now I am hearing you."

"What are you saying?"

"You sound just like your father."

Dante leaned out over the plane. He put his face close to Sabino's.

"I could punch you in the face for saying that. I am nothing like that man."

"Don't you remember how he used to drill you in the history of Spoleto?"

"Yes, but I am not drilling you. I was going to tell you so you will know that this marvel of engineering was designed by Alessandro Marchetti and we got a look at it just six years ago. 1933. You should take pride in it. It is the best in the world. Marchetti named it after himself and after the Royal house of Savoia. Look at it, man. Look at it. You fix it but you don't pay attention."

Sabino stepped away from the fuselage. He looked at the plane.

"It is very nice."

"Nice? This is not a nice plane. This is the fastest, sleekest trimotor there is. Look at these. These trimotors have three Alfa Romeo nine cylinder air-cooled engines."

"I like the colour. Though I think the red will be easy for the British fighter planes to pick out of the sky."

"It's fast though. No dorsal hump, no gondola. It was meant to race. You remember the race?"

"Ah, *si*, Paris-Istres. I read about it."

"This makes you proud to be in the Regia Aeronautica, doesn't it? They spared no expense. I love to work on this plane, Sabin. It is simple and clean, no doors or windows. It is our best, this S-M 79 and here we are, right inside it."

"You are in it. I am underneath it."

Dante ignored his friend. He had worked hard and for once contained his rage so that he could be posted to work among the Elite Twelfth Stormo pilots, the select few chosen to fly these planes. He was one of the "Sorci Verdi," the Green Mice.

Dante ran his hands along the plane's curving contours. "Italy won that race from Istres, in Southern France, to Damascus, Syria and back to France. Attilio Biseo won the race and Bruno Mussolini, Il Duce's own son came second.

"Those planes, all of them that flew in '37, six of them were S-M 79s. When we landed in Paris, the Savoia took the first seven of eight places in the race and would have taken all eight top spots if one plane had not crashed upon landing."

Sabino had put his tools down and was pretending to fall asleep.

"This aircraft, Sabin, its maximum speed was four hundred, twenty-eight miles per hour and its maximum distance on full tanks was 10,000 kilometres. No one else could do that. No one in the world."

Dante waited for Sabino to say something.

"Speed and distance records. A bomber this fast does not even need fighter planes to protect it. Even when it's fully loaded and armed, I don't think any other pilots could present a serious threat. Sabino, they could not in their wildest dreams keep up."

"*Scusa, signor?* I think it is time to break for lunch."

Lunch did not stop Dante from speaking.

"It is so fast that Biseo, who won the race, told Mussolini they should send it across the Atlantic to the Americans."

"Why would we send it to America?"

"Because of the war. Because we don't want America to get any ideas about joining the war on the Allied side."

"Ah, *si. Capito. Allora.* And?"

"And so we heard in the mess, where were you? We heard that Biseo put it to Mussolini. Since we have the record for speed and distance, let's bomb America to keep them out of the war. Teach them a lesson."

Sabino looked confused. "Bomb the Americans to keep them out of our business?"

"Yes."

"But wouldn't that force them into our business."

"Ai, Sabin, you know nothing of strategy."

"What did the Duce say? Are we going to bomb America?"

"No. Listen. He said it was a great idea. I have this from Biseo's own cousin. It is a great idea, but that we should not use bombs but lemons. Lemons. Can you believe that?"

"*Limones?*"

"*Si*, and attach to each of the hundreds of beautiful Sicilian lemons a tricolour parachute—the Italian flag. We let them fall gently on the streets of New York to let the Americans know that lemons could just as easily have been bombs, and will be if America does not stay on its side of the ocean."

"I have never seen America," Sabino said, as though Dante were not acquainted with this fact. "I might like to see the streets of such a city tacky with lemon zest."

"It is a true story."

"I have always liked your stories, Dante. Tell me another one."

Dante cleaned his hands on a rag. These hands that had touched Angelina.

"I will tell you about a girl."

"I already like this story better than the lemons."

"There was a girl walking on a warm day in Rome."

"Was she beautiful?"

"She was tall, almost as tall as me. Small at the waist and curving at the hips. Her hair was brown, very dark and her eyes were green and grey."

"One each?"

"No, both at the same time."

"Mouth?"

"Yes, she had a mouth."

Dante stopped. She had lips, he wanted to say. Lips like, what? Honey? No. Like basil and thyme. She did not seem sweet. Not at all.

"Keep going."

"A soldier met her. He spoke to her, but she would not answer him, not on a street in Rome when she had never laid eyes on him before."

"Absolutely not. What was the soldier thinking?"

"Only that he must speak to her."

"Ah, *si*. So, love at first sight."

"*Io non so*. But something. She would not talk to the soldier, but he persisted, walking as fast as he could a couple of steps behind the two lovely *ragazze*."

"Two?"

"Yes, one was her cousin. I forgot about her."

"You could save her for me."

Dante did not say to Sabino that Angelina's dress rippled in counterpoint as she walked. Her brown hair glistened, pinned and neat behind her. It would be long, that hair. He would like to take out those pins. See what happened.

"Well, what happened?"

"The soldier kept asking her questions while her cousin covered her mouth, laughing. He kept asking her questions as though he were a tourist in Rome and she was a native, someone who could show him around, show him the sights, tell him where to find a good meal."

Dante had coaxed her. He could see that she thought he was a hooligan, a wastrel, who would speak to girls out for a walk on a sunny morning in Rome. He had persisted. With courtesy, sometimes stumbling on words, he asked her about this or that building or ruin. When Angelina finally answered, she sounded like someone who had been sleeping in the sun on a sandy beach. A deep voice, pleasant and woodwind. Few words and direct.

"She turned in the street. Stopped her cousin with a hand on her forearm and turned, irritated. She had been hurrying up the hill toward the market and this soldier, following her, pulling away from the shade of the low garden wall and stopping her and turning her in her tracks. She asked him, '*Que devi fa?* What do you want to do? Follow me all the way home? Go back to your friends and leave me.'"

She had spoken to him. She turned her grey-green eyes to tell him these things. Deep eyes under dark, arching brows, eloquent, disinterested.

"The soldier was smiling, looking at her with his own deep blue eyes."

"Blue eyes. Hah! Your blue eyes?"

"Not so unusual. But still, she sent her cousin on to the market and went for a walk with the soldier. She answered first one question. Then another one."

"Is this a true story? It happened in Rome?"

Dante nodded. "Her name is Angelina. And now she is writing to me." He unbuttoned his shirt pocket and presented his first letter from Angelina.

"You are too lucky. You want the Green Mice. You get the Green Mice. You want the girl, you get the girl. I am sick of talking to you and I am going to take a nap."

Sabino pulled his cap down and lay down in the shade of the plane's long wing.

He had turned. He had seen her walking with her cousin. Dark hair, firmly pinned, eyes calm. Neither frightened of him, nor amused by him, nor even curious about him. She appeared to regard him as though he were a cow in her father's field. Ought he to be fed, watered? He was a fact she was taking in.

That was three months ago. Then he went to see her in San

Placido. He had three days' leave and it had taken him all of the first day and the morning of the second to get to her. He had a couple of hours to see how she would be, to meet her family, and see if what he felt in Rome was still there. He had finished his training at Ciampino and he would head to the Balkans soon. In his bunk at night, he ignored the rattled snoring of the sleeping men around him and tried to hear again her voice. Her dimples deepened before she smiled. They were crescents, these dimples, not dots or divots but perfect half circles of amusement. He had to see her. To see her in her home where she would be comfortable to speak to him about the matters that occupied her mind. He had leave before being deployed and he made the long trip to San Placido. He saw her, but she was so quiet at first.

He took Angelina's hand under the bowed trees at the entrance to the San Placido where its light and shadow, its sweet filaments of fragrance, honeysuckle and dogwood, tomatoes full and ripe on leaning stakes and smelling green and vibrant, cast a web around them. She traced the pitted stone of the bench where she waited, drenched in scent, and faint in the afternoon heat.

He asked her what she did on the mountain.

She helped her mother in the kitchen when she had to. Otherwise, she was with her father in the field or the barn or the garden.

Did she like to read?

On the mountain, there was not much time to read. In the summer when the days were longer, she sometimes looked at the magazines that Stefania sent from Rome.

Did she enjoy music?

Yes, she enjoyed music. She listened to the radio last year at Stefania's.

She did not ask him about the war or about his family, his interests, his point in coming.

"This is a very hot day for travelling," she said.

Dante agreed.

He had danced with lots of girls. In his life, so far, two young women had thrown their arms around him, sobbing against his neck, begging him to remember their names. In the warmth of the day, he could barely recall them or the reason for their urgency.

Angelina had skin tanned from working in the field. She was not dainty. She was something the foaming sea would crest against. Dante sat beside her, put his warm palms on the stone, one hand next to hers. He courted her skin, put his fingers so close to hers, let her feel the skin of his hand as a magnet. Surely, she would feel the pull as he did.

Sabino said, "That was a good story. It put me right to sleep." He dodged the spanner that Dante launched at him, resettled himself and began to breathe deeply. While he slept, Dante took out his pencil and paper.

He wrote to Angelina,

"*Carissima,*

"*The memory of you keeps me company here in this noisy world of men and machines. It is interesting to work on the planes and they are all good fellows here. They get up early and they work until the job is done. Ready for anything the enemy will send our way. We have the fastest, sleekest planes in the air. I imagine that you would like to lift off from the ground with me, to soar above San Placido and see all the people far below. When I think about you, I feel that I am already in the air and have to work hard to concentrate so that I do not cut myself open with a lack of attention.*"

Dante hoped no one but the censors would read this. On paper, it looked like nonsense, but it was all true. He was there under a plane, inside the cockpit, in the bomb bay, and he would think of Angelina and forget what he was doing. He had gotten into a lot of trouble for this and he would have to be careful or he would spend the war in the brig, or worse, be sent to Russia.

Angelina

In the San Placido garden, there were olive trees, fig trees, almond trees, hazelnut trees, apple trees, persimmon trees, plum trees, *nespole* trees, yew trees, cypresses, tall and casting long afternoon shadows over the old stone benches. The path's worn cobbles were trimmed in moss and the pool at the centre was refreshed by an underground spring. The cornflowers grew wild among tall crisp grasses that moved in the slow August breeze. After months in Rome working with her uncle and aunt, Angelina had finally come home to San Placido. Questo turned and flipped himself, joyful tail bruising against her legs. His hot tongue leaving a trail wherever it landed. He did not seem to be the worse for her absence. Her mother must have been looking after him. There were no soldiers here. Not yet. Just the old men and old women and a few of the children. Berto and Nico were still home, but they were getting too large for their school desks and in September, she worried that they would join the groups of young men she had seen walking in Rome, waiting to go to war.

There was also Dante. She knew that he would be stationed in the Balkans, which was safe as such postings go. There were always the bombers to worry about. The British were never that far away.

She kept track of events on her trips into Visso with her father and she prayed for Dante and began to write him letters. He had held her hand in Rome. He had kissed her wrist. Such small things, but they stopped her in her tracks, in any task, at any time of day. The moustache, his moustache, had tickled her hand. She remembered the feel of bristles in front of warm lips.

When Angelina was a small child, she would go with her mother past the almond trees and beyond the wisteria hanging down the side of the houses of the village. Angelina's mother always took her shoes off before she went near, bowing and crossing herself as though approaching an ancient, holy place. She went, still and quiet, wiping her hands carefully on her apron. They would leave the house holding hands. Her mother would work in the garden, in the plot of sun, just down from the spring where they grew tomatoes and lettuce. Her mother would turn the soil, lifting the shovel and breaking the dirt with her hands. Angelina would splash her hands in the pool.

She would move to the shady bench, tracing the pitted stone with her fingertips and she would think how right it was in her village and how she knew every bump in the road for as far as she could see up and down. She always thought she would stay in San Placido. Her brothers might move away or they might not. But for her, everything she knew and wanted seemed to be close at hand. Then she was eighteen, back from Rome, and Dante was climbing up the hill to see her and she did not know what to think.

Angelina knew how difficult it was to get there. He would have to take the bus or the train from Rome to Ancona. Then he would change trains for Visso. Once he got there, if he was lucky and the town's one taxi was not off on a run or parked beside a tree on a country road with the driver asleep in the shade and wine uncorked beside him, and assuming he had some money and could negotiate a fare, then Cecco will drive him halfway up the mountain, until the switchbacks became too steep for his old engine to manage.

Angelina waited for him. Smoothing her dress. She had not ironed it, but the heat from the sun and from her own body helped to press out the creases against her skin. Questo lay outside, regal and alert, in the shade of the spreading hazelnut tree watching as Signora Martinelli came up the lane.

"*Ciao*, Angelina. A young man telephoned to our house to say he was on his way to visit with you and your family. You know this man? Dante, something. I forget."

The Martinellis had the only phone in the village. Signora Martinelli fanned herself with her hand while Angelina poured some cool water into a glass.

"*Sì, signora*. I know him. I suppose it will take him about an hour."

"I suppose."

The *signora* stood in the doorway, still fanning.

"Would you like to sit down?"

Angelina offered her own chair.

"Ah, no thank you, Angelina. I will just have this sip of water and get back home."

Angelina tidied the clean kitchen counter, moving the plates to the left and then to the right.

"So? You met this fellow…"

"In Rome, *signora*."

"He is a friend of Stefania's?"

Angelina would like to have said yes. Yes, he is a friend of Stefania's, a cousin of her father's best friend. Something to establish Dante's connection, his family tree and his history and to justify his visit to a girl of San Placido, a girl that this good wife, indeed all the good wives and some of the husbands would watch out for. If they were all but related through Angelina's uncle, then the neighbours might mind their own business. This was too slim a possibility.

"No, *signora*. I met him in Rome, *sì*, but Stefania was with me. He is a soldier now from the De Angelis family in Spoleto. Do you know them?"

There was no reason for the *signora* to know anyone from Spoleto.

"Now that is a city known to host snobs and art lovers, you know that, Angelina."

In San Placido, this was nothing less than a mortal indictment.

"I don't think Dante is either of those. But you will see for yourself soon."

"Ah, *si*." Signora Martinelli finished her water and then smiled as though she had made a discovery. "My sister's husband's brother owns the shoe repair there in the main square."

Angelina thought, now it might be all right. By the time the *signora* gets back to her own kitchen, she will have told everyone along the way that a man was coming and that he was from a good family in Spoleto that frequently needed shoe leather.

Dante had ridden and walked, she knew that. It had cost him probably two days of his leave to turn up on her front doorstep. She turned her head when she heard that step on the path. She turned to see the face of a virtual stranger who had come to make a claim.

In April, she had met him. He had made her late for dinner at her cousin's. He had touched her forearm, the sleeve of her dress, and felt the strength of the arm beneath. He bought for her *gelato* in the hot afternoon. As the day cooled, they stopped at a coffee bar where he ordered her hot milk with chocolate and when she sipped it, a bit of the cream frosted her upper lip. Leaning forward, Dante would have tasted that cream from her lip with his tongue, but she stuck her own tongue out and that was that. She did not have a fever in April but her skin felt so warm. Unusually warm for spring.

When he turned the last corner, she took him in. He walked at a good pace. Not too quickly, not as though he were trying to sneak in, but not too slowly either, as though he thought himself to be a man of leisure. Questo had run partway down the lane and then back up to stand guard beside Angelina. She patted his silky ears to soothe her own nerves.

The quiet of the village deepened, as though even birds came to perch, bright-eyed, to watch a man walk up the mountain to meet Angelina. Nothing stood out more in San Placido than a man in a suit and tie. It did not matter if his clothes were dusty from the high summer grit that rose up onto him with each step to the upper reaches of the village. Angelina watched him pass all of the San Placido neighbours who had found some urgent reason to clean the front steps or the windows facing onto the lane. They were busy, but not too busy to say hello.

Signora Martinelli was the first to shake hands and introduce herself. Even Father Paolo stepped out of the church on some errand of mercy and almost walked directly into Dante. Angelina waited, nervous and happy, watching the people look out for her. She was happy until she saw Anselmina sitting, black and still, on her immaculate bench with a look of vicious pity on her face. Angelina met her gaze when the old woman turned to her. While Dante was talking to Father Paolo, Anselmina went into her house and came out with two small carpets. She draped them over the bench and began to beat them in the sun, raising the business end of the beater and whaling away until Angelina could hear her breathing labour in and out. She seemed a force of fury and the limp carpets bore the brunt of her.

Angelina walked down the road toward Dante. As she passed Anselmina, she wished her a good morning and received in return a grunt. At least it was not a curse. Anselmina narrowed her eye, but Angelina looked away. There might be truth to the power of her evil eye. There might not. Dante was here for the first time. She had not seen him in months. This was not the day to test Anselmina's power. Just as she passed the old woman, Angelina heard her ragged voice say, "Do not mind how you pass by my door, girl. I let the young grow up and be broken. I do not need to curse you, girl. Time itself will do that."

Angelina was about to turn when Dante smiled at her. She moved toward him and stopped short, not certain how to greet him.

He put out his warm hand to take hers and kissed her on both cheeks.

"*Ciao*, Angelina. I am happy to see you."

"You found your way."

"Yes. Yes, I did. How is it with you?"

"*Va bene, grazie*. It is well with me. And you?"

"Very well now."

They faced each other for a moment as if to refresh memory, to take in the contours of the real face before them. The particular skin and eyes and certainly the mouth. Their hands held fast. They had forgotten to let go.

"You will meet my mother and father?"

"And your brothers, too. Are they big, those boys?"

Angelina laughed and took back her hand.

"I suppose they are, you know. I have been giving them orders for so long; I forget how big they are. Come and see for yourself."

They turned away from the glaring Anselmina and walked back toward Angelina's house. Angelina looked back over her shoulder to see the poor Father step across Anselmina's doorstep on a pastoral visit. She thought she had never seen anyone as brave.

As they passed Carlo's house, the boy came and stood in the doorway. Angelina turned with Dante.

"Dante De Angelis, this is Carlo Montefiore."

"*Piacere*," they both said, shaking hands.

"Carlo has a trick that he does with a stick."

"I do. I can show you."

Dante said, "I would like to see this trick."

"Hold the dog, please, *signorina*."

Angelina had forgotten about Questo. She bent and pressed him against her.

Carlo got two sticks this time. "I'm up to two. Soon I'll be able to juggle three."

He tossed them, caught them three times without missing, and then took a bow.

"Congratulations," said Dante. "I think this dog would like to join your game."

"He ruins it, *signor*. He always wants to run away with the sticks."

Angelina's father and mother stood in the kitchen when Dante stepped in. Angelina performed the introductions, trying to keep her voice calm. She was light-headed with nerves and scolded herself. *He's just a man, a friend visiting. These are my parents. Everyone will get along. Settle yourself.* But she could not. She looked at Dante, amazed really, that he should have put forth such effort to visit her village. To visit her. In Rome, she had come to believe that soldiers would whistle and watch any woman who passed, except perhaps for a nun or a *bis-nonna*, a great grandmother. Their attentions to her she disregarded utterly. But Dante was here. Not flirting with her on a side street in an anonymous city. He was here before her declaring an intention, forming a connection. To be fed by Angelina's mother in the house of Angelina's father would, no matter what, connect them always. She watched her father clap Dante on the shoulder. Graziela brought him a steaming plate of the best *bistecca* before he could sit. At his right hand, there stood a sturdy glass of Alfonso's new wine.

The house was small, the table taking up most of the kitchen and the kitchen itself taking up all of the main floor. It was a place to eat and sit. The stove there for warmth in the winter and the tiles cool in the summer. In the window above the sink there were pots of fragrant rosemary and basil. There were two small lemon trees that her father pruned and watered tenderly. Angelina's mother had been cooking a fine lunch for their visitor. She had had an hour's notice and so had sliced the meat thin before marinating it in oil and garlic with some clippings off the rosemary plant. There were potatoes and carrots, a small salad and hard-crusted bread for dipping in the sauce of the meat.

They were good to strangers in San Placido. They fed them well and let them chew their meat before asking too many questions. They spoke to each other while Dante ate.

"This weather," Angelina's father began.

"Ah, *si*," said Graziela. "What weather."

"So hot," Alfonso said.

Angelina had to speak.

"The calves are doing well?"

Angelina knew the answer to her question before it left her mouth, but honestly, the weather.

"They are growing strong. We haven't lost a single one."

Dante spoke up. "It's a beautiful place, San Placido."

They accepted this as obvious. No one spoke for a moment.

"You are from Spoleto, Angelina says."

"Yes, my father is a clerk in the mayor's office there."

"Do you know Signora Martinelli's brother-in-law's brother?"

"I am sorry, no. I have not met him. But I understand he is the best cobbler in Spoleto."

Graziela had gone to the trouble to make a cake, to fold in the zest of a lemon and use the day's eggs and dear sugar for this guest of Angelina. It had to be thin, this cake, so it would bake quickly, but it melted against the tongue, just pulled from the oven. She cut him a generous portion, and Dante moved to pass his full plate to Angelina, who held up her hand.

She told him, "This is for you, Dante."

"*Si, mangia,*" said Graziela. "I hope you like it. Please, have another piece before the boys come in."

Berto and Nico were arguing on their way in. Dante stood to shake hands with the large brothers of Angelina. The kitchen was by now quite crowded with the six of them. Angelina's brothers stood with plates of food and asked Dante about the war.

"Where will you be stationed?"

"I am not exactly sure. Possibly Yugoslavia for a while and then somewhere else. Wherever the bombers go."

"The air force?"

"*Si.*"

The boys looked at one another, nodding. "Angelina, it is our duty to tell you that the air force is the best."

"Why is that?"

"They have the snappiest uniforms."

Angelina's father smacked them both on the head, but this only made them laugh harder. Nico almost dropped his plate and Berto choked on a mouthful of his mother's fine lunch. Graziela stood to beat Berto across the shoulders until he could finally catch his breath.

In all the commotion, Angelina stepped to the door and announced that they were going on a walk to the garden for now.

Angelina was quiet as they walked away.

"That is my family."

"Those are big boys."

"They grow big on the mountain." She was looking for something clever to say.

"Perhaps I should stay and then I would grow, too."

"You look fine as you are." She turned, blushing, away from him.

Dante and Angelina walked past Anselmina's house, each one looking at the road and feeling the heat rise from it.

The path ahead looked as though it came to a sudden end. Low bushes and tall trees with the branches bending down formed a solid wall of green. Dante slowed his pace, but Angelina kept walking.

"It only looks as though it ends here. But the path goes up to the garden once you turn the corner."

She thought Dante must be tired after coming such a distance. That might be why he walked a bit behind her. Angelina did not imagine that such a gesture would be for him both a courtesy and a pleasure, that the way she walked might give a man pleasure until she turned quickly to see him contemplating her back, and not only her back. She was naïve, she knew, having spent her life wrestling with her brothers and growing up as a kind of sister to all the boys in the village. Yet here was a man from Spoleto walking behind her and seeming to enjoy the view. She blushed again.

"It is certainly a warm day."

"*Certo*," he said.

"Do I walk too fast for you? I forget that I am used to the mountain and you are not."

"No, *signorina*, I think I can keep up. Though a man can certainly stretch his legs around here."

Dante took a handkerchief and wiped the sweat from his brow. Angelina slowed down for him. It would not do to be seen walking through the village with a man panting like a beast behind her. She must remember that the air was thinner on the mountain than it was on the Via Tre Donne in Rome.

The last house on the high street, the one beside the gardens and the cemetery beyond was inhabited by Francesca, Zia Anselmina's sweet-natured sister.

Francesca was watching them. Angelina waved to her, the

pleasant face hanging out over her small window watching them stroll toward the shade of the garden. Francesca waved the back of her hand at them, as though pushing them forward. "*Avante, avante.*"

To Angelina, Francesca said, "Come, *carina*, come after your walk and bring the young man to drink something cold after all this dust you are stirring up. I will go to press the lemons for you. Come back and we'll have a chat. Ah, so peaceful you make an old woman feel. So happy to see you."

Francesca saw Angelina every day of her life. The excitement, clearly, was Dante. Francesca was pleased by nothing so much as a courtship. The word itself flashed in Angelina's mind, wiping it clean. She walked beside Dante and could think of nothing to say.

The silence was immense. Everyone in San Placido had stopped talking. Not even a breeze flapped the white sheets that hung from the clotheslines that they passed.

Angelina said, "I visit Francesca. Mamma and I, we make some cookies or we take some prosciutto, whatever we think she might like, and I take them up to her."

"She wears black," Dante said.

"*Si*, her husband has been dead many years, but she talks about him as though her were in the next room. She wears black, but I think she wears it well."

Angelina never thought of Francesca as a widow in mourning. She spoke of her dead husband, yes, but she talked of the happy memories he had left for her to contemplate. She was a woman who could make black seem a lively colour, neat as a pin, fresh and pressed.

"She never complains."

"I admire that very much."

"There are some in San Placido who would be so wealthy if one could be paid for complaining."

"How does she live?"

Angelina would not have guessed that her friendship with Francesca would save her. She could talk to Dante about Francesca all afternoon. She lost some of her nervousness. They crossed the path into the garden. At the bench, Dante waited until Angelina had seated herself. Then he sat down quite close to her. She stopped speaking for a moment.

"How does she live?" Angelina repeated. "She has a little garden behind her house and her neighbour has some cows. Every once in a while he sells her the bit of meat she needs and a few eggs. Beside her tomatoes and peppers, she lets the daisies grow and the wild orchids."

Francesca's house was beautiful. She grew the flowers and then cut them, put them in jars around her house.

"I like her house very much. She wears black, you know, but everything around her, the small woven mats, the curtains, and the table covers, even her plates and cups, they are bright with colour. You will see. We will go there. You will see how pale her skin is, like someone from the north, and even her eyes are such a bright blue. Like yours," she said before her mouth closed.

Angelina would bring him along to Francesca who would talk until dark if need be.

On the way back they sat for a while in the sunny enclosure in Francesca's back garden. Francesca grew wisteria around the broken pergola at the entrance to her garden, the vines and flowers concealing the erosion of time and weather. She grew crocuses and daffodils around the back door. She served them lemon squash and they sat in silence.

Finally, Francesca leaned forward and picked one of the blossoms.

"Look, Angelina, Dante. Look at this."

They both examined the flower. Perhaps there was a strange insect in its depths.

"Think, now. Why should a petal grow to this shape and length and colour and know to stop? Why should it start? Why germinate at all? I tell you this frankly, though you may think I am a mad old woman, I find the garden a mystery. That something like a flower should grow and feed the bees and cheer my old eyes. That we should see such things and have the wit to enjoy them. Is this not a miracle? Well, I think it is a visitation from the Blessed Virgin, if not from the Almighty himself."

"You should talk to Father Paolo about such things, *zia*."

"This I could do. I am just that cheeky in my old age. I could tell him to come sit here with me if he wanted to learn about comfort. And really, he is so kind to come and give courage for the day to an old woman. May the Lord bless him and may the blessed Mother of God shower him with her mercy today."

Francesca was not lonely. She was not like Anselmina, whispering malignancies to every passerby. She was happy to see the young people and give them a cold drink, to sit in her bright garden with the possibility of new love.

Dante sat with his boots and his knees turned toward Angelina who looked straight ahead. At Francesca, or at the roses or at the cloud drifting below and far to the western horizon. Cesca told them about her husband, Antonio, whom Angelina remembered so well. When they were first married, she had wanted flowers in their garden, but he thought them a frivolity. In the dawn after she had cried, a foolish youngster, for colour and beauty and whimsy, he had gone in the damp morning collecting seedpods on the hillside, seeds of wildflowers that he, without telling her, made a space for behind the kitchen. In the spring when everything started blooming, she knew he cared for her so much.

"He could keep a secret, that man. And he could make a surprise for me." She looked at Dante. "You seem like you might be a surprising fellow as well."

"Given the chance, *signora*, you never know what a man might be capable of."

She asked them to stay for supper, but they said they could not. Angelina had, of course, to help her mother cook. Dante turned toward her at the door to help her step out of Cesca's house, but such courtesy was strange to Angelina, unexpected and unnecessary and she passed by his hand before she understood why he held it out.

She had never been mistreated. When she was much younger, her father had one day whipped the donkey to get it moving. The day was hot and the hill steep. The donkey, dim-witted and sluggish. Angelina stroked its back and spoke to it. *Andiamo, piccolo*, let's go. She did not know that her father was lifting his arm. He did not see her hand on the donkey's side. When the whip came across, it raised blood on the back of her hand. Her father said only, see what happens to you when you do nothing wrong. Imagine what will happen to you if you are bad. No apology. She could not even imagine that. The priest himself might as well be wrong as her father. She accepted the lash as her due.

She was not mistreated, but her father and mother spoke little to each other and, to their children, even less. Instructions, reprimands, orders. They said *Buon giorno* in the morning and *Buona notte* in the evening. If Angelina or her brothers left town for a few months, as Angelina had just done, they were greeted with a dry whiskered kiss on each cheek and a pat on the back. They might be offered a glass of water before being told to pick the beans or the tomatoes or to draw water from the well for the cows. To go feed the ugly chickens whose necks Angelina twisted swiftly. She was used to this life. Her family passed plates of food silently around the table. They talked only of the weather or of sick relatives. They did not thank Angelina for making the day's bread at five in the morning. They ate the food to keep themselves working and they worked to keep the food, the artichokes and mushrooms, the *insalata*, *zuppa*, *pasta asciutta*, *carne*, and, rarely, the sweets that finished the meal when the priest came to visit, moving around the table where they sat, *alla famiglia*, bound not by words or niceties, but by something else.

And here was Dante, deferential, a man who would stand at the door holding it for her, though it was already open to the cooling afternoon breeze, and here he was with his other hand suspended in mid-air to support her elbow as though she were frail instead of sturdy and as though she were teetering on high city heels instead of standing with her feet firm on the earth. She did not laugh at him and his fineness as she walked past him into the bright light. She did not want to keep him at a distance, but she could not make her mouth work to bring him close. Whether she spoke or not, he would be posted somewhere in the great world. San Placido was high and hard to get to, but talk of the war, whether they should invade, when and how they should invade, whether the Germans were good allies, such talk buzzed in the kitchens on the mountain as it did everywhere else in the country. She knew he would be in danger. He and his smile and his fine manners. She must not rely on these things.

As they walked down the path to her house, he stopped. "Will you write to me?"

Angelina looked at him. There was not much call for writing in her life. Paper and pens she would have to find. Postage. The people she knew, the people with whom she must communicate were all within shouting distance and had been for her whole life. He looked so hopeful. The sweat on his pale brow. She stood above him on the slope of the mountain.

"*Scrivo voi*? Write to you?"

"Yes. Tell me about your days, about the peace of this place. I think there will not be much peace where I am headed."

"The war is not too peaceful."

He laughed.

"Angelina, you have made a joke."

"I will write to you. I think the letters will be not too long."

He wanted to pay her a compliment.

"I have never met a woman to look me in the eye as you do."

Angelina let her breath out. She picked up her nervousness, finally, as though it were a peevish cat in a small house, and set it aside to meet his gaze.

"You should spend more time in San Placido. That is how we speak to one another here. Unless we are lying."

"Liars? In San Placido?"

"Not so far in this century. But the last one was terrible."

She smiled now. She put out her hand to shake his. He put his hand on her strong shoulder and leaned to kiss her cheeks.

He held her hand.

"*Buon viaggio*, Dante De Angelis. I will write to you."

"Angelina, you give a man hope."

"*Lo so.*" I know, she said, dimples deepening.

"Here," he said. He handed her a small paper. "You write to my squadron. Put my name on the envelope and this information and wherever I am, your letters will find me."

"I hope they find you well."

Angelina could feel her mouth warm and her dress pressed damp against her skin. He would leave now. She put out her hand again and stepped toward him.

With her face very close to his, she spoke softly to him.

"I will write to you. Be careful."

If he stepped into her, they would embrace. If they embraced, Angelina, so strong and steady, felt that she might faint.

"Angelina."

"*Sì*."

He waited. Breath between them, commingling. Distance closing. On the edge of his vision, at the turn of the path, and crossing it like bad luck, Dante saw the old bent woman in black.

He kissed Angelina's cheek, first one, and then slowly the other. He said goodbye.

Dante left her at the base of the path before the switchbacks down the mountain. She waved and turned toward home. The sunset behind her washed the valley in rose. The leaves were pink, the stones and grass, flush, wafting warmth. Down the long basin of the dale, she could hear the echo of a train whistle, vibrating in all the hollows of ancient mountain rock. She looked behind her, but Dante was gone.

She wrote to him.

Carissimo Dante.

The intimacy of the address. She stopped writing.

Dear Signor De Angelis.

It would have to be *carissimo*. Dear one. Just a formality. But more, she knew. And he would too. It rolled off onto the paper, off her lips as she spoke the words that she wrote. My dearest Dante.

Fine.

> *The harvest is in and stored. We have plenty of food, in spite of the hardships that we read about in the cities where there are more and more of our German allies and fewer of our Italian young men. The Germans are a very hungry people. I think that they sent their*

young men here so we Italians could feed them good food for a change and send them home strong. Stefania and her mother are well, although my zia has had to turn in her wedding ring to support the war effort. Some of the women do this gladly. Mussolini is very persuasive and appeals to women especially. I am glad I do not live in Rome any more where the only thing a person can talk about is the war. It is getting bad enough in our quiet village. The old men sit on the bench in front of the church and speak of how they would run campaigns. Then they go inside to eat their soup and take a nap. Zia Anselmina—you must remember her—utters curses of vengeance on us all, but we do not know why.

My father goes carefully to Visso and Ussita.

I do not know where you are stationed, but I hope it is comfortable and that your work is going well. The garden is bare of fruit and flowers now, but still when I go there, it is beautiful. You should come sit with me on the bench soon.

With much affection,
Angelina Fiori
Your Angelina.

She put down her pen and prepared the letter to mail. She had surprised herself. It was easy to write to him, much easier than to speak face to face. How long would a letter take to find him? She did not know. She addressed it to his unit and walked down to the town to mail it.

She slipped behind her house to take the steep path down. As she followed the turn on the path coming out from behind the gorse bush, she felt a sudden sharp shove. Angelina stumbled off the path and onto the rocky mountainside. She grabbed for the gorse branches to stop herself and fell just short of a steep drop. When she caught her breath and looked up, there was Anselmina, leaning heavily on her cane and stepping down toward Angelina, so careful of where she placed her feet until she stopped just above the girl.

"*Senti*, you. Listen to me. I see you with that soldier and I know you for what you are."

Angelina's elbow was bleeding and the letter for Dante had

dropped out of her pocket onto the rocks. She wanted to reach it before some breeze took it from her. She leaned on her good arm and reached for the envelope.

"I am not lonely and I do not want any husband grunting over top of me, spilling useless seed everywhere for me to clean up."

She poked Angelina with her cane.

"Don't get up or I will knock you down again. I am strong enough for that."

"*Signora*, why do you do this?"

"Shut up, you witch. I am telling you something to save you. It is a shame that my only sin was to kill my husband. A tragic turn of events. A thoughtless moment. But I could not say that I miss him now that he suffers the earned indignities of a vigorous stint in purgatory, God rest his soul some day, but not too soon. If that fellow dies in battle, that one that came to see you, that would be a blessing, eh?"

Anselmina's voice croaking, grating to the ear. Angelina, her elbow bleeding, but her letter back safely in her pocket, was frightened to get up. If she provoked Anselmina, the old woman might die right there on the mountain. Her breath was coming in gasps from the effort of her attack. Now it seemed she wished to utter some awful judgment, but Angelina did not know why. Had she finally gone mad?

"Listen you. You are a vicious girl who should spare God and us all and do away with yourself. I have a knife here, Angelina. You are hurt on the mountain now. Why not slit your own throat?"

Anselmina dug in the pocket of her sweater. In her fist was a long, thin knife used to flay rabbits.

"Here, Angelina. Look. Come a little closer, child, *vieni qui*. There's a sweet girl."

Anselmina held out the dagger, bent and offered it, leaned and gripped Angelina's forearm with an untoward strength, pulling her up near her own breath, the moulded onion smell of it, choking her. She lifted the fingers of her other cold hand, this terrible woman, and she pressed the arthritic tips against the pulse in Angelina's neck.

"*Va bene*, child, cut here, cut fast and deep and you will feel better immediately. You will meet Mary and the angels and you can pray for us here. Just be quick, my darling."

Angelina felt the ancient fingers pressing against her neck, heard the voice coaxing, muttering endearments such as Angelina had never in her life heard. Endearments more frightening than the strident abuse she would usually hear, listening to a crazy woman try to woo her toward death, toward unconsecrated burial and hell itself.

"*Adesso piccolina*, take the knife. It will be a mercy, darling, *carina*."

The sun was shining in San Placido. It was a brilliant fall day. Behind her out of sight, Angelina could hear the women at the well. All she had to do was call out, or stand up, but Anselmina gripped her and held her. The scrape on her arm throbbed. The blood beaded and seeped into her dress. She noticed that her ankle hurt. That her foot had swelled against the laces of her shoe.

Angelina twisted and took the knife. She held it, not to her own neck, but to the neck of her straining captor.

"*Signora*, can you hear yourself? Can you hear yourself trying to breathe? Can you feel your lungs closing? You are not long for this world, but I swear, I will take this knife and cut you like the pig that you are if you ever speak to me again. *Capite?*"

Anselmina was taken by a fit of sudden coughing and Angelina threw the knife down the mountain.

She stood up placing as little weight as she could on her right leg.

"We will not speak of this again. Can you make your way back to the path?"

Anselmina had no words. She had fallen herself and was wiping her damp eyes, trying to catch her breath.

Angelina did not wait for an answer. She pulled herself back up to the path, ignoring the pain in her foot and ankle. She would mail Dante his letter. Then she would go home and cheerfully kill a chicken to roast for supper.

Dante

Within a few weeks of Dante's sending his letter, he and Sabino were drummed out of the famous Green Mice Squadriglia for neglecting to set properly the propeller pitch on the S-M 79. Dante was livid. A moment of inattention and he had misread the specs, miscalculated. No second chance with the Green Mice. He wanted to blame Sabino, always laughing and talking nonsense. Or worse, singing. Dante had to get away from him. He ran three full circuits around the base before returning to his quarters. The lieutenant summoned him with new orders. Dante held out his hand for the vegetable peeler, but was instead, along with Sabino, sent to Yugoslavia to join the occupying force and keep the fighter planes in trim. Dante arrived after Prince Paul had signed and then been forced to renege on Hitler's non-aggression pact.

As they loaded ammunition into the planes, Sabino said, "Non-aggression pact? Is that why we are here?"

Dante lifted two of the smaller crates and dropped them on the floor of the cargo hold.

"Such reasonable demands from the Führer. He only asked permission for his brave German troops to travel freely and peacefully through Yugoslavia to attack Greece. For this, he would offer the cooperative Slavs the province of Salonika. The Prince agreed, but his Serb officers declined. They turned Hitler down."

"I think one does not turn Hitler down."

"And so we have Operation Punishment. Almost four hundred bombers and dive-bombers on Belgrade. Fifty fighter escorts, Panzer divisions from Austria, and our Italian fifth, sixth, and eleventh corps, backed by the Luftwaffe. It took a week and a half, the Royal Yugoslav army was demolished and every bridge across the Danube destroyed. The Yugoslavs signed an unconditional surrender and here we are."

"Here we are," Sabino agreed.

Dante wrote to Angelina.

> *Today for the first time we have had our hands on the best that our enemy has to offer. You should have seen the fellows, Germans and Italians shoving one another out of the way, to see the Hawker up close. We all know how inferior the RAF is, but this British fighter has been giving us all so much trouble. There it was when we took charge of this area, sitting solidly on the runway. About a dozen of us clustered around the tires, propeller, wings. Three men climbed on the wing and, with the engine cover cracked, leaned on top of one another to get a look inside.*

He could not tell her the specifics. He stopped writing and looked up at the Hawker. He hoped she would not mind hearing about the aircraft. He did not wish to bore her or to talk about things that must seem so far from San Placido, but when he ran his hands along the fuselage, the contours of the craft slipped warm under his palm. Could he write that to her? That the warm skin of a plane made him think of her? Probably, a woman would not like to be compared to a plane, but still, he kept his hand near the nose for a few moments, smiling. He finished his letter and folded it away until he could get it into the post. He rejoined the men in their close examination of the alien plane.

The plane had four guns built into each wing, maintaining

considerable speed and accuracy. It had caused a certain amount of grief to each man on the tarmac and they were fascinated by its appointments, at the same time familiar and strange.

Dante had looked closely at the Rolls Royce engine and shouted down to Sabino. "1200 horsepower, maybe more."

"It looks like a bulldog."

"What?"

"The monoplane. It looks like a stumpy bulldog. How is the armour?"

Dante rapped his knuckles against the fuselage and shook out his hand.

"Good."

"If it is heavy, it will not be as fast."

"It will not climb like the Messerschmitt. I do not think it will manoeuvre quite as well."

"Want to take it for a spin?"

"It would not do to crash this treasure."

Sabino looked disappointed.

"Besides, there is only one seat. No cargo, no storage of any kind. We will keep our feet on the ground for now and figure out how best to beat this thing."

Dante stayed in Yugoslavia until June. He received orders to report to the base at Pantelleria and went back to the barracks to pack. Sabino sat on the edge of his cot, watching.

"You got orders?"

"Pantelleria."

"You are leaving Yugoslavia."

Dante did not answer.

"Your luck is holding."

"But I'm not in the Sorci Verdi any more."

"No. That's true. But you are on your way to warm sunshine. Fine food, too. They speak Italian there, don't they?"

"Don't hold it against me."

"Perhaps I will join you."

"Sabino, are you related somehow to the Italian high command? Are you Mussolini's illegitimate child?"

Sabino laughed. "No, but I am your sidekick. I helped you with your first bandage and I should be there to help you with your last."

"In other words, you will be lost without me."

"Leave me Angelina's address. Maybe she would like two soldiers to write to."

"How would it be I leave my bayonet in your throat?"

"So, you have learned how to attach it to the end of your rifle?"

Dante was finished packing. He put his hand out. Sabino shook it and rose and kissed him on both cheeks.

"*Arrivederci, mi'amico*. I will see you on the beach."

"Pantelleria has no beaches. Stay warm, Sabino."

Dante joined the truck convoy out of Belgrade and through Sarajevo and southwest to the Adriatic. He brushed shoulders in the back of the troop truck with men being deployed through Europe. For the first time in years, Sabino was not with him. Each morning, he had opened his eyes to find Sabino already pulling the sheet and blanket tight across his cot. His boots shone like black beetles and his belt and trousers held fast his neatly ironed shirt. He was fit and ready for service. For a man who had arrived at the military school with his socks sticking out of his luggage, he had made great strides. Dante was always slower in the morning and no matter how he arranged his kit, he always appeared dishevelled at breakfast, unpolished and unkempt. Sabino was not a better mechanic. He could not fabricate missing parts on the fly the way Dante could, but he was a better soldier. Dante envied that and wondered if, without his friend beside him, he might become better himself. As far as he knew, there was no one from Spoleto on the truck. Not one neighbour or familiar face except a few men with whom he had bunked or sat with at the mess.

He put his head down and said to his shoes, "You've been gone one half hour. Think about something else before you start crying."

Dante made a habit of smoking one cigarette a day, both to make the package last and because in truth, the smell bothered him, upset his stomach and put him off his food. He smoked one now. He was alone with these men and on his own. He would have to make sure he did not contract some plague, as seemed to be his habit as soon as he left what was familiar to him. He looked through the canvas flap at the receding road. On either side lay heaps of rubble, splintered wood rising in hectic memorials to the Führer's strategic response to the Slavs. Farther out there were forests of trees, dark and light greens and greys on the valley floor. The leaves looked misty and indefinite. Behind the truck, the dust roiled in grey clouds as the trucks rolled through and the men on the transport shouted at him to drop the flap, but he held it, looking back at the distance and wondering how he would manage without Sabino.

Dante arrived at Pantelleria on a troop ship. He had seen the island on the map, a cork in the bottle of the Mediterranean, plugged primly in the blue water between Sicilia and Tunis in the strait of Sicily. He knew Pantelleria's value stemmed from its coordinates. Heaved up from the sea long ages ago in a place so strategically valuable, the island and its people had been the unfortunate victims of repeated assault and seizure. Dante was going there to support the bomber battalion. In that summer of 1940, the island was the jumping-off point for the North Africa campaign. Better to be on Pantelleria, the Black Pearl of the Sun, he thought, than heading for the desert of Tunis and beyond. The wind hit him as soon as he got off the ship. It whipped around the cliffs and crags that made the island such a natural fortress.

There were no beaches to land on and no harbours at which to dock. Men stationed there came ashore in dinghies and pushed their way up the cliff. After one good night's sleep, Dante was put to work on construction.

The Italians constructed airstrips on Pantelleria by levelling a mountain. There were too many hills altogether, fertile and exposed to destruction. Dante saw the remains of the Neolithic village, obsidian pottery and rough tools turned up here and there while Dante worked alongside other soldiers, both Italian and German, as well as conscripted political prisoners, some perhaps from the

Rocca itself, to turn the island into a fortress. Around the caldera in the centre of the island, the Italians and Germans embedded more than one hundred gun emplacements in the rocks. They built pillboxes and turned a mountain itself into an aircraft hangar. Surrounding him were the volcanoes, Montagna Grande and Monte Gibele. He was held as though in a bowl, a spacious and naturally occurring foxhole that made him invisible to enemies he had not yet encountered in battle. Dante felt safe there. The island was unassailable.

He worked with his unit, pounding at rock and pouring the concrete to implant machine guns in caves and crags along the shore. With his shirt off, his back burned in the sun. Beside him, the other men worked at the rock or took cigarette breaks with their faces bare to the sky. Eyes closed and taking deep drags. Concrete work was familiar—they might have been mixing and pouring in their own gardens. At the knees of their grandfathers and fathers, they had built stairs and walls, imprinted the names or code names of girls in the village, left the mark of their young hands in the wet cement. This they did now again, as men at war under the sun. They left their mark on the battlements, flinging grey drops from their fingertips at each other.

Two of the men were from a village near Rome, cousins who teased each other about the fat girls of the town and which of them had fallen for the fattest.

"You, Eduardo, you took a shine to the niece of the storekeeper. She was good with that broom, wasn't she?"

"Not as good as your sister."

Eduardo's fierce cousin dropped the trowel and pushed him into the wheelbarrow. The concrete slopped over the sides and the men stood by, laughing.

"You are a pig and not a man."

"*Si*, but she could really sweep, your sister." *La sua sorella.*

Dante helped Eduardo out of the wheelbarrow. He rose, shook himself free of the bulk of the muck, and then climbed down the cliff to the water. As he disappeared over the edge, they could hear him, still laughing.

"*Allora,* you couldn't fall too hard for that one. Soft, plump thighs to break your fall."

"*Sbrigatte*! Hurry up!"

"And arms to hold you tight!"

"*Basta,* eh?" That's enough!

On the plateau above them lay the airstrip. The hangars had been dynamited out of the sides of the mountain and the planes secured within. It ought to have been impregnable, but the Italians discovered themselves ill-prepared for the wind and the humidity.

Dante had been shipped to Pantelleria to repair the Duce's dive-bombers, but once he arrived, he realized that there was a critical problem with the airstrip. The Italian planes, it seemed, were having trouble getting off the ground. Dante was ordered to determine what the problem was. He must resolve the issue and urgently. With the planes grounded, the British war ships navigated freely around Malta and the Axis supply ships in the strait had no air support to protect them. He headed toward the airstrip. The wind lifted his hair, cooled his skin. The island was an easy posting, he thought. He could mix and pour concrete, bend and hammer and stand straight in the sun. But he could not keep the hair on his head organized. The wind blew his fine hair every which way. He greased it but it would not stay put. The major would see him coming across the tarmac with the tool apron pressed against him and his hair standing on end.

"*Guarda,*" he would say to the men gathered around him. They watched, laughing, while Dante pulled his comb out from behind his ratchet and pulled it again through his misbehaving hair. He would bend and chase his cap and fix it uselessly on his head, proceed a few steps until the wind swirled again.

Dante was preoccupied, with his hair, with the pillboxes on the island's cliffs, and with finding his way around. With the unusual sensation of a runway that seemed to push back against his boots when he walked across it. He was unprepared to see the familiar, square figure in the distance, waving.

How had Sabino managed again to be stationed with him? Dante had left him behind in Yugoslavia, sitting on the edge of his cot outside Belgrade. He thought he was clear of his old friend. Yet here he was, one man shorter than all the others in a sea of short and dark-haired men, smiling and waving as though waiting for Dante was the point and structure of his life.

"*Ciao,* Dante." Always the same "*Voi caffé?*"

"*Ciao*, Sabino. What are you doing here? I thought you had a nice clean job babysitting the Slavs."

Dante embraced his friend, bending to kiss his cheeks. Sabino stood back to look at him.

"Belgrade? No. Too many cars." He patted his stomach, hard as ever. "Too many potatoes there. Would you look at this place? *Guarda*, Dante. Now we get paid to go to the beach!"

Dante did not know how Sabino managed to be posted here. He offered no explanation. Dante did not ask. He was annoyed and relieved when he embraced his friend again. Sabino brought with him all the history of his home. The man had seen him weak and sick, bruised by his father, babied by his mother, browbeaten by Signor Giallo, and dressed down by every commanding officer whom he had encountered. How could he take his place among men in the presence of this fellow who regarded him, and whom he regarded, as a *ragazzo*, a boy in bare feet?

He told Sabino how it was in Pantelleria, about the work, preparing the artillery, the concrete.

"You will like it here. But I should tell you, there is no beach."

Sabino seemed content to have work to do in Italy. Or, at least in a place where the inhabitants spoke Italian and knew how to cook proper food. It wasn't like his mother's, but it was close. Dante's irritation dissolved like sugar in good hot espresso. He had been fine without Sabino, he told himself. But some of the tension seemed to ease out of his shoulders, sitting in the sun and talking again with Sabino. He laughed at Sabino's sad story of transports breaking down, changing tires in inches of muck, making it to the coast finally to have his boat sink. It had belonged to a local fisherman until it had been commandeered as a troop ship for an afternoon and run aground in crashing tides around the forbidding island.

"I swam to shore with my pack on my shoulders and my boots on my feet. You are lucky to see me alive, my friend."

"You can't swim, Sabin. With or without your pack. Unless it was full of hot air."

"*Allora*, I scrabbled ashore somehow. And here is my kit to prove it."

He held up the sodden pack.

"What happened to the boat?"

"Lost at sea."

"And the fisherman?"

"He has decided to give up fishing. It turns out the *maggiore* has a sister in Sicily that the fisherman would like to court. And now the major feels guilty. So..."

"All ends well."

"Now and forever, let's hope. *Deo volente*."

"Amen."

Dante did not want to admit that he had missed Sabino. He was fine, he was. Getting along well with the other men and thus far keeping out of the brig for a change. The light on Pantelleria was stinging bright and in it, he seemed to see a little more clearly. His nights had been more difficult. Since he had arrived on the island, he had been dreaming. In his dreams, he stood alone under a dark sky. No men from his unit, not even the enemy around him. No moon or stars guided him to his last breath. In his dream he was again and again startled by the sweetness of the dark air, at first pleasant and soothing, and then suddenly cloying and close. He kept falling, as though trying to find legs to stand on in the shift and tilt of a fun house floor. In these dreams, Dante was always alone. It was good to have Sabino with him again.

He did not write to Angelina about his dreams. He told her about Sabino's arrival, about the ocean turning every which way and the gulls dropping and rolling as though they were caught in waves of air. She would laugh, he thought, at his nonsense. And he would not be there to see it. It had been months since he had seen her and it would be months at least, or more, before he made his way up the mountain again. He wished to see her. He regretted not holding her hand sooner and longer. Why let go at all? He had looked at the palm of her hand, had kissed it once. Once. When he had the luxury of hours, he took time for one kiss. And the palm. Not even her lips. He tried not to worry whether other soldiers, perhaps friends of her brother Nico, had hiked the trail to San Placido and found treasure there in Angelina. The fellows in his unit sometimes opened slim letters from a wife or girlfriend. Letters that drove them to long and solitary walks and that moved the other men to clap the sad soldier on the shoulder, to enlist him in acts of rowdy fellowship, drinking and card-playing till heads were sore from the work of forgetting. Dante had no claim on Angelina. He had not even kissed her lips. She was a free soul who might do anything with her affections. As though affections were like sticks one might throw to a dog. There was harm, though, he knew, in time and distance.

All manner of worries and longings would torment him if he did not find some way to discipline himself. The major's commands helped. Most days he had to pick up a rock as though it was the burden of his imagination. He would hold it, volcanic, faceted, black, and gleaming. He would imagine he might still feel the heat coming off it. Dante would say his own sort of prayer. *Questi oggi sono i miei pensieri di voi. These today are my thoughts of you. I will carry you in my pocket for a while and then I will put you in a safe place.* Nevertheless, sometimes Dante had to pick up the rock and set it aside to get to his proper work. To follow orders now, to comply with demands. Once upon a time, he would have done anything to escape orders, expectations, and limitations on his life in the world. He had once contracted typhoid in his attempt to escape such demands. Now he bent his back to fulfill them.

On Pantelleria, Dante rose on time. He made his bed and tidied his belongings, squaring the trousers and shirts of his uniform against the corners of his trunk. He was shaved and present at roll call and on time for breakfast. He offered dagger-sharp salutes to his superiors and did his best to manage the ratio of gravel to concrete for maximum strength. He followed the orders that were given him and became, of all things, a good soldier. At least for the moment.

The morning after Sabino's arrival, Dante went out to the hangar. He had completed his attachment to the detail of men embedding anti-aircraft guns and building pillboxes. That work was urgent and for the most part, finished. He was now ordered to return to the planes. After breakfast, he walked down the runway, taking his time in the cool of the morning. He had taken several steps before he realized what was happening. He remained still for a few minutes and then stepped to one side. There was the imprint of his feet in the ground beside him, slight but defined. No mistaking those feet for anyone else's. He could have laughed. The squadron was finding it difficult to get the planes off the ground, and no wonder. Dante examined the surface for twenty minutes or so, long enough to convince himself. Pacing, standing, apparently lost in thought, and then stepping backwards or sideways, as though in a very slow and solitary dance.

Somebody's head would roll for this. Unless the fellow who paved the runways had an aunt or uncle or cousin close to Mussolini himself—and there were more of these relations cropping up every day—somebody would be shot for this calamity. Dante decided to wait until after lunch to inform the base commander that his runway would have to be excavated and repaved with a compound that would set firm in spite of the humidity of Pantelleria. He had to report it, but how to do it without becoming the one whose head rolled across the soft tarmac and into the turning ocean below?

It was well known that the major was severely constipated. Each day the men found some reason to occupy themselves outside the hangar and to watch the rigid senior officer walk briskly toward the latrine with a book or a magazine in hand. Sometimes minutes, sometimes nearly an hour would pass. In silence, the groans of the unevacuated major carried across the tarmac before he, having given up, returned with more bile than ever to his desk. Dante would wait for lunch before breaking the bad news.

In the meantime, he took Sabino with him to have a look at the SM 85 Bombardier aircraft, the Flying Banana. The plane was so ungainly that the Regia had built them and then scrapped the plans for the dive-bomber. Of the thirty-six that were built, Dante had a dozen to inspect and maintain at Pantelleria, and when he saw them for the first time, walking into the hangar from the brilliant runway, he no longer wished to laugh.

"That is an abomination."

"*Come?*" Sabino had not heard him.

"Look at this. This thing could not possibly fly. Could it? Look at the lines. They are off-kilter, my friend."

The plane was long and large, underpowered for its size by twin Piaggio 500 horsepower radials. That would be bad enough, but the body of the plane itself was constructed entirely from wood. The sea air and heat had made an assault on the airstrip, softening it to the point of inutility, but this was nothing compared to what the elements had wrought on the Banana. The wooden dive-bombers had warped in the heat. Wings sat slightly askew; the fuselage bulged or sank according to a drunken builder's whim. It was terrible to see. Even without such a catastrophe, the Flying Bananas would have been aptly named, for they resembled nothing so much as great bananas, but these ones, exposed to the elements on the island, could not fly. All the planes would have to go back to Sicily to see what could be salvaged.

"This is not going to help the major's intestinal problems."

Dante walked with Sabino out of the hangar and down the soft runway. At the path to the major's office, they shook hands and Sabino wished him godspeed. The news would have to be broken and Dante was the one to break it. How had the landing strip been built without someone noticing the problem? Perhaps it only manifested itself in the new hot summer. And the Banana. Surely they could have foreseen that wood planes would not be resilient in the sun and spray of Pantelleria. Dante had not been there when the tarmac was laid and had had nothing to do with the construction or deployment of the bomber, but that would not matter now. The major was the sort who would have no difficulty shooting the messenger and Dante resigned himself to a long stint in the kitchen. He knocked on the tin door.

"*Permesso, maggiore.* I am sorry to interrupt."

The major was sweating at his desk, grey skin and dark eyes. Lips pinched together in a line.

"What do you want?"

Out the window, Pantelleria looked beautiful to Dante. The men outside played cards in the sun with their shirts off, sitting on overturned crates in the sharp grass beside the runway, carefree. As though the machines that brought them to the island and reason for their stay were insignificant compared to the next great hand the dealer was now passing out. They looked lucky.

Dante told the major about the runway and about the warped Bananas. The base and the planes both would have to be scrapped or rebuilt.

"Can you fly?"

"*Si, maggiore.*"

"Then take one up in the air. See what you can do with it. I hear you are a wizard with the plane. Perhaps there is a simple solution. Perhaps you are wrong."

He wiped his brow and neck with a damp handkerchief. He moved on his chair as a man who cannot get comfortable. One cheek, then the other. Dante kept his face straight.

"I do not think it is possible to fly the bomber. With the runway soft as it is, it probably would not get airborne."

With the runway in such bad shape, he imagined that the nose would hit the ground. He would probably break his jaw and have to present himself to the infirmary, left out of the action for a good six weeks. He would keep his feet on the ground, however soft it was. He had not been ordered yet to do anything.

"I will check the plane again, sir, and see if I think it would not kill me immediately, provided I got it into the sky."

Dante sat with the men. They dealt him into the card game. He did not want to look at the Banana again. He did not want to take it up. He had to survive at least until he saw battle. He had been to Rome and met Angelina. He had been to her home and seen her mother and father and brothers. He had sat in the garden beside this haunting girl. He would tell her about the warped planes and the poor major. Dante had a tic above his eye, which he pressed with the back of his hand. It was hot and he sat, looking at his cards.

The adjutant approached to give Dante word that the Banana was not to be flown. The major had changed his mind. It was not safe. It would stay on the ground and so would Dante. Direct orders.

Dante made a bad play. Lost the hand and kicked at the stones at his feet.

The stillness of the morning, the men around him grinning at their cards and at the pot of pennies in Emilio's hat, his own bad playing suddenly made his hot skin itch. That old feeling he used to have at his father's table, at the military school, when given an order that pinioned him, it was like a sharp release of adrenaline that set him trembling and impatient. The Banana was not safe. As though the Regia Aeronautica could build a machine that he couldn't fly in his sleep. The major was a *signora*, an old woman who needed a long and hearty shit in order to be able to think straight. Dante looked at the hangar and back at his cards. He rubbed his hand along his jaw. Probably he would be all right. Beside him, Sabino sat quietly, rearranging his hand, shuffling his cards. His fellow card players, scratching their balls like dogs in the sun, yawning, and digging in their noses. He looked back at the hangar. Perhaps he could get the plane off the ground. Now that the major had grounded him, flight was what he must have. The plane must be tested. It was the only sensible thing.

He threw his cards down, a bad hand anyway, and said, "Sorry boys. I am off to *il cielo*. The sky awaits; enjoy the dirt here, will you?"

"*Basta*, Dante. *Vai, vai!*"

It seemed they wanted him to leave.

"Just leave your money behind!"

Dante strolled into the hangar. He would have to be fast down that cursed runway to get any lift at all. Faster than usual. He looked askance at the plane, its strange line from nose to tail that waved as though refracting in bright sun instead of the cool shade at the heart of the mountain. It did not look like much on the ground and he knew from experience that its weight and load would make it difficult to maneouvre in the air. All in all, a bad business. But still, better than playing cards. He threw some tools into the gaps around the seat and shook his head. He could hardly repair the thing while he was flying it. Even a wrench would add to a load he was not sure the plane would carry. He leaned in to retrieve the tools.

Sabino stood behind him on the ground beside the fuselage, his silence startling.

"What? Sabin?"

"I'll come with you."

"Want to run away from the warm ocean breeze? Sorry, my friend. I cannot help you. This plane is not likely to get off the ground as it is. It is too heavy. Look, I am not even taking my tools."

"Take your tools. Take me. You should not fly by yourself. You have no sense of direction and you are not much of a pilot, either."

This was true.

"Sabin, I would take you if I could, but, number one, you do not have permission—"

"—Neither do you—"

"And number two, look at you. You are built like a tank, man. We will not get off the ground."

"*Certo*, we will."

"How do you know this?"

"Look. There is nothing in the bomb bay. You are empty. No cargo. I will be your cargo."

"What about the major?"

"The major is, sadly, constipated. He has taken a stack of manuals to the privy to see if he can't work something out."

They grinned as though they were boys in short pants.

"I'm afraid I am going to have to commandeer your services, airman."

Sabino, with one foot against the wing mounting, flipped himself up into the small space behind the pilot's seat. When Dante turned and saw him folded into the space as though calmly waiting for one of the Duce's very prompt trains, he started laughing. He shut his mouth quickly so that no one would come over to see what the joke was. He had spent enough of his military career in the brig.

He tossed his tools back in and cheerfully contemplated the

current trials of his constipated major. He cranked the propellers, jumped into the seat and adjusted his goggles. He pulled on his *cuffia* and taxied out of the hangar.

His card-playing friends saluted as he went past. Ground crew began chasing Dante, waving their arms and shouting at him to stop. One tripped on his left, toppling the other three behind him. It was as funny as anything he had seen in the cinema. To his right in the distance, Dante could see the door to the privy swing open and the major stumble out, his pants in one clenched fist and his newspaper in the other, thrusting it into the air in order to provide emphasis to a command that Dante was disinclined to hear. He couldn't hear the men laughing, but he could see it. The major reaching to pull up his trousers and the enlisted men looking away too late.

He got up some speed and held on while the Banana creaked and banged its way to something approaching lift. The nose and landing gear rose off the strip only to bounce back down. It lifted and bounced twice more. Dante, in spite of the helmet, could hear terrible groans and felt the shudders of the plane that had sat too long in the wind and sun. Still, it rose into the air.

He turned to look at Sabino, who was grinning.

They circled the island and moved southeast toward Linosa. The sky was clear and balmy. No cross winds troubled them, thank God. Dante looked out across the horizon, wishing he could turn the plane and head north to Angelina. Not yet, but maybe soon. Not too far beneath him, the blue ocean lapped and turned against itself, lace froth collecting and dissolving in point and counterpoint. It was lovely. He must only mind the wings, which seemed to be at odds with each other, one looking for lift, one driving for land. It was tricky, but not impossible.

Sabino tapped Dante's shoulder, shouting over the engines.

"*Ugualmente vicino a Malta!*"

Too close to Malta.

Dante nodded and circled north just as a blaze of fire shot past him. The plane shuddered again, shifted to starboard. Dante lost altitude. He pulled back on the throttle with both hands. He was sweating with the effort of keeping this piece of lumber in the air.

When he levelled off and turned, he saw Sabino reaching for something, a gun perhaps. The bomb bays were empty and the Banana was not equipped with artillery. A swift cloud shadowed the plane and turned the ocean to steel. He knew the water might as well be steel if he did not get them away from anti-aircraft guns at Malta. He had been a fool, an idiot to be thinking about Angelina in a plane like this in a place like this. They would not need searchlights. With the range finders, he would be an easy target, joyriding in the middle of war within sight of enemy guns. If he had been aware of it, such news would surely loosen the *maggiore's* bowels.

Behind him, Sabino had a wrench gripped in his hand as though he were thinking about throwing that at one of the guns.

Dante knew he had been foolhardy, as well as obstinate. It better not cost him his life or Sabino's life. Another flash went by. With no manoeuvrability and no weapons, he was moving as fast as he could to get out of range before the interceptors came after him. They must have some powerful guns on Malta to be able to come so close from such a distance. The flak had only just missed him. He wondered if the lumbering speed of the Banana was confusing the range predictors so that they couldn't make quite accurate calculations. He patted the instrumentation, grateful for the perversity of the bomber's design. He pulled back and gained some altitude and some breathing space.

He could see no destroyers in the near vicinity, nothing to worry about there. He must be just barely within reach of the guns.

When it seemed as though he was going to make it out of this scrape with his life, he wondered whether he would be put back in the brig. It would be better than peeling potatoes. He would rather pound away at the tarmac in the afternoon heat than be stuck in the back of the mess hall bent over a mountain of rotting skins. The water shone below. The plane's shadow rippled along the waves below, dark on bright. They were safe and following a modest heading toward Sicily. In the flashing light of sun on water, Dante's eyes teared behind his goggles. Sabino tried to shift behind him and in shifting, altered the balance of the plane. Dante corrected and kept on north. He could see Sicily in the distance on this clear day. Sicily, where there would be a restaurant, where he could perhaps buy something to read besides his manuals. He pushed forward.

He could probably land the thing. He looked behind him again, but Sabino was looking at the sky.

Flying time to Sicily was pushing his luck, but after the encounter with the Malta guns, he felt lucky. He approached the southeastern coast, hoping to slip in and slip out of some field. He saw a patch of green on which he thought he might survive a landing. He pulled back on the throttle and began a choppy descent.

The plane hit the ground hard, cutting through the tall grass while Dante pressed both feet on the brake and prayed. When the Banana finally came to a stop, he turned and saw blood pouring from Sabino's head.

Sabino, with his hand pressed against the wound, was laughing.

"Where did you learn to fly?"

"Ai, Sabin!"

Dante slid the canopy back and pulled some filthy rags from under the yoke. These he pressed to Sabino's head.

"That's good axle grease. That will stop the bleeding faster than anything."

"You should travel with *grappa* if you're going to fly like that."

They sat for a minute, breathing.

"*Allora*, what are we doing now, *signor* pilot?"

"*Adesso*, now, now we are going to look around. We are going to find some wine, some meat, and some bread. We are going to take a little rest and then we are going to search high and low to find some treasure we can bring back to the Major so that we can keep our precious asses out of the brig. Let us have a look at that skull of yours. *Certamente*, Sabin, you have been blessed with the *testa dura*, the hardest head in Italia."

They heaved themselves over the edge of the plane. Dante ran his hands along the fuselage, looking closely at the undercarriage. The plane was as sound as it could be and lay still in the furrows it had gouged upon landing. They should be able to take off again. His hands were not even shaking. And the blood had stopped seeping from Sabino's head.

They walked to the edge of the field and pushed their way through the fence of young oak trees and chestnuts. Sabino picked up a rotting chestnut and threw it at Dante's head.

"Ai! Sabin! What are you doing?"

Sabino threw another chestnut, stinking and soft, at Dante's shirt.

"*Grazie, signor.* Such a gentleman."

Sabino threw another. It hit Dante's back with a dull thud.

"Enjoy yourself, fellow. You won't provoke me. I have been shot at by worse than chestnuts today."

Sabino bent and collected a dozen chestnuts more in his big hands. He threw them all at once, a barrage of odour that hit Dante's head, shoulders and backside, leaving a peppered brown trail down his uniform.

"*Finito*, eh?" Dante dodged behind a tree and picked up his own ammunition, but when he stepped out to fire back at his friend, he saw Sabino collapsed in a heap on the ground.

His head was bleeding again.

"Sabino, taking you anywhere is like taking my *nonna*. *Piano, piano, mio amico.* Take it softly, my friend. Stay there on the ground for a while, will you? Here, put your feet up on this rock. Good thing you didn't hit your feeble head on that when you hit the ground."

Dante sat beside his friend, waiting for Sabino's head to clear and the blood to stop. The shade cooled him while he kept the pressure on the oiled rag that served as a bandage for Sabino. He could see the Banana at rest in the field. Though he would not say so, he could not believe they had survived the landing, never mind the takeoff. There were fourteen of these things sitting in the heat of the island. Fourteen to deploy against the British on Malta. It was madness, he knew. A joke that would see the pilots and bombardiers ordered to man them obliterated. Orders would kill their own men and for nothing.

He looked at Sabino, lying still and pale with his eyes closed. A little rest and he would be fine. In the mean time, he had to get back to Pantelleria and somehow keep himself out of prison. But really, in spite of the major's caution, it *was* his job to discover the problems with the bomber. These excuses, compelling as they had seemed when he was moving down the runway and gathering speed, thinned to transparency when he thought of going back to face the poor major.

Sabino sat up in stages, first on his elbows and then on his side. By the time he was standing, the sun had moved across the sky.

"Are you ready to look around a bit?"

"*Certo*. But what are we looking for?"

"Some kind of treasure."

"Treasure," Sabino agreed.

The men headed west around the field, moving slowly. Sabino was not weaving, but his colour was not good. They found a stream about a kilometre in and both dropped to their knees and sank their faces in. Sabino bathed his head, unwrapping the makeshift bandage and giving that a rinse as well. The cut was ugly, jagged, but not too deep.

"Head wounds are the worst for blood."

"*Sì.*"

"You should wear a helmet in the plane."

"*Sì.*"

They moved upward through the forest and came out at the crest of a hill looking out over an orchard below, drenched and dusty green in afternoon light.

"You know what this is, Sabino?"

"They are cherries."

"No, my good friend, that is our treasure."

They moved in among the low-hanging fruit. Dante found a small crate that he lined with his shirt. He and Sabino picked and ate sweet cherries, filling their mouths and the crate.

"How's your head doing?"

"*Va bene.*"

"Does it hurt?"

Sabino looked at him as though he was the one who had split open his head.

"*Allora*, Sabin, let's get out of here."

On the far side of the orchard, they could hear dogs barking.

Where there were dogs, there might very well be cherry farmers who may also be carrying guns. The men turned with their booty and jogged back up the hill.

The trick was to arrange Sabino's legs in such a way so that the cherries could be accommodated without being crushed. He gamely climbed back into the cramped quarters in which he had made the outward journey and held the crate pressed against his chest with his knees on either side.

Dante climbed up into the cockpit. He put on the leather headgear, closed the canopy and started the engine. He gave Sabino the thumbs up and slowly turned the awkward craft around.

The dive-bomber rattled down the field, banging against the furrows and tilting this way and that while Dante tried to gain the speed he needed. Behind him, Sabino cradled his head with one hand and the cherries with the other, chin down and braced. He might have been praying. Dante nearly offered a prayer himself as the twin engines groaned and the plane approached the end of the makeshift runway. He pulled back on the throttle and the plane, as though on the wings of drunken angels, lifted off, taking branches off the tops of the oaks at the edge of the field.

Dante concentrated, bent over the controls. He had to look out for the anti-aircraft guns mounted on the British ships in this part of the Mediterranean. He did not want to find himself in such grave danger again and he scanned the horizon for Pantelleria. In spite of the pain in his shoulders and between his eyes, Dante's shoulders started to shake with laughter. He could not help himself, nor could he get his breath. The dive-bomber itself seemed to join in his unseemly amusement, shaking and shifting on the capricious breeze. He did not look back at Sabino, who, if he was still alive and had not crushed the cargo into liquor, would surely be laughing too. Dante directed the plane to the south and navigated back to the base.

Before he landed, he could see the military police, binoculars pressed to their small faces, watching for him. He turned the plane and circled around the landing strip. He rolled the cumbersome craft to a perfect stop beside the jeep that was waiting to take them both to prison, lifted the canopy and waved to the men.

"*Buona sera, signori. Come va?*"

He and Sabino climbed out of the plane and held out their hands for the irons. When they arrived at base command, the major was waiting for them, bent over his desk and still sweating in the cooling evening. Dante and Sabino waited for him to speak.

He put down his pen.

"You are charged with dereliction of duty, *signor*, among other things. You will be held in the brig until a court-martial can be convened and then you will be sent off to hang. Frankly, at this moment, I wish I could join you."

"May I speak, major?"

"Speak carefully, *sergente*. Your head is all but in the noose."

"I have some cargo in the bomber that may interest you. As we were arrested on our arrival, I have not had the opportunity to retrieve the treasure and bring it to your attention. However, I think it will offer some relief."

"Relief?"

"*Sì.*"

Dante met the major's glare.

"About face, *signori*. Let us examine the contraband you have brought with you and let us hope that it will not land you in even more trouble. Of this, I have doubt."

The major himself drove them back to the Banana, which the ground crew had taxied into the hangar and left unexamined. When their handcuffs were loosed, it was Sabino who hoisted himself into the cockpit and retrieved the crate. The cherries were whole, warm, and red. In the months on Pantelleria, the men had been on rations of tinned meat and pasta and potatoes. Fruit was scarce and supplies had a difficult time getting through. The major was not the only one suffering from constipation.

The Major took the crate and jumped back in the jeep, leaving Dante and Sabino in the hangar. They did not wait for the military police to notice their absence, or for the major to recall the charges against them. They strolled instead to their quarters, washed up and went to the kitchen to beg for some bread.

"Too bad we did not save some of those cherries for our supper."

Sabino pulled a small ratchet case out of his deep front pocket. He stretched out his arm and tapped Dante on the shoulder.

"Dinner is served, my friend."

Dante grinned, bowed, and daintily plucked two sweet cherries from the greasy container.

"But where are the ratchets?"

"I think they are rolling around in the bomb bays. We'll find them in the morning, I am sure."

In the morning, the Major emerged from his tent, whistling the national anthem.

"He's had a good night, finally."

Sabino nodded over the mounting pile of potato peels.

Dante sat on the low stool. The mess was peaceful in the early morning and the sun warmed his back and neck. He took the knife and got busy, peeling, slicing, and dropping the naked potatoes into the tub of water between them.

To Sabino he said, "Potatoes are better than prison."

"Or the firing squad."

"Or the gallows."

The major approached. Brisk and pink in the cheeks.

"De Angelis!"

Dante and Sabino jumped to attention.

"De Angelis, do you know what is the hardest compound known to humanity? The hardest material on earth?"

Dante wondered what was at stake. He had not checked the plane for flak marks. It would not do for the major to discover just how close they had come to being shot down.

"Sir, I think it is the diamond, is it not?"

"No, De Angelis, it is not. Would you care to take another stab?"

Dante kept his eyes forward. The sea was calm beyond the rocks in the far distance. The rocks themselves could not be harder than diamonds. He was sure that nothing could be.

"No sir, I would not."

"The hardest compound on the earth, De Angelis, is nothing more and nothing less than the material out of which God has manufactured your thick skull. Your *testa dura* beats out diamonds, steel, anything you choose to mention. And if that head leads you into any more trouble while you are in my command, I will see that it is removed from its resting place atop your shoulders and sent by courier to your mother. Understand?"

"*Si, maggiore. Capito.*"

Dante walked away, rubbing his good hard head.

In the major's favour for now, Dante was put in charge of detailing men to repair the airstrip. The poor wooden dive-bombers would be left to rot. It took a month of work from all the men working three shifts per day, the strip was torn up and relaid. The men and machines that had regrouped at Trapani returned to Pantelleria. Once the construction detail was complete, Dante was back with the planes. The Germans had supplied their allies at Pantelleria with the pride of their offence, the Junkers Ju 87 Sturzkampfflugzeug.

Sabino looked at him when he first heard Dante try to pronounce the name.

"Pardon?"

"Stukas."

The major came out to inspect the fleet.

"Keep these in trim, De Angelis. Kesselring has ordered that Malta be wiped off the map."

With Pantelleria's airfield finally organized for defence, the Germans supplied its newly built hangars with dive-bombing Stukas, over which Dante hovered, calibrating, measuring, and cleaning the engine parts and instrumentation with the devotion of a novice priest. These planes were beautiful and ferocious. Dante sent them out, watched them lift off to stymie the Allied presence in the Mediterranean.

The problem, Dante knew, was Malta. However many sorties they flew, however many bombs the German and Italian pilots dropped, they could not gain the upper hand in the Mediterranean as long as the Allies held Malta. The small island proved a thorn in the side of the Axis. With the Allied anti-aircraft guns based there and aircraft carriers docked there, Malta was causing more trouble per square foot of area than any other place on earth. The Stukas would be launched again and again against the poor island and its inhabitants. The Stukas were perfect weapons. Their pilots strolled across the tarmac, the best of the airborne division. The 208th and the 207th flew high overhead, dive-bombing the dockyards and the cities around them. This was good news for the ground crew. This was the object of their work. The strikes were strategic, surgical, necessary—every one of the thirteen thousand bombs that the Stukas dropped on Malta. His country was at war. Dante did not have to convince himself. He worked carefully and tried not to think about the returns for his labour. He would not think about fire or wreckage.

Until the church.

Dante had helped arm the planes. Seen them lift off at the end of an airstrip he himself had built. The Stukas took off in formation. He listened to the engines firing, the rhythm and grind of the motors, loud, deafening, and eloquent. The fighters went up with them, fast and light, so light that the wind lifted them, collected under the wings and drove them on. It was marvellous to see. It was so difficult to think of the mission as destructive when it was born of such beauty and ingenuity. He had not built the engines, but he had rebuilt them. He knew them inside and out, and he sent them on their way, waving. Thirteen thousand bombs. Dante had never been to Malta. He had come too close for comfort, but he had not seen with his own eyes the mess his fine Stukas were making of it.

They all heard about the church. The news went out on the radio that the Stukas had dropped a bomb on the Mosta church, the biggest one in Malta, where the parishioners must have been kneeling over old wood benches saying prayers. Dante imagined them, three hundred heads bent, some with kerchiefs, most grey, all certain that Malta would not fall. They would look just like the humble souls in the Duomo at home.

The news was nothing short of miraculous. The radio announcer was spitting into the microphone, too excited to pretend cool distance or objectivity. So much hardship had Malta endured, so much loss and destruction that the people had gone to pray. And what had happened?

Those souls had gone to pray for salvation. When the five-hundred-pound bomb crashed through the high ceiling, the gilded faces of the saints around the dome must have remained serene, as though knowing that all would be well.

The massive bomb bounced off the floor, hit the west wall, and skidded down the wide aisle, coming to rest near the altar, as though waiting for divine blessing. The people would not even have had time to hold their breath.

The announcer continued. When the noise stopped, a few of the ladies fainted. Mothers held back their small children from getting a closer look at the new supplicant. The people waited, wondering if their lives would be over this minute. They waited. Then someone started laughing. Soon, the whole congregation, including the trembling priest, tiptoed out of the church into the sunlight, laughing or crying, and calling upon the British to defuse the latest addition to the church.

In spite of Dante's efforts and the innumerable sorties of the Stukas, Malta, the most bombed place on earth, held. He could not fathom it. He knew that people across the world were falling victim to artillery and ammunition, the machines of war, wherever they struck. Why should this church be saved? What kind of joke was that?

Sabino made the sign of the cross. Dante heard him whisper, "*Grazie.*"

A small relief.

Angelina

Angelina's mother stayed in bed one morning. It was too late to start the bread so she sent Angelina with a few lire to go buy some from the neighbours.

"What is wrong, mamma?"

"*Non so.* I have a pain in my side. It must have been the fish last night."

Angelina had cooked the fish in a sauce of tomatoes and basil. She had also, when her mother's back was turned, slipped in a pinch of sugar to sweeten the dish. She and her brothers and her father had all eaten the trout, pulled that morning from the deeper water where the brook met the river. Angelina herself had cleaned and filleted them, cooked them with some rice. Her mother's skin was not right, not the right colour, but it could not have been the fish.

First, she went for the bread, Questo on her heels. On her way past Zia Anselmina's she greeted the sweeping woman, who spat on the brass handle of her front door, the better to polish it. Angelina walked stiffly. She wished she could laugh at this woman, but she was shocked by Anselmina's malice. How could she spit like that? Angelina had held a knife to her scrawny throat. She could not concentrate on the old woman, distracted as she was by the turn the morning was taking. The black-clad and bent widow no longer frightened her.

Back in the kitchen, Angelina found her mother sitting in a chair and leaning against the cool wall.

"*Va bene*, mamma?" Is everything all right?

The morning was still and Angelina's mother did not answer. She only crumpled forward, and rolled off the chair onto the stone floor.

Angelina stretched her mother out on the floor. She checked her pulse; she ran her fingers down the older woman's spine. There was fever, certainly, but no broken bones. She thought she could probably lift her, but when she tried, her mother was heavier than she expected. The dog whimpered and then wagged its tail.

"What good would you be to me, dog?"

Questo looked at her and then disappeared. Angelina shook her head and turned back to her mother. She put her arm below the woman's shoulder and lifted, but could not get purchase. She did not want to pull her forward. There was nothing she could use for leverage and time was passing so quickly. She must get someone to help her. She looked up as though to ask heaven for assistance when she heard the dog scrabbling toward the door and, in his haste, banging into it. Behind that noise came the polite double knock of the good Father.

"Thank God, thank God, Father. Please help me with my mother."

"Angelina, what's happened?"

"I do not know. She did not make the bread this morning. She could not answer me before. She just fell over."

"We will get her to bed and then you run for your papa and then off you go for the doctor. I will look after her until you return."

"*Grazie, Papa, mille mille grazie.*"

"*Allora, signora,*" he said to her mother, "*andiamo piano, piano.*"

The doctor came from Visso. Angelina had travelled this path a thousand times, more, and never had she seen every stone, every weed, every divot, every beetle and ant, so slowly did they seem to move.

Finally, they crossed the threshold. There was Father Paolo.

"Angelina, *dottore*, the *signora* is resting a little easier and has had a little tea. I hope that is all right."

Angelina waited with her papa and the Father while the doctor examined the patient. She looked around the kitchen for something she could use as payment. As the doctor came down the stairs, Angelina wondered how many faces had turned up to him just like theirs, how many expectant hopeful faces, waiting to hear that it was nothing, a stomach cramp, a sudden inexplicable fever never to be felt again as though we would all live well and forever. She lifted her face waiting for the doctor's good news.

"I am very sorry to say that your wife appears to have a tumour of the stomach. I have told her not to worry, that the pain will pass and that she will feel better soon, but in all likelihood, she will not be well again."

When her father stood silent, Angelina spoke. "Is there a medicine, perhaps surgery for her?"

The doctor frowned. Angelina knew their house was small, but with the doctor there, it seemed too small to hold such news.

"You would have to get her to the city. And not to Visso. To Rome, maybe. If she could see a doctor there, they might be able to give her a few more months. But the chief tumour is large and there are others in her stomach and under her arms that I can feel with my bare hands. I will leave you some morphine. Use it very sparingly and keep her comfortable and happy."

Angelina's father leaned against the new paint on the door. She moved to the cantina to get the money jar down and take out more than she thought they could afford.

"If this is not enough, *dottore*, I can bring you some vegetables and a chicken or two in the morning."

The doctor took the money. "This will do."

As though having dropped the news, he was now in a hurry to leave. Father Paolo saw him out and escorted him back to the path down to Visso. Angelina tried to take in the news. How could her mother, who had been fine yesterday, now be upstairs needing morphine? Never to recover. The doctor's coat was worn. He needed a shave. He was only a Visso doctor, not a Rome doctor. Angelina wanted to believe that he did not know really what he was saying. He had felt some things and decided on the basis of a few lumps that Graziela would have to made comfortable. That there was nothing to be done. That she had tumours. More than one.

The doctor was unshaven because he most likely had not had time to shave. Or to buy a new coat. And what would he use for money? If all of his patients paid him as Angelina did, then he would not have the means for new fine coats. Angelina apologized to the doctor, though he was long gone.

Finally, Angelina's father spoke. "Perhaps if we could get Graziela to the city? But, Angelina, how could we do this? She can't walk down the mountain the way she is. I don't think she could stand even the donkey's back. Then the train trip." Her father looked at the door as though calculating the distance and the possibility.

The doctor had rinsed his hands and shook the water into the sink. He had said "*Signor*, I am telling you, my best advice in the circumstances is that you keep her comfortable and happy."

Angelina looked at the vials of morphine that the doctor had removed from his bag. Surely her mother was not as bad as that. Angelina would not believe that her mother's condition was so desperate. She needed a rest. A rest would bring the swelling down and ease the pain. Graziela, truth be told, had been sick before and always she had gotten better. She might be ill, there might even be tumours, but they could not be as serious as the doctor said.

Her father went back to his sons in the field. Angelina went upstairs to her mother.

The San Placido garden was not a place for leisure and Angelina's life was not one of idle reflection. The produce from the cultivated land on the incline of the mountain fed not only Angelina's family, but also the people who purchased the surplus from her father's stall in the market square at Visso. In the last few months, there had been a few dozen German officers stationed in the town. Not many, yet, and not inclined to pay for market goods as they strolled among the stalls and chose what they liked.

In the spring, Angelina and her father planted potatoes and wheat. They planted rows and rows of beans which grew sturdy and tall, drenched in sun, like a dream of green. These were her father's best sellers, sweet and crisp, and the small dark ladies of the town collected at her father's stall and discreetly elbowed each other or tried to distract one another from the business at hand to some triviality in the square behind them in order to procure a more congenial place in the cluster of women with families to feed and reputations to maintain.

"Ah, *guarda*, Elisabetta, the balloons at Alfredo's barbershop. Has he come into money that he can afford such nonsense? *Guardo*, the bread is finally pulled out of the oven at the *pasticceria*. If you hurry, you can get the first loaf, warm. Look, Alfonso's tomatoes are huge this year. You can smell them from here."

And Maria or Antonietta, or Luisa, if she were not sharp, would turn to see and perhaps shift her feet and the next woman would sigh as though faint from waiting and shift her weight from one foot to the other in a way that somehow placed her closer to Angelina's father.

The women were devoted to Angelina's father's beans. She did not think it was crazy. She knew how much better they tasted. The ladies tried to pry from him secrets he might have about the soil or whether he put sugar in the water or ground rose petals into the earth up there on the mountain.

Sometimes, in a good mood, extravagant and flirtatious, he would answer.

"Ah, *signorine*, the heavens open above my fields and the rain comes down gently and sweetly, as though dropped from the fingertips of the Blessed Virgin."

At this, the ladies of Visso might gasp, "Alfonso, you go too far."

"*Mi dispiace, belle signore*. I'm sorry, ladies, but what can I say to you? The Lord himself smiles on San Placido in spite of its poor people."

With this, the women would be content, knowing themselves better off than the ones up the mountain and knowing that if the villagers had the smile of God, that was nearly all they had.

In a bad mood, Alfonso would be short.

"*Signore*, these beans are seasoned with my sweat and blood. I should be charging you ten times as much. Enjoy. *Buon appetito*."

Surly or gallant, it did not matter what he said or how he comported himself. He was cleaned out by breakfast time and the ladies went, sweetly or gracelessly, to their own kitchen pots to cook up the best *fagiole* in town.

Angelina stayed quietly behind, taking the money. Some of the ladies would say, "*Ciao, Lina*," which she hated. She answered, "*Ciao, signora, come sta?*" Sometimes they would ask her about boyfriends and her father would answer for her.

"Angelina has too much sense for that."

Her father, in his sparse references to romance or love, presented it as a trial of life, a thing to which one would have to succumb and endure eventually, as though it were a head cold. For her part, she was content to plant the beans, tie them to stakes, prune and weed and water. She saw none of the profit, but she did not think about money. She did not need it. She left her father in the garden early enough to make the lunch and mix and make the pasta they would eat for dinner. She fed the pig, the lambs, the cows, the donkey, the chickens, and rabbits, and made sure they all had enough water.

How much sense did her papa think she had? While she did the work of cooking for her family, she kept pressed and fragile in her dress pocket the latest letter from Dante. He spoke to her about good men he worked with. He described his days the way any labourer would. He did not talk about bravery. He did not write of extraordinary deeds. The men of Italy were doing a job and when it was finished, they would come home. His letters said he would come home. And by home, he meant to Angelina.

She did not have too much sense at all. She kept Dante's letters as treasure in a box under her bed. She kept the envelopes whose creases she slit with sharpest knife in the kitchen. She read them alone. For the first time she felt the cloth of her nightgown against her own skin at night. It was rough, having been dried in the sun until it was stiff and it took some time before the fabric warmed and softened against her. It felt fine around her abdomen and breasts, her thighs and ankles, intimate. Lying under the covers, she stretched as long as she could and the nightgown slipped around her and she covered her mouth to stifle a sigh born of the beginnings of bliss. How much sense did she have? Enough to wait for Dante and to pray for his safe and quick return.

Angelina stoked the fire in the stove, to bring the warm ashes to life and add the kindling and wood shavings to bring the flame. She prepared the supper. Her mother's side had begun to hurt, the weakness to come for her when she stood too long. There was pain and more and Angelina understood none of it. A tumour of the stomach would not be cured by excellent broth. Angelina had washed the bloody rags in the late evening when the cistern was vacant of the chatty women of San Placido. Anselmina sat at her door on the bench, her hands folded over the cane that kept her upright, watching Angelina head to the water at such an unusual hour. Angelina kept her eyes down. She would not discuss her mother with that woman. Anselmina was getting worse and worse. Everyone in San Placido, except for Father Paolo, gave her a wide berth. Angelina would not explain. Anselmina smacked her lips together as though tasting the air for scandal. It would be awful to speak to her now, but it might be worse to ignore such a vicious woman. The worst of the stains were turned inward, but still visible. Perhaps on the way back, she could wish Anselmina a pleasant evening. She could perhaps summon the courage to do that.

She hoped her mother would be all right. Perhaps the doctor was wrong in what he said. Her mother had refused the hospital. In spite of her collapse, she kept saying she would be better in the spring. She had the winter sickness. Sick of the cold, that is all. When spring came, she said she was longing for the summer heat to take the ache out of her bones. She would soon be put right. She would race Angelina, as she used to do, to the garden and back again. But summer had come and still Angelina's mother rested up. Waiting for a season to turn and the pain to ebb.

Each morning Angelina took the pot to the cistern, filled it with water, and carried it back down the path to her house. From the upstairs bedroom, her mother called out, *Buongiorno?* Hello?

And Angelina replied, *Mamma, sta Angelina qui.* Come on, mamma, she said. You know it is I. I am putting the water to boil for the pasta.

And her mother's weak reply would come, "*Finalmente,*" as though she had been waiting days to be fed by her keeper. The word was released gratefully, as though for her mother the pain itself eased in Angelina's presence.

The sausages warmed in the pan in which Angelina had cooked them that morning. Over the other pan, Angelina rubbed fresh rosemary between her palms and added a bit of salt to the potatoes as they warmed over the fire. The water would take an hour to boil, but the pasta, drying and ready on tea towels on the table and the credenza, would be ready minutes after she dropped it into the pot.

She left the house again and walked up to the garden. She cut some lettuce and a cucumber. The dog followed at her heels and sat while she pulled a few weeds and dusted off her hands. The black dog watched, its pink tongue dripping onto the earth beside the garden. He watched her hands and then looked at her face, watching and gathering himself for the catch.

Suddenly, Angelina turned and tossed a small piece of sausage that she had slipped into her apron pocket. It arced high over the rising corn. The dog leapt up and snapped his jaws around the scrap of meat, which he chewed with concentration, then licked his lips, sat down in the shade and rolled onto his back, bracing his legs against the air, abandoning himself to contentment. Angelina put her hand to her mouth to cover her smile.

"This dog, *questo cane,* is a lunatic," she said to the tomato plants. "But he cannot be fooled and he is always ready to eat. He will fit in well with my brothers who eat without question or complaint whatever comes their way."

Angelina heard Father Paolo behind her. "*Signorina, come?* I beg your pardon?"

"*Mi dispiace*, Padre. I'm sorry. I was speaking of *questo cane*, who follows me, waiting to see what bits of meat I will feed to him. Once I do, he rolls in the grass or runs like a crazy fellow around the garden, as though he is playing a secret game."

Father Paolo looked at the dog, whose hind and forelegs pawed at the air while he twitched on his back in the cool grass, turning suddenly to snap at his own tail.

"It looks like a delightful game, Angelina. Bless you for taking care of God's messenger."

Angelina believed Father Paolo must have been walking too long in the sun.

"Father, you think *questo cane* is a messenger of God?"

"No one knows where he came from. Like the Holy Spirit and the wind. And no one knows where he will go or what he might accomplish while he is here. Already, you smile more than I have seen since that young soldier was here."

Father Paolo walked away. "Yes, child. I think that this dog might have been sent straight from heaven."

Angelina was sure the Father would not be speaking blasphemy, but to look at this lazy dog and compare him to the Holy Spirit signalled a peculiar streak in the good Father, one that Angelina, weeding the garden, could not work out. She would not think about whether she was smiling more. Had Dante made her smile? The dreamer who saw magic where there was none?

Set on the earth, her feet were. Loose inside her father's unlaced shoes.

And now, every time she came to her garden, she could hear Dante's voice in her ear, feel him watching her. The hem of her dress lay across her calf. Her ankle below.

"*Il giardino ora è così bello,*" he said, knowing he sounded so thin in the rich afternoon.

The garden is so beautiful now.

She had pondered the utterance of the young madcap beside her. The war had clearly hurt him in the head and she understood that she must not draw attention to this.

"*Sì.*"

Dante laughed. She looked at his hands, hands that were so clean. He had not gardened. He looked as though he had freshly scrubbed under his nails to wipe out the traces of his work, as though he had scrubbed and nearly flayed his skin to be clean in San Placido. When she followed his gaze, she saw that he was looking at her ankle. And there was her ankle, fine and still, and there her calm hands. Her quiet breast. She breathed evenly.

Angelina tilled the soil. She and her father worked in silence in long parallel rows, turning the earth and crumbling it. In San Placido, though everyone knew about the war, they could not hear the tanks move on Abyssinia or Prague or Albania. If they turned on the Martinellis' radio, they could hear Il Duce from his balcony exhort the poor masses, warn them of their ignorance and their need of a good strong leader.

Signor Martinelli turned up the radio to listen. The Duce spoke.

"*E' l'aratro che traccia il solco, ma è la spada che lo difende.*" It is the ploughshare that traces the line, but the sword that defends it.

"*Fascista e colui che sente viva dentro di se' la poesia maschia dell'avventura e del pericolo.*" The Fascist man is that one who feels inside the male poetry of adventure and danger.

"*Sempre avanti ad ogni costo per la grandezza della patria!*" Ever forward no matter the price for the glory of the fatherland!

Signor Martinelli took the risk of shutting off the radio before the latest speech was finished. He poured coffee for his neighbours who commenced a discussion of these notions, epigrams that Angelina believed as substantial as the dust she shook out of her rag on a Saturday morning, which, if she were careful to mind the wind, might provoke a sudden cough in Zia Anselmina, who could hardly scold a girl for being clean. Her father read the speeches as they were published by the national newspapers.

Signor Martinelli said, "You know those editors have been handpicked for excellence by Mussolini himself."

Angelina's father did not think it could be as bad as that.

Down in Visso, when Angelina went with her father, she heard the words of Mussolini discussed in the coffee bar as the men, those too old for war, put Rosella's dainty cups of scalding espresso to their lips and tossed them back in firm agreement, or hot derision of the Duce's pronouncements.

It was outrageous, one said. The woman on the next street has lost two sons. Two! Her husband is long dead and the last boy is nearly old enough to deploy. Then what will she do?

"Listen, if you are going to be a force in this world, you have got to claim some kind of empire. You have got to gain ground. You cannot just sit around and have the goods of the earth handed to you. Sometimes you have to sacrifice."

Angelina's brothers were safe at home so far. Her mother was there. Her father sat at the supper table each evening. Their family had not yet had to sacrifice anything, or any of its members, for the war. They were a bit poorer, but the animals were fine. There was enough food and the clothes could always be mended. Angelina did not feel that she needed anything that she did not have. The Germans took up more and more space in Italy, but they were still rare in Visso and unheard of in San Placido. As Angelina sat quiet by her father, she felt her legs weaken. Nico and Berto were babies she had raised. They were needed at home. Angelina teased them about being useless, but what would happen if they went to drive the machine of war? Could she stop them somehow from entering that terrible march forward to which all the young men seemed to be drawn?

"Our boys are in Africa. They are in Russia. Places no one gives a shit about. Wilderness and snow. Deserts and nomads. Can you grow a crop there? Can you build a house? No. So tell me, what is the point, if not to swell the head of our fatheaded Duce?" Signor Martinelli slammed the table.

Alfonso placed his hand on his friend's arm. "Watch yourself, you do not know who is listening, old man."

In a corner of the café, dark and bent, Anselmina sipped her coffee. She crushed a *biscotto* into her coffee and spooned the gruel into her mouth.

"Exactly. I am an old man. If I cannot speak my mind now, what use am I? I cannot see well enough to fire a rifle, not even to catch my supper. My granddaughter feeds me. My wife keeps me clean. I tell you this, I have seen the war that they said would end every war. I have lost my cousin and my brother. This one will follow the same stupid path as all the others and the vultures will get fat and we will get thin."

Strident opinions struck against others like flint in the raucous bar.

Angelina had seen her brothers growing restive in the village. She watched them now as they kicked at stones outside the café, their fists deep in torn pockets. They could not hear their father, his pleasant calm voice unheard in the storm of voices within.

Angelina and her father left the café and collected Berto and Nico and the donkey. They had sold their load of charcoal and mended a fence on this trip. They had a bit of money and Angelina wished that her father would give it to the boys and tell them to go buy something, some treat for themselves, as though a pastry might satisfy them. Might keep them close. She was surprised at the force of such a desire. She wanted nothing more than to keep things as they were. And if she could by wishing it bring Dante back to Italy as well, she would light a thousand candles and pray on her knees for a month.

She watched in the dusk as her father put his hand in his pocket and jostled the change inside so that it made a tuneless little song. He did not pull any out. He did not make a gift of it. Such a gesture would not occur to him and Angelina certainly could not ask. Behind them, Nico and Berto were trying to trip each other on the darkening path. Perhaps they were still too young. Sixteen and almost eighteen. That was surely too young to go to war. Her father rubbed a massive hand over his skull once or twice as though to clear his head and then he pulled at the old donkey and pressed home. The higher they climbed, the less urgent seemed the possibility that her brothers would leave. Angelina felt better. How could flimsy things like the thick air of the café or words on the page of newspaper make such a devastating change in her family? Such ephemerals could not change the sweetness of the beans under the warm sun. The words of war and glory that had so pricked the men at the bar to noisy discussion slipped from her mind, drawn by gravity to the small stones beneath her boots.

By the time she turned the last corner before home, Angelina could no longer recall the details of the day's speech by the Duce as it was printed. She was peaceful as she ate her dinner in silence. Her mother's appetite was good. Her colour was good. Perhaps the doctor was wrong. Angelina hummed a tune as she served them all, watched as her brothers dipped bread into the last drops of sauce or drippings from the meat, every plate cleaned. Outside, they could hear the dog turning and turning on the mat by their boots and arranging his long black nose so that it lay with the bar of light across it that streamed from the gap in the front door. Angelina laughed at him. That dog, sniffing at light as though light were fragrance. They did not talk about the war. They talked about the beans.

Angelina and her father worked the garden. From childhood, when he rose, she did. He took a hoe, she tried even as a toddler to hoist the long shovel and work alongside him.

"*Cosi*, Papa? Like this?"

"*Si*, Angelina, just like that."

For fine work among the plants, Angelina still used the small shovel that her father made her when she was a small girl. The shovel and the pruning fork no longer fit her hand but she used them, cradled them, and paused in work to think for the first time how lucky she had been to have grown up here, to have had a father who knew enough about magic to point out a bright caterpillar or spindly spider, letting it crawl on the back of her hand. He took her hand and laid it flat to the ground so the creature would step on it. He didn't speak; he didn't explain. The minute footsteps tickled her palm, but she stayed still beside her hushed father, watching.

Dante's voice had got inside her somehow when he came to San Placido. He had stayed for the afternoon and then he left. He was away, now, far from Italy. She did not know where or doing what exactly, but she thought of him. She wondered if he was frightened. If he were here, she might even venture the question. During his visit on the mountain, her throat was too dry. She had barely spoken to her own father in all the years of her life and here was Dante, a river of language washing away her calm. She would listen to him as he sat pointing things out to her that were right before her eyes and growing in her own garden, as if she'd never seen a red tomato or a green bean or a yellow zucchini flower and thus had to be formally introduced. The motion of butterflies, as though she could not see for herself, on the branch before them the struggle out of the chrysalis that made the blood flow into the fragile wings, strengthening them, paper-thin and enduring. It was amazing to him, so that he must narrate it. There were hummingbirds that came to sip nectar from the honeysuckle that grew wild along the ancient wall and Dante was astonished to see them and so he talked to her about his astonishment, invited her to marvel at something she had seen each warm season of her life.

She thought he must have been dropped on his head as a baby. Not to be able to see that the butterfly and the hummingbird were not doing miracles; they were doing what they had to do to survive. Work hard to get out of your egg. Fly fast and hover to get the food you need without being killed by a hawk or a cat. For these commonplaces, she sat still on her own bench and looked where he pointed.

She should have stood. She should have stood and thanked him for making the long walk up the mountain. She should have shaken hands and thanked him and returned to the garden to weed. She instead looked away and nearly smiled. She looked down. The pattern of pink flowers on her skirt was faded. She smoothed the fabric across her thighs. If a man wanted to walk miles and scale a mountain to point out the obvious and discuss it from all angles, so much hot air from a bellows, let him behave like a poor *buffo*. She would sit. He had kindled her interest. How much could he speak before collapsing? And how could a man walk so far in the afternoon heat and smell so fragrant, shaved and clean?

In the end, she watched him walk away. She promised to write. She gave him a photograph. His words had filled her. She did not know she had been empty. She said under her breath as he disappeared, *ritornato a me*. Return to me.

She did not know, but she would like to find out. He wrote her letters. He told her he was well and that being at war was more like doing a job of work than anything else. He liked his co-workers. He did not sound like a man who feared for his life. The words on frail paper summoned his voice in her head and she read them and reread them for nothing more than pleasure.

Dante

From Pantelleria, Dante's unit was posted to the North African front. Before deploying, he and Sabino had twenty-four hours in Rome. Not enough time to make it to San Placido. He might, if he were lucky, have time to get there in order to wave and to turn around. Instead, he compelled Sabino to follow the path of Dante's first meeting with Angelina.

"Here, I first saw her."

"Here, I took her hand."

"Here, we had *gelato*."

Sabino yawned, leaning against the iron rail around the Borghese gardens. He dodged Dante's punch.

"I could use some ice cream myself."

Dante did not notice his friend walk away. It made his throat hurt to be there.

"In a minute, I will start crying like a baby."

He found Sabino and bought them both *gelati*. They walked on, but Dante said nothing more about Angelina. Instead, they got a paper and sat on one of the shaded benches to read the news of war.

Dante had followed the career of his leader from the earliest days. Because of his father's position in the town, he was aware, before the war was declared, that Mussolini had been the delight of the world. His father had struck him, lightly for once, had thrust the newspaper in his face and said, look, look at this. Churchill declares Mussolini to be the saviour of Italy.

Everyone loved the Duce. He was short, all thick jaw and forehead, bright eyes and a staccato delivery that hailed his people, stopped them in the street. He was irresistible, Dante thought, until his alliance with Hitler. Dante had been pressed by the throng, listening with his parents and thousands upon thousands of others in Rome in the Piazza Venezia until he nearly fainted. He had felt the urge to raise his arm in some kind of salute to a power he could not comprehend. He had felt it, though. His parents talked about how things would be better now. They already were. There were pensions, there were jobs, there was construction everywhere they looked. They were solid, paying bills and looking forward to thriving retirement. All because of Mussolini. It had to be good.

Then came the inspired notion of a second Roman empire. And Hitler.

Mussolini had said, "Italian people, rush to arms and show your tenacity, your courage, and your valour." Dante listened. Mussolini would invade Egypt. He would hold Libya, Eritrea, Italian Somaliland, and Ethiopia. He would, he insisted to the world, establish a new Roman empire more glorious and more enduring than the first.

Dante and Sabino stopped before the billboard. Dante had not seen it before, this tremendous map of Europe and North Africa, an emblem for the people to behold. The Mare Nostrum lay spread out before them showing all the countries whose shores touched the Mediterranean under Italian control. If Dante wondered what Mussolini's interest was in such a wasteland, as Africa seemed to be in his imagination, this map detailed it. The Duce had colonies now in Eritrea, Libya, and Italian Somaliland. He wanted more.

"Do you think this will happen as the map says?" Sabino asked.

"I don't know." It was impossible for him to contemplate such vast movement of weapons and men across such terrain. "Who will stop it? Japan invaded Manchuria and no one in the world had said anything, not even the League of Nations."

"Is the League so frail, then?"

It seemed that it was. That men had decided to expand the borders of empire again. Mussolini, who had done so much that was good for Italy, good to give a young man like Dante hope for a prosperous future, was now asking this of his citizens. Before Dante stood the representation of a kingdom. He did not know if he would choose to fight for such a picture, but the choice was out his hands.

Were these the dreams of men? The agglomeration of territory? The forced submission of races of people whom no one in Italy had heard of or cared two figs for? Dante had listened to Mussolini encourage his people to greatness. Before the declaration of war, before he began down a rhetorical path that would see him hanging upside down in the city square to be spat upon by the mothers without sons, Dante had seen him walk the streets of Rome, blessing the children, smiling at the mothers and shaking hands with unemployed, unshaven men. They greeted him warmly. They travelled on roads that were now maintained by the government, on trains that ran as they should, they visited the hospital when necessary and if they needed a pension, one was made available to them. When Mussolini started talking about the empire, they turned to listen. He had done a good job of stabilizing Italy. Perhaps it was time to help the other poor nations. The warm Italians, Dante included, turned to Mussolini, up on his balcony or striding in the square, they turned to him, repeating, "We are strong now. We can fight and take what we want."

It was tempting to believe.

Dante had read about the parade that the mayor of New York threw for the Italian pilot, Italo Balbo. Everyone in Italy knew about Balbo's accomplishments. The man had flown a record twelve thousand miles round trip between Italy and the Chicago World's Fair. With twenty-four sea planes, he had landed on Lake Michigan. Dante had read the headline to Sabino.

"Balbo lands in Chicago, takes the town by storm!"

"That would be something, Sabin. To fly like that with the eyes of the world watching you. Look at this."

Dante held out the newspaper. "They are comparing him to

Marconi and Columbus. He is going to have lunch in Washington with President Roosevelt!"

At the military school, everyone followed Balbo's career and everyone noticed the change in newspaper coverage of the hero of the Italian air force after Balbo's trip to America. It seemed that perhaps the Duce offered the newspaper editors new guidelines: Only one article on Balbo per newspaper — not on the front page. Now, if they wanted to find out about his latest exploits, the men had to find them buried in the mid-section of the newspaper.

Within two weeks of Italy's declaration of war on Britain, Dante and Sabino were learning the ropes at Ciampino, still reading about Balbo who was back in his plane, now flying reconnaissance over North Africa on Mussolini's orders. Dante thought, such a good soldier as Balbo was would do as his commander ordered him. The North African campaign started strong and was going well for Italy. The ground soldiers covered territory so rapidly and now they had Italo Balbo with them, flying overhead. Dante wondered not about Balbo's courage, but about his modesty. If stories about him, just stories, were printed in obscure parts of the newspaper, among the confirmation and baptism notices, then it could only be because the Duce had ordered it. No one in Italy was unaware of Mussolini's domination of the front pages. Dante wondered if perhaps Balbo lacked discretion, a salubrious modesty that would serve him better than bravery. Anyone could see that Balbo was a handsome fellow, carved out of alabaster and charming, a man over whom both men and women had fawned. His accomplishments were manifest on an international stage and all who met him loved his joy—joy in flight, in pretty girls, and fine cigars. Dante thought he seemed like a man to speak right to your face, to embrace you and drink to your health, and your wife's health and perhaps the health of your mother-in-law and your beautiful daughters.

The newspaper report was sketchy. From his post just north of Rome, Dante read the brief article. He was curious about anything to do with the North African campaign because he would be heading there himself. He had admired Balbo so much. The famous pilot was one of the first ones into the sky over Africa. On June 25, 1940, Balbo took off to observe the British garrisons in the northwest. Over Tobruk, he pulled the plane on its side to greet his compatriots below when anti-aircraft flak hit the plane's left wing and fuselage. Balbo's plane burned in the blue sky and crashed to the earth. The war had barely begun and Balbo was dead. The news was stunning. Dante felt robbed of the chance to see for himself the great flyer. The official report published in all the Italian newspapers, which Dante read with sorrow, reported that the friendly fire was the result of a tragic accident, of Balbo's well-marked and quite famous plane having been mistaken for a fighter of the British squadron. War had just been declared. Balbo was its first casualty and he had not even met the enemy.

Balbo was gone and his death was suspect. Under this shadow, Dante was deployed to North Africa. He had joined the Regia and placed his life and fate in the hands of men for the good of his country. He understood that some of the men were the type to savour any meagre authority. He also understood that he was a man who had to learn to follow orders for the sake of his unit, for the safety of the men around him, and for the success of the war effort. This he learned in classrooms at the military school and, more often, in the small cell to which he was confined because his failure to comply with those orders. Such compliance was drilled into him and in more ways than one. Dante was beginning to believe that it was good for him to obey orders, that his physical survival might depend on it. And now here was Balbo, obedient and bold, blown to smithereens before his time.

Dante wondered about the accident. The markings would have been clear. To have made such a stunning mistake was almost inconceivable. He had heard the rumours, that Mussolini, jealous for glory, had himself arranged the mishap. But such an act was too unpalatable to consider. Dante supposed it was possible that a young gunner, too eager, too nervous, might have fired on Balbo's plane. It was possible. Perhaps in the desert, the eyes do not focus as well. Dante would have to mention this to the fighter and dive-bomber pilots. He wondered if they should paint the undercarriage, mark it, so as to avoid such mistakes.

The news report added that a British plane did fly over Tobruk later in the day; that it passed unharmed above the guns and crossing over enemy lines dropped its only cargo, a note of condolence from RAF Commander Sir Arthur Longmore who sent it upon hearing of Italy's loss of the famous pilot.

Dante's specialty was the instrument panel of the Ju 87 Sturzkampfflugzeug, the Stukas that formed the heart of the German Blitzkrieg. Dante's squadron had taken delivery of them from the Germans. The dive-bombers were offered to the Italian air force to fortify their advances in North Africa. By the time Dante arrived, the battle for Tobruk had been engaged with wins and reversals on both sides. Graziani had been facing off against the British commander, General Wavell, attack and counter attack, with forces on each side pushing forward and then falling back.

The road that Dante travelled had been built by Mussolini, under his orders and with the sweat of Italian men and forced Eritrean labourers. The desert road ran a thousand miles to Tunis. In North Africa, the Italians who arrived before Dante had dug in. In Benghazi, they planted hedges and gardens, which decorated prim white houses built in tidy rows. The gardens were full of flowers and fresh vegetables, bougainvillea and eggplant. He could well imagine the drive to make a place in the wilderness. As though it lay in the very beat of their blood, they got to work building aqueducts along ancient plans. They had collected run-off and had fertilized the desert soil. They needed water, water for the gardens and water for the pasta that was included in their ration packs to sustain them. What parts of Libya and Egypt they occupied, they made over in their own image. They built oases for the officers who wore scented and brilliant uniforms in their daily duties.

Dante's Stukas would assist Marshal Graziani, who had got his troops as far east as Sidi Barani. They had just established their position when Wavell counter-attacked and, with inferior numbers, managed to push the Italians back into Libya. The Italians had marched east so easily that the retreat, when it was forced upon them, was swift and shameless.

Now Dante was posted at Derna with his squadron and the other reinforcements to take back the territory the Italians had lost. On his first night, he looked up.

There was the night and there was the moon, hung large in the sky, as big as God's earring, if God were also a woman who understood the allure of a cool round pearl kissing the line of the jaw. This moon filled his eyes. Provoked questions in a man who could not believe where he was standing.

What is the path to North Africa? To the shifting turbulent desert where carrion die falling from the air on their way to a decent meal?

There was too much to which a man must become accustomed. In the desert morning, Dante recalled with fondness early mornings at the military school where he had turned up in pyjamas to salute the Italian flag. It had been cold then, as now, but the fragrance of the air, the dawn's moisture seemed after only weeks in the desert a foreign and extraordinary thing. For the first time, he knew constant thirst.

The officers did not make the men stand at attention for too long. In the morning parade the sand sifted over the tops of their boots and kept rising and would keep on rising if they stood long enough, until they were buried and the memory of them had ceased. New sand, young and sharp, old sand, sphered and soft against the skin. All of it, eroding the flimsy hide that contained each one of them. They stopped long enough to get orders, to salute, and then kept going.

Dante went where they sent him. Behind every task and duty, he composed letters to Angelina in his mind. If he could narrate his days, perhaps they would take perceptible shape. If he could know them as a story to tell this woman, a story to amuse her and keep her attention, then he could manage the dreariness of the days.

The sand collected in every crease of Dante's uniform, between fabric and skin, within folds of skin, at the base of the hairs on his arms. When the storms whipped up the sand and moved it in billows and with force, he and his men were nauseated—the static electricity, unless the men could find some way to ground themselves as living breathing conductors, made them sick.

Storms were good for one thing only. When the wind whipped

up, the flies left him alone, flies as determined as grains of sand to get next to his blood. Black biting flies covered him. He and Sabino found some netting to tuck in along their helmets and around their faces and necks. Dante tried to keep gloves on as he worked, but for the fine tuning, his hands were exposed and the flies lighted on fresh meat. The wind set him free from that plague.

The best that Dante could say about the passing of days in the desert was that he had a commission. To have a task to accomplish, to spend days with men focused on a task, to see the edge of the empire in person and not on a map on a building in Rome, to see with his own eyes the ladies of Africa, their brilliant clothes, in their daily undertakings and to know himself strange to them, these things gave him courage so that he did not complain.

In the day, he strapped on coveralls and an apron to crack the hatch of the pride of the Luftwaffe. Dante loved the Stukas. He had great respect for their power, their elegance in the air; he was mortally glad to know that he would never look up at the business end of the dive-bomber screaming toward him. The pilots were beginning to notice his work. Pilots who required that the throttle respond almost before they touched it as they moved out of their steep and dreadful dives. A young prodigy, Hans-Joachim Marseille, was a frequent visitor to the card games that Dante and Sabino staged on barrels between the bombers. He asked questions, provoked Dante into answering, provoked his curiosity about what the Stuka might be able to do in the hands of a crazy young German.

At night, Dante wrapped himself in his overcoat against the cold. He sat watching the meagre water begin to steam over the fire built in a hole in a place forsaken by God. His rifle beside him and he himself almost swallowed by darkness. He could hear the low voices of the others from their posts along what remained of the Italian line. He could see the quick flare of a cigarette end. He was out of cigarettes himself and so had decided to quit them, but he breathed the cold in deeply as smoke drifted by and drew some comfort.

"Sabin, have you got a smoke?"

"*Mi dispiace*, my friend. I'm sorry. We need another pilot to stop by with an engine problem."

"I don't think this water will ever boil."

Dante pulled out the blue packet of dried spaghetti and broke string after string into the tepid water.

"I hear the Germans are coming."

"The miraculous Afrika Korps. *Si*. Herr Rommel is coming faster than your uncle comes to supper. He'll be sprinting through to Tobruk with us doing the heavy work to clear the path."

"Look," Sabino said, pointing west, "I think I can see the dust rising. That must be Rommel."

Dante stirred his pasta, hoping it would soften enough to eat.

"I have seen the maps. We'll have to push through to Tobruk. If we can get there, we'll have enough provisions to make it to El Alamein."

"The German officers will telegraph to Cairo to say they will be there for dinner. They will save the day, have their pictures taken again in all the papers and newsreels."

"It will take at least a division."

"Listen to us. We've been a month in the desert and we are already strategizing our way to an Italian victory."

Dante picked up his fork and saluted his friend. The retreat would end, and an advance would begin, enforced by German air power and tanks. Dante squared his shoulders. There would be more fighting, more holes, and when his spaghetti was gone, more potatoes.

Dante was careful. His hands did not shake. He had not been in the brig since he arrived in Tunis. He had learned not to lose his temper, not in the heat or the cold, nor in the dust that plagued them all. He watched Sabino work, his patient, smooth gestures, clearing the sand, then cleaning the tools, he would caress the parts and blow the dust away. That Sabino worked alongside him with equal ease was calming. Dante often, on the edge of fury, would look at his tranquil friend, grease-covered and concentrating on the stripped bolts and cracked gaskets, and would contain himself. He would look up from the desert around them or at the men with whose lot his had been thrown. Good men, every one. He grew peaceful himself. When a storm blew up, he and Sabino covered the engines of the planes they worked on and gathered their tools. Dante had organized his work apron so that it had a pocket for everything and everything was put exactly in its place. He had taken long, dull afternoons to stitch seams along the front, so that the wrenches and screwdrivers, hammers and gauges each fit neatly into a slot easily and blindly reached.

Because of his care, the two friends rarely ran out of cigarettes. They even had a bit of chocolate sometimes. Dante became the unofficial lead mechanic, a valuable acquaintance for the princes of the Luftwaffe. For the first time in his life, men's faces turned to him for answers, for assurances. Perhaps Mussolini had been correct about war making Italian boys into men. It was a terrible truth, if it were truth. Perhaps war was not the requirement. Dante looked at his hands. Tanned to the colour of old horse hide and greasy. But they knew things, these hands of his. He thought his obstinacy had stood him in good stead. His hard head had brought him to the desert and wisdom seemed to be seeping in. Not just sand.

The pilots were the elite and among the soldiers in North Africa, the Stuka pilots carried themselves tallest and with most ease. They wanted Dante to work on their planes and argued with one another about whose gauges took priority on Dante's schedule.

They brought him small gifts, wooing him, hailing him, making friends with him. They brought him clean socks or a bit of wine or some honey. When they found out that he was confounded and compelled by curious sounds that the engines might make, he suspected that the pilots might have begun to embroider their stories to capture his attention and perhaps skip the queue.

"Dante, I was just going into the dive, the British supply line spread out below me lazing about, when suddenly the tach started to twitch and ting. I had to pull up. Not a single kill this trip. You've got to look at it, man. I've not heard anything like it before."

"Dante, I was flying low over the desert when the horizon started to spin like it had drunk too much grappa. What do you think can be the cause of such strange behaviour?"

The German pilots learned some Italian, and spoke it to comical effect. Dante's German was serviceable, but he let them blunder through sentences composed of German verbs and Italian nouns.

It was young Marseille who kept him the busiest. He had arrived from Yugoslavia in April and caused nothing but trouble for Dante and the mechanics since he got there. He could not keep himself from diving nose-first into enemy formations. If he did not crash the plane he was flying, then he returned it so that the sun shone through a spangled array of bullet holes. His *Geschwaderkommodore* was furious and Dante knew that his pilot friend was in danger of finding himself grounded.

Most recently, Marseille had coaxed Dante into fueling up the Macchi 202.

"Come on, Dante. You are always bragging about these Italian planes of yours. How will I know if the boast isn't an empty one unless I can fly the thing? It doesn't look like much."

That was challenge enough for Dante.

"The Regia Aeronautica is at your service, sir."

He and Sabino fuelled the plane and watched as Marseille taxied down the airstrip.

"Will he crash this one?"

"I don't know. He is used to crashing German planes. You've seen him. He takes ridiculous chances. He dives straight into the line of fire and looping around, cutting the turn too close. It is amazing that the boy is still alive."

"The boy?" Sabino asked. "You are not much older than this boy."

"Maybe not in years, but, well, look at him."

In the sky above them, Marseille was taking the Macchi into a dive, a hard right bank and then looping back up. They watched him, the sun behind the plane causing their eyes to water.

Sabino looked at Dante. "Does he know about the landing gear?"

"*Dio mio*! I forgot to tell him."

They watched as Marseille, finished playing in the sky, turned to approach the runway. There was no time to get to a radio. Dante watched the perfect undercarriage of the Macchi strike the packed surface of desert that they called an airstrip. They had forgotten to warn Marseille that, unlike the Stukas, the Italian Macchi had retractable landing gear. Marseille did not deploy the landing gear. The plane skidded along the ground and crashed into a storage tent. Its nose mashed in and smoking. The men ran over and pulled the unconscious pilot free of the wreckage. Four of them carried him to the infirmary.

It wasn't long before he came back to consciousness. A concussion, not too severe and some abrasions.

"You must have a clover in your ass." Dante stood by Marseille's cot waiting for him to open his eyes. "Come on, fellow. You'll have a headache, but you are remarkably well preserved for a fallen angel."

Marseille groaned. He pushed himself onto his feet to stand, but fell back on the bed. He would have fallen right off, but Dante caught and held him.

"Perhaps you need a few moments."

"What happened?"

"Landing gear."

"What about it?"

"Marseille, listen to me. We Italians, we know aesthetics, aerodynamics. We are not like you Germans who don't mind a few lumps on your machinery. The Macchi is a work of art, on the ground and in the sky. The landing gear, you see, retracts in the air and when you bring the plane to earth, you must engage it again."

"You should have told me."

"You should have known."

Marseille swung a weak fist, but Dante only caught it and patted his hand.

"Come on, now. Let's try again. The nurses require this cot for people with real injuries. *Andiamo, ragazzo*. Let's go, boy."

With Dante's help, Marseille remained on his feet and walked with care out into the sun. Waiting for him were all of the Italian aircrew on the base, cheering and applauding, congratulating Marseille on his first Italian flight.

"Don't mind them," said Dante, smiling broadly.

They whistled him all the way back to his tent where Dante left him and his ego to suffer in the din of Italian superlatives inspired by his brief flight and spectacular arrival.

As a fellow who had himself spent considerable time in the brig, he understood the pilot's impatience with his cautious and sedentary commander's expectations. The young man wanted to fly, really to soar. Shooting down enemy planes, doing it faster and with more precision than anyone else on either side of hostilities would be only part of the thrill for Marseille. If planes were destroyed, what did it matter? That, Marseille believed, was why they were built.

Sabino stopped working one day and cleaned his hands, rubbing the rag over the left and the right and around each finger. Dante watched him as he seemed to collect his thoughts and bide his time before he finally turned to speak.

"Why don't you have a word with Marseilles? He could learn something from you, I think."

Dante stared back. Often, he thought that Sabino's tranquility was the result of a slower wit, a mind operating with less intensity than his own. He was pleasant to work with, easygoing, but Dante always assumed that Sabino lacked the insight necessary to ignite what he believed to be righteous anger. Now Sabino was telling him what to do. Suggesting. Dante swallowed. It was true that Marseille needed some help. He would be punished, grounded, soon if he did not learn something about strategy. After all his knocks and bruises in the academy, Dante had stepped into his uniform with an inspired understanding of the planes, of strategies, and of possibilities. He ought to have been a fighter himself—and would have been if he could have borne the lieutenant for one more day. He knew that Marseille respected him and the work that he was able to do to keep his poor planes in the air. Sabino was right.

Dante risked an approach.

"*Senti*, good fellow. You have got to take measures to avoid so many bullet holes. One of these days, the poor Hurricanes are going to get lucky, miss the plane and hit you instead. Spend some time, figure out where you are in the sky and what are the possibilities for the planes around you and the anti-aircraft guns below. There are elements to keep track of. And, of course, you have to hit the planes that you are shooting at. *Capisci*?"

Marseille brushed off his uniform. He had just returned from another failed sortie and now having been forced to land with another damaged plane, he looked at the dusty man before him.

"*Ja, gut.* What can you tell me?"

"*Penso che*, I think that," Dante hesitated. He had flown planes, but he was no fighter pilot. He looked at the young man before him, probably one to break the hearts of women with those light eyes sparking and the curling mouth. This was no matter for amusement. What had kept Dante alive this long seemed to him to be at least partly his sense of how the wind was blowing, who was sitting on his left and right, what sounds were coming at him and the direction they were coming from. He would have to teach the boy. He looked at Sabino who was smiling.

"I think that you should spend some time on the ground first, listening, looking, noticing everything that you can. Think about where you are and what you know about where you are."

Marseille looked doubtful.

"No, listen. What do you know about where you are right now?"

"I know that you need a bath, my friend."

Behind Marseille, Sabino checked the undercarriage of the plane, to all appearances very amused by what he saw. Or heard.

Dante agreed. "Nothing could be more certain. That is good. Your nose is working. What else?"

Marseille was quite still. He told Dante everything that he knew about the environment.

"I can feel a breeze around my ears. An itch in my armpit. The poor Messerschmitt beside me might not be reparable. I need to change my socks. Over your shoulder, I see a dust cloud gathering far in the distance. It will most likely come to nothing or be driven by the west wind to Tunis. To my left, a few infantrymen are playing cards and smoking cigarettes. There are a few coins on the upturned fuel can. A game of high stakes." He smiled. "I hear footsteps—"

He stopped. These were not just any footsteps. It was a particular step he suddenly knew he could pick out of a crowd of soldiers.

His eyes widened at Dante just before he turned.

He saluted the Kommodore.

"Marseille." Neumann eyed the broken BF 109E beside him. He did not acknowledge the salute. "I see that you have returned to the Luftwaffe another limping aircraft for the magical Dante to fix."

Neumann was in command of the fierce Jagdgeschwader 27, which was claiming air superiority in North Africa, keeping the British hemmed in and scoring kill after kill. They were superb fighters and this headstrong playboy of a pilot before him, an insubordinate man who listened to American jazz music and flirted with any girl, with every girl in a one-hundred-mile radius of the camp, was going to mean the breaking of them. He would not have it.

"You will either organize yourself and your skill to further the purposes of the Afrika Korps or you will be grounded and sent to train pilots who know how to follow orders."

Dante had moved to the other side of the plane. The boy could not follow an order to save his life. He could not stay in formation as a winger. He would break formation to make a kill and thus could not be relied upon. Worse, when he expected to be rewarded for initiative, he was instead publicly and instantly dressed down and passed over for promotion. Dante would see what he could do for him.

"What skills you have are keeping you alive, sir. See if you can't improve upon these to keep the planes alive, too."

Neumann strode on.

Dante walked out from under the cowling.

"The offer still stands, my friend."

"All right, De Angelis. What did you have in mind?"

Dante sat down with the pilot. "There are some exercises to start with, things you can do to improve your awareness of where the plane is in the air. I think we can minimize your response time, make you even more like lightning than you are right now."

Dante looked at Marseille. He was a handsome fellow, a prime example of German good looks.

He said, "Take off your sunglasses. Make your eyes accustomed to the light. And stop drinking. It's milk for you, young fellow."

Together, Marseille and Dante worked out the details of a

training program. Dante drove him around and, having had Sabino place targets here and there, Marseille then mounted the gun and tried to hit targets while bouncing on the hard desert scrabble. There was no question that Marseille's speed and accuracy improved in short order, but the outings were nevertheless curtailed by Neumann after a time. Petrol became too precious to waste.

They switched the training to the more physical aspects of strengthening Marseille, his vision and endurance. Dante told him that in the clear desert air, one's ability to spot enemy fighters is greatly enhanced and that this cuts both ways.

"You can see them, but they can see you, too. There are not so many places to hide as are provided by the clouds and fog of Europe."

Dante built up Marseille's strength to handle the g-force of the Stuka's deep dive. He rigged a wood and leather mechanism that would enable Marseille to hang upside down and lift himself from the waist. He timed the laps that Marseille began to run in order to strengthen his legs. When he could get up into the sky, Marseille practised his assault. In the air, he twisted tight S turns, spirals, shooting from high angles and short range.

Dante offered him some strategy. "When you come at the Hurricanes, come at them from high above instead of trailing behind trying to catch them. Come at them above and along their flanks, shooting down at an angle. You will see. It will work beautifully for you and they will not be expecting it."

Marseille had been training with Dante and had not had a kill for four months. Dante waved to him as his plane lifted into the sky. He and Sabino played cards, waiting for Marseille to return. As the time passed, Dante's neck began to ache with the strain of looking east to see the boy's colours returning. When the familiar firing of the engine, smooth and fierce, came at him over the desert, he dropped his cards and hurried to the landing strip. He watched with his palm to his brow as Marseille taxied the plane to a halt. The aircraft was in perfect condition and Dante wondered at first if the pilot had encountered any enemy planes in the air.

Marseille was grinning as he jumped out of the cockpit. He held up his gloved hand, four fingers in the air.

Dante clapped him on the shoulder.

"Congratulations, Marseille, and well done!"

"Four of them, Dante! Four in one sortie. And look at the plane. The Kommodore will be so pleased!"

Dante maintained Marseille's plane as his first priority. By Christmas, the young German pilot marked his thirty-fifth kill. Neumann was pleased to bring him news that he was being awarded the German Cross. He brought Dante a bottle of *grappa*. The men sat down, Dante, Sabino, and Marseille, to listen to the pilot talk about his victory.

"It was the most thrilling thing. I tell you, Dante, it is as though I see everything. The enemy planes below in the distance, sixteen of them, man. I dive, I just dive in to the middle of them. I turn, oh so tightly, so beautifully, and fire, I keep firing. Ten, twenty, sometimes sixty rounds, but the plane goes down. I turn and fire, I climb and fire, I dive and roll and fire and, never, never the same way twice. I blow them up from the inside. Dante, the planes go down! It is beautiful."

Dante poured him another shot. To hear the boy speak, one would think he was playing a game after which the players, gentlemen all, would shake hands and go home to martinis instead of burning up in the sky or being blown to fragments on the earth. He poured shots for Sabino and himself. When the Kommandant went by, he called him over. Neumann unbent sufficiently to pick up a drink and salute the Star of Africa, as Marseille was now being called. It seemed a fine moment.

Marseille continued. "I got myself into a spot. Two Hurricanes came at me. I do not know how they caught me on my own like that—"

Dante winked at Sabino.

"—but there I was, and here they were coming at me and firing. No way out, I tell you. Two of the Regia pilots, fantastic, the Italians, don't you think? Came out of nowhere and took on the Hurricanes for me. I would not have survived without your fighters. I have sent them some champagne and now I lift my glass to you, Dante, and to your fierce fighter pilots. Show them a fight and they do not back down even one inch."

The men drank to this, warmed inside and smiling. Dante stretched his legs out, unnaturally relaxed in front of the Kommandant who seemed himself to be rather at ease.

"Tell me, what is it like up there? How do things look?" he asked Marseille.

Marseille paused, circling the alcohol around the edges of the glass. "You would be surprised. You can see the Mediterranean. You can see its waters cresting the shores of three continents. It is amazing to behold. But in Africa here, the battlefield is small, only about ten miles between us and the British forward defences. They are huddled back as far as the sea. From the sea there are the limestone cliffs, the *djebels*. They crumble underneath tanks and so you cannot navigate across them. There is the desert, gritty with shale or dusty with sand or both. There is the limestone plateau where most of the ground fights seem to occur. And there are *wadis* and hills, the Tel el Eisa and the Tel el Makhkhad. The British hold El Alamein and the hills around it. We've got the Ruweisat Ridge in the west."

"What is at El Alamein?"

"Nothing. It is a corrugated metal sign propped up in two barrels and held on two-by-fours. On quiet days, you see the Bedouin with their sheep and camels grazing as best they can."

"I have heard that the fight will be there."

"It is the narrowest point of the front. To the north is the sea, to the south is the giant Qattara depression. Below that are the great rolling dunes across which no land vehicle can travel. The only road is the Via Balbia, the east-west route from Tripoli to Sollum. Otherwise, there are caravan routes and native tracks. Not much to navigate by. And El Alamein is at the bottleneck. Take it and you have taken the whole of North Africa."

Dante listened carefully, mapping the geography in his mind. He felt fortunate to hear from the mouth of the bird what the eye of the bird had seen. Marseille's excitement was clear and magnetic, and Dante for the first time shared it. He wondered at himself. He had learned to obey orders and now, in the middle of the desert, he was eager to be only exactly where he was, to be finally in himself bringing all that he had to bear upon the enemy. The dry air seemed sweet. The grappa was delicious. The potent liquor loosened the knot in his shoulders. The blood flowed warm and slow through his veins as he sat face to the sky, thinking about home. Home at its best. And the past mixed with the pleasant present. He sat happily in the presence of brave, even stalwart men whose company was now so valuable to him. He looked at the faces. Neumann, Sabino, and Marseille, a good boy. He was a marvellous fellow to soldier with, it was too bad he was a German, though the good will augmented by thick wine made Dante forgive him for that.

"Now, listen, Marseille, and I will tell you about the Spitfires. I saw one in Yugoslavia."

"They do not use them too much, those British, over here."

"You will see them sometimes and you had better be ready."

"They cannot outrun my beautiful Messerschmitt."

"Not in speed. They will beat you at distance and they will manoeuvre all around you. If you see one, you have got to be fast."

"I am fast!"

"Yes, I know, but your armour is not as good. You have that great 20 mm cannon, but if the Spitfire gets to you first, your armour will not hold as long as his. Those Hurricanes will seem like average beasts, disappointing foes, once you have engaged the Spitfire. But I will tell you a secret."

Marseille leaned forward, as though hearing a ghost story.

"They are not fuel-injected. They cannot loop upside down. If they try, they stall."

"You know this?"

"I took apart the engine myself."

"So I get in, flip over, dive through and fire with the big cannon."

"That will finish the game."

Dante felt the pride of an elder brother as Marseille went on from strength to strength. He admired Marseille's account of his meeting with Hitler in Germany that June after he marked one hundred kills. He had received the highest honours, both the Swords to the Knight's Cross with Oak Leaves from the Führer and, in August, from Reichsmarschall Göring, the Golden Pilot's Cross with Diamonds.

Marseille was most pleased to show Dante the Medaglia d'Oro. He had gone to Rome to receive it from Mussolini himself.

"Look, you. It is your country's highest decoration for bravery."

"*Si.*"

"And I have got it. It is a beauty, isn't it?"

"Is it your favourite?"

With a thick German accent, Marseille pronounced, "*Certamente!*"

Angelina

Angelina walked to the garden with Questo weaving back and forth across the path behind her, his nose to the ground here, leg lifted there, a zealous sentry for whom the slightest beetle movement presented a threat to the human he adored. There was a tidy shed on the garden's edge for the few tools Angelina required. There were old, broken rabbit hutches waiting for repair and there were watering cans to be filled at the cistern. Questo inspected everything. Everything Angelina touched or lifted. He circumnavigated the structure, snapped at a mouse and sat, finally, tongue draped with some elegance at the side of his mouth, satisfied.

This dog, she thought, is enough to make the angels laugh.

Angelina turned the dirt between and around the rising tomato plants. She plucked out the snails and crushed them under her father's old boots. She watered. She went back and forth to the spigot with the pails. Questo lay down, watching. The earth, so thirsty on top of the mountain. Angelina bent and poured and watched the leaves grow plump before her eyes, verdant and stretching. Always more sun and more water, by the grace of God. A good garden this year. She looked up. And a good dog to watch over it. She took the biscotto from her pocket and tossed it to the drowsy dog whose jaws snapped open and shut on the treat he seemed to know would come his way.

He watched as Angelina put the pail and hoe away and was on his feet at the entrance to the garden waiting for her. He dodged back to the shade and then back out to the entrance, around Angelina's legs, running larger circles around her and kicking up dirt and grass as he went.

"Your fun ends here, dog, if you break one of my tomatoes."

The dog stopped short, crouched low with his hind parts up in the air. He looked at her, brown eyes sombre. He looked up from the ground where he had planted his face between outstretched front paws, abasing himself, acknowledging shortcomings and foolishness. Angelina frowned at the dog, finger raised.

But the dog's backside was pointed to the setting sun and his eyes looked very worried. She smiled suddenly and the dog's nails dug in as he dodged off again, tore around her, and trotted down the path, ears up, tail up, as though he had successfully pointed something out to Angelina that she had not known to be true.

When she entered the low door into the kitchen, Angelina did not at first see her small mother at the table. She was standing up, bent over and rolling out what looked like pastry and Angelina started at the sight of her.

Angelina's house was the third to last at the top of the narrow street. There was no place for a car, an unthinkable luxury in any case. The steps first went down to the door and directly into the kitchen. Two shelves and an ancient credenza for the dishes and the linens, the stove and the pantry and in the middle, her mother, out of bed and preparing food.

"*Que fai*, Mamma?"

"*Faccio queste pannettone per Nico.*"

Why would her mother be out of her bed to make pannettone for Angelina's brother? It would cost them precious sugar and eggs. It was neither Easter nor Christmas, and, as far as Angelina knew, everyone in the village was still alive today. Outside the door, Questo licked his lips. Angelina turned to the sink. If her mother chose to so exert herself this day, perhaps a good thing was happening. She did not tremble as she drew water from the tap. Perhaps it was a good thing. For a cake to be made in the middle of the day in the middle of the week, there must be some cause for celebration about which Angelina knew nothing. Her mother, breathing, table rocking on the stone floor under the force of a rolling pin wielded by an invalid who had found new strength. Angelina would not ask why.

Finally, her mother said, "Nico is going to Roma."

Going to Rome. And not for a holiday.

Angelina sat down and watched her mother's back. She had not listened when the honourable members of the Fascist Party, young men so funny and smiling, had come to her district school to talk to the children about the love that Il Duce had for them and to tell them what the only sensible response could be. Angelina was almost finished with school when they came and she had looked out the window and watched branches bend in the spring breeze. Nico and Berto sat behind her, as far to the back as the teacher would permit. They must have been listening. Italy and empire first, family second, self last. She knew the boys would eat as many cookies as the Fascists could give. They would nod and chew while they were asked what they could do to further the empire.

Nico was the oldest boy in the school. After Dante came to San Placido, Nico had missed weeks of lessons to follow his father behind the plough. When their house burned down, it had been Nico's job to go through the still warm ashes and pick out the nails, nails that his father had fabricated himself, for re-use on some future project. Nico was well behind children younger than he and the only student to squeeze daily his young man's body into a desk made for a *piccolo ragazzo*.

Nico always had a sweet tooth. He would have eaten up the talk of honour and glory along with the cookies. Of course, he would be the personal enemy of Churchill. Nico had pushed himself out of his chair and stepped forward.

Angelina tried to remember.

Signor Gianelli had said, "You're a big boy for such a small chair. I can see that you are a thinker of big thoughts as well, thoughts too grand for such a small room. You will help your country, your leaders, your family, and yourself. Have another cookie and I will tell you about a future you could not have imagined for yourself."

Nico had listened. Angelina did not think it was just the cookies. She knew that her brother thought he had one too many mothers, that Angelina treated him like a child to be sent on errands and have his face pinched or his hair messed. He was her little brother and she did not think that such gestures would compel him to go to battle. She sat at the table as her mother made a special treat for Nico. She did not know what would happen, but each day she woke up and made breakfast for her family. She could account for all of them, see them, touch them, speak to them. They were safe. She looked after things, made sure there was enough food for Nico's massive appetite. She teased him or ignored him and now he would leave. His chair would be vacant.

Signor Gianelli had shaken Nico's hand as though Angelina's brother were a grown man. He said that he would escort Nico to his future, that Nico would look back at the small desk and chair behind him and laugh.

"What will happen?" Angelina asked her mother.

"He will go to Rome. They will send him somewhere. My boy." Graziela could not speak further. She left the pannettone to rise and went up to her room.

He signed up. He would go for training and then to one of the fronts. Some theatre of the future.

When Nico came into the house, Angelina stood.

"Nico, *que fai*? What are you doing?"

She knew her voice was thin and hard. It rasped against her throat.

"Are you angry with me? Do you think I can stay in San Placido all my life?"

"Yes. That is a good idea. Stay in San Placido. It's not too late. You know mamma and papa need you here."

"Lina, they have you and Berto. They will be all right. I'm too big for San Placido now. Look at me."

He stood tall and straight, taller finally than his older sister and beaming. She grabbed hold of him quick and hugged him close.

"Now, what are you doing? All this emotion so early in the day. It will be all right, you'll see. The army supplies paper and pencil. I will write to mamma and papa. At least I've been in school long enough to do that! I will go away and help the Duce, I will write some letters, and then I will come home."

Nico turned away.

"Where are you going now?"

"Where all soldiers go. I'm going to Visso to see if there are any girls in the piazza!"

"Don't be late for supper. Mamma is making you a treat, you spoiled boy."

Angelina watched him wave and run full out down the path to Visso.

Angelina's mother washed her face and came down the narrow stairs to make the pasta that no one, not even Angelina who had watched for years, could replicate for its lightness and flavour. Nico would be fed properly before leaving at dawn. His mother would see to that.

Angelina's father said nothing at supper. He gave Nico his watch.

"It's a few minutes slow."

"*Grazie*, Papa. I will take good care of it."

Berto wanted to go, too. "I'll be happy to leave school and even San Placido for the good of the empire."

"We all have to make sacrifices."

"You have to stay here to help Mamma and Papa."

"They have Lina. They're fine."

Angelina did not like that abbreviation of her name. She thought she probably could do the work of both of them put together, as well as her own, as well as the cooking. She was almost as tall as Nico, taller than Berto and likely as strong, but as she had not their capacity for distraction, she believed things would run more smoothly if they both left. Though she did not want them to go to the war.

In any case, she had no say in the decision.

They ate their soup in silence.

Nico said, "You can't expect Angelina to do everything while we're off having fun."

"Think how easy it will be here if I join the army, too. There will be fewer people in the house, less work to feed them, less cost to feed them, more space, more rest for mamma. And papa, you would be happier, too. If I were in the military, I wouldn't be here to keep on wrecking your tools. You know how careless I am."

"Yes," Nico said. "It would probably be better for the Italian army if you joined the British forces. You could be our secret weapon. The one who sneaks in and destroys all of the British efforts, all of their tanks and planes and guns. That is an inspired idea. You could be a force of ruin and destruction and Mussolini himself would give you a kiss on both cheeks to thank you. Berto, I'm afraid it's the RAF for you."

Berto leaned across the table and punched Nico's arm as hard as he could. No one scolded him, not even Nico. Angelina passed him the beans and he piled them high on his plate, asked for the sauce and more bread and pasta and the last piece of chicken—the neck—and ate it all as quickly as he could, sucking the marrow between his front teeth.

"If you are going to keep me at home and in school and working the land, you will just see how much I can eat."

The next morning, Angelina's mother woke up paralyzed by the pain. Her stomach was hard and hot to the touch. She could not get out of her bed. Angelina sat with Graziela while Nico came to her in the breaking dawn. She brought hot towels and heated rocks and pressed these against the sheet where the pain was worst. Sometimes the heat worked to ease the attack. Angelina helped her to sit up so that she could embrace her son. Angelina pulled her shawl around her shoulders and tidied her hair. Nico knelt at the bed and leaned over his mother, kissed her cheeks.

Angelina heard him whisper, "*Ciao*, Mamma. Don't cry. I will come back to you and give you all my medals in a necklace. You'll be feeling better then. Don't cry. I won't be gone long."

He had to duck his head under the doorpost. His boots were heavy on the stairs, and slow. A slow drum of descent that Angelina could hear in her ears for a long time afterward, almost as though she could hear his footsteps all the way to Rome. For the next few weeks, she rose earlier than usual. She cooked the breakfast and left early. She took the bedding to the cistern before the other women arrived and forced her, out of politeness, to answer their questions. They were good to her, these neighbours, and went a little later, it seemed, to the well.

Eventually, Angelina spoke to them, giving information they most likely already had.

"My brother is gone to the war where he imagines something good will happen."

"My mother is not well and will wait here in bed for a necklace. My father collects iron scraps today to melt down and make parts to repair the gates of the wealthy in Visso."

"I have not heard from Dante in quite some time."

"Yes, the mail is slow."

"I do not know where he is stationed. He may not say."

"I am sure he will write when he can."

"Yes. I am sure that he is well."

Down the narrow street the boy, Carlo, was already outside throwing a stick up into the sun, high as he could, watching it revolve in the morning air. He flung it above his head, and caught it behind his back. Angelina was watching the boy. He would toss the stick and do a cartwheel in the dust or a back flip while the stick turned in the sky. He would land on his feet or on one knee, extend his hand and the stick, as though tied to a string, would smack back into his palm. He tossed it higher and higher, all his body upthrust and no one to witness but Angelina on her knees at the cistern letting the sheets float and furl in the cold water while she watched the little trickster.

She thought she should warn him. He was a boy of perhaps seven or eight years old, that Carlo Montefiore, the only son of the new people whose family only came to San Placido a hundred years ago or so. She thought she should warn him to be careful, not to risk an eye or a limb with such foolishness, but she was enjoying the show. Questo sat tense and still beside her, his front paws dug into the ground, his head jerking up to follow the spiral of the stick with his tongue out and his eyes jumping. The two, girl and dog, held themselves still, waiting for Carlo to drop his baton.

He turned at last in their direction, stick in hand, and took a bow. He waved to Angelina and took a step toward her before his mother called him in. He did a final cartwheel in which his shoes came off and landed courteously at the front door of his house while he went inside for breakfast.

Angelina twisted the water out of the bedding. Questo looked first at the space where the boy had been performing and then back at Angelina.

"You want me to throw sticks?"

Questo licked his muzzle.

"I do not throw sticks for lazy dogs. You need not make your eyes so big. And keep that tongue inside your mouth for once."

Questo swept his tongue along the finger pointed at him and trotted away toward Carlo's house.

Dante

That September of 1942, Dante kept Marseille in good form while he lifted off into the record books, with as many as seventeen enemy aircraft shot down in one day, eight of them within ten minutes of the attack. Marseille was promoted to Hauptmann, the youngest captain in the Luftwaffe. He brought his medals back and he and Dante toasted each one. Sabino put the blocks under the wheels and sat down on the ground beside Dante. With enough *grappa*, even the flies crawling around their nose and eyes were bearable.

Sabino wiped his eyes. "At least they're flies and not maggots."

"Maggots would be a definite sign that something was amiss."

"Maggots, my friends, wait for us all." Marseille raised his drink to them both and tossed it back.

"*Si, capitano. Ma, spero che non questo giorno.*"

"Not today. Maybe tomorrow."

Dante wished the young man would not speak so. Marseille's fair skin was pink with sun and liquor and brilliant success. He knew Marseille was not reckless, not careless with his life, only certain that he could twist and turn the plane at will and that it would respond finely and flawlessly. That he could point the guns and shoot and hit, get in and get out. Of his skill, he was certain. Not reckless with the plane, then, but rash with words. Perhaps it was the *grappa*. All this talk of today and tomorrow and maggots. Dante would warn him away from such thoughtless talk at the front, in battle and in the presence of men who knew the awesome truth of it. But it was not his place. He wished the young man a pleasant evening and went to sleep.

Days afterward, Marseille came by to check on his old plane. The Messerschmitt had been through some terrific dogfights, but was still air worthy. Dante was working on the gauges, Sabino on the carburetor.

"How does she look?"

Dante pointed to the fuselage. "These few bullet holes we call beauty marks. Nothing to worry about. But it must have been noisy in there."

"I cannot hear a thing."

"*Veramente?*"

"I see the throttle, the gauges, I see what's on my wing, and what's ahead. I do not hear anything. Though I suppose if something went wrong with the engine, I would hear it soon enough."

"That is a comfort, my friend."

"De Angelis, have you had a chance to look at the new fighters?"

"Ah, *si*, the 109Gs. The Gustavs. I have seen them, but I have not yet worked on one. Are you going to take one up and wreck it for me?"

"I think they are ugly. I do not like the look of them."

"The cowling is different." Dante pointed across the encampment. "See, they had to accommodate the new cooling. The guns are bigger. It's altogether an unpleasant-looking machine."

"Die Beule."

"*Si*. The Bulge. It might be faster."

"Hard to manoeuvre."

"Possibly."

"What about the engine?"

"They are having some difficulty with it."

"I will have a look at it."

Marseille took a few steps away, turned, and walked back. Hand on the wing, he spoke softly.

"You know, Dante. I love flying this plane."

"I know it."

"It is like art, I think. I am high, high in the air. I fly with the bombers. They drop their bombs. I shoot at hard targets to keep them away from the bombers. There are explosions, fires, there is noise and smoke and the sounds of engine parts grinding or exploding. It is really spectacular."

Dante waited.

"I kill the planes, you see? They bleed oil and grease and fuel. Sometimes the plane, smoking and in pieces spirals down to hit the ground in flames. Sometimes an enemy pilot pops the canopy and out he comes. His parachute blossoms like a lily of the air and then he turns and twists his gentle way to the earth. I do not shoot at him. I take off from friendly territory and then I come back to it."

"Yes."

"In what I do, there is no blood. No sons of mothers, no husbands, fathers."

Dante could think of no reply. In what he did, there was no blood either, and yet he knew that gallons of it, rivers of it, soaked the black earth on every day of battle.

"Do you know what we say about the Italians?"

Dante braced himself. He had heard it all. No stomach for fighting, only for pasta. And worse.

"We say, do you know the reason why we think they are such brave soldiers?"

Dante waited.

"Because they are willing to go to war with the equipment they have. Those tanks you drive, they are like moving coffins."

Dante knew.

"And the planes. Have you seen the Banana?"

"*Si.* At least it is not in the air any more."

"That is a good decision. But you are still flying the Fiats, the CR 42s. Biplanes against Hurricanes. Underpowered, underarmoured, and under-armed."

"I know."

"Poor Regia."

Marseille walked on and Dante turned back to his work. The boy meant well, he thought. No matter. Dante focused on the task at hand. He knew the engine was failing on the 109Gs and that they were having trouble pinpointing the problem. There was difficulty with the engine running at maximum power. The only thing to do was to scale back the assault speed, a deadly option for a fighter pilot, especially one like Marseille.

Sabino came from under the propeller.

"Is Marseille all right?"

Dante wiped his hands on the rag in his pouch. That was a good question. The pilot had been wreathed and celebrated by the whole camp. The star of the nations, he was. Even his enemies respected and envied him. He had so many laurels laid upon him, it was a wonder he could still see.

"Well?"

"I do not know, Sabin. I think they are going to make him fly the Gustav."

Sabino looked across at the half dozen new planes that Kesselring had brought in for the Afrika Korps. So far, Marseille had avoided them. They stared back.

"I knew a German named Gustav once," Sabino said.

"Good fellow?"

"He had a broken nose."

"How did he come by that?"

"He met my fist head on."

"Terrible mistake." Dante regarded the hands of his friend, clasping the wrench.

"Could have been worse."

"*Si. Sicuro.*"

He wrote to Angelina on brittle, thin paper, letters aligned on the vertical, standing at attention as he put his thoughts on paper and sent them into the ether, hoping they would arrive at the doorstep of a woman who might read them or who might use them to soak up the oil away from battered and fried zucchini flowers. He had sat with her in the very place those flowers bloomed and when he was with her, he had tried not to stare at her ankle. He had sat, confused. Rows of vegetables, orderly, green and swaying, verdant in the afternoon sun. The birds slept. Even the bees moved slowly, drunk with pollen. Dante had watched the idle ground.

Finally, he had spoken to her.

"*Signorina, grazie per questo tempo con voi.*" He held out his hand, but she stood without taking it.

"*Niente, signor,*" it was nothing.

Indeed.

As they walked back down the path from the garden, he held the stillness in him. He felt rested. They stopped at the well for a drink of the cold water.

"*Guarda,*" she said. "Watch out. The water is spilling down the front of your shirt!"

And he had laughed and agreed. There was her voice, finally. Watching out for him. For his shirt. Her voice speaking to him. He would have jumped into the cistern for the joy of hearing it again.

"Ah well, it will dry quickly in the sun."

He had moved his hand around in the water.

"How long have you had the water here?"

"My uncle tapped the well water more than twenty years ago. The town collected money for the spigot, this head of a lion, and it pours water into the cistern. Then this water, running over, flows down the mountain to Visso."

Dante had wished to jump in. He had to keep himself inside his skin with this woman beside him. He could not look at her. He would have to leave. He had seen women before. Lots of them. All so jolly with the soldiers, especially with the airmen, big-eyed and tender and turning toward him with their arms open and ready to dance.

Why should he be compelled to look at Angelina as though his eyes were composed of iron bearings and she were true north? Because of her nice legs? He had to leave before he fell to the ground, prostrate and absurd, declaring eternal love to a woman whose life was hobbled to the garden and the kitchen. Was there courage in such a life?

He had hopes. He hoped to live. To go back to Italy, to Angelina. To find her heart soft toward him. To see her walk to him and speak to him. Such a vision would make the blood pound in his head. The sand adhered to the ink before it dried on the page. In order to give the censors little to delay his letters, he refrained from writing about where he was, thus the letters were very difficult to write. Where he was, was everything. The vicious sun and creeping unjust cold of the night. The supply lines were these days frequently interrupted or non-existent. The war in the desert was becoming not just a war against the British, but also, a war against the elements. Dante and the men suffered a ravaging lack of food and water. Rations were limited to half a cup of water a day. Drops, mere drops. He barely pissed. He could not tell her that. Even the stream of gifts from Marseille and the Stuka pilots was drying up. They, too, began to steward their limited fuel for essential engagements. They were otherwise grounded and sat under the shadow of the wings playing at cards or dice or, like Dante, writing letters.

He told Angelina about conversations he imagined having with her about her garden. Was it growing well? No, of course not. The harvest had passed and the garden was finished for this year. Now, in October it would be still and luminous on the western slope of the mountain, sunset red radiant against the harvested earth.

"Sabino makes us laugh," he wrote. "This is not easy, what he does, or maybe it is. I have never tried. He can turn his helmet upside down and balance with his hands on the tipping edges. He can lift his thick legs into the air. He turns them this way and that, as though he is dancing on the sky and we toss him a few cigarettes. Even the sergeant stops to look. He does not smile, though, or toss even a stub of a smoke. It is amazing what can keep us entertained here."

He wrote to her about the tasks of the day. Stand to, breakfast, clean up, digging out, digging in. The tools of his trade. He did not talk about the planes or the particular difficulties of keeping them ready to go, keeping the instruments and gear free from the worst incursions of the sand. And everything in the desert wants your blood, he could have written. The scorpions, the flies, the enemies, and even the tools that cut and scraped his skin so that he sprinkled the pale sand with red.

He had to stroke out the word "sand." Instead he wrote "environment" and hoped she knew the word. He did not tell her about the constant maintenance of the thing they called the latrine, which was really just a modified trench at the edge of which they squatted gingerly and with a fierce eye on the horizon. Haunches aching, heart pounding, the soldiers followed the string at night from their post to edge of the latrine in order to find their way back in the dark.

She would not know about these indignities and he would never talk about them. He would not write about the *sergente* who made them stand in the sun when the *tenente* was otherwise occupied. He would call them out to raise the flag or clean the big guns. He would take pleasure in their aching shins and dizzy heads and talk and berate them until one or the other of Dante's friends collapsed in the high afternoon. They got him back, though. One night they re-tied the latrine string. Instead of leading the sergeant and his loose bowels to the edge of the latrine, the string took him through it. They could hear his curses across the encampment. The lieutenant must have had some sense of what was going on. He neither investigated nor punished the likely perpetrators and the sergeant was persuaded to better behaviour.

Instead, Dante wrote letters to amuse and engage Angelina. To woo her. To win her to the notion that he was a good man, worthy, one in whom she could place her hard trust. He wrote with her picture, a rare photograph and hard-won, in front of him. When he was with her in San Placido, he had asked her for a picture.

"Angelina, honour me with a photograph to take with me to battle."

"*Perche?*" Why?

"To keep before me. To think about you, to give me hope that I will come back to see you, just as you are, unchanged."

He dared not say lovely. She would have laughed at him

"I do not change."

She did not request a photograph of him.

"Would you like this picture of me to keep?" He offered her a posed picture of himself, taken by a Roman photographer, backlit and serious and uniformed, a photograph Dante himself had arranged and paid for with the intent of leaving his image with Angelina.

In the garden, they were secluded by the bending branches of the almond tree. He would leave. First for Pantelleria, then for the Balkans, and finally to the North African front. He might not come back. Italian boys were dying by the hundreds every day. He might not come back. Did she not wish to have a photograph of him in order to remember him?

"*Se li ricorderò.*" I will remember you.

He slipped the photo back into his breast pocket.

I will remember you.

"Still. I would like your photograph. I would like to keep it with me. I will write to you and I will look at your face and wonder how you are and whether you are thinking of me. Will you write to me?" he had asked her.

Dante waited while Angelina considered his request. Every house had a pen and some paper. San Placido was civilized, after all. The walk to Visso to mail a letter, to receive a letter. The walk back up the mountain. The time and effort it would take from the chores that formed her daily life. She considered all this and looked at Dante.

"I will write to you."

"You will?"

"*Gli ho detto.*" I told you.

"*Grazie*, Angelina. You give a man hope. Now, if I had a photograph as well, I could leave a happy man."

He looked at the picture. Shadow and line. Her hair prim and contained. She looked askance at the lens, its imposition. As though such a machine could hold her.

She told him, "This photograph was taken in Rome. My uncle had a customer with a camera who made a bit of money taking pictures. Stefania made me sit, sit still, turn my knees one way and my head another. It seems to me that Romans have very little sense. So, I have the photograph now. But why do you need it? Either you can remember a person or you can not."

"*Signorina*, think of me at war, at some remote front with only ugliness before me, and have a little mercy."

He was joking with her a little. Teasing her, and she smiled at him. But now, it seemed to him that his words had been prophetic. Now he could take out Angelina's picture and be reminded that she was beautiful. That the image of her face was worth guarding. He had pleaded with her lightly. Perhaps she wondered about his mental stability, but she handed over the picture.

Dante hunkered down in his trench. He wrote to her.

"I imagine you in your day, in the kitchen, in the garden, safe and warm. I miss you, Angelina, and thoughts of sitting with you on the bench at the top of the garden keep me company in the night. Bless you. *Con tanto affetto*."

Dante could not prevent himself from explaining things to someone and Sabino was most often on hand.

"The Stukas," he said, "come in formation. All moving parts, engine, throttles, propeller, everything coated with thick grease to keep the miserable sand at bay."

"I know this, Dante."

"Listen, the Stukas come in formation. The pilots are gathering wind, checking gauges, altimeter, pressure, coordinates, and they are gathering courage for the sudden descent, the commitment to the dive. The Stukas come on slow and steady. They are classic, precision bombers that absolutely require the company of the faster, versatile fighters to keep them safe. They drop bombs on roads, bridges, supply convoys, ground forces, tanks, and ships. The blitzkrieg, the lightning, they bring the storm screaming into dead silence."

"They are dreadful," Sabino agreed.

"Listen, the hearts of those English sink and grow cold as they wait to see how close they are standing to Stuka target."

Sabino wanted to know what Dante was doing.

"There was a short in the connection to the autopilot."

"Autopilot? Are these planes so smart that they do not need people?"

"They need the pilot, *si*. He has to decide when to activate this. The Askania autopilot, here." Dante jumped down from the bomb pay and pointed out release gear, the elevator controls, and the dive brakes.

"It brings up these flaps and the autopilot sends the plane right away into the dive. Everything is connected." He interlaced his fingers. Though he was a good Italian and had trained on the Savoia Marchettis, the beauty of the German foresight and precision delighted him. This was a machine with a single goal, the pilot barely necessary.

Dante's hands roamed over the plane, the controls, the moving parts. Exquisite. He sounded the klaxon on the undercarriage, which started up its harsh scream.

"That was Signor Hitler's idea. As if the thing, swooping like an eagle was not terrifying enough. Now the siren, the Jericho trumpet, sounds a scream descending upon the poor British who shit in their proper trousers.

"Once he sets the bomb release height, all he has to do is push this button. See? On the control column, here. The autopilot takes over. The elevator trim tab is adjusted, the plane's tail is as heavy as your aunt Sofia and the nose comes back up. Just as well. When he is diving, the pilot can hardly control anything. Sometimes he passes out and this sweet plane, of which everyone is so frightened, pulls itself out of the dive at just about four hundred metres from the earth and everybody goes home happy."

"Except Signor Churchill."

"*Si. Poverino* Churchill is not happy."

Dante pointed out the bombs secured under the planes' wings with faces of Churchill painted on them.

"So, we will win the war quickly with this one and we will go home."

"Ah, Sabin. If we can keep the fighter planes away from the greenhouse canopy, keep the pilots alive and the fuel running, we will go home soon."

Behind them, the armourers were pushing the cart. There were four men, two to pull and two to push and steady the bombs before loading them onto the swing rack.

"Look, Sabin, even the bombs themselves have whistles."

The bomb fins were fixed with whistles so that not only the aircraft, but also the agents of destruction themselves would fall screeching to the earth.

"And the *inglese* don't have this?"

"They do not."

"But we do."

"*Si.*"

"Do we have enough?"

Dante jumped off the strut and landed on the ground.

"Only God knows that."

"Do you think they will send us to Russia?"

Both men had read the pamphlets that the Allied bombers had dropped, inviting them to surrender.

> *Tomorrow your men may be invited to die in Russia. Act before it is too late. In the icy and bloody battlefields of Russia they are finding dead young people from Italy. Some weeks ago, as you know, Mussolini made a visit to Hitler in Russia, and promised to send other young Italian militia to die in Russia this winter.*
>
> *Why must these Italians suffer this agony and die like this? Is this what will happen to your husband, son or loved one on blood-filled snowy steppes where wolves roam looking for meat? Or if he is made a prisoner, the Russians will send him to Siberia, where it is all ice and desolation for five months of the year.*
>
> *Do not allow this to be how your men will die! Mussolini has never told you how many Italians will die in Russia this winter. But one of your dear ones could be among them. What significance is it if Hitler boasts of victories in Russia if your son is in the one killed by a Russian tank?*

The pamphlet invited them to surrender. To tell their commanding officers that they wanted the war to end. They wanted peace. It told them, "*Agito subito.*" Act quickly.

They knew the pamphlet was meant to inspire fear. They had read it carefully. Dante had folded one into his pocket for a souvenir.

He did not think he would be sent to Russia. The Italian planes there were open-canopy and the pilots were freezing to death. He stroked the wing of the Stuka.

Toward the end of September, Marseille found his way back to Dante's station. Dante was wrapped in his greatcoat, which was belted tight over his coveralls, the fur collar up around his ears. The mornings were colder and he pushed his hands deep inside his pockets. He and Sabino, also thickened with the layers of his jacket and coveralls against the morning chill, had the plane's gauges spread before them on a ground sheet. The wires laid out and ready for testing. There was a short somewhere.

Marseille handed him the tools that he needed.

"Will you know how to put all that back where it goes?"

"Sometimes there are a few extra parts, but no one seems to mind."

"I have to fly the Gustav."

"Have to?"

"Generalfeldmarschall Kesselring has ordered me."

"Kesselring. The smiling one. *Allora.*"

"Dante, you are always saying this. This '*allora.*' It sounds like a woman's name. What does this '*allora*' mean?"

"In this case, my friend, it means you are screwed."

"I am to fly it on the next mission, escorting the Stukas."

"You will be fine." Dante wished to believe this himself.

"I will?"

Marseille seemed to take a little comfort from Dante's assurance. He looked relieved.

Dante warned him. "Just watch the power. Try not to overload the engine. You may not mark as many kills, but you will come home alive."

Sabino said, "Home?"

Dante laughed. "I have been here too long, *mi fratelli.* Go carefully, Marseille. You know the Italian? *Piano, piano.*"

"And so I'll be dodging Hurricanes and thinking about pianos."

"Just go softly."

"*Piano, piano*, eh? I will be dainty as a ballerina in the air. I shall see you in time for lunch."

Marseille tossed off a salute and turned to his mission. Dante stood with Sabino watching as the planes, fighters and Stukas, took off in formation. The agitated sand cast out enormous billowing clouds behind the craft. There could be no take off in secret this morning or any morning.

At lunch, he and Sabino opened the checkerboard and set up a game. The encampment was dead quiet, apart from the droning flies. The Stukas had dropped their bombs and returned, but the fighters did not accompany them. Dante and Sabino watched the planes come in.

Dante moved poorly and in minutes Sabino had been kinged and kinged again. The red and black squares blurred and he blamed the blasted flies. Sabino gathered up the checkers and folded the board.

Where were the fighters?

To fill the time, they decided to wash their uniforms. Dante got the petrol and mixed a bit of it with sand. He took off his trousers, shirt, socks and undershirt and crouched in his underwear, cap and boots to scrub his drab accumulation of wardrobe. On the other side of the can, Sabino did the same. Petrol-cleaned clothes would give them a few hours' relief from the lice at least, if not the flies. They laid the laundry out on the wing of a Stuka and waited.

Dante had gone to the mess hall to occupy himself with what passed for coffee at the front. He was there when the pilots who had flown out with Marseille came back. Everyone on the base made their way to the gathering of men near the officers' tent. Dante stepped among the men, still hoping to greet his friend, though he had not seen Marseille's Gustav come back with the others.

The pilots were talking. The planes had gone out and met with no opposition. They were returning to the base when Marseille's cockpit filled with smoke. Dante hung his head, cursing Kesselring. It was Pottgen and Schlang, Marseille's wingers, who were telling the story. Marseille radioed them to say he was going to have to bail. It was all right, they thought. They had made it back behind German lines and could easily spot the white mosque at Sidi Abd el Rahman. They would be safe, now. The wingers spread out to give Marseille space to jettison.

"We moved out. Marseille turned the plane upside down, as you do, but the plane went into a dive and I do not think Marseille realized it. Maybe the smoke. We don't know. He did not say anything except that it was too much and he had to get out. We think he was caught in the slipstream. The plane was nose down and moving fast. Rainer saw him hit the stabilizer and go limp. When we found him on the ground—"

Here Schlang covered his eyes. "When we found him on the ground, his parachute was not even opened."

The men were silent. Marseille never knew what hit him. Of all the ways to die at war, each man hoped for the one they never saw coming, never knew had arrived. But the waste of it, of Marseille's life, not given in battle, not laid down for the notion of a greater good. Marseille was dead because Kesselring wanted to test the airworthiness of a poorly designed plane when he already had a complement of brilliantly operative fighters.

Marseille was twenty-two. How could anyone expect a boy to know whether his own nose was up or down? Dante cleared his throat. "Where is he?"

"They are cleaning him up and putting him in his dress uniform. I think he is in the sick bay."

"Where is the plane?"

"About seven kilometres south of the white mosque. There is not much left of it."

"I will not need much."

Dante, Sabino, and a few others, including the Kommodore and the wingers drove out to the crash site. There, scattered in a surprisingly narrow pattern, were the remains of Marseille's Messerschmitt. Dante would go over every scrap, every gauge and gear and cog that he could find. Neumann expected him to inform a hastily convened committee of inquiry into the crash. Marseille was a national hero. There would have to be explanations and these had better be thorough.

They would find their way to the desk of Hitler himself.

His back and legs aching in the afternoon heat, Dante bent to the task. The men with him brought to him every component, those that could be identified and those that could not. They pieced together the fragments of the plane that had become a terrible puzzle, the solving of which would grant no one peace, unless peace would be granted to the dead.

"Look, Sabin." Dante held the differential gear, still in one piece, but the ring gear was damaged and covered with oil.

"A leak, then?"

"*Si*. And look here." The spur wheel in his hand, teeth broken.

"There would be sparks."

"Yes."

"And a fire."

"An oil fire. No wonder he had to get out."

"Poor fellow."

Dante was silent. He turned and faced east. It seemed the wind was changing. He blinked to ease the dust out of his eyes.

Marseille's body lay in state in the sick bay. The men of the 27th Jagdgeschwader sat in sorrow while the camp's troops, mechanics, infantrymen, cooks, medics, pilots, drivers, gunners, and officers filed past slowly, paying their respects. The flaps of the tent were closed tight against flies. His wingers had music playing, Marseille's favourite record, the "Rhumba Azul." Dante filed through with the other soldiers, all equal for today in this room. He paused beside the young man's pale face. Marseille's head was bandaged to conceal his crushed skull. Dante placed his hand on Marseille's heart and bowed as though in prayer. There was no blood in evidence and no enemy to blame for this one death. But this was the cold skin of a mother's son. The men waited at a distance. Most of them had seen the boy laughing with Dante, his arms stretched out, reenacting the dogfights he had blazed through with such brilliance. They waited for the mechanic while the pianist's fingers tripped over the piano, the guitar and double bass, echoing, rapid-fire, dipping, rising, perversely joyful.

Dante whispered, "Let the day suffice, *ragazzo*."

He and Sabino filed out and found the last ounces of the last bottle of grappa given to them by Marseille. They sat on low upturned crates outside the back of the mess and drank the thick liquor. Dante lifted his arm to drink, an arm that felt weighted, arthritic, ancient, a hand he could barely lift to his lips, he was so tired. He sat with Sabino and drank without pleasure, hunched over and watching the ground beneath his feet until the alcohol warmed his fingertips. He kept drinking until the skin of his face grew numb.

They escorted Marseille's body to the heroes' cemetery at Derna. Kesselring, Kesselring who ordered the boy to his death, gave the eulogy, after Geschwaderkommodore Neumann, who had been at once so angry with Marseille for the risks he took and so proud of him for his brilliance. Dante had been given leave to attend. Sabino as well, as he had serviced the Hauptman's plane and formed part of his crew.

Once the brass had left the heat of the burial site, once the ceremony was over and the crowd had dissipated for a cool luncheon in Derna, Dante hung back. From the distance, he could see the trucks coming, full of Italian soldiers and engineers. They climbed out of the transports and got to work. Over the course of two days, they built for Marseille his own pyramid in the desert. Sabino carved the epitaph in stone. Only one word: Undefeated.

Sabino said, "We are here, Dante. *Noi siamo qui.*"

"*Si. E vero*. It is true."

"*Ma, perche*? Why?"

"You heard the field marshal. 'No other area of the globe is of such strategic importance.'"

"Yes, I heard him."

Dante turned and looked around at the graves. He worked on the planes as he was ordered. He would say that he enjoyed his work. He carried heavy objects and drove trucks to and from the encampments. He rarely fired a gun, or even held one. He placed stones for Marscille, layer by layer, engineering a pyramid that would last for a time, marking the life of only one of them, too young and no more. Sabino worked alongside him in silence. He had not felt so vulnerable before. In the plane over Malta, it had seemed like a game, dodging too close and barely getting away, as though he were a boy throwing stones at a shop window. He had not doubted that he would escape, not really. Now Marseille was gone, so uselessly. Sabino was beside him still. Dante wanted to speak, but he could think of nothing to say. All around them, the sunset desert lit itself up and the absurd roseate light entered his eyes. Sabino standing before him took on a pearl's sheen. The stones themselves glowed in the late afternoon. Dante turned to the edifice they had created in the desert, its declaration of death.

The stones would most probably stand at least as long as Marseille himself had lived. Dante dusted his rough hands and turned away from the marker.

As the days and weeks passed and the hardships in North Africa increased, Dante noticed that a vague unrest was spreading through the Italian cohort. He had heard rumours of military action against families back in Italy whose fathers and sons were at war. The Germans, Italy's allies, were making their presence felt in the cities. While not a fully occupying force, the officers did not hesitate to assist local authorities in the execution of proper authority. The Italian wives were ordered to donate their wedding rings. Reports came in that the soldiers' families, their grandparents and children, were jailed for being out after curfew. The Germans had moved into their hometowns as governors and enforcers. There was no friction in Dante's unit among allies, but the men, hungry and thirsty and tired, began to wonder at the larger purposes driving the eastern push through the desert.

"What do you think, Sabin?" Dante had asked his friend after the slim rations had been distributed in the evening.

"I think that Mussolini has maybe stopped eating *capelli di angeli*. I think he has given up the tresses of the angels to eat sauerkraut and dance the polka."

Dante thought about this. He was so far able to endure the grim repetition of the days. He wrote to Angelina to rest his mind and he thought of her always as safe in the mountains, ensconced with her family in a place unaffected by battle. He wondered how the German allies were treating their Italian friends. Where he sat and worked and lived, the exigencies of the locale demanded camaraderie. But what about the peaceful towns at home? Then he was disturbed by another idea. He wondered if Angelina knew any German soldiers. If they had moved as far north as San Placido and found what Dante most treasured. If she were in danger or if some German was courting her. He could not let his mind run in that direction and took comfort for once from the fact that it was so difficult to make Angelina smile. No stranger would be able to stroll into the village and win her in Dante's absence.

These were the thoughts with which he wrestled in the long nights on watch. He and the men sat in holes dug at intervals in the desert expanse, guarding a front that not one of them could demarcate or present a sound argument for. The sunsets had been extravagant, blazing and glorious. Layers of vermilion, orange, and gold, illuminating, gilding the tanks, planes, guns, and faces of the men lifted toward the eastern front.

Marseille was gone, and with him much of the heart of the Stuka pilots. He had led them, challenged them. He had not cared about the division of Italians and Germans. Pilots and infantrymen. He had spoken to everyone with equal curiosity and his presence seemed to bring good fortune. The other Germans had tried to follow his example. Now that he was dead, and Dante was sure that this must be a coincidence, things seemed to become more difficult. Disagreements broke out, the clash of foreign languages and soldiers lacking good will to make an effort. The hardships of the desert seemed more odious. Morale was low, almost as low as the water ration. It had been a long time since the squadron had taken any ground.

When the sun dropped below the far horizon, the stars appeared, myriad, cold, and beautiful, and adding not one gleam to the utter darkness of the desert. In the vast distance, they seemed to cast shadows that moved back and forth. Eyes straining to determine whether what was before him was a trick of the dimming light or the advance of an enemy as shadowy as the air, Dante listened to the cracking sound of the rocks cooling. It sounded to him like a gun scraping against a stone. Was there an advance? He shifted, jittery and striving for stillness. He turned his compass and took a bearing against the need for the latrine. There was no light by which to orient himself should he need to leave the trench. No one was there. He was safe for the moment. In the deep darkness, Dante sat with Sabino, stretching his mouth, grimacing, frowning. Smiling, even, in his effort to keep himself awake.

"What are you doing with your face?"

"What are you doing with yours?"

Sabino looked at his friend, pondering the question.

"The best of my knowledge, my face is sitting still, whereas, as far as I can see, yours looks like it is trying to escape from your head."

"Listen, Sabin, *senti*. I have to stay awake. You, too. If we fall asleep, we're done for."

"The lieutenant will certainly ensure that we both wake up dead."

Dante snorted. "Or, the lieutenant will wake us up before he pulls the trigger to give us the pleasure of making sure we know that we are being hauled off to the firing squad. Now, what do you see over there?" He laid his hand across the small pile of rocks they had made on the edge of the trench for some slight protection. Dante had placed each rock himself—she cares for me, she cares not for me, she cares for me—.

It was very late, the last watch of the night. Sabino followed Dante's finger to a point on the horizon. There were the stars, beginning to fade in the indigo sky, hanging close to the desert. There was the desert, purple itself and barely visible, evident only in the distance as the place where the stars stopped. But lightly, rising from the surface, they could just see clouds of sand, small and barely discernible. It could be a coming wind on the windless night. It could be a storm, a *khamseen*, coming from miles away.

Or it could be troop movement.

Dante ceased exercising his face as the two men concentrated. They were there, alert among their sleeping brothers, but uncertain. To wake the lieutenant for a few clouds of dust would not result in court martial, but it would not increase their water ration either. They watched the cloud, counted seconds waiting for it to die down or turn itself into a storm or an invasion. There was no pointing squinting. The binoculars at this time of night were useless, even if the lenses had not been scratched with sand from months in the desert. The men waited, breathing. The cloud loomed, suddenly billowed, and rose high, blotting out constellations.

Dante and Sabino, galvanized, scrambled to their feet, shouting, "Storm! Sandstorm! Wake up, you idiots! The storm is coming!"

They kicked and shoved the men around them. They roared the word down the line and grabbed the ground sheets, secured them as tightly as they could while they cowered in the slit trenches and the sand came on.

Over his head, the wind screamed and sand filled his eyes and nose and swirled around his ears. He could feel the bodies of the men packed close together in the hole around him and it was some comfort. Dante tried to breathe as shallowly as he could, as though that would make a difference. He could, in spite of the wind and furious sand, feel his own heart beating, the pulse in his fingers gripping the thin sheet that kept the worst of the storm out of his lungs.

There would be no dawn that morning. The sand had swallowed it. Perhaps it would swallow everything.

To have left his father's house in a rage, to have screwed in lightbulbs at the academy, to have learned the tools of his trade and the calibrations of the fine motors in the Savoias that the Green Mice flew, and then to end up here, all but buried alive. He huddled, his back to Sabino, straining to breathe. He had eaten the cookies of the Fascists in school and they were delicious. But did that mean he had to eat dirt, too? To work in the middle of this place on which God himself had turned his hind parts, loading cannons and firing rifles, some of which had not seen action since the 1800s. To sit among weapons, rusting, ancient, or ill-suited to the desert and to hear Mussolini's words ringing in his ears:

Chi se ferma e perduto. Sempre avanti.

The one who stops is lost. Always advance.

Absurd.

They curled, back to back, holding the tarpaulin against the wind as best they could. They could not speak. The wind would likely not kill them, and it did ensure that there would be no attack for the moment. Even the war stood still before the storm. The bruises on Dante's legs, desert bruises and sand sores earned on the planes or tanks against which he had bumped a shin or a shoulder, were aching. They required precious gasoline in order to cleanse them and help them heal. There were scratches on his arms that would not heal until he could manage to get himself out of the sand. A dream beyond imagining in the blasting wind.

Sabino stirred.

"Keep still, man."

Dante imagined he could hear the movement of men beyond the dark veil that he clenched around him. Had the British somehow managed to manoeuvre in this storm? Had they got round behind him? He wanted to call out. He pressed his back against the solid Sabino and forced himself to be still. He kept his lips pressed tightly and tried not to breathe. The wind lifted the tarp away from them so that it billowed. The sand came in like coarse air filling every fold and furrow and he could not stop it. He thought he might scream.

Sabino started singing.

Tutto nello Stato, niente al di fuori dello Stato, nulla contro lo Stato…

Everything in the State, nothing outside the State, nothing against the State.

Stunned, Dante almost let go of the tarp.

"Now you're singing Fascist songs? Now?"

Sabino shouted back. "I suppose Il Duce has not encountered sandstorms."

"I suppose not."

The wind blew itself out finally and the men emerged from beneath it, coated in silt and sand, so that they looked like red-gold statues rather than men, barely animate in the exhaustion that followed such wind. Dante turned his back on the rising sun to see to the planes. They also were covered in sand. There had not been enough time to protect even the engines before the storm came upon them. As he and Sabino walked toward the aircraft, their shadows extended before them, the fresh blossoming sun against their backs, the light casting an aura around them. Dante looked down at his hands and gestured to Sabino, who looked as well. Then both men looked up at each other's faces. They were golden, lit up, as though from within.

"We look like saints."

"I see your halo is askew."

"Look, our shadows on the sand cloud."

In the retreating storm, they could see their shadows projected, large and growing larger even as they dissipated. Massive phantasms, burlesques of their own bodies were silhouetted against the roiling sand cloud, stretching toward the southwest.

"What are we doing here, Sabin?"

"We are finding out about ourselves, Dante. We are learning something new in this place."

Dante shivered in the new morning. He looked at Sabino as if he was crazy, as if the sandstorm had robbed him of reason. Sabino looked strong, as though the wind had blown its own strength into him. Dante wondered what Sabino was learning in the desert. He folded his arms across his chest. Whatever new thing Dante was learning, it was not a thing to generate heat. Beside him, Sabino put down his weapon, took off his greatcoat and laid it around Dante's shoulders, his arm kept firm around Dante until he warmed enough to stop shaking.

He felt calmer, but these tricks of the sun, the shadows burgeoning, the blazing light after the darkness of the storm, spun Dante's head and he would have fallen had not Sabino caught and held him.

"Ascend, my friend, ascend. It is heaven you are meant for, not the other place."

If Dante thought about all the turns in his path from the green military academy in Spoleto to the brown desert, it might have seemed that the hand of destiny had directed his steps and brought him to battle. But he did not hate anyone. He did not want to kill anyone.

There were faces before him, of men in trenches, barely concealed behind the shifting surface of sand. Faces stippled with sand so that one had no notion where whiskers ended and the desert left its mark on each man's face. This was the marker of distance, of time served, the indicator of risk. The closer to the front, the dirtier the man. Farther behind and closer to the trickling supply lines of food and water, the men looked bored but kempt. Dante was brown, corroded and pocked by the sharp sand.

Sabino, thank God, could still make jokes.

Dante watched as Sabino bent to wash his hands in the sand, rubbing them together and splashing handfuls of it over his head and back and under his arms.

"The only thing that takes the stink away, my friend. Wash up now."

"It will take more than the sand of ten deserts to scour the stink off you, Sabino."

The men were on guard, perched in and out of the slit trench outside the encampment. During this exchange, one of their squadron, a new recruit, Nunzio, who had arrived at the front only days ago and was still complaining about the wind and dust, sat on the edge of the hole, smoking. He was thirsty and had not yet learned to savour small drops of water from his half-full canteen. He was still pissing with enviable ease at the side of the foxhole.

He invited them to watch as he arced the stream out across the desert and gave himself a satisfied shake. Nunzio buttoned up his trousers and took a fresh cigarette from the package in his shirt pocket. He tapped it for effect and not for the usual reason of knocking out some small percentage of sand.

"Soon, you will find there is more desert than tobacco in your cigarettes."

"Come on, men. We'll soon be finished with these British. We'll be going home before you know it. Deal the cards, man."

Nunzio jabbed his elbow into Sabino's side.

"Don't you think they'll finish up with this front? In Italy last week, Mussolini said we had just about taken over Cairo." He looked at the hand he had been dealt and threw it down to the dirt.

Dante did not know how to respond. He had heard the officers trying to encourage the men. They had renamed Marseille's JG 27 the Marseille Staffel, trying to improve morale. But as the Italians were not part of this, it had very little effect. Rather, they were now directly in the line of fire, facing the enemy at the front. Dante had been posted to a fighting unit after Marseille's crash; they all had. The planes did not have enough fuel to fly and so they did not need to be maintained. In the meantime, the British were coming on.

It was Sabino who answered Nunzio.

"I hope you are right. I hope the Duce is correct. We have not heard that we will be sleeping between sheets in the Windsor Hotel in Cairo, but perhaps we will. You never know."

"The Windsor Hotel?" Dante shook his head. How did Sabino know about these things?

Dante turned his back on the men and bent to pick up his rifle. He heard the unmistakable pop of gunfire and dropped flat against the hole. Sabino was already in and firing back, as were the other two men beside him. Dante worked himself to the edge and took a sighting to the east. The explosions of rifle fire, staccato, startled him. He braced himself against the rim and took aim. In the distance, he saw shadows through grey clouds of dust and gunfire. Behind him, the heavy guns boomed bursting into the sand and setting it on fire. Sprawled in the hole, his head barely above ground, Dante shot at the invisible horizon. Anyone facing him must be his enemy. He loaded and reloaded. He could feel his pulse in his throat and taste blood in his mouth. His fingers moved, cold against the heat of the rifle. Around him, the grey smoke of the cordite obscured all visibility. He could barely hear the voices of men shouting orders. He was too frightened to sort the sounds into meaning. He loaded, took aim, and fired. He would kill whomever he could. Dante kept his breath shallow. He paused finally to listen. The gunfire around him slowed and ceased and a sudden vast silence overwhelmed him.

He felt for Sabino on his right.

"*Va bene?*" he whispered.

"*Si. Penso che.* I think so."

The haze of smoke and dust dissipated with terrible slowness. Each of the men in the hole spoke their presence softly. All but one.

Nunzio lay, the smoke curling off the cigarette still wedged in his knuckles, half in and half out of the hole, balanced between shelter and storm.

They could hear the sergeant shouting and men firing from the other holes on either side.

"*Aspetta!* Don't fire unless you have a certain target!"

Dante peered through his gunsight once more. Perhaps it wasn't over. He corrected for the wind and waited, looking for his enemy across the waste. The sergeant was right, of course. Even caught off guard, they could not fire at will. There was not enough ammunition in the unit to keep them going if a sustained fight were engaged. He waited, not looking up at the hanging dead face beside him. The men waited for more fire. Dante scanned the distance. But there was nothing. He waited, wrapped in his great coat as the cold deepened. In spite of the temperature, the flies crawled across Nunzio's eyes, burrowed into his uniform, crowded for warmth around the viscous hole in his neck.

In the still night, they finally climbed out of the hole. Sabino placed Nunzio's hands across his chest in a posture of peace. Dante thought, we do not die peacefully here. He could see no reason to mimic a serene departure. Sabino reached again and closed the man's eyes, stroked his face tenderly and tried to close the gaping mouth.

That fool of a Sabino washing himself in dust and Nunzio laughing at us. Bickering like old women. Nunzio with his wizened dick pissing in the wind. Dante had been so bored. He could have fallen asleep. They had been playing cards. Everlasting cards in the everlasting sand, anxious and restive until the very symbols on the cards came to seem meaningless. There had been a sudden fierce argument among the men in the hollow beside them over pennies. Over who would take the pot. Now they were shouting for the medic. Innumerable stars shone over their heads, some bright, some dull, clouds of witnesses. Dante knew the stars did not weep and yet there was a singular mourning in the air despite the multiplicity of loss, a startling dampness in the desert as though the air partook of lamentation and sorrow, as mere men had no time for it.

Dante did not ask what turns had brought him to a head-high trench in the sand. He could see them perfectly. From his father's house to the *scuola motorista* in the officers' training school, to Pantelleria, Albania, and now here. To squat over his helmet playing cards and trying to shake enough sand out of his cigarettes so that he could smoke them, another futility since his lips and tongue were coated in sand and every breath he took made him less of a man and more of a desert rat. He did not count the potatoes that he ate every day. He did not think about the number of times he climbed out of his hole in the earth to risk a crap in the light of day, his bowels now moving water. He did not count the days since he had a clear recollection of dignity or privacy. He drafted sweet letters in his mind to Angelina, committing them to paper when he could scrounge some. In her last letter, she had described the new residents of the town below San Placido. Angelina, from her kitchen table, had written to him. Had she written slowly, making the letters as she had been taught in school? It did not matter. The words came to him as though from a dream.

> *Papa sold all of the beans. He has stopped going directly to the market and now he just sees a few families on the edge of the town.*

She did not say why. Dante suspected that the Germans had come to Visso to assist with local government. There would be men in authority whom they had to avoid if they wanted to earn a small bit of money.

> *Mamma is feeling much better. It is cooler now and her legs are not so swollen. She went very slowly to put flowers on the grave of her father and mother. They have been gone a long time, but her eyes still look for them in the corners of the room. I helped her back into her bed and brought some good clear soup to give her strength and calm her stomach.*
>
> *The dog stays near the house. He is restless this day, up on his*

feet a thousand times and listening to the angels know what. He had the bone of the soup right in front of him, but something has climbed right up his long nose, where it will remain, I suppose, until he has a good sneeze.

There is a German officer who comes to San Placido with a camera. He has taken some photographs of the buildings and the valley, as though they were worthwhile things for a visitor to remember. He speaks to me, but I do not understand what he says. The dog must be tied at the back of the house for the uniform makes the creature frantic. He will not live long if he gets hold of the officer's shin.

I hope you are well. Here, things remain the same but with you, I imagine things are always changing. I hope that is agreeable to you and that you remain in the care of God.

Angelina Fiori.

She would have folded the paper and placed it in the envelope. Perhaps she had never seen her name written out. First and last.

Dante let his eyes rest on the name. Angels and flowers. He could use a vision of these in his hole. He worried about the German photographer. Did he take photographs of Angelina? Would she smile for something so pernicious as a camera? Those Germans and their cameras. At least she had the dog to protect her. He longed to see her. He held his face in his hands and held his breath.

Most days he sat in his hole, within the maze of trenches heading from the makeshift command to his place at the front, with his gun and his eyes scanning the desolate waves of sand, stretching east of Tobruk. He should be back with the planes. Back behind the lines. There should be fuel to get them airborne. But there was none. Not enough to make the sorties worthwhile. Instead, he had got himself caught up in this face-off at Alamein and there was no getting out of it until some resolution had been reached. Now he was waiting. Waiting to see the British tanks upon which he would fire, the British soldiers he would kill, or who would kill him. He sat, turning cards over, relighting his cigarette, stretching an arm or a leg to relieve a cramp.

"Dante, fellow. What are you doing here? There are no planes for you to fix here. You need to head back to Tunis. You're wasted here, my friend. Any fool could point and shoot one of these!"

Dante looked up from his cards. Eduardo, with whom Dante had been stationed on Pantelleria, had arrived with the new recruits from the high command. His uniform was clean and he himself still round. Round of face, round in the middle still, and, as he smiled and reached for Dante, he was round and soft of hand. He would be pared down soon, bleaching sand and wind and sun would peel him until he was as thin as Dante. Perhaps he would be killed quickly and would make a succulent meal for the vultures that had travelled so far to dine. Either way, Dante could not summon a smile though he welcomed the conversation of one whose throat was moist enough to waste words.

"I am working on the trucks now."

"With what? No parts, no tools, no supplies, no fuel? Are you a magician now?"

"Yes, I am. I am Dante, master of the miraculous. I concoct auto parts from dust. Like God, I create working motors of destruction for the glory of Rome. And look, I make flame from dust." This was more than Dante had said in one conversation for three weeks. Dante added to his fire the dry brush and scrub that blew at all times and in all directions.

From his conversations with poor Marseille, Dante knew that Alamein was a mere crossroad, a train siding with a meagre grey station corroded by desert sand and a half-buried compound of barbed wire, the sign hanging, turning and waving in the wind, held fast by crooked poles that had themselves been battered this way and that. It did not look like anything, certainly not like the prime object of anyone's desire, military or otherwise. Now that they were close enough, he knew that such a suggestion was laughable. There would be broken crates and barrels, stacked or scattered behind the station, the detritus of men at war. The building itself would be pocked with bullets, the result of target practice or prior engagements or, more likely, indolent soldiers shooting from passing trains at the only target for miles. At El Alamein, he knew, there was nothing but the sign, barely visible, that read Alamein, a name around which the force of a storm was gathering that would shape the Axis effort and his own position in the world.

He sat on the edge of the trench one morning. He had cleaned his rifle as well as he could. He felt the shadow fall over his shoulder before his colonel spoke. The *commandante* had come to order Dante to take one of the five-tonners and drive more bombs to the garden. He did not have to ask where it was.

Southwest of El Alamein, Field Marshal Rommel was planting a garden.

Rommel's desert garden, the Devil's Garden, was an antitank, antipersonnel minefield, laid with care in order to channel the attack of the British along specific lines for the Gazala Gallop. Dante had seen the engineers at work, obeying Rommel's orders, orders to be carried out by the Italian infantry, men with whom Dante was passing every day, to lay thousands of these in specific corridors. The plate mines, the size of dinner plates, had several pounds of explosives. Dante watched them lay tripwires for some of them and for others, a tank fuse so that a soldier would not detonate the mine, but a tank would. The S mines were anti-personnel and although they looked to Dante like nothing so much as a tin of baked beans, each one came equipped with a lethal, three-pronged detonator that set off two explosions.

He had asked one nervous fellow how they worked.

"What will happen when the English step on this?"

The soldier dusted his hands and smoothed his hair before answering. Nervous habits that he repeated before and after every installation.

"The first burst flings the mine into the air and the second causes it to explode at about waist height. From inside it shoots hundreds of ball bearings, compressed hot steel. These will bisect the soldiers to the right and left and front and back of the fortunate one who had triggered the mine and whose life will have ended most painlessly."

Every airfield, well, verge, and encampment was encircled by these S mines. No one got up in the night to piss without guarding every step.

"Won't the British sappers catch these? Mark them?"

"There, my friend, is Herr Rommel's genius. Look. We plant the garden in layers, so that there is a plate mine near the surface and beneath it, the anti-tank mine lurks, hidden. When the careful Allied sappers come along on their hands and knees to remove the plate mine, they will explode the one beneath."

"What if they don't remove them? What if they simply mark the spot?"

"That will be perfect. You see, in this way, Rommel channels the British advance toward our guns. Nothing, absolutely nothing is more exhausting than mine sweeps. The sappers go crazy. Look at me." He held out his shaking hands. "And I know where they are going. Imagine if I were working blind. I'd be wearing a dress and dancing a waltz with the field marshal himself before too long."

The soldier wiped his dry hands on filthy trousers.

"The sappers have to work at night. They have to be protected by the infantry, who have to be backed up by armoured divisions. All those men, all that hardware. Exhausting and costly. We have the benefit of dread as it works through the ranks of the enemy who must bend tenderly, anxiously, and slowly, to the task of marking a safe route through the mines, as though they were caring for the most fragile orchid on the planet."

Dante had never cleared a minefield, but he had seen his companions working in an agony of cramped muscles and fierce headaches. He knew the sappers could only take half-hour shifts, bent over the ground on their knees, slipping their bayonets, flaying the skin and flesh of sand, tenderly.

The soldier continued, glad for the break. "Those nomads, those tribesmen you see walking around the German and Italian encampments, they blow up so often from the fruit of Rommel's garden that they have reversed the tradition of millennia. Now, you watch them, you'll see, now when they travel the deserts, the women precede the men."

Dante stepped gingerly away from his new acquaintance.

"Be careful, *mi amico*, and God speed."

"Thank you, but somehow I don't think this is work for which God pours out a blessing. I will be careful."

The moon waxed full in the last week of September. The men looking after the camp watched as Rommel's aides travelled from base to base, telegraphing the Führer, the Duce, anyone who would listen to their pressing needs for petrol, food, ammunition, and spare parts. Without them, Dante could not repair the aging trucks that were stranded, immobile in the brush, wheels stripped. He grew weary, waiting through the long days. Even Sabino was reduced to silence. He neither sang nor joked. Dante watched him play solitaire in the shadow cast by the carcass of a truck. He felt faint. Dried out and hollow. His tools lay useless in a pouch he barely had the strength to lift. He could not maintain the equipment, never mind himself. He poked a new hole in his belt and cinched his coverall tightly. For a while, the feel of the buckle against his belly might fool him into believing his stomach was full.

The colonel had looked at him one day. Said, "De Angelis, for God's sake, find something to eat, will you? You're nothing but ribs and a prick."

He had no will to argue any longer.

They had been deployed as an offensive force and indeed, had ground their way east with little resistance until El Alamein. Now they were being pushed back with disgraceful ease, back down the empty supply line. Soon they would be back in Tunis. Six hundred and fifty miles so far, and unless Rommel and his friends moved expeditiously, more backward miles were coming. They had gone forward and now were going back. If Rommel came, they would push forward again in a brutal tug-of-war over a span of the earth that would not sustain a dog. They had been pushed and pushed. Captured and pushed. They could not consolidate. They could not form a line. They had been brave, Dante felt, listening to the quiet voices that spoke at intervals across the desert. They had camped in holes without complaint. They had survived on slim rations, without baths, without cigarettes, without any comfort. In their fear, they had remained and fought as ordered. They had fired old weapons and shot at what enemies they could see. They had cleaned the guns and repaired them when they jammed. They counted bullets and used them judiciously, abandoned the trucks and tanks as they seized and choked and sputtered to a fatal halt. They had been brave men, all of them.

Months passed before Angelina's letter, crumpled and fraying, came to Dante, to the desert. To have another letter from her, from a mountain in Italy, from a woman who lived there right now and who thought of him was almost unbelievable. The date seemed implausible to him. Where had he been three months ago? He smelled the paper. He considered eating it. She had stopped in her work to sit and compose. The writing, looping and curling across the page. She thought of him. He was filthy. He had worked on planes and trucks in coveralls with giant pockets, pockets packed with tools and bolts, hoses, knobs, needles, gauges pilfered from other dead or dying planes because you never knew what you might need. He jangled, walking from machine to machine. The men laughed at him, shouted at him to borrow the kitchen sink or the bicycle pedal that he kept in his trousers. They had laughed, but, with almost everything he needed at his fingertips, he had always been the fastest to have his planes back in the air, and the pilots swore and complained if he was occupied and unable to tend to their equipment. Now he was at the front, in a hole and embracing an ancient rifle and opening the miracle of a letter from Angelina. He wondered how the mail had gotten through when so little else had.

She thought of him. He looked down at his own body. Grease and sand were his aftershave. His cologne was his own weeks-old sweat. He could count his ribs, marching in the night to stay awake with his arms wrapped tightly around him for warmth. She had signed her full name so that the impress of the letters nearly tore the thin page. Her full name as if there might be several Angelinas on the earth with whom he corresponded or for whom he cared. He held the paper in his hands for minutes before he read its contents. It would have taken time, this careful letter. She would have been waiting for a pot of water to boil, or for the iron to heat. She would not have been sitting idle while she wrote to him. The beans were canned, the tomatoes as well, by this time of year. It was comforting to think about her moving to and fro on such mundane tasks. Life was proceeding normally somewhere, if not here.

Dante's commanders conferred. They were gathering will. He could feel it. The petrol was strictly rationed. Even Rommel himself had been nearby, moving among the troops, short, square and strong, miraculously clean, urging them to patience and courage. Dante could barely listen. Something would happen soon. Angelina hoped he would be safe. She had hopes. For him. In his hole in the desert, he thought about how and when he would make the climb up the mountain to see her again.

In the afternoon when the sand had died down and the worst of the weather had blazed across the cluster of men, Dante went from hole to hole until he found someone who would trade cigarettes for paper and pen. He wrote back.

Carissima Angelina,
   Thank you for your letter. I am well. Camp is good fun and there is work to do that I enjoy. The men are good fellows, each one funny or brave or generous or all three at the same time. The days are quiet. We do our work, we play cards and we wait. This is the most difficult. I think of your dog, watching and waiting, and I am glad you have a fierce companion to care for you until –

Here he stopped. Until what? Until I can come to look after you? As if such a suggestion would be welcome. He picked up his pen.

   – until I get back. The truth is, I long to see you and walk again to your garden. I hope you will save me a seat on the bench.
   Con tanto affetto,
   Dante.

He placed the letter in an envelope—no point in sealing it as it would have to be read by the censors before it went anywhere. The quartermaster, with whom Dante was friendly and to whom in richer times he had made gifts of cigarettes passed on from the pilots, would get the letter out for him as soon as he could.

He looked at Sabino who was trying to clean his boots with spit and a dusty rag. He did not ask what the point was of such an exercise here and now. The waste of spit. He admired Sabino. He kept his hands moving. He wrote to his mother and sisters. He kept his rifle clean. Dante was full of notions about a future away from war. A future that he would build with Angelina, if only he could make it home. He wondered what Sabino hoped for and was ashamed of himself because he had never asked. He watched Sabino's hand strike back and forth across the cracked leather, as if a shine were possible. Dante imagined his friend at the church on his wedding day, how clean and pressed he would be.

"Sabin."

"*Si*, Dante."

"What will you do when you get home?"

"I will eat my mother's pasta. I will drink my father's wine that he put down before he died in 1928. Do you have any idea how good that wine will be by now? I will eat cakes. I will go to confession. I will ask my next-door neighbour's daughter to marry me. She will say yes. The babies will come, fast and many. You will be the godfather. If Angelina can still bear the sight of you, she will be the godmother. We will make our own wine, you and I. We will grow fat and slow. Our faces will shine with the wine that is the blessing of God."

"*Veramente*? Really?"

Sabino looked down at the boot in his hand. His toes stuck through his sock.

"Remember the hermit?"

Dante said, "Of course."

"Me too."

"What about him?"

"*Io non so*. I don't know. He stays with me." Sabino touched his hand to his chest.

The men were silent. Dante raised his head and looked across the trackless distance. Field Marshal Rommel had told them they were at the epicentre of the world's conflict. North Africa was the Mediterranean, the east-west supply conduit for the warring armies. They must hold. He looked around. *Wadis* in the middle distance, barbed wire, hills, the gritty surface of the desert. The epicentre of nothing, it looked to be. As though, by this light, God's imagination had for once failed.

When he looked at Sabino, he was not surprised to see him smiling.

"Well?"

"*Come?*"

"You know what. Why are you smiling? Sometimes I think I have to knock that smile off your face."

"I was just wondering."

"*Andiamo*, Sabin, wondering what?"

"*Allora*, I know Herr Rommel is a brilliant leader. I know the Duce is a visionary. But I was wondering how this brilliance and vision will expand the physical properties of petrol so that an allowance for one hundred kilometres will permit us to travel the three hundred kilometres we need to meet the British at El Alamein."

For this, Dante had no answer. He sat down and began a careless swipe at his own boots.

Angelina

Nico had written home. In the letter he wrote, he tried to make the news sound exciting. He was going to see Russia. Imagine. Going as far away from San Placido as Russia. He described the transport itself as an exotic adventure. He asked his mother to send him mittens. Perhaps a scarf.

Angelina knew that this was the worst possible news. Of all the theatres of war, the Eastern front was the one that was most futile. So many Italian soldiers had died in Russia. The news was just coming back about the cold, the resourceless units struggling with no ammunition, little food, and no heart for the battle. She didn't know how Nico would survive.

Angelina read and reread the letter after her mother laid it down. She was looking for something, but she didn't know what. He sounded well and brave. She could not believe the man writing in such terms about such a place was the brother she had tested her strength against, throwing him to the ground when she could, outrunning him until his legs grew longer than hers. She had watched him try to flirt with the Visso girls. He was so funny and so bad at it. Offering them cigarettes he didn't have, hoping to catch their attention. She missed him so much.

Angelina packaged up Nico's mittens and scarf. She found a good warm hat in his bedroom and put that in, too. She had no idea how food would travel, but she took a chance and wrapped some biscotti in waxed paper to put into the box. They might not make it, but if they did, Nico would think it was Christmas. He would have a little feast of cookies.

Cookies were a rare enough treat these days. Angelina's neighbours had begun to tighten their belts. In that early spring of 1944, everyone was becoming lighter, if not of heart, at least of foot. Alfonso pulled cracked leather through his belt buckle until the last hole, the Mussolini hole. They were supporting the Duce's war effort with their plain wedding rings and simple crops and hard labour. The people of San Placido were as thin as they could hope to be, as small of waist as their belt leather would permit, and still the trousers of the *vecchietti* hung loose and flaccid.

The garden's soil, in spite of Angelina's care, grew coarse and dry. The fall of last year yielded a crop so scant, so little to put in the pot, that she thought she might have to learn to savour the taste of boiled water. She had worked every day, but even the weeds were meagre and thin on the ground. She turned the soil, watered it, brought espresso grounds used and re-used to nourish the dry earth. Questo followed her, thin as well, but having fared slightly better in his ranging on the mountain. Satisfied with himself, smiling and glossy, he had on occasion left a hare limp and cold at the door, its neck politely broken and its hide otherwise untouched. Angelina had opened the door to step into the grey frosted day of late fall and bent for shoes only to find the soft creature, just cooling at her feet. She had crossed herself more than once, regarded in silence the strange heavens above and the care provided by means of a stray black dog. Too pleased with himself in the world. She skinned and cleaned the carcass, made the meat tender and swimming in herbed gravy and oil. She fed it slowly and in small pieces to her slight mother. She made the rabbit last, boiled every bone and sinew and cooked every organ. She took soup to Francesca while Zia Anselmina watched out her window, all *malocchio* and furious. She left a small bowl of stew with Father Paolo, just inside the priest's door.

She patted the dog and scratched his cocked ear.

"*Signor cane. Ringraziamo.* We thank you."

Questo sat still, pressed against Angelina's leg, permitting himself to be caressed.

They could keep clean, if not fed. After all, the mountain spring would not fail unless the mountain itself fell to the earth. They could launder their clothes and bathe themselves. They were the cleanest starving people in Italy. But no amount of water would heal the earth of the garden, which, Angelina knew very well, had been overplanted and not left to rest as it ought.

In Visso, the German command had moved the swastika into the mayor's office and taken over the large walnut desk within. The mayor was invited to use the secretary's narrow alcove and to bring his new boss some coffee and pastries. Somehow, the Germans had manoeuvred a half dozen panzers through the narrow streets. The soldiers moved in stomping ranks, dark and gleaming. The sun struck their helmets as they moved through Visso. The townspeople ran ahead of the tanks and men, dodging into alleys and doorways seeking shelter. There was not one Italian soldier in sight. They stood in the beautiful piazza, with their backs to the church of Santa Maria Maggiore. Angelina watched from the path as the units saluted and dispersed. She watched as the mayor left the bakery with two boxes of sweets which he had packaged himself at the bakery. The woman behind the counter had stepped away, refusing to assist.

In the corners of the *piazza*, in the shadows of the great church and the old town hall, young men collected, hands in their pockets. Some of these were acquaintances of Angelina's, sons of the mothers who bought her father's produce. They were men who, for one reason or another, did not go to war. Flat-footed, asthmatic, men with poor eyesight wearing thick spectacles, frail, thin men with heart murmurs who clustered, whispered. Passed packets, kept their heads down, and moved in silence among the citizens who went about their business and pretended not to notice. Occasionally, there would be a new face, a new man among them, sometimes forgetting to bend in ill-health. A man the others were perhaps assisting or hiding from the Germans. Angelina did not ask. No one did. But she had the sense from the way that they never spoke of this, never looked in his direction, that everybody knew. She hoped the Germans did not.

Angelina gave the German soldiers as wide a berth as she could. They did not step aside to let the old ones pass. Everyone in the town had to walk around them and into the gutter if necessary. One soldier, his camera case tight under his arm, seemed to follow Angelina, no matter what backstreets she took on the errands on which her father sent her. She had been up and down every street of Visso since she could walk. She was able at times to lose him, or to slip into the town without being seen. She would go to the back door of the *alimentari* and knock softly so that she did not have to use the main entrance off the piazza. She would make the slight purchases she required and follow the same track home again.

Afternoons were the best times. Just before the grocery closed for the long lunch, most of the Germans seemed to be occupied elsewhere. But one afternoon, he was waiting for her. She was glad, at least, that he found her before she got to the door. Perhaps the grocer would not get into trouble on her account.

"*Ciao*," he said, putting his fingers to his helmet, as though tipping it.

Angelina kept her eyes down and stepped to the left. He stepped with her.

"*Buongiorno*." He tried again, the Italian words coming rough out of his throat. "*Mi chiamo* Helmut."

Angelina stepped to the right, but he put his hand on her arm.

"Hello," he said. "Hello, *signorina*."

She risked a glance. He smiled.

"*Buongiorno. Scusa. Sono in una fretta terribile.* I am in a terrible hurry."

He seemed to ponder her statement. She said it again, slow this time.

"Ah, *si*," he said. He moved out of her way and held out his arm for her to proceed.

Angelina walked past the store, past the piazza, and out toward the switchbacks on the main road to San Placido. If he was following her, she did not want him to find out where the path was. She was afraid to turn back and see if he was there. She hoped he believed her to be a resident of Visso. She hoped he would not follow her to her home. Her shoulders and neck were taut with the strain of not looking back. She could not. But she had to.

She risked a glance. He was behind her. Not more than a hundred feet.

Angelina's stomach turned inside her. Once she had threatened to kill Anselmina. That little mean woman. Now there was a big man behind her with a rifle. She turned to face him.

He stopped on the road and saluted.

"May I escort you to your home? These are dangerous times, *signorina*."

She did not understand what he said. His pronunciation was so strange. She was too anxious to walk away. He caught up with her and put out his bent arm for her to take.

She understood.

"*Non capisco.* I don't understand."

Angelina did not know if the soldier saw that she was afraid or if he was suddenly tired of the effort to communicate with an uncooperative girl. She wondered if he could grasp the effect of his presence. Her throat was so dry. San Placido was still far away. Below her, Visso spread out like a picture postcard.

The soldier stepped toward her. Angelina moved back. He reached toward her arm and she stepped backwards again up the hill. She wondered if this bizarre dance would take her all the way home. He seemed to give up. The soldier dropped his arm and shook his head. That was fine with her. Let him believe her to be stupid. Just let him leave her.

He said "*Auf Wiedersehen*," and turned away.

She did not tell her father. When she got home, he was reading the newspaper.

"*Ciao*, papa. Is everything all right?"

Angelina rinsed her hands under the cold water at the sink until her fingers were numb and still.

He did not look up. Instead, he shook the newspaper. "The war is not going too well. You can tell by what they don't say. The

Canadians are not good fighters. The Americans abuse our women in the south. What I think they mean is that there is an invasion force coming up from Sicily. I think the Germans mean to hold them off in Rome. They hold the north. They hold us, it seems, now that they have liberated Mussolini from the King's prison and can pretend that he is in charge of things here."

Angelina sat with her father. If the Germans held them, what could they do? She did not ask the question. She knew the partisans were at work in the mountains. They had got some Jews out of Visso. Not all of them, but some. She had seen Father Paolo disappear at odd hours down the mountain path that ran behind her own house.

He rubbed a hand over his face. "No one is talking about an empire any more."

In the morning, Angelina opened the door to see the man, the German officer, at the far end of the lane. He had a camera with him again and was pivoting around in a halting circle, taking photographs of the village and the valley and Folignano, above. He bent and photographed what must have been the small flowers that grew between the rocks on the mountain, the wild thyme and buttercups. He seemed captivated by everything he saw.

Angelina slowly closed the door. He did not know where she lived. He had seen her on the mountain, but she could have been heading to Folignano for all he knew. She closed the door and the shutters and prayed that he would not be in the mood for visiting.

When she looked again, he had passed the Martinellis'. He was heading directly for the path to the garden. If he passed her house, it might be too late. He must not find the garden. She felt that he must not set foot in it.

She stepped outside. He saw her and waved. He pointed to the camera and then at her, as though asking a question.

This would keep him from the garden. She was so ashamed to have her neighbours see her. She could not nod at him or gesture. She simply stood like a door ajar. He pointed his camera and shot her. Something in the look on her face must have spoken to him. He waved again and moved away, up the road to Folignano. There would be snow still on the mountain. He would be able to take some nice pictures. If only he were a tourist. Angelina almost felt bad. If he were a person, just a man instead of a black-suited German officer, would she have smiled? Would she have offered him some water?

She could not eat her breakfast. The Germans were rising like a doleful tide. If one found San Placido, surely more would come.

The next day, the *postino* came up the mountain. He was walking when Angelina saw him. She smiled at first, thinking that he must have parked his bicycle at the last switchback so that Questo would not attack him. The mail carrier was uncharacteristically early on his route. He walked, solemn in his uniform holding before him a single envelope. She waited in the doorway as he passed all of her neighbours' houses and came directly to hers.

"*Signorina*," he said at the doorway, "I have this for your father."

Angelina took the paper from him and said thank you. She put on her shoes and carried the envelope to the field. Her head was light and buzzing. A telegram. A short message. Would it say that Nico had been injured? That he was being discharged? Was he coming home? Or not. It would be unbearable. Her father and Berto looked up from the cattle. Angelina's throat was too dry to call out to them. She could not lift her arm to wave. Instead, she walked to her papa and handed him the telegram.

He held it, unopened in his big palm. He nodded at the ground, as though telling himself something with which he would not disagree.

"Is your mamma asleep?"

"*Si*, papa. She fell right to sleep after I washed her."

Angelina thought, just do not open it. *Lascilo*, papa. Just leave it.

Alfonso slipped the paper out of its sheath and read the abrupt announcement of his son's death in Russia. Nico Fiore. Stop. Missing. Stop. Presumed dead. A day, a place. A word that Angelina could not pronounce when her father handed the telegram to her and she read it for herself. It had taken a month. Angelina thought, I had just sent him mittens. He would not even have had a chance to wear them.

Berto took the paper and moved away from them to read it.

Alfonso opened his arms as though to the heavens and Angelina stepped into the circle they made. Her father bent his head to her shoulder and gasped to catch his breath.

Over his shoulder, cresting the rise, Angelina saw the good Father coming toward them. He had his own handkerchief out and blew his nose into it as he walked.

"It's Father Paolo, papa," she whispered to Alfonso.

Her father used his sleeve to wipe his tears. He turned to Father Paolo and embraced him.

"Alfonso, Alfonso. I am so very sorry. Angelina, *cara*. Are you all right?"

Father Paolo looked at Angelina. He said, "*Poverina*. Again the world forces us to be strong. You especially. I am so very sorry. He was a good boy."

The priest went over to Berto and whispered to him. Angelina did not know what he could have said, but Berto turned back and came with them to the house to tell Graziela what had happened. When they returned, they found the kitchen table burdened with food. The ladies of San Placido had slipped into the house. They had already taken away the laundry and washed the breakfast dishes that Angelina had left. Two of them were upstairs with Graziela who was just waking up from her sleep. Two were downstairs to embrace Angelina and Berto and fuss over them as though they were small children. Angelina and her brother climbed the stairs and got onto the bed on either side of their mother. They took her hands while their papa came and told her the bad news of her son.

The morphine proved merciful. Though Graziela seemed to hear them—she covered her mouth and tears flowed from her eyes—she dozed off again shortly after. The small room was crowded, but no one moved or offered to give up their place.

Signora Martinelli said, "We will stay, Angelina. We will look after everything. You can rest or eat or go to the church. We will be here."

Angelina lay back against her warm mother. She did not want to think about Nico alone and cold on the steppes of Russia without even woollen mittens. She wanted to think about Dante in Rome.

Dante in San Placido. About a future beside him, with him. A safe future with a house and a garden. Laughter and wine and plenty of good food. The war had forced itself upon her family. The edicts of a man in Rome, a man in Berlin, a man in England had taken her brother away forever. What reason did she have to dream? She closed her eyes and folded her arms against hope or anything like it. If the world would be hard, then she would be hard, too.

Francesca pulled her chair close and stroked Angelina's arm with such gentleness that Angelina fell asleep in the bed of her mother and father while the ladies kept watch.

Dante

Dante marched. He marched as he had been taught. Eyes forward. He marched along the desert road and then he stopped. The sand swam across the hot trail, almost lifting in the thermals cast up from Mussolini's road. It slid in curling waves so that Dante staggered on solid ground. He had to look hard at his own boots to make sure they were fixed on the earth.

He spoke to himself.

Guarda! Idiot. The ground does not move. You stand upright, good fellow. Try not to fall down.

He shook his head and saw below him minute pink flowers with dusty green petals blooming in the gap between the desert and the desert road. He tried to blink sand out of his eyes—the trick was not to rub—but when he looked again, the fine petals had become suddenly larger, though the whole flower would fit ten times over into the palm of his had. He bent to one knee and shielded the blooming flowers with the palms of his hands as though cradling a fragile small fire, only just ignited. His eyes began to sting.

The flower faded in moments. Kept out of the wind and sand, the petals curled and closed in on themselves, bent and collapsed. Dante had seen the bodies of his friends and enemies do the same thing. After having bloomed and burst in the waxing heat and sudden cold, they subsided, became forms too small for the uniforms that had once adequately contained them. They did not look real, but they did not come from any dream or nightmare he had ever had.

When he looked down again, the flowers were gone as though they had never even been. Dante made the sign of the cross, in spite of himself.

He stood to rejoin the marching line toward the deserted railway station at El Alamein. It seemed possible that in advancing so far without secure supply lines, the Desert Fox had outfoxed himself.

"And screwed us all," Dante whispered to the place where the flower had bloomed.

On parade, in conversation, and speeches to the men, Dante listened as Rommel cajoled and encouraged and challenged. Dante and his compatriots listened in awe. That a man, their leader, could look around with his own two eyes at his men, hungry and sick and going nowhere but to the latrines to lose what little food they had consumed. That he could stand before them, confident, to all appearances, clean, upright, look them straight in their eyes and tell them things that could not be true. It was awesome to behold. Dante took a tentative sip of his water ration and contemplated the hand that held the canteen, the wrist, the forearm, the skin, fossilizing, petrifying before his eyes. It seemed to him that they were far from being on the brink of victory, though for a moment Dante had taken a deep breath of belief. He knew that the British tanks were grinding across the distant desert. They were advancing toward the Axis high ground. He listened to Herr Rommel with his face lifted.

They were out-manned, outgunned, and all but out-manoeuvred, but no one would guess this from listening to the man who stood before them on the jeep, who tried to persuade tired men to step beyond what seemed humanly possible. Every soldier's face turned toward him, exhausted, stubbled, wind-blown, and bent, listening as though the words themselves were weapons that would lead them to victory.

To the Italians, he said, "General Von Thoma has told the Führer that one British soldier is worth twelve Italians, that you men are good workers, but that you do not like to fight. It is too noisy for you. But I know that you are exemplary among soldiers. That your courage matches that of your German comrades, that you are fleet of foot and quick of eye and that your hearts are trimmed, ready for battle. You are willing, unselfish, good comrades, and considering the conditions under which you have been compelled to serve, you always give better than average. It is my honour to serve with our Italian brothers and to stand against our enemies, shoulder to shoulder. You are all tired. You have all excelled beyond what ought to have been asked of you. We ask you now for one more effort and the day will be ours."

Dante stood on the stones and sand among the dry scrub in the empty heat. The men around him, worn to shreds, had given to the war every ounce of their force and personality. And still they marched. He had seen in the men profound courage to stand each day and move forward. Dante knew the field marshal's reputation, the high regard in which command on both sides held him. But here, among the ragged men of his country, he was ashamed of Rommel. And ashamed of himself for listening. He looked to his left and right at the weary, saluting soldiers and bowed his head, honoured to be among them, even in such straits. There were low hills in the distance, Gazzala, Mersa Metruh, the high ground they were desperate to hold. The brilliant pale sun defining all the contours of the ground, the faces of the men, the shimmering evanescent waves of heat rising. His bowels cramped and turned inside his skin and he hoped the field marshal would soon be finished with his encouragements. Dante's hands in front of him, not stone any more but incandescent and blazing.

Dante had dug in with the units at El Alamein. In May and June, before he arrived, Rommel's army had pushed its way across the top of Africa and had now been forced to a standstill carrying out skirmishes for a few square kilometres of dust and rock. The Allies stood at El Alamein. They were entrenched in the high ground, with infantry divisions in position to hold the coast road, the railway track, and the water supply. A brigade group was holding the Deir el Quattara and Jebel Kerag. Dante could see them in the distance. Both offered natural defensive positions so that they could easily turn back any approach by Rommel's forces to the ridge of Ruweisat and Alam el Haifa. Dante could almost see them at work, constructing pillboxes to hold the anti-tank guns. He knew enough of pitched battle to know there would be observation posts, trench lines, barbed wire, and belts of mines. Dante had felt the thunder of the antitank guns.

The Panzerarmee with them had been decimated that July by the Allies' aerial bombardment. They were down to twenty-three tanks. The next day and the day after that, Rommel drove the infantry forward behind what tanks he had, only to be repelled and held in place south of the Ruweisat Ridge. Dante had followed with the infantry behind the line of tanks, barely breathing through the rag he had tied around the lower half of his face to try to filter out the worst of the sand. He did not know what would happen, what could happen. The ruthless New Zealanders had descended, screaming, and had overrun the Italian Ariete and Brescia divisions. In the clouds of dust, Dante had seen the grasping hands of the dead. Looking upon them no longer as men, but meat for the fat vultures, he felt hollow and weak, overcome by the pointlessness of such sacrifice.

The Allies had been moving by night, raising the usual massive dust clouds as they prepared their lines. There could be no secret manoeuvrings in the desert. In his retreat, Dante passed German Panzers, idle in the desert, sometimes fired on by his own men to prevent the British from making use of them. Word came that the Australians had taken Tel el Eisa, smashing the Italian Sabratha division. The 21st Panzer division came to prevent any more British gains, but the Allies came on. The Australians struck again, taking the Trieste Division. Dante watched as Rommel gave orders to move units and tanks as best he could, scrambling with the slender force he had to hold position. Dante knew they were in bad shape. The infantry was depleted, there were not enough field guns or antitank guns to withstand any sort of incursion. He could see that Rommel was no longer shaving and appeared more vulnerable to the sand and wind. There was a rumour going through the ranks that the supply ships had been sunk at sea, that Kesselring had promised an airlift of supplies. Without them, Dante could not see how any of them would survive. Rommel, he knew, had wanted to march with the Panzerarmee to the shores of the Nile.

Even with such limited resources, Dante's unit was ordered to fight back. They engaged a line of tanks set primly on a rise within range of the Panzers. Dante was with the infantry behind the tanks, which spent all day firing on their British counterparts. All through the long day, the tanks burned. Dante had seen the British Grant tanks. They ran on high-octane fuel and when the Panzers, with their seventy-five-millimetre guns, fired on them, the Grants exploded. The crews had no chance to escape. It burned his eyes to watch. Dante was disturbed as well, wondering why the British would be foolish enough as to park a line of Grants directly in harm's way. He was waiting for the order to advance when he heard the planes overhead. The RAF were coming in, Hurricanes, Spitfires, Wellingtons, and some that Dante did not recognize from the US air force. They were under attack on three sides. The British were coming at them from behind the line of burning Grants and around to the south. Now they were hitting them from the sky.

Dante ran and fired his feeble gun. In the smoking dark, he sought cover. He retreated with Sabino and the other men, tracing backwards from foxhole to foxhole, spending rounds to cover the retreat and then running as though chased by the demons of hell. Dust, burning flesh and metal and the strange blinding light of the blazing flares assaulted him, confused him. Somehow, Dante got turned around and began running for the Allied line. He heard boots churning the grit behind him and forced himself to run faster, his throat blistering, desperate for air. He was tackled from behind, dropped to the hard ground and held, his arms pinioned and flailing until he heard Sabino shouting.

"Dante! It's me. Stop, my friend. Look at me."

Sabino held his face. Dante put his hands up to cover Sabino's own. He felt something tear inside. Something was finished. He hoped it was not his hammering heart.

"Sabin," he said, gasping. "Sabin."

From the ground, he could feel the tremor of the British advance. Sabino stood and held out his hand.

"*Andiamo*, my friend. *È tempo di andare*. It's time to go."

He let Sabino pull him to his feet. In as much haste as he could manage, they rejoined the retreat. Around Dante, trucks and tanks burned through that night, illuminated by the flares that the Luftwaffe dropped on open ground.

By the last week of October 1942, the Italian and German divisions had retreated west of El Alamein. Dante waited through hours for a battle from which he had no escape. He still had his skin and this was a marvel to him. He wished to write a letter to Angelina in these dull moments, but could find no paper and, since the night he had run toward his enemies, he could not assemble his thoughts. On the radio after that last engagement they had heard Signor Churchill announce the end of the beginning. The British were strong and tricky, setting up those Grants and drawing the best of what Rommel could offer. Everyone had been told again and again that they must conserve. They had been ordered to shoot only at hard targets to preserve ammunition. There was little fuel.

Dante heard the rumours of Mussolini's visit. The Duce was coming, flying in his SM 81, the tortoise, and bringing his horse with him for the victory march on Cairo. The bad news, he thought, must travel much more leadenly than the good. Dante thought, we are empty here. We have no petrol for the tanks, we have bad rations for the soldiers and we are growing more and more ill. He knew that Herr Rommel had been in tight spots. He knew that there was great and, as it seemed to him now, quite ridiculous faith in the man's ability to steal victory. Dante believed that Mussolini and his tall horse would wait quite some time before they galloped into Cairo. There would be quite a wait before Herr Feldmarschall would pull a victory off. Like a magician with a top hat and a rabbit out of emptiness. Dante regarded his superior officer with pity as he received reports and sent urgent requests into ether. He sat in the shade of the burned-out armour of a tank. It must be a terrible thing to have such an excellent reputation, thought Dante.

The third and final battle at El Alamein began on the evening of the twenty-third of October. Herr Rommel had paid visits to as many of the units as he could, encouraging, challenging, and even joking with them about how petrol was more important than water. Both were in such short supply that the men did as much as they could to avoid thinking of their thirst. They kept their gaze away from the inert Panzers. Dante sipped from his canteen and held the water in his mouth, held it against his own instinct to swallow, felt it slide around his teeth and tongue before finally opening his throat to the trickle.

They were dug in for the night, wrapped against the deep night cold and almost soothed into a ragged sleep. Colonel Liss, shorter than any of the Italians and often seen clipping his stubbled moustache, had been by to inform the men that no major British offensive was expected. Dante had heard the Panzerarmee commander contradict this, in the privacy of the officers' tent. He had walked by and heard the argument. He did not know whose intelligence was more reliable. The weakness of his body on that evening compelled him to trust the untrustworthy Liss and he hunkered in his trench beside Sabino and, while the desert moved around him, he drifted away from wakefulness, a rocking rowboat in a choppy sea.

He did not look at his watch. His eyes were still closed when he felt the trembling and throbbing in the earth. The Allies had begun a furious artillery assault on all fronts. The Afrika Korps, the 90th fighting division and the 20th Panzer division all sending out the message: *We are under attack.*

Dante was now awake and watchful, waiting for a target upon which to fire. He could see the flash of muzzles and the flares going up to light up the front at El Alamein. Their unit had been taken by surprise. He and Sabino leaned over the trench, breathing together and waiting for a clean shot.

Sabino spoke into his ear. "Not like looking after planes."

Dante was too frightened to answer. No, it was not. Beside him scrambled soldiers who had taken their boots off in the early evening to air out their socks. They grabbed now for laces, no time to dump out the desert, no time to check for scorpions. A couple of the men just leaned with loaded weapons. What difference if they died with their boots on or not?

Under the eerie light of the flares, they could see the desert, pockmarked with shell holes, the barbed wire blown to bits. The tanks of the British were barely visible in the far distance, but they could hear them, and feel them. Behind the barrage, the infantry would be advancing, the men at whom Dante and Sabino and the soldiers with them would take aim.

The advance troops held off the British as best they could. The land mines, meanwhile, were doing their terrible job. Dante could hear them in the distance. The thundering and blasting masked the screams of those not instantly killed. He held still. He had seen them lay those mines, which were not mines at all. Herr Rommel had been so short on fuel for the Stukas that he had ordered that some of the aerial bombs, bombs meant to be dropped from thousands of yards in the air, be buried just below the desert and fused with trip-wires to trigger explosions that would blow the arms and legs and brains out of entire units of men and tanks. It was terrible to behold. Fragments of men fell like hailstones, hard on the brittle desert.

In the smoky dawn, Dante and Sabino waited.

Dante said, "What day is it now?"

Sabino had to think. "It is the twenty-third."

"It was my birthday yesterday."

"*Buon compleanno.*"

Sabino stuck his hand in his pocket and pulled out a silver lighter.

"Here, my friend. For your birthday."

Dante flicked the lid and struck the flint, but the lighter did not ignite.

"No fuel," Sabino said.

Dante was surprised to laugh. One more device in need of reinforcements.

"Thank you, Sabino."

"*Niente*," he said.

The previous evening, column after column of German and Italian prisoners had been taken. They knew that Rommel was mounting a counterattack, lining up the Panzer divisions so that they had the least possible territory to cover, thus saving fuel. They started shelling on the morning of the twenty-fourth. No one had to tell the infantry what was going on. They could see the planes coming in formation. The Stukas came in on frequent, heavy, and destructive raids. The noise they made, the screaming of the dive-bomber and the bombs they dropped echoing in the dust and smoulder of shellfire. Dante had seen the Grant and Sherman tanks abandoned in the back-and-forth of attacks. They were fuelled by aircraft fuel and turned into fire bombs when they were hit. A Stuka dive took out not only the tank, but also all the infantry following behind it. The bombers hit a column of supply trucks in the distance, loaded with petrol and shells, which raised their own flourishing pillar of black and oily smoke.

The twenty-fifth was quiet. Men digging in, cleaning weapons and refitting as best they could. In a clearing between trenches, the German priest was holding a mass. Across the field, Dante watched as men bent knees and bowed heads. Bent and supplicant, they prayed for peace, these kneeling soldiers. The ones who carried rosaries took them out and told them quietly. They were too exposed, too upright, scattered like cardboard targets, dark against the desert. Sabino was among them exercising an unfortunate piety. Dante hoped it would not get them killed. One fellow looked over his right shoulder toward the east and the enemy. Dante stuck to his dugout, his insides turning. No one prays more urgently for peace than a soldier. These ones who know the loathsomeness of war. Dante's legs twitched as though they would of their own volition jump out and kneel. The priest's voice carried across the plateau.

"Though a host encamp against me, I will not fear; though war arise against me, in spite of this I shall be confident. One thing I have asked from the Lord, that I will seek. To dwell in the house of the Lord all the days of my life. To behold the beauty of the Lord and to meditate in his temple. For in the day of trouble he will conceal me in his tent. In the secret place of his tent he will hide me. He will lift me up on a rock and now my head will be lifted up above my enemies around me. I will offer in his tent sacrifices with shouts of joy. I will sing, yes, I will sing praises to the Lord."

The priest standing before those men, his voice, vibrating, carrying. He spoke in German and Italian. He sang the *Non nobis*. He blessed them in the name of the Father and Son and Holy Spirit. He dipped the crusts in sour wine and offered the men lined up before him communion with the sacred body and blood, elements with which they were all too familiar. The soldiers said the amen. They returned their helmets to their heads and their thin bodies to their posts. Everything was familiar in what the priest said. The enemies, the rock, the tent. As though the holy words were ordinary words, scribed by some poor soldier. Everything was there except the beauty. Dante recalled the desert flower, blooming with no one but himself to witness it. Lasting only moments and only in the worst of conditions. He did not think it was adequate compensation for desolation. But it had surprised him when he thought there was nothing in the broken world that would.

From his quiet hole, Dante watched as Rommel paced. Their unit had been promised supplies. Kesselring himself had promised that a fuel tanker was on its way. They could not afford to wait, he knew. They were sitting ducks. But they could not move without the fuel. Word came late in the day. The RAF, coming in straight and level at seventy feet and 140 knots across the Mediterranean, had released torpedoes at about a thousand yards, torpedoes that moved almost without resistance into the hull of the freighter, exploding its contents to the heavens, exploding the possibility of a Rommel victory at El Alamein. Exploding the possibility of survival. Dante would have to find paper. He must write something to leave for Angelina.

Before he could start to look, the adjutant was at his side. He handed Dante, Sabino, and three other men in the hole new orders. They were being sent with a unit to support the gunners of the Folgore division. There were not many of them, but unlike the rest of the Italian cohort they had a reputation for being aggressive and accurate. In the longer and quieter days when they were back with the planes keeping them serviced and ready, Dante and Sabino had all the time in the world on their hands, they had taken some time to hone their aim and speed, loading, firing, and hitting targets at great distances. They thought it was a game. They did not expect, as airplane mechanics, to join the paratroopers and gunners at the attack.

"We are learning all kinds of things."

"Sabino, things we never wished to learn."

"It will be a good skill for hunting rabbits when we get home."

"Your mother keeps the rabbits in a cage behind your house."

"Grouse, then."

"*Si*, grouse."

Dante smiled. They would be home some day. He thought he would not have the heart to kill a single rabbit when he got there. Maybe not even a chicken.

With the men of the Folgore, they held off the British. The *capitano* had been up and down the line, furious, spitting at them, laughing in the noise at the eye of the storm.

"Hold, you men! Hold for your very lives!"

If he was crazy, it was too late to do anything about it. The British were firing everything they had. The Folgore line held, but it cost them, an entire mortar platoon and six anti-tank guns. Dante could not believe he was still breathing. He advanced with the front lines and moved forward at sixteen hundred, crouched and firing, and even the *capitano* was astonished to find that within thirty minutes, they had taken back all of the territory they lost in the Allies' surprise attack.

Dante rested with Sabino in the hole they had dug with such haste. It would be sufficient, he hoped, to see them alive to the next morning. He drank a little water, seasoned with chlorine and the taste of petrol and blood. It was delicious. He smoked a cigarette and looked out over the ruins around them. Safe, for the moment. The British counterattack would come and probably fiercely. The Folgore men did not have much, but they were blessed with a supply of paper and Dante had equipped himself with all that he needed. The day was quiet. The sun not warm enough. Dante patted his shirt pocket to feel the letters he had written, one for his mother and one for Angelina. In the dim light, he took out the photo and looked into Angelina's eyes. They looked back, clear and calm. A smile skirting her mouth, reaching her eyes. Her hair in a dark crown around her head. He held the photo close to his face, so that it was all he could see. Not Sabino, not the desert, the wire, the tanks, or the guns. He would just have to live.

Sabino said, "It will be all right, my friend."

In the darkness, Dante smiled.

"How do you know this?"

"The hermit told me."

"You received a letter from the hermit? Our hermit?"

"Not a letter. He told me in a dream. He came to your wedding, we both did though we were not invited."

"Ai, Sabin, as if I would have a wedding and not invite you."

"Still, I stood in my uniform with the hermit. Outside the church, we watched. It was very bright."

Dante did not know if there was comfort to be found in his friend's visitation. He was confounded by how little time it took for a man to recover a ridiculous sense of hope. Let the guns stop firing for a few hours. Let him sit, absurdly comfortable in his hole. Look out at the wilderness around him. As if one moment's peace could provide a foundation for the next moment and the next and so on into a future that included a wedding celebration on a sunlit day. He gave himself minutes to imagine a wedding suit, the itch of new wool, the starched shirt, Angelina in a dress to bring out the depth of her eyes. To rest soft against her radiant skin. Such a thought could take him at once far from Africa, far even from his own hunger and fear. He was grateful to Sabino for his dream. Even if it did not come true.

In the morning, they received orders to join the seventh battalion to counterattack against the British foothold in the line. They advanced with the big anti-tank guns, dug in and fired on the British throughout the day. The British retreated, a mere five hundred metres away, to regroup.

They began their counterattack the next day, moving with more and more accuracy toward the position of the battalion commander. Dante could no longer hear Sabino, singing while he fired on the British. The anti-tank guns had deafened him and the shells coming from the British guns had blown holes in his ability to sift through sound for meaning. He moved as quickly as he could, loading and shooting and loading again. The sound of guns and blasting mortars, of Panzers grinding, turning, firing, recoiling, echoed through him, through his chest as though it were hollow. Throughout the night, they fought off the advances of the British.

Dante had lost all sense of futility. Whatever else he was fighting for, he knew he was fighting for his life. Sabino had turned his head with talk of weddings and hermits. It seemed an immensely long time since he had seen Angelina, and it was longer still since he and his friend had scaled the gorge to be blessed by the holy man. His hands ached. Covered in cordite and oil, his fingers stank. Still, he loaded and fired and wondered whose son he was killing. In the waves of shimmering heat, the shapes in the distance were distorted. The artillery was firing, the tanks were moving forward under shellfire. None of them could see the battle. There were the cries of men, the grinding of the tank tracks and the booming of the guns. All was noise, dust, stench, and throbbing silence.

On the night of November second, their battalion was ordered to retreat. They marched fifteen kilometres through the night, after having burned or destroyed every piece of equipment that they could not in haste carry with them. They were out of water, out of food, and worse, out of ammunition. And still the British, in advancing armoured car squadrons, came after them. And with them, lifting over the *wadis* and cliffs, across the pure desert, came the sound of bagpipes, keening. They would not make it to Fuka.

The battalion commander called Dante and Sabino to his jeep, now serving as command headquarters on the run.

"De Angelis, you are fast, eh?"

Dante was unsure how to answer. He remained at attention, exhausted, before his commander. He did not look at Sabino.

"We are finished here. I need runners, two of them, who can get a message to Rommel. I can provision you with a pint of water each and a few rounds that you will need to do yourselves in if you get lost. Do you think you can keep this vehicle in motion long enough to deliver a message?"

"You are surrendering?"

"*Si*. There is nothing for it. Will you go?"

There was no question of accepting the assignment, though surrender, the possibility of a rest, of food and water, took the heart out of them.

They saluted Capitano Bianchini and headed to the tattered vehicle that they would take to Axis command. They drove past the bodies of men, Italians, British, Australians, still holding weapons, dusted in fine sand, ground down to basic elements. Only flesh and blood, only men's bodies to do the work of machines, to take ground. Young men, blood still, hearts calm at last. There might be aerial bombs, artillery barrages, there might be fire and movement, tactics, precise weaponry, but nothing gets done, Dante thought, without the bodies of young men. The ground was thick with them. Sabino drove on, eyes front. Dante looked around him, bitter and hopeless. He did not expect to live.

He heard Sabino's voice.

"It will be all right."

"Are you my mother?"

Sabino didn't answer.

In the lower distance behind them, they could see the men of the Folgore surrendering to the Allies. They had run out of ammunition. Not a single bullet or mortar among them. They stood and walked out of their trenches, heads up, and no white flag. The British stood to meet them.

"*Guarda*, Sabin. Our boys are keeping their weapons."

Sabino pulled to one side of the bare track. He kept the jeep idling to look back over his shoulder. "Ah, *si, onore delle armi*. The honour of arms. Those British, they eat bad food, but they are gracious."

"Gracious in victory, as we must be in defeat."

"I wonder how Herr Rommel is doing."

"I think he is up a creek of shit."

"And we are the oarsmen."

They drove on in silence.

They found headquarters north and just east at El Alamein. Dante delivered the message to the colonel's tent, surprised to find Neumann of old within. He greeted the former Kommandant, saluting him and finding his right hand crushed by the big German.

"Dante, you are alive! I am shocked." Neumann was grinning, pumping Dante's hand up and down as though he expected to draw water. Dante was pleased as well to see him, the man with whom he shared the loss of Marseille.

"Not more shocked than I am, sir."

"How goes it with you?"

Neumann was still shaking his hand.

"Very well, thank you," Dante replied with a straight face.

"Good God, I can't believe you are alive. You have seen some action, I imagine."

Dante did not know what to say. Action. Was that what he had seen?

"Yes, sir."

"You have news of the Folgore?"

"Yes, Kommandant—I mean, *colonello*. Here is the message. General Von Thoma will dine with Montgomery this evening. The Folgore division has surrendered. The British have made headway through the line and will most likely come up on the south flank to attack."

The colonel listened to Dante, his face shadowed in the dim light.

"I will take the message myself to Rommel." Neumann could see Sabino through the flap. "Take your colleague there and retire to the mess. See what you can find to eat."

Dante saluted and walked with Sabino to the mess tent. Men were scattered at tables, bent over the rations before them.

Sabino asked, "What is going to happen?"

"Herr Rommel will mount an attack, provisioned by plenty of oxygen and blood. And we will sing with the angels tomorrow."

Sabino chewed the hard bread.

"*Allora*, we will learn to sip tea." Sabino stuck his small stubby finger out as he lifted his canteen. "We will be dainty, *allora*."

Dante would have laughed. "Have you heard the Führer's order?"

"Ah, *si*. The top-secret command. Everyone knows." The other soldiers in the room nodded, grim. "'El Alamein will be held to the last man—no retreat, not so much as a millimetre.'"

"What happened to Herr Rommel's *Fingerspitzengefuhl*?"

"His what?"

"You know, his sixth sense. He is always ahead of them. Always planning moves ahead as though he knows what the British will do. Now, they are the ones fencing him in, up from the south, pushing us north and east. We'll be floating in the Mediterranean soon."

"If he listens to his Führer, we will not be going anywhere."

The men in the mess looked toward the command tent. Dante knew there would be no one left, not one, if they followed the order. The British were coming on. Unlike the Germans and Italians, the enemy had supplies, petrol, water, food, and ammunition.

"What is left of us here?" Dante asked.

One of the Italians at the next table spoke up. "There are about eighty tanks left. The British are fielding about six hundred. I do not know how the Stukas are doing. Rommel is frantic for fuel. In the meantime, there are seven hundred miles between us and Benghazi. Twelve hundred to the ships at Tripoli. How are your boots holding up?"

Seven hundred miles. Twelve hundred miles. Dante looked at Sabino who was looking down at his feet. They knew that the Germans had transports, trucks, jeeps, a few ragged motorcycles. The Italians would be on foot. The German infantrymen behind them said nothing. That was all right, Dante thought. Perhaps Sabino's instincts were accurate. He could walk. He and Sabino would sing all the way to Tripoli. They would get on ships and go home.

Just as they were about to leave, the Colonel came into the mess. The men rose to attention until he returned their salute.

"The field marshal has determined that a retreat is in order. The Führer has agreed that we are to retire to Benghazi where we are expecting supplies. Men of the Brescia and Bologna divisions, those that are left, will hold positions here to make retreat viable. The rest will mount transports and head east in the morning."

He left the men standing.

Just before dawn, the transports starting heading west. There was one road and every tank, truck, and soldier had to get onto it in order to retreat. The colonel approached Dante who stood straight and saluted, staring into the middle distance. He wondered what Neumann could have to say to him. He knew he was being left behind to hold an impossible position. He could imagine that Neumann was disgusted by the order and as trapped by it as Dante was himself.

He waited for Neumann to speak. This took some moments while the man looked like he was wrestling with a decision.

"I have a truck for you, De Angelis. You will drive it to Tripoli. You are the only one I know who can get it there in one piece."

"A truck, sir."

"Yes."

"I am ordered to stay and fight."

"I am ordering you to take my truck."

"Yes, Colonel."

"It is important to me. I have items in it. Personal items I would not wish to see decorating the halls of Herr Montgomery."

"*Si*, Colonel."

"Take your friend with you. Find your squadron and head out with them. I will meet you at Bardia." The colonel would be departing in his much faster jeep, leaving Dante and Sabino to push along in the truck, which, should the wheels, petrol, and radiator hold out, would grind forward dangerous and slow. An easy target.

"Yes, Colonel." Dante paused. "And thank you, sir."

"Don't thank me, Dante. I am ordering you to fulfill this mission. You will not fail me. You will keep your skin on."

"Yes, sir."

Dante saluted. He would not be left behind to fight. Neither he nor Sabino would have to face the onslaught of crazy Australians and tea-swilling pale British. The colonel had some items. Dante could keep a truck going.

He went to find Sabino.

"*Andiamo*, good fellow. Let us find the road home."

"*Come?*" Sabino was cleaning his rifle. What was his mad friend saying?

"The colonel has ordered me to drive a truck to Bardia and then on to Tripoli. One with some items in it."

"Items?"

"*Si*, he is taking back loot. I am the only one here he can trust. We will keep the wretched gears turning, the wheels moving. We will not end our days in a slit trench, not today anyway. Pack up, man, and let us get moving."

They collected what belongings they had in a matter of minutes. They loaded canteens. Now that the Afrika Korps was in full retreat, the storehouses had been opened and Dante and Sabino took the opportunity to store litres of water and petrol in the truck, and to load some rations for the long trip. Dante's hands shook as he threw what he imagined they might need into the back of the truck. He took care not to examine the cargo. Neumann, he knew, was saving his life. Perhaps for the sake of Marseille. Perhaps for old times' sake. He did not care. These blessed orders would take him out of the way of bullets and mortars and mines. The flies would come with him, but perhaps if the truck ran well and the wheels held, he might outrun even the flies. He hopped in before light had crossed the eastern ridge. When he turned back, he saw Sabino running toward him.

"*Vai, vai, mi'amico.*"

Dante rolled the truck forward and Sabino grabbed the handle and jumped in. He tossed a canvas satchel that clanked between them on the seat.

"What have you got there, gold?"

"Better than gold. *Guarda.*"

Sabino pulled back the flap to reveal two bottles of champagne he had lifted from the officers' supply tent.

"One for each of us."

"For services rendered unto the empire."

Sabino uncorked the bottles with care not to spill one golden drop. He passed one to Dante.

"*Salut*, my friend. To your very good health."

"*Bien sur, mon ami.*"

"You speak French?"

"One must, when drinking champagne."

Sabino shook his head and took a long draught from his bottle. The sun was up, as was the dust of the desert, marking the path behind them. They did not look back.

Dante headed west to join the long line of retreat. Soldiers, transports of all manner, converged at the Halfaya Pass near the border of Egypt and Libya. West of Sidi Barani, east of Bardia, he was well aware that the pass provided the only access point to the coastal road that ran across a five-hundred-foot-high plateau. The entry point was utterly clogged. Dante pulled into the line of transports trying to join the retreat. There were burning trucks and tanks left abandoned at the side of the road, the black smoke rising into the sky offering the RAF strafers precise indications of where to fire when they made their salvoes. There was no doubt of the hazard, but no choice either, unless one were prepared to cross a trigh, a native desert path that might come to a dead end or to a minefield.

Between a slow-moving Panzer and a motorcycle that was limping along behind, he saw an opening. Just as he was about to move into position, a jeep roared up on his left, the engine revving in an unusual waste of fuel. When he turned to look, he saw pointed at him the black muzzle of a Luger and behind it, the ugly face of a German officer. He put his foot on the brake and the clutch and stared.

"I am next."

Dante let him go.

It took him four hours to gain access to the road. In the dust and noise, he struggled to keep calm. He had been imagining release. The sea, a bath, perhaps some food. The colonel had, he thought, moved ahead with the squadron and Dante wondered how he would find him to restore to him the contents of the lorry. He waited, breathing, thinking about Angelina and watching the road. Sabino tapped the bottle he held, whistled lightly, as though he had some pleasant melody in his head. He sipped champagne and kept his eye on the air. They waited, keeping the truck running and worrying about the fuel. Finally, Dante put his foot on the gas pedal and they found a place in the column of slowly fleeing soldiers. El Alamein lay behind them, Fuka, and finally the Halfaya Pass. They would be all right. If they could avoid the Spitfires and Hurricanes. If they had any luck left.

Dante was thinking about luck when smoke began to curl out from under the hood. At first, he thought it was a trick of the light. Perhaps the sand was causing some trouble. He waited for the smouldering to get much better or much worse. Sabino, who had been slouched and drowsing against the window, sat up and nudged his friend.

"I know. I see it."

"Radiator?"

"Most likely."

Sabino opened the truck door and leaned out into the dust of the vehicles ahead of him. On the front of the truck, the radiator cap had come off and Dante was certain that the engine was running dry. He slowed the truck to a walk and Sabino jumped out and hopped onto the front bumper, adding water as they drove. He spilled a great amount of it over the bumps and debris on the road, but he managed to fill it up enough to stop the smoking. As the day ground on, Sabino would resume his position, clinging to the truck with one strong arm and adding liquid to the radiator. When they ran out of water, Sabino improvised and Dante drove the only truck in the long retreat to run on incandescent champagne. They did not have to stop or lose their place in the column. Sabino would climb back into the cab, ever dustier, his white teeth smiling from behind gray lips. It was enough to make Dante laugh in the middle of the desert, in the middle of retreat. He had not felt like a boy for a long time. Sabino raised his eyebrows and a small avalanche of dust shook out of them, down his face, as though part of his skin was sliding off like silk. He laughed.

"You think this is a game, don't you?"

"It might as well be."

"*Ai*, Sabin, what will I do with you?"

"I don't know."

"What was that? Listen, Sabin."

Dante looked over. In the noise of the engines in front and behind, he had not heard the planes coming. But he could hear something beyond the trucks, some register of sound, staccato and penetrating even the din of the retreat. The sound of shots firing. Such noise had become part of the long day of retreat, engines backfiring, blowing up of their own accord. The champagne had made him stupid, careless. Sabino was bleeding, the blood mixing with dust and dirt to form a terrible muck on the side of his face.

Dante shouted, "*Sabin!*"

He jerked the steering wheel and almost went off the road into the soft sand shoulder.

"Watch what you are doing."

Sabino was struggling to breathe.

"Keep driving. Do not stop."

Dante said his friend's name. They were clear, they were home free. There might be other battles, more planes, more deployment, but they were leaving the wretched desert with their skin on. Sabino. You will be all right.

"You said it will be all right. Are you all right?"

He saw the bullet holes in the door. How could he have missed it? What had he been thinking about? Sabino turned his head a bit. He was breathless. Blood streaming, washing away the dust. His shirt was steeped in blood. It pooled on his thigh and poured down. So much of it.

"You are all right. Head wounds, they are the worst for blood."

He waited.

"You banged your head in that plane, remember? Maybe you bashed it again and the old wound opened up."

Sabino managed a smile. Still Dante drove.

"Let me try to find a doctor. There must be a doctor in one of these trucks."

"Who will drive while you look? Keep going, my friend. It will be all right."

Dante was shaking his head. His throat hurt so badly, he put his hand to it. Perhaps he also was bleeding. His face was wet. His neck. His eyes burned. Was it blood?

"Sabino? Talk, my friend. Do not sleep."

"Do you remember that hermit in Spoleto? How we haunted him."

"I remember."

"*Pulirà ogni rottura dai loro occhi e ci no più lungamente sarà tutto il dispiacere.* Remember? 'He will wipe every tear from their eyes and there shall no longer be any sorrow.'"

"No more sorrow, my friend. We're on our way home. Stay awake now and tell me what else you remember."

"That hermit had good food."

"The best food I ever tasted."

Sabino seemed to sink into sleep. When Dante glanced over, he saw Sabino leaning against the door, his eyes closed, his hands limp in his lap.

He reached across to shake him.

"Sabin, wake up! I am not joking with you. Open your eyes. You're missing everything."

Dante kept his hand on Sabino's shoulder, digging in his fingers.

"Wake up! You goddamned fool. We are almost home!"

Dante moved his fingers to Sabino's throat. There was a pulse there still, thready and lean. He did not want to shake him any more. He did not want to weaken him, make him lose more blood. He kept driving.

Sabino released a long breath. His throat did not rattle. He breathed in again and then out.

Dante drove. He managed to close the truck windows. He would at least keep the flies off his friend. He drove at the pace of a snail in sand, which is to say, hardly making headway. He drove with his eyes forward. He sipped champagne and spat it out, warm, into his hands to wipe the filth out of eyes. He had to keep seeing. The haze of dust around him enveloped him. He had scant glimpses of the truck bumper in front of him and he followed it with devotion. If that truck went off the road, so would he. Beside him, Sabino had cooled. He was gone, his death so quiet that Dante had not noticed.

He limped into Bardia with smoke roiling out from under the hood of his truck. He drove it down a lane, at some distance from the squadrons of men reprovisioning for the last legs of the journey. He sat for an hour in the truck with Sabino. He touched his hand and held it. With his left hand, Dante rubbed his own forehead, but he couldn't feel the skin. For a minute, he thought he had no face. Then he realized that his fingers were numb, having clutched the steering wheel for the past several hours. He let go of Sabino and got out.

Dante got a spade out of the back of the truck and under a palm tree, within earshot of the waves coming in at the Gulf of Sidra, he dug a hole. The ground was softer there. Not as rock-filled as the desert across which they had travelled for so many months. He lifted Sabino out onto a tarpaulin that was covering some of the colonel's treasure. Underneath it, he saw a chest and some artifacts that he knew came from Alexandria, mementoes from one of the British officers who had left Fuka or Marsa Matruh, or Sollum even, in a hurry. He did not care.

Dante took what was left of the champagne, tore the tail off his ragged shirt, and rinsed the blood off Sabino's face. The liquid frothed, antiseptic against the wound. Dante looked at the face, the skin dried by the wind and the cold and the irresistible heat. The cheeks sunk deep, collapsed against the architecture of bones. Dante washed off the dust and composed his friend, now gray and cool, wrapped him in the tarpaulin and laid him in the grave. It took hours. He was certain that his colonel would be frantic, wondering what had happened to his booty and why he had wasted his trust on a man such as Dante. A man who would probably find himself once more and finally in the brig, if such a hasty retreat permitted prisons.

He sat with his back aching. His chest and arms sore from the effort of the day. On the ground with his knees bent and his head down, he understood that he had been defeated. Against the only loss he feared, the loss of his better self, such as it was, he could not imagine joining his squadron. He could not get on a transport plane and leave this place. This man.

Sabino, so calm. Telling him to drive.

There were no stars in the sky. He looked up. He did not expect comfort. He did not expect the heavens to declare to him the glory of God. It remained for him to speak.

"I will look after your mother. And your sisters. I will find them all rich husbands. And I will tell all of their noisy, sticky children about their uncle who stole champagne from the German high command. They will hear all the stories."

"I will make sure," he said to the sweet air.

"I will see you at my wedding."

"You and the hermit. He was right about you, at least."

Dante lay on the ground beside the mound of earth. There was the sky above him, certainly. The lack of stars in the November sky he could not explain. What did it matter? He stretched his hand across the grave. In the hand were Sabino's identity tags. He would give them to his friend's mother, he thought. Or he would keep them. Either way, he would tell Sabino's family about their son.

Let there be no rain upon the earth, he thought. Let the earth itself dry to crumbs and disappear among myriad constellations. He cursed the inexorable tide as it broke on the shore close by and then he held his breath for a moment. He fingered his sidearm. Pulled it from the holster and dropped into the sand.

Let the weapons of war perish.

The war had beaten the anger out of Dante more effectively than any blow from his father, any discipline from a superior officer. He saw now that he had come to the Regia as a stripling boy, wet behind the ears and swaggering. In the vacuum created by the desertion of his rage, he found an encroaching consolation. In battles, in dust storms, in the obstinate mundane boredom of the desert, in the gasping blood rush of advance and retreat, Sabino had been with him. The man had not been angry; he had not lost patience. For months, Dante believed that he had been carrying his friend, keeping him alive. Now that Sabino was dead, he knew the truth.

———

In the night, the sand swayed across the surface of the ground, curling and drifting, wiping away Dante's footprints. Beyond the rise, he could make out the curving shore of the bay, the thin tide rolling in and washing the crescent clean. Water and desert looked the same to him, each rocking, and he rocked with them, wrapped his arms around himself like an orphaned child and wished himself for long moments sealed under the surface of one or the other. Sealed and swaying. Sabino was submerged now and perhaps listing. Who was to say whether the depths of the desert did not enjoy their own ebb and flow? The earth itself would hold Sabino now. And he would move with its movements until he vanished.

He woke up, startled. The first drops of rain began to fall at dawn.

Dante looked around him. He thought perhaps a bird had dropped its breakfast on him, but he was wrong. A bird would have made more sense. A flock, perhaps. But this was rain. A sudden rain that would, if it continued, let his fellows get away entirely from the pursuing English. He would have to find the colonel. He would have to return and join the retreat. Dante patted the earth beside him.

"I have planted you, my friend, and now the heavens themselves water you. A November rain, out of order, but there it is."

It would be a conceit to think that God himself was weeping. But he properly should be. The earth had closed over Dante's friend almost as seamlessly as though he had never lived. A world gone while he was not even paying attention. Worried about the radiator, about the dust, about the rubber on the tires. As though a truck could not be replaced. Leaving Sabino to hang out the door and pour liquid into the cap.

The rain came on stronger and Dante returned to the truck. He looked back at the palm tree, marking it in his mind. He did not expect the truck to start, but it did. He found his way back to the main road and then on to the encampment. The rain was coming down thick and fast and the wipers for once cleared water from his view instead of sand. He made it back to the squadron and went to find the colonel. His souvenirs were safe in the truck, if a little damp.

"De Angelis, the colonel was looking for you."

Dante was disinclined to explain. He looked at the man before him in raingear, excited by the strange weather and the possibilities for survival that it opened up.

"I was separated from the squadron at Halfaya. It took me hours to get on the road. Where is the colonel now?"

"He has gone back along the desert road to search for you." The soldier appeared to size him up. Dante had no gear, no weapon, a torn shirt and he was filthy from top to bottom. The soldier shrugged. "Why is the colonel looking for you? Are you his best friend? His cousin?"

"I am nothing to him, but I have some of his belongings."

"Will your transport make it to Tripoli?"

Dante was so tired. He was alone under the awning of the colonel's quarters. Around him, men were scrambling, draining the fuel from ruined tanks and trucks to use for the remaining vehicles that still ran. Others were under hoods and in tanks making sure that they left nothing behind for the British Eighth Army to use. The aide was waiting.

"There is a problem with the radiator."

"Will it make the trip?"

"*Si.*"

Dante would drive the damned truck if it killed him. It would be no more than his due.

All around the staging point, Dante saw soldiers, vehicles, and provisions being mobilized. The storm could not have come at a better time. The limping Axis forces could go into full retreat now that the pursuing Allied forces would be bogged in sudden mud. There would be streams in the desert, rivulets, and waterfalls running through the desert while jeeps and trucks and heavy guns slipped and slid. The trenches would fill with water and the vehicles would sink to their hubcaps. With clouds so low to the ground, with all the electricity of the storm, desperate communiqués for towing, for assistance of any kind, would not get off the ground. The Allies would be well and truly stuck. Rommel's remaining forces were just as wet, the vehicles just as bogged, but they had the advantage of higher ground and the unexpected boon of nasty weather. They were ahead and travelling light, leaving heavy guns and limping trucks behind to escape with their lives. Dante watched as the engineers used the time that the storm had bought them, time to mine the roads and destroy equipment that they could not haul with them.

Dante stayed back with the men laying the mines. They laid a few and then dug up the road and put empty tins in the holes. Then they laid a few more mines. This, he knew, would frustrate and slow the British sappers with their metal sweeps. They would find when they came along tin after empty tin. They would become careless or angry or both and trigger a real mine. The other men were laughing at the excellent joke, but Dante only bent to the task.

He drove the colonel's truck as far as it would go, which is to say not far at all. The radiator gave out completely west of Derna. He had been moving slowly, counting the pebbles, it seemed to him, as he passed. The rain had put an end to the dust clouds through which Dante normally drove, but it did not give much assistance to the cracked radiator. Without a companion to keep the water flowing, the truck groaned and shrieked to an utter stop. He got out and watched the disappearing line of vehicles heading west. It seemed that he was the last man of the Axis forces making his way to Benghazi.

Angelina

Angelina's father had been ordered to supply produce to the German army. Over the last few weeks, since the telegram, he had loaded his small crop and carried it to the market at Visso. The birds were noisy on the way down the mountain. Angelina would have liked to shoot them into silence. Once in Visso, the Obergefreiter, so shiny and well fed, commandeered their cartload of vegetables for his hard-working officers. She and her father had gathered everything they could, winter potatoes, damp-blackened carrots, musty beets, and turnips, only to see it all taken away by laughing young men, both the crop and the cart, and Alfonso, standing alone in the piazza, his cap in his pocket, had not dared to ask for payment. Angelina was with her father when the officer told him at pistol point to bring more.

That last time they had come to Visso, bringing what was left of the stores of the San Placido garden, the man called Helmut had been there. The same man who had taken pictures in San Placido had stood before Alfonso's empty cart and held out his hand for Angelina to shake. When she pretended not to know what he meant, he had reached for her hand and put it in his, then moved her hand up and down, grinning.

"*Ja? Ja? Ja!*"

Angelina did not know where to look. Her strong hand had ached.

With no more food to bring, Angelina came into town with her father to help with the repairs. Father Paolo had spoken to the Visso priest who hired Alfonso to fix the iron gates beside the church. She had walked beside the mule, wrapped in her shawl against the spring cold, in step with the animal's slow front hooves, swaying with him, her hand on his warm back. Her father walked, quiet, beside her. Inside the pack, his tools tolled against each other. She could not explain to him her reluctance to come along. She could not add another worry. Nico was dead. Their mother was sick. Berto was gone for hours at a time. She would not add one more worry. She would look after herself. She had looked after herself.

They were on a side street when her father heard the commotion from the piazza where the church stood, where the gate lay on the ground. Angelina was moving toward the noise. If there was shouting done in San Placido, it was done behind thick walls and closed shutters. She had not ever heard sounds like those coming from the square. She could not take in the evidence of her own ears. Around the corner, she would see with her own eyes what exactly was going on. Alfonso stepped quickly forward and put one of his great hands on her shoulder.

Ferma!

She stopped. Alfonso pulled her back down the narrow street and into an alcove. They were close enough to hear the soldiers shouting at civilians with their shopping bags and worn purses, the grandfathers and grandmothers and the children. They moved just to the left where they could see the piazza through the small gap between buildings. The German soldiers stopped everyone who walked by. A dead officer lay stretched out on a makeshift gurney, two chairs from the café facing each at the head and foot and one in the middle underneath the torso. His brother soldiers had not covered his body, not even his bloodied face, and the quiet people of Visso kept their eyes down out of scrupulous respect for the dead and out of a terrible fear.

The German officers clustered in the piazza, facing the *gelateria* and the *pasticceria*, across from the leather goods store. They had taken out their weapons and lined up ten Italians.

One of the officers was screaming as he walked around the ten, shouting at all the people. Angelina tried to listen to the translator whose voice shook as he echoed the words of the furious officer.

A German soldier had been found dead in the tall brush under one of the bridges that crossed the narrow river that ran through the town. It appeared that he had been hit, like Goliath, by a rough stone, a direct hit to the temple. The stone, bloodied, had been found beside him in the grass. The Führer's orders were standard and clear. Ten for one. A woman fainted.

Angelina gripped the stone pillar behind her. She knew that German's face. Ten for one. It could not be. She stepped forward. She would not let those people die because of her. She stepped forward and felt sturdy hands on her shoulders snatch her back. Her father held her, pressed her face into his shoulder. Angelina pushed him away. She had to stop this. It would be unbearable. She fought against her father, the two of them dead silent and holding their breath.

Alfonso looked at her as though she were mad.

The Germans were methodical. They stood so straight. Angelina could see them, pressed as she was by her father. They looked so proud, sure of their orders and their place on the cobblestones of the town. They spat gutturals at the confused and frightened people. From her hiding place, Angelina could see them, the two men in charge extending their hands, their fingers clamping onto the forearms of passersby, rippling the fabric of a woman's best shawl, the one she might wear into town to show she was a person worthy of respect. The Germans were not afraid. They were not slow or uncertain. The soldiers formed a parallel line before the Italians, their military backs to the statue of the Blessed Lady with her blue cloak and her open arms. There was no time for begging. Before they understood what was about to happen, what kind of reprimand they faced, the Italians were dead on the ground. Bullets slammed against the cars and carts parked around the square. The people, out in the sun and doing a little shopping, were dead, left in a mound of shabby brown clothes. The soldiers ordered those dumbstruck and standing near to clean up the mess.

Angelina leaned her face against the stone wall. She had seen blood before. Last night, she had washed it out of her clothes, seen the mountain water turn pink and then clear again under the dim moon. She knew about blood. She had killed her family's chickens and rabbits and helped her father with butchering the cows. She knew Dante was at war somewhere in the frayed world, in places she could not and did not imagine when she looked out of her window at night and saw only her own reflection in the glass. And Nico, poor Nico whom she could not bear to think about. In Rome, she had seen the soldiers on parade. She had even remained with thousands of others in the Piazza Venezia listening to Mussolini, watching him so calmly. But here in Visso, she had seen an awful thing. A violence that contaminated the street with blood and the body itself with the certainty of hell, not distant but close, around the corner. When she had thought of the war, she imagined only lines of men all dressed in the same clothes and firing on each other without much precision across an ill-defined distance. She had not imagined the battle would be drawn and engaged down the road from her home among people whose faces she recognized and whose voices she knew.

People began to move in the square. Her father left her to join them. Angelina collapsed to the ground. She was alive. And wretched. She could not imagine standing again. Her legs shook. She leaned over and vomited, wiping her mouth and nose and eyes on the hem of her skirt. It could not be possible that such a thing had just happened. She turned to look into the piazza. She saw the mayor of Visso come out of his office to see about the commotion. Angelina watched as the man stumbled on the step in his haste to return to the safety of the building. He disappeared behind the door.

Along with some of the others, Angelina saw her father remove his own coat and cover the bodies of friends and strangers. German soldiers still stood with rifles drawn while her father and the others bent below the hard end of the machine guns and lifted the victims. They stood, the pairs of old men, straining against the weight and unsure of what to do next. One by one, the people stepped forward from shops and alcoves to direct their steps, to take the dead home to be washed and mourned and buried.

She looked across the street at the high wall opposite her. There was a poster, a soldier in uniform, helmeted, gun resting over his back, muzzle pointing up. There was a dark shadow on his right shoulder and below his waist, darkness. Only the top of his sidearm was visible. He was smiling, blue eyes and a square jaw, his left hand over his heart, his right arm outstretched and his hand open. The caption read, "*La Germania é veramente vostra amica.*"

Germany is truly your friend.

Concealed within the alcove, she kept her eyes away from the piazza. Busy ants at her feet continued untroubled. She would not harm them. Of all the possibilities for the morning, this one, this execution of her neighbours, was not one she could have imagined. She leaned against the wall while her father helped to arrange the final rest of the new dead. People who happened to have an errand to run, a *nonna* to visit, perhaps they wanted a quick taste of the prosciutto for which Visso is so famous.

Angelina and her father left town, but not by the road. They climbed up the hillside until they were far enough away so that Visso was small beneath them. She could barely walk. Her father stopped and put his arm around her waist. They limped together up the path, their stomachs turning and queasy. Angelina clamped her teeth against the rising sickness, the bile encroaching on her tongue. Those people, familiar to her in one way or another, had stood, bags and purses and newspapers in hands. She would stand, too. Until she died, herself. She reached a stronger arm around her papa. Whispered to him. She could not say, "It will be all right." It would never be all right. They moved through the dusk back home to tell their neighbours that misfortune was headed their way.

That night the candles were lit behind drawn curtains. Angelina went for Father Paolo, who already knew what had happened. He had been through the village, warning the people to prepare. To hide thoroughly what they needed and to keep themselves hidden if necessary. Though the war rationed meat and milk and coffee in other parts of the world, the people in San Placido had not yet suffered any severe shortage of food or wine. They looked after themselves, harvesting their gardens, milking, collecting eggs, milling small quantities of wheat, and making thick soups out of the root vegetables they had stored beneath the floorboards. The Father told them what Angelina had seen. Told them that their enemies were coming. Angelina knew for sure that in spite of the alliances of the clown, the *buffo*, Mussolini, not one person in San Placido believed that to host a *Tedesco,* a German, was to host a friend. The curtains were drawn against them and the candles were lit so that the men and women and children of San Placido could in privacy find places to hide their food and to hide themselves. Solid walls moved, revealing shelves of preserves. In the cool caves at the back of the garden, they moved stores of bread and aging cheese and wine. They moved blankets in to make the space comfortable for the young women and children and they waited until noon the next day for the sound of the soldiers.

Questo was at the doorway, up on all fours, his hackles up, nose curled and ready to strike. Dead quiet, he stood guard against something. Angelina did not know what it was that he could smell. Perhaps the rising stench of men in ribboned uniforms, smoking foreign cigarettes in the square and spitting with impunity on the church steps. Not in San Placido, but down the mountain in Visso. After what she had seen today, she knew the worst was not over. The Germans would come up the path and pick the fruit of the village, whatever they had harvested, and wherever it had been concealed. But she knew it was not only provisions they would look for.

Dante

Dante pulled the broken body of the British pilot from the fuselage. He covered it with the parachute he had unpacked from behind the young enemy. He took the boy's tags and lowered the body into the slim and paltry grave he had carved in the rubble and sand. The propeller came away from the nose with fortunate ease and Dante used it as a makeshift marker. It was enough.

Dante went back to his truck, which performed the miracle of starting up right away. He did not get very far before he heard the snap and twang of the broken fan belt hitting the hood. He kept going when the steam rose from the cap, when it billowed out from under the hood. He kept going until the engine seized, the block cracked. He stopped, an abrupt and utter end to his journey.

Dante had to make it to the main line of retreat. He should never have left it. He walked as far as he could and then tried to rest for a moment. Dante was staring, waiting for a truck, a stray as his own had been, to pick him up, maybe get him on a transport out of this place. He tried to make the time pass. He did not wish to think about Sabino. Instead, he considered the things that he had seen, the Bedouin, their spitting camels. The Italians and their gardens, cultivations that his officers had planted and kept. He could not now imagine the surfeit of water, the riches of liquid it would take to keep lettuces alive in Tobruk.

They had set their minds to some crazy tasks, Dante thought. Here he was now, in the middle of the desert, walking toward the Duce's monument, the Arco dei Fileni. Sitting there, not in Paris or Rome, where it appeared to belong, but rather on the border of Cyrenaica and Tripolitana in the middle of the frontier. Near the bottom of the arch in the shadow as Dante passed through, he saw that someone had taken his knife to carve the words, "*Vive* Mussolini." He thought that Mussolini would live. The damnable always endure. Another thug would be along after the Duce was gone, flying one flag or another. Dante took out his own knife and bent to the stone.

Let Mussolini live. In Dante's memory, another name would endure.

He stood up, slow and weary. Walked away from the monument with its new epitaph:

Vive anche Sabino.

Even before he was sent to Sidi Barani, to Bardia, and to El Alamein, before he spent months living on half-rotten potatoes and warm, rationed water, his features were lean and sculpted. He knew he had the physique of a scholar, not a man to push much weight around. He knew that he looked as though he should be in a library, lifting books off shelves, annotating cards and replacing the sources in perfect alignment with the volumes on either side. But he had survived the worst that had been cast upon him to endure. He could move across the desert and through the heat and cold with grace. He could not account for his own survival. He wished he were walking in the gardens of the Villa Medici at the top of the Spanish Steps. He would go again, at least in his mind, with Angelina. He smiled to think of it. The two of them, with icy *gelati* and shy posture, glancing more at the earth than at each other. Such wasted time. He ought to have stared into her face. Why not? It was a beautiful face. He wished he had provoked more conversation, heard her voice so that it stayed with him through the years of war. He could hear it sometimes, catch a whisper of expression in the letters that she wrote, but he longed for the sound itself to break on his ear and against his chest, to break him and make him whole. Gentling him. Piercing him to perfect stillness. A voice he would not argue with, a face that would enlarge him for any task at hand.

Dante walked away. He put metres and kilometres between his sore body and the stone monument. Between himself and the wreckage behind him. Dante had seen men leaving the battlefield, their pockets full of the small belongings of the dead, items pulled from the pockets of the loose uniforms of enemy soldiers. Of all the redundancies of war, this seemed the most glaring to him. As though the men around him did not comprehend that they too had pockets, that they too were unsafe, facing bullets and mines every step of the long retreat, that their bodies, under the right circumstances, would expand and collapse in the heat and cool of the sand and that their pockets, too, would be sifted in their turn. Dante understood that these tags, documents, letters might offer some slim strand of intelligence, but this pushing and pulling at the dead sickened him and, truth be told, frightened him. He turned away to see a man's hand extended toward him, black and grasping. It could not be the hand of a living man and yet it moved. He stepped closer and realized that the hand was covered in a moving mass of maggots, making it appear to close in on itself, having reached toward nothing at all. As he walked by, the flies rose in a cloud from the corpse and settled on him. He moved faster.

The sand shifts, as everyone knows, and it is more that one colour. It is green and grey and brown and sometimes the colour of roses. Sometimes the sand is black and it is always in motion. It shifts and turns and forms light and shadow where no shadow could possibly be. Dante walked, trying to orient himself against the stars of night and the shadow he cast in the dawn. He had lost his hat and the cold sun scuttled his thinking. He fell to his knees and rested with his eyes closed. He only had to keep walking west and north and someone would find him. If he stopped, he would die. He pushed himself to his feet and walked some more. He had no voice left with which to talk to himself, to reassure himself of his sanity. He thought about his home. About his father. The drills he had endured. He spoke inside his mind.

"Matteo Gattaponi. How long? A thousand feet long. What year?"

He could not recall.

He took a few steps and stopped.

"Fourteenth century. That's as close as I can come."

"Who? The Medicis, the Barbarossas, the Borgias, the Aldobandinis and the Viscontis —" He paused. "And Dante and Sabino. We are the famous people who crossed the Ponte della Torre in Spoleto, Italy."

The sun burned, but he was cold. Dante wrapped his arms around his body as he walked.

"*Grazie*, Papa."

Dante walked and squinted against the light. A city appeared in the middle distance with towers and minarets, flags held firm by the breeze. He did not want to blink for fear that he would lose the only vision of hope in all the miles he had crossed. The desert rose up and blazed before his eyes, surrounding him, entering him and lighting him up from inside, until he himself was a pillar of light moving toward light. Who was making all this sand? Was God himself so fascinated? Lichens, crystals, streams, rivers, lakes, windblown sand, skeletons, rocks ground by time and distance, across continents and millennia. In school, the year before the fascists came, he had read the English poets, Blake among them. Now, in the desert, Dante could have told him he was right. He could see a world, he could hold infinity in the palm of his hand, it seemed to him, and for a few terrible moments, he lost his fear.

He wished Sabino were with him. He would say, *Ai*, Sabin, what terrible things we will have to remember.

He could hear Sabino's quiet voice in his ear. It would be much more terrible, my friend, if we were to forget.

Dante sat down on the slipping ground. He was dizzy so that it felt to him that the earth itself was rocking him to sleep. He did not have one single decision to make. He felt just as he had when he was recovering in his bedroom from typhus. Dante imagined that he could see the doorway, his father's frame filling it. He was at rest. The day would unfold. He could go to sleep. He went to lay down his weapon and realized that it was already gone. He had already dropped it. He closed his eyes, tranquil at last.

Angelina

Without telling her family, Angelina had come down into Visso the evening before she and her father witnessed the murder of the ten people in the town. She had been in the garden in the chill afternoon, leaves earth-fragrant and wet under her feet after the long winter. Spring was coming home to San Placido, but she had not heard from Dante for a long time. She did not know if somehow she would be told if he were dead or wounded. She had written him every week letters that she now wondered about. Perhaps he had grown tired of receiving them. There had been nothing in any of his letters to her that would suggest such fatigue. It must be the irregularities of the mail. She would have to wait, uninformed and alone. In her pocket she carried his last letter. She read it again on the bench in the infringing dusk.

She read endearments. *Carina, inamorata, bellissima. Aspetto qui.* I am waiting here until I can come to you. Angelina was warm in the cold air. Dear, beloved, and beautiful. She would have laughed to think of herself this way. But words on paper, words written in the hand of Dante, carried weight with her. In Rome, she had felt his hand on her elbow. Met his gaze. She wanted suddenly and urgently to taste again the hot milk with chocolate that she had sipped with

Dante. He would have taken her hand, she would have let him. They had walked into the café and stood at the bar. She rested her hands on the polished wood and waited, shy. Dante ordered the sweet chocolate and they took it to a table at the window. It seemed a long road from her village to that café.

Now, back in San Placido with Dante far away, she felt bereft of the one thing she had not even known she wanted. What if he did not come home? Angelina would write him a letter this very night. She would tell him that he must come home. He must be careful. She would write him tonight. But first, she would take the money she kept in a drawer, just a few lire would do, and she would go for a walk into Visso and drink that chocolate and milk together. It would ease the ache she felt. She would be quick.

After the main road into the town, she circled back behind the piazza. She did not want to draw attention to herself or to her unusual extravagance. Along the Via Castelsantangelo, the German, Helmut, addressed her from the black shadow of a doorway.

"Fraulein."

Angelina kept her head down and stretched out her long legs, moving toward the lights in the piazza. The soldier followed her. He called to her again in the strange language, but she did not slow down. He did not raise his voice. The Germans always raised their voices when there was real trouble. Maybe he needed to light a cigarette, maybe he wanted directions. He would find what he wanted somewhere else. She was nearly at the bridge when he caught her by the shoulder. His fingers dug in and the quick bruising pain shocked her. She tried to shake him off and run, but he had her, and with both hands, held and turned her.

"*Piacere*," she said, and then, "*Aspetta*," as though she could ask him to wait. Wait for what?

There was no one. In the middle of town, she could hear the music coming from the bars. Off the stones of the square and the buildings around it, voices, laughter reverberated.

She pushed at him, her elbows pinned. She said, "*Piacere*," please. "You cannot want to do this."

The man, drunk, clutched at Angelina. He was big. A gun

strapped to his back. A utility belt that was digging into her. He crushed her against him.

She scratched at his face, tried to meet his eye.

See me, she wanted to say. Look at me.

He would not look.

He pushed his blunt nose and wet lips and tongue and teeth into her neck.

"*Ja, ja.*"

He sounded like a monstrous infant repeating meaningless sounds, tonguing at skin. Hair rose on her arm, bile in her throat. She turned and twisted but he had her, in strong terrible arms, he pinned her and then tripped her and she thrashed on wet grass. Screaming would bring more of them. Give them a show. She would not. He pressed a massive hand over her mouth and nose and she lost breath. She went limp. She would turn to air, disappear from under him, be far away and he would not even know.

She was abruptly calm.

He straddled her and pushed her skirt higher on her thighs and he said his "*ja, ja,*" again.

Fate was working in his favour, he smiled, his face just above hers, stinking.

He could not with one hand get his trousers undone. She could feel between his legs all his vulnerability hardening to a centre. Angelina found purchase. Shifted her hip quickly and shot her knee up into his groin. She squirmed out from under him as he collapsed in what she hoped was magnificent pain. She pushed and rose and grabbed with both hands a rock beside the stream.

Angelina swung the rock down, swift and keen, on his sallow temple, once and then twice, and he was still. His skull was splintered and the white underneath bursting out. She sat down beside the body, listening to the music from the square. Her hands shook. She folded them on her lap. Beside her, the German Helmut's hand still reached out toward her. She would have liked to push it away. She had touched dead things before. Blood fell out of the wound, no longer pushed out by any heartbeat, it only seeped and stained the ground, moving toward Angelina. She must collect herself. In his hand, he held a fragment of her blouse. She took it away and put it in her pocket.

Angelina hauled him toward the stream. She pulled him across the mud and leaves. She kept stopping. He was so heavy. Dead weight. She put the bloody rock underneath his head. Maybe they would think he fell and struck his head. Maybe the other soldiers would know him for a drunkard and a coward and be relieved.

She tied up the torn fabric of her blouse across her chest. She could sew it or patch it. The backs of her thighs were scraped. Her neck bruised with thick fingers. She would wear a scarf tonight and claim to be coming down with a cold. She would not have hot chocolate. She would not think about Dante. No one would know, she thought. She went home in the dark, listening to the sound of her heart, tripling beats against her chest. She kept her hand over it, as though to keep it in.

That night she lay in her narrow bed curled against her fear. She was finally tipping into sleep when she woke to cold consciousness.

What if the restless Anselmina had seen her leave? And worse. What if she had seen her return?

Dante

Into his dream, a dream of water and light, of trees and sweet fruit, a dream that he had not known was a dream, came the grinding sound of an engine. He lay in the sand, indistinguishable from it. In his hand, he held Sabino's dog tags. The sun had bounced off the tags and into the eyes of the driver of one of the last Italian trucks in the retreat. Weary infantrymen fell out of the rear of the truck and hoisted Dante in as though he were cargo. And none too precious, at that. He lay still while the truck ground west toward Tripoli. The men spared a little water and Dante gradually came to consciousness. They told him where he was and where they were headed. He lay back, exhausted.

The colonel's treasure was lost, left behind in the truck for the British to find. There was nothing among the canvas-covered loot that Dante wanted. No souvenir or memento of this tour of duty would come home with him, should he make it home. Other soldiers had collected British helmets or weapons, some had insignia or even whole uniforms tucked away in their kit. Dante did not think about how they would have come by these. As the clouds above him, laggard and slow, moved east, the jerk forward and back as the truck geared down and up came to be a comfort to him and he fell asleep.

At Tripoli, he rejoined the 208th squadron. The colonel had disappeared, probably captured by the British and taking tea with the officers by now. At least, Dante hoped so. The colonel had saved his life with that truck. He had almost saved Sabino. In the streets of Tripoli, Dante could not get his bearings. The city was swarming with Germans and Italians mustering themselves for deployment to Italy or to other fronts of war. Everywhere he looked, on the docks and among the squads of men, Dante saw supplies of all kinds, armaments, ammunition, tanks, planes, fuel, and fresh soldiers. He had come from the front with the fabric of his uniform worn away from his skin, blown almost to dust by extremes of weather and sorrow. There were new faces, crisp kit and lustrous gun metal. Dante suffered the certainty of his own shabbiness. The leather of his boots had cracked in the heat and cold. He no longer bothered to empty the sand out of them. He was out of place among the crowds of soldiers heading east in the Afrika Korps's new thrust. Rommel must finally have got the supplies he needed. It seemed to Dante that they had come too late. He could not imagine heading back to Alamein with anything but a waning heart. The moment for victory had been lost and he could not say why, nor could he now draw any conclusion about whether this was good or bad.

Let the British have North Africa, he thought, and let me go home.

Dante could not bear to count the cost. He could smell coffee, onions and burning oil, cinnamon, and garlic. All of it nauseating on his hollow stomach. He left the busier streets and found his way to the shore. Walking along the coast road toward the port, he took a last look at the desert beyond the civilized, crowded streets of Tripoli, at the deepening blue of the evening sky, and the rocking Mediterranean. He sat under a palm, his back against the rough trunk. He was prepared to grieve; he would weep here for Sabino. He would reassert his promises. He would rage against God, so cold and brutal. He would pound the earth and moan and tear at his shirt. All was lost and it was time he said so out loud. Dante was still, preparing for the deluge of feeling to overwhelm him. He waited, looking out over the sea. The tide lapped in and eased out. The palm behind him swayed, delicate in the breeze.

He yawned, stretching his jaws until he heard them crack, so tired it took moments for him to realize that a rock was pressing into his backside. Dante shifted, only to move himself onto another larger stone. He turned and knelt, smoothing a proper seat in the sand, and composed himself again to weep. Dante felt his insides roil. He could not recall the last time he had eaten. He should find his way back to a restaurant or find the mess once he got to the dock. That his appetite should foist itself upon this memorial moment insulted him. He looked out at the sea. His stomach made a noise, loud and percussive. A fly bit his cheek and he slapped his face. Too hard. Blood spattered across his nose. Dante lifted the tail of his shirt to wipe the blood off, but the fabric, worn by months in sun and sand, tore away into his hand. In the still evening, the sound of the tearing fabric was huge and he looked around to see if anyone was around him, if anyone heard the noise.

His undershirt was like a net and his skin gleamed through the holes. The stark white of his belly looked like a graft from another man's body. Dante placed his brown arm against it to see the contradictions in his own skin. His nose hurt. Life, while his breath moved in and out, compelled notice. He heard night birds squawking in the high palms. The tide moved out leaving a phosphorescent froth behind it. He watched the ocean for a long time, his limbs slack. In his hand, he held the calm sand, turned it over from his palm to the back of his hand, felt it trickle away. The moon rose. Dante sat, hungry and frayed, breathing deeply and suddenly, inordinately, content. He turned his head to smile at Sabino who was not beside him.

Angelina

In the switchbacks up to San Placido, she could hear the German soldiers' motorcycles whining. Angelina could see the smoke seeping out their engines. It looked like even the powerful German machines were having difficulty managing the inclines. Some of the soldiers had given up and were making their way to the village on foot. Angelina knew what was coming. The Visso priest had clambered up the mountain before dawn to warn Father Paolo, who told the Martinellis, who told the Montefiores who told Alfonso. Angelina sat in the dark kitchen with her father, taking in the news. She could not stand, not even when her father asked her to make some coffee for the Father, who fortunately declined.

The Germans were looking for partisans, particularly the ones who had killed the soldier in Visso. There was worse news. They seemed to believe that the men responsible for the death of the German in Visso were part of the same band that was responsible for the Via Rassela attack in Rome. According to the priest, they had turned Visso upside down looking for the guilty parties, but they had come out empty-handed. Now, they were moving up the mountain.

Angelina turned her face away. Let him think she was overcome, horrified or frightened. She was, but there was more. Anselmina might have seen. She might speak. The number of breaths left to Angelina might be numbered in the hundreds, but she felt ready. She was exhilarated. Pleased, to think of herself as a partisan. She was in the war, too, now. A soldier who would most likely die a soldier's death. She had hoped to see Dante again. To see him every day for the rest of her life. She had believed that he was the vulnerable one, the one whose life lay exposed to wounds and looming death. She had been frightened for two days and now she turned away from the grim news brought by the priest, turned to walk down the hill before the soldiers arrived. She would go to the small church. She would light a candle in the nave for Dante and say a prayer.

"Let there be courage here today."

Angelina had read with her father the report of the assault by partisans on the SS troops in the Via Rassela. They set bombs to go off during the daily march in the narrow street. Angelina had strolled up that street before. It was tucked behind the Fontana di Trevi and not far from the Piazza Venezia. The bombs went off at 3:45 among the 156 Germans. Thirty officers died. There was gunfire and a massacre of Italians afterward. Ten Italians for each German. Angelina should have known that the wretched Helmut's death would exact the same price in Visso, so close to home.

Father Paolo had come to the house on a pastoral visit. Angelina was already in bed, but she could hear his voice and her father's easily.

Father Paolo said, "There are no crematoriums in Rome. No way to handle three hundred dead at once."

Angelina's father said over again, "My God, my God."

"They took them, the prisoners, the ones who had violated curfew, the ones visiting the ones who had stayed out too late, they took them all to the caves."

Angelina had gone to see the caves on a day off when she lived in Rome. She had stepped into them and shivered. She had leaned against the wall of the labyrinth and felt the encroachment of the cold into her hand and wrist and arm.

Peopled already with centuries of the dead, the catacombs would provide the perfect place to execute vengeance.

Father Paolo knew details. Angelina couldn't breathe, listening.

"Even Germans have trouble killing that many people at once. The Kommandant, Kappler, gave them cognac to make it easier."

"My God, cognac. No. Father. No."

"They could not aim properly. They stacked them up, the living upon the warm dead and shot legs and arms, and finally chests."

Angelina heard her father's chair scrape across the tile. She could hear the wineglass on the table and the liquid pouring in. Two glasses.

"They mined the entrance of the caves. Brought down the roof upon the bodies."

She wanted her father to ask, "How do you know these things? How do you know?"

But he didn't ask. Really, he didn't have to ask. The shadows she had seen in the night, dark men in dark clothes moving from tree to tree until they disappeared around the bend that led to the San Placido garden. One man in a skirted cassock leading the way.

She could hear truck engines on the mountainside. Transports with soldiers. Questo was already circling at the front of the house. Growling and whining. Then he did the unimaginable. He crossed the threshold of the house to Angelina's side and pasted himself to her thigh.

"*Que fai, cane?* What are you doing, dog? Everybody knows that dogs are not allowed in the house. Out you go. It is just a few trucks coming. A few hungry Germans. Whose hunger will have to go unsatisfied. Out, Questo."

She would not think about the one she had sent to hell. The blouse was long gone, irreparable and burned with the sticks and leaves cluttering the garden. She took one of her mother's out of the closet. Asked, may I have this, mamma. Even the patches are shredding on my blue one. She wore a slack brown blouse now, as everyone in the village noted.

She would not feel guilty.

"I killed as one would kill a wild dog. Better for everybody."

Questo looked at her, head tilted, ears up.

"Forgive me, dog. I meant as one would kill a wild pig."

There was no blood on her hands. She did not rinse them off at the cistern. She was clean.

When the dog did not move, Angelina grasped the thick fur at the back of his neck and tried to haul him toward the door. His nails dug into the wood floor, deeply scratching the planks. He wrestled his head away from her grasp and ran up the narrow stairs. When she climbed them herself, she could not see the dog anywhere. She had left the window open. Surely the foolish dog had not jumped? She leaned out onto the valley side but could see no sign of the beast. She did see the fog of dust trailing behind two German transports and a couple of motorcycles. Angelina ran downstairs. Her father was gone for the day, gone to the distant fields to find wood to sell to the richer houses in the town. Without crops, without ironwork to do, he was trying to make a bit of money as a woodsman.

Angelina closed the front door. She could still hear the vehicles grinding up the mountainside. Out the kitchen window, she could see them just at the last switchback, steam coming out of the radiators. Even the motorcycles could not gear down any more. The soldiers left the transports where they stopped, formed ranks, and marched up the lane.

Angelina could see for herself that there was no one in sight. This seemed to halt the Germans as they looked around from door to window trying to see someone. Only Questo, descended from the upper floor where he had been hiding, prowled the threshold of Angelina's house, all his hackles raised. She was afraid he would launch himself and be shot where he stood. She tried to whisper to him, as though he could hear. *Calma, calma.* The dog sat, his backside against the door, growling low in his long throat.

A few of the *vecchietti* were sitting, legs spread and feet planted in the dust, on the low walls beside their houses. Angelina watched them look at the soldiers as though they were insects, as though the old ones of San Placido did not want to miss the sight of sweating, perturbed Germans.

One of the officers shouted. "Where has everyone gone?"

The old ones sat. One of them, Piero, a grand-uncle of Signora Montefiore, leaned over and spat. The old ones, Angelina knew from experience, could pretend deafness very well. But she was worried that the angry man might swing his rifle around and crack a head or two to get them to listen. If they were looking for partisans, they would be frustrated by these old men.

One of the soldiers took aim at Questo, who had left the doorway and was pacing in the middle of the street beside Angelina's house. The soldiers were mostly on foot and the dog did not seem provoked to attack. But he was circling, head low, tail still. Angelina watched as Old Corrado bowed his head and waited for the worst. Then Piero beside him set his cane in the dirt. He was going to shift his weight to stand. Angelina would have to go out. She would have to distract the soldiers. She saw Corrado put his hand out as though to say, *non parla, amico, non parla per questo cane*. Do not speak for this dog and lose your own life.

The soldier lost interest in Questo who trotted away into the bushes.

German officers came up the path, shouting, in spite of their breathlessness, ordering the citizens out of their homes. Angelina wished her father was there. But maybe better that he was not. Upstairs her mother slept, full of morphine these days, and not in pain, at least. Berto was out with her father, thank God. If he were here, he would surely act the fool and get them all thrown into prison or worse.

She listened to the Germans shouting. Sounds never heard in the village before, sounds of "*Raus*" and "*Schnell*," spluttering out of the mouths of these overheated men. She would not be able to hide in the kitchen. They would come for her with their red faces. In the high sun, she could not possibly slip away. In San Placido, none of the houses had rear doors. This seemed a terrible oversight now. Angelina watched as the *vecchietti* stepped slowly with their canes and showed themselves willing to comply with orders they barely understood and whose outcome seemed dubious. They stepped off their benches at the sunny side of the church wall and moved slowly to San Placido's centre. Angelina, along with her neighbours, walked into the sunlight.

Dante

He sat *against the tree*, limp and languid. If Dante had any strength to comment to thin air, he would have expressed his own surprise at being alive. The bark of the palm scratched an old itch between his shoulders. He rested his hand in the sand as though offering a blessing. The soreness in his chest, across his shoulders, the soreness of burying Sabino gave him comfort. He had carried the weight of loss and now his body properly ached. Sitting at the base of the palm in the deepening night, he wished to lay the burden down. To cast his care somewhere where it would be kept safe. The ground sustained him. The tree, the sand, the air. He rested, held himself with his own folded arms and thanked the unknown God for having known Sabino.

Dante left the palm tree and took a last look back. He followed the tangle of dusty streets back to the hangars at Tripoli. He found some provisions, indeed, more than he could manage. The Führer and Mussolini had opened the larder and provided the men in Tripoli, maybe everywhere in North Africa, with all that they needed now that it looked like it was too late. He found a seat and with his plate full of pasta and his arms full of fruit, he commenced to break his fast to the point of sickness. He had water and a ration of wine to drink.

The conversation of his fellow soldiers moved around him, the familiar language rocked him, the words of those living and breathing ones in communion. The talk was all about retreat, deployment to Sicily. They were getting out. They had pulled back from hell and they would be heading somewhere else, somewhere there might be trees and fresh rain, the scent of rubbed oregano or warm gorgonzola. This started a cheese-naming contest in the mess.

One said, "Friulano."

"Bel Paese."

"Asiago."

"Fontina."

More and more men joined the circle. They sat back with their legs outstretched. There was silence for a moment.

"Mascarpone."

"That's easy. *Va bene*. Mozzarella."

"Ah, mozzarella. Parmigiano reggiano."

"That's two!"

"Pecorino."

Dante closed his eyes on the game. He had dreams of cheese. He had cheese and warm bread visions while he sat on a bench and leaned against one of the posts. His eyes flickered closed and he slept.

Dante woke up with a bang. The soldiers around him had risen quietly and tipped the bench. He was on the ground and the boys around him were having a good laugh. It was the sort of act that would have affronted his dignity, on his ass on the earth floor of the mess, he would have burned, humiliated. He looked up at the faces around him, some men he recognized, some were strange to him, but they all had the withered look of those who had spent long days burning and freezing, underfed, dehydrated, and frightened. To see them in pain with mirth and full stomachs, gasping for air at their fine joke was a pleasure. One Sabino would have enjoyed even while he helped Dante to rise.

"You men are geniuses of comedy, I see. *Va bene, ragazzi. Adesso andiamo a casa.*" That's fine, boys. And now, let us go home.

They boarded the transport for Italy. Dante was deployed first to Varese on the Swiss border to assist with the reorganization of men and materials. The new planes came, the Reggiane 2000 planes with the eighteen-cylinder motors. They were then flown across Sicily and the south of Italy to the coastal town of Taranta to meet the Allied invasion.

Keeping the planes in the air was more difficult in Taranta than anywhere in North Africa. They were there battling against the American fleet, American fighters, and American carpet bombing. He had thought he was out of the frying pan of North Africa, as indeed he was, but Dante found himself in the full fire of the American invasion. The Germans were trying to stand firm, but the attack came on too many fronts. Finally, they heard the retreat. Kesselring gave the order to evacuate Taranta. Dante would head north with his unit, falling back as the German units laid mines and bombs.

Dante asked what was going on. He could see the sense in destroying equipment in the desert, but his fellow-soldiers were mining homes.

The fellow turned. "We destroy Taranta. There must be nothing left to assist the Americans. No food, no water. No sanitation."

Dante asked about the residents and the German infantryman pointed to the sign posted on the street.

The order invited any Italians who wished to leave the town, which, the paper stated, because of the exigencies of war, must be destroyed. The town was to be evacuated by noon and its residents were restricted to taking along only necessary items of clothing. Dante read the order. They were directed toward Suloma by the main road. Anyone who departed into the hills or along back roads would be considered a member of the partisans and would be subject to the treatment established by German laws of war. Which, Dante knew, meant no law at all. Kesselring was fighting for his life, and fighting tooth and nail. Dante spent enough time in and around Taranta to see what the German friends of Italy were doing to the countryside. He had heard, as well, rumours of houses bombed or grenaded with the inhabitants, generations of families from very old to very young, locked inside. Of those who survived being shot before they could reach any kind of safety.

He did not know what he could do, nor did he understand what he had become a part of. The North African campaign was gentlemanly, courtesies offered on both sides to all prisoners with varying degrees according to rank. Here, in Italy, the Germans were giving no quarter to their supposed allies. Dante considered sabotaging the planes, but as it turned out, there was no need. The Americans bombed the airport outside Taranta, destroying much of what was left of the Axis fighters and bombers. Dante had not seen so many sorties, nor witnessed the destruction of so many planes and pilots in all of his months in Africa as he saw in those few weeks at Taranta.

He would soon be of no use there because there would be no more planes to maintain. In the middle of the attack, the King and his entourage rolled into the small airport to which Dante's squadron had withdrawn. Victor Emmanuel raised himself to his full small height on the floor of his open car and saluted the remains of the last fighting squadron in this sector. Dante could see that the King's hand was shaking as he saluted the troops and encouraged them to do their best for Italy. Outside the hangar, the drone of incoming enemy planes approached. The pilots and mechanics scrambled and the King was left standing, saluting the empty parade ground.

Shortly after this, Dante read the news. From the safety of his palace, the King declared that Italy was now allied with the Americans. He removed the Duce and signed an armistice, an unconditional surrender that ought to have brought peace.

Dante wondered if that meant the war was over. What would change? Would the Germans politely leave? He doubted it.

Dante's squadron was depleted after the last raid. The German senior officers withdrew in the night, leaving their juniors to the mercy of the invading force. He was astonished at the efficiency of their disappearance. In the base, there were always engines starting up, always trucks coming and leaving. But the morning after the King signed the armistice, every German, not only the officers, but every one in the camp was gone. Dante's *maggiore* ordered the Italians left to lay down their weapons and support the Allied cause in the liberation of Italy. Dante looked around at the men. Most were weary and ready to comply. They had seen the work of the

Germans and seemed relieved that they would no longer have a part in the devastation wrought on their own people.

Dante had fought alongside Marseille. He had seen Rommel pull victory out of his pristine hat. Many of the Germans he had worked alongside since he arrived had comported themselves with courtesy. These were the desert soldiers, ones schooled in the etiquette of victory, ones who had received courtesy in capture. Dante could not fight against these ones. He would not repair the planes that would destroy these men. Most of the Italians were pleased to lay down arms against the Americans, but there remained a handful who would not switch sides. Who would not, having fought together with the Germans, now expend their efforts to fight against them just because the Italian high command had thrown its lot in with the Allies.

The *maggiore*'s face reddened. Huge and brawling, he stood before the fifteen Italians, Dante among them, who refused to take up arms against the Germans. He lifted his fist and grabbed the shirt collars of those who did not move quickly enough and punched their faces, knuckle on cheekbone exploding.

"The *stronzi* Germans! The *stronzi* Americans! I hate them all!"

He kept swinging until the other men finally held him still.

The *maggiore* caught his breath and straightened his shirt. He cradled his large fist and ordered the men before him into the brig.

"*Ottengali dalla mia vista*. Get them out of my sight."

Nursing a red, swollen face, Dante joined his fellow soldiers for one last stint in the brig. He did not hold a grudge. The *maggiore* was plainly a man at the end of his rope. Left without dignity or support to face the coming Americans. Dante waited in the brig, peaceful and light. He had not been shot. He could spend the rest of the war in prison if he had to. He played cards with the other men, the same as he would have outside the prison walls. He played cards and won and lost a fortune in pennies. He ate the good food that was brought in twice daily. From the window, he could see the commander's office. Dante watched as the man soaked his hand every day for two weeks in salt water.

On the fifteenth day, the *maggiore* rose from his desk and walked across to the prison. He unlocked the door and stepped to one side. He was shaved and clean, ready for foreign guests, it seemed. The door was opened wide. He released them all.

"Go home if you want, if you have somewhere to go. Just do not let me see your faces again."

Angelina

In the small square at the centre of San Placido, Angelina waited before the semi-circle of German soldiers. She could see the boy Carlo and his mother and her neighbours down the path. To her left and upward, she could see Anselmina and higher still, Francesca.

The German officer was shouting, but no one could understand him. He called forth one of the rank to stand with him. The translator spoke.

"We are here to find the criminals who set off a bomb two days ago in Rome, as well as the one who killed the German soldier in Visso two days ago. Reprisals have already been executed for the criminal acts. Now we want the criminals. We are going through your houses. You will offer no resistance or you will be shot. Step into the square immediately."

Most of the villagers were already at the small square in front of the church. They stood, grim and silent. Questo was nowhere to be seen. The soldiers began to enter the houses. Sounds of crashing glass, pots, overturned furniture shook the silence of the afternoon. In the square, one of the old men fell to his knees, damp with perspiration even in the chill of March. When Francesca moved to help, the soldier nearest her stepped forward and slapped her face so that her head snapped back and she fell on her side. Francesca's skirt had flapped up so that her slip and the bare tops of her legs were exposed. The soldier poked at her backside with the barrel of his gun.

He told her to get up. "Fat pig," he said. "It is not quite time for the slaughter."

Francesca pushed herself up and smoothed down her skirt, dusting and straightening. She rose slowly to sit up and Angelina moved to help her. When the same soldier raised the butt of his rifle to end such assistance, Angelina raised both hands and grabbed it from him. She threw it on the ground as though the metal burned. The young soldier, stunned and embarrassed, picked it up and with one arching swing, landed it across Angelina's head. She dropped, her head bleeding into Francesca's lap.

From behind the *chiesa*, Angelina watched as Questo charged at the soldier's throat. He landed, paws first on the man's chest, knocking him down. His teeth closed hard around the pulse point. The young man had no chance to cry out. Others hurried into the fray, beating on the dog's head, kicking him, so many soldiers trying to loosen Questo's grip that the ones who had kept cool, who had their rifles pointed at the centre, at the dog's large head, did not have a clean shot. Questo let go of the man's neck. He was snarling and furiously fast, dodging the rifles and biting the hands and ankles and even the scrotum of one unlucky German officer. Someone fired a shot into the air to clear the chaos and execute the black dog. But the echoing noise startled even the soldiers in the square for a moment and Questo raced away. He had heard that sound before. A rifle shot did not frighten him. It launched him.

Tired, hot, frustrated, and bleeding, the soldiers looked around at the small population of San Placido. Some on the ground, some standing.

The officer spoke. "A more pathetic collection of humanity, I have never seen. Have you in this godforsaken place lost even the sense to purchase for yourselves new clothing when the old things wore out? Look at yourselves. A street cleaner in Berlin would spurn to wear such garments."

He spoke to his fellow officers. All of the soldiers had gathered back in the square. They stood, bent together and empty-handed. If they had found any evidence, they certainly were not holding it as they stood before the humble houses of the village. Angelina's head throbbed. It had not taken them long to go through every dwelling and break and smash what they could. Perhaps the Germans thought their homes insignificant, their lives trivial. All the better. Who could believe that courage would thrive in such a shabby place? Angelina regarded her neighbours, motley and still. She wanted to laugh, but could not. The war had taken a toll on them. But even if it hadn't, there had never been much vanity in San Placido. If a woman needed shoes and she could afford them, she got them. Sturdy ones. Skirts and sweaters passed through generations.

The Germans held their weapons at the ready. Questo had attacked a German soldier. Angelina knew that someone would have to pay. She hoped it was only one and not ten. He was not dead yet. That young private, so anxious to knock down civilians, lay in the back of a transport down the road, carried by his fellows and ministered to by them. He was bandaged and losing blood. She heard what she thought was the word for hospital.

Angelina lay, bleeding onto Francesca's skirt. Felt the woman's gentle fingers on her forehead, moving so slightly. Felt the vibration of her own erratic heartbeat, or the heartbeat of Francesca. She could hear the swallows in the trees above the gardens. The trees were faintly green with tight buds starting on the branch tips. With her eyes half-closed, she listened to the unusual quiet in the village. Her neighbours waited, arms at their sides or hands folded as though praying on the sly. She wanted to sit up, but there was a weakness in her ankles, in her knees, up her spine and to the back of her throat. Around the people, in various stances of arrogant leisure, eight soldiers and one officer stood with their hands on their weapons. Angelina could see them, stroking the sight or the trigger while they watched the hushed circle of inhabitants. One young man had very blue eyes. One had a badly sewn scar above his eye. She could see the blood on the rifle end. Her blood? Or Questo's? She could see that it did not matter to these men. Whether they were tall or short, handsome or ugly. They were not smiling. If anything, they were bored, ready at a command, it seemed to her, to walk away before killing them all or after.

The Germans in San Placido and her father, thank God, far away. He was a big man, big enough to carry the burden of iron or wood or even the loss of his son. What would he do if he saw his only daughter, not small herself, levelled by such animosity? She looked at the cross on the church and said a small prayer of thanks. She wondered about Dante, far away and working alongside these brutes. He was perhaps friends with them. Had perhaps learned some German. She would not think about that. She wondered where the dog was and if he had got away. She could not bear to look around and see the dog's dead body being spat upon by bleeding Germans.

The conference ended. The captain was methodical and would not himself have chosen to hit old people with a rifle. He wanted the partisans and he wanted to make sure they were not concealed in the kitchens of the virtuous San Placido matrons.

The captain called Carlo forward. His mother held on to the boy's shoulders, held her head down, repeating, "*Piacere, piacere.*" Please.

"*Schnell, schnell, junge männlich.*"

The translator waited.

Carlo shook off his mother's restraints. Stepped forward.

"*Si.*"

"You have a church here, boy."

Carlo said, "*Certo*," thinking the poor German would soon tell him that he had arms and legs as well.

"You have a church, but you have no priest?"

"Of course we have a priest. Father Paolo. He is very tall."

"Where is this priest?"

Carlo lifted his shoulders. What was it to him where the priest was?

"Probably he is at the other parish in Folignano."

"Folignano?"

"*Si*, he is there all the time. There are younger girls there. Single ones. He's not much of a priest, really. I've seen things."

Anselmina wheezed. All of the people in the square, the Germans and the worried villagers, turned to look at her.

"Are you well, *Frau*? Have you also seen the priest?"

Angelina waited. She felt Francesca's arms tighten around her. Zia Anselmina folded her arms. Her eyes rested on Carlo and then on Angelina. Her mouth moved. She wanted to speak, that was clear. If she had had anything in her stomach, Angelina would have lost it. Anselmina would speak. She had their death warrants. If she had seen Angelina come back from Visso that evening, her blouse stained and torn, Angelina would be the first one to be shot. If she knew where Father Paolo was, if she knew where Berto had been in the long days of his absence, she would surely speak.

Angelina had threatened her once with Anselmina's own knife. There would be reckoning for that now, but shame on Anselmina for using the Germans to pay her back. She would not faint; she would not sicken. Angelina pushed herself upright to face Anselmina.

"I can tell you some things," the old woman said bitterly. "That boy, Carlo, is a liar, a good-for-nothing who breaks windows and runs away. His mother is a whore. The priest is a vagabond begging at every honest door."

Anselmina spat into the dust. She was just warming up.

Anselmina straightened her shoulders so that she seemed almost tall, larger than before, blacker. She appeared gleeful, calming herself with deep breaths. She looked ready to cut a tarantella, to turn a little dance in the square. Everyone watched her and it was plain to Angelina that she was enjoying this moment. That she could see them all looking at her, the whole town in the palm of her hand.

"A parish at Folignano, indeed. As if anybody there went to church. Go on, take your cars and your guns up there and see if you can find anything worth bothering about. Good-for-nothing boy, ragged and breaking windows at a whim. Who would bring a child into this world?"

Anselmina looked at Carlo's mother. "Your husband gone to war in some godforsaken place. And you, struggling to keep food on the table. Couldn't you raise your boy with some decency? What reason do you have to stand with your shoulders straight?

"That Father Paolo. He's a disgrace. I have never liked that man. No good would ever come of a priest like that. I told them. I told them all and I told him to his pretty face." She spat again.

"It would be a mercy if you stinking Germans lifted your weapons and finished off the whole village."

Angelina met the old woman's eyes. Francesca kept her arms around Angelina while she stared at Anselmina. Her face had such a look of sorrow, as though at a dear one lost to hell.

The German soldiers stood in a circle, listening to the translator who rendered Anselmina's curses. They looked confused, unsure for the moment about how to respond to a woman who invited execution. It looked as though they took offence, that they would not be ordered in such a fashion by such a woman. They lowered their weapons out of spite. This woman wanted an execution, they seemed to say. Well, she will have to do without. They spoke to one another, shaking heads. One officer waved at the whole population and walked away.

Anselmina looked back. She spat again. She opened her mouth and closed it again, pressed her empty gums together and sucked in her sagging lips.

Finally, she screamed, "That priest has gone to hell, as far as I know! As far as I hope, if there is any justice."

Angelina fell back to Francesca's lap. She could feel the woman breathing out. Around her, the people of San Placido concealed their relief.

The German officer spoke. "Well, boy?"

"*E vero*," said Carlo. "That priest likes to visit when my mother is bathing herself at the sink in front of the kitchen window."

His mother covered her mouth, eyes round.

"It is true, mamma. He walks by so slowly, even though the curtain is closed. In the evening. You know."

His mother crossed herself and kept her eyes on the ground.

While Carlo spoke, he picked up the stick on the ground and spun it around his fingers. The officer stepped back to watch him and with more space, he began his tossing tricks, spiralling the stick into the air and catching it, as before, behind his back and under one leg. He tossed it high and swiftly circled behind the officer to catch it behind his back. Carlo laid it on the ground and did back flips over and back. The soldiers stared, then finally smiled.

"Congratulations, boy. You will be a credit to the Italian army some day. They at least know what to do with such a modern weapon."

The soldiers nudged one another and laughed, as though at a joke only they could share.

The Captain retrieved a sweet from his pocket and gave it Carlo, who reached for it, grinning.

"Citizens of San Placido. We know that the partisans have run like hares to this area and we know that they are concealed somewhere in the godforsaken hovels you call home. Tomorrow at oh-eight hundred, you will evacuate your homes with whatever measly possessions you can carry, whereupon your houses will be blown to bits and all the partisans within them dispatched to their Maker. This is the order of the German high command. If you remain in those houses, you, too, will be sent to eternity."

The soldiers collected themselves to some purpose, laughing at the stick tricks of the ragged boy. One of them turned to assist Angelina to her feet, even offering her a handkerchief, which she received into her open palm, too shocked to close her fingers around it. The next breeze lifted it away and still she stood, bleeding down her shoulders and back.

They were gone and the scant population of San Placido exhaled together and, shivering, dropped their aching shoulders. Carlo spat out the German's candy.

They gathered around Carlo who was holding on to his stick. His face was wet with tears.

"Mi dispiace, I am so sorry I had to say that about the Father."

"Good boy, good boy!"

Carlo's hair was a mess from the old men rubbing his head. His cheeks were sore from the old women pinching him.

"It is all right, my boy. The Father and, indeed, God himself, knows you were born for that moment."

"And many more, good fellow. Do not worry a bit."

"God bless you, young man."

"They did not go to the garden."

"No, they stopped at Francesca's house."

"Of course. The bend in the path."

"Ah, *si*. I had forgotten that you cannot see the garden from the lane."

Everyone in the village seemed to want to speak at once. They moved toward the Martinellis' house, where they were offered a toast from last year's fine wine. A toast to survival, a toast to the blessed dead of Visso, and a toast to the San Placido garden.

To a native, the way to the garden was merely the way to the garden. They gave no thought to its twists, bumps, stones. Concealed by evergreens and a sharp turn in the path, the garden remained sacrosanct. The shed, as well, was safe from the searchers. Angelina was certain that whatever was inside was safe. Every hoe and shovel and every man concealed among them, including the good Father, tightly packed with rough strangers. She offered a small, quiet prayer for the men, and for her brother, who lay in safety.

Angelina, still with her head in Francesca's lap, began to weep. She was bruised and aching. But she was alive. Everyone in her village had survived. But the people in Visso on a market day in the sun, they lay dead because of her. Though Francesca held her, though she soothed Angelina and reminded her that the worst was over, Angelina could not elude the horror of her own survival.

What if she had let him? He was only drunk. But even the other path, the other choice, to lie back and spread her legs for a man, her first man, to be forced and *fottuta*, whether this was worth murder or not, she did not know. She knew only that her heart blasted when he grabbed her, that some fire coursed through her. The rock leapt to her hand; her hand smashed into the head of one who was less than nothing to her. She wept for the ten dead, for the three hundred dead in Rome, for Nico, for her mother, and for Dante, who was surely lost by now. She lay on the ground, half-held by Francesca who had her own losses to mourn, and she cried until her throat was hoarse and her eyes nearly closed.

Francesca waited until the worst of Angelina's grief ebbed. Angelina used the hem of her dress to wipe her face. She looked up at

Cesca and nodded.

"*Grazie,* Zia Francesca. *Grazie.*" She could hardly speak.

Angelina went with Francesca back to her house where the woman washed and wrapped her head. She helped Angelina out of her dress, and gave the girl one of her own. Angelina waited while Francesca carried it to the cistern to clean it.

Old Francesca had taken a hot needle and thread and stitched Angelina's head at the kitchen sink where she had sat, cold cloth to her mouth, teeth clamped against the pain, while Questo circled outside the door with a fresh-killed grouse hanging from his jowls. The wound had stopped bleeding, but the cut was jagged, hot, and swelling. Francesca did her best to mend it. Angelina's eyes teared up and Francesca told her not to wince.

"I don't want to sew a crooked line, my dear. Stay calm and it will soon be over. Look at that dog. I didn't know he was a *partigiano*, but I should have known."

"The partisans should be glad he joined them."

The dog sat on his haunches and dropped the bird.

"He is fast on his feet, that dog." Angelina used the cloth to wipe tears from her eyes. "And a handsome fellow, too."

Francesca said, "Not as handsome as some. You know what the Father told me. The Americans are heading north. The war must soon end. That young man will be coming home as fast as his feet will move him. Perhaps making a stop in San Placido."

Angelina could neither nod nor speak. What if she should see him? What if he should be safe after all, and on his way to her? She had put his photograph in her pocket the morning of the Germans' ascent. It no longer seemed a vanity to her that a man should pose to have his image recorded. She hoped it had been spared any bloodstains. She would have looked at it again while Francesca leaned over her. She wanted to check it again as she had on that morning, as though it might give her courage to face what would come.

Angelina leaned with her head over the sink so that Francesca could wash her hair, a task she performed lightly, rinsing all the blood away. Angelina sat with her chin in her hand while Francesca took a fresh towel, squeezed the water out, and then combed out its full length. Angelina rested, meek and hushed like a child who has had a bad fright and has sobbed herself to stillness. It had been years since anyone had combed her hair. Her arms and legs felt heavy, thick, and warm all at once. She could have fallen asleep as Francesca pulled the comb through and sang to Angelina as though she were a child.

She said, "My brave girl, let me brew you some tea to help you sleep."

"*Grazie,* Francesca. But I don't think I will need any tea. I must go and put my sore head on a pillow."

She looked in Francesca's small mirror by the door. Turned her head this way and that.

"Lovely. It will be as good as new."

In broad daylight, she climbed the stairs to her room. She dropped Francesca's borrowed dress on the floor and lay down on her bed. Alone, finally, she held Dante's photograph up to the light coming through the window. There he was. Polished and sepia. But also he was not there. His eyes gleamed, but Angelina wondered whether that was just a trick of the light. She turned the photograph this way and that, but the expression did not change. She was losing him. If he didn't come back to her soon, he might be gone altogether. It had been so long since she had seen him, spoken to him. That first moment in Rome when she saw his reflection in the store window and she turned to find the real man standing before her, that was a moment to raise the hair on her arms. If she took out her memories, examined them as though they were firm stones that formed the foundation of her love for him, if she unbuilt them all and reassembled them, would he come back to her? Would she know him better, or see something she hadn't seen before?

She could only wait.

When Angelina's father came in from the field and forest that night, she had composed herself. She turned the visit of the Germans, the malice of Anselmina, and the bravery of Carlo into a story to tell him. She was no longer trembling when she took thin soup to her mother who had sat in her bed while the Germans rifled through her small room.

"They poked the mattress with bayonets! Very nearly stabbed my leg. They asked me if I had a partisan in bed with me."

"No! Mamma! What did you say?"

"I said nothing. Them with their guns. But I could have said, 'Wouldn't that be nice?'"

Alfonso looked pleased with his wife. He leaned and kissed her while Angelina shook out the sheets, and tucked them in crisply against her mother's thin legs. Her head hurt, but her mother had surprised her and made her laugh aloud.

By some miracle, they had all survived. Even the dog.

Berto, though, had still not returned.

"What will we do about tomorrow?" Angelina asked.

Her father had never uttered a sacred scripture in his life. That was the priest's job. But Alfonso looked at her and said, "Do not worry saying, 'What shall we eat?' or 'What shall we drink?' or 'What shall we wear?' For the pagans run after all these things, and your heavenly Father knows that you need them. But seek first his kingdom and his righteousness, and all these things will be given to you as well. Therefore, do not worry about tomorrow, for tomorrow will worry about itself. Each day has enough trouble of its own."

"Papa, you have been listening to Father Paolo again."

"No harm in that."

This day had certainly had enough trouble. What on earth would the morning bring?

Angelina knew about the storage area beneath the boards in the shed in the San Placido garden, but apart from her father, she had believed that not many others did. She should have known by now about the way secrets are kept in a village, which is to say, not at all. She had seen Signor Martinelli go up toward the garden that very morning. She had waited, keeping watch while he tucked Berto, Father Paolo and the three unnamed guests into the space beneath the shed, slid the boards into place, and rearranged the rakes and spades and hoes and buckets haphazardly to conceal the opening. He then gathered the dry lucky dust from the edge of the garden and sprinkled it over the surface of the floor. The light that morning lay in pinstripes across the floor, the implements, and across Signor Martinelli's happy face.

To Angelina, his accomplice, he had said, "I think I would make a good spy."

He had left no trace of anyone having been in the hut. Everything looked as jumbled and dusty as usual. He went out, putting on his most ignorant and lugubrious expression, to meet San Placido's Nazi invasion, face to face.

When Angelina came up the path at dusk with a sack of provisions for the men in the garden, she found them waiting. Father Paolo's cassock was grimy. Berto's face, paler than usual and streaked with dirt. She forced her brother to give her a fast hug before he pushed her away, embarrassed by his sister. Father Paolo sat with the men, filthy, stooped, and deathly quiet, but in very good spirits. She would not have thought the cavity large enough to hold the five men. She gave the Father her package.

"*Panini con capicollo, formaggio, mele, mio Padre.*" Her head was still aching and she spoke softly.

The Father nodded, as did the men. One of them, the tall one, turned to the Father.

"Your path ends here, Padre. We cannot thank you enough. People will say things. They will tell you we should never have done it. I tell you we would have lost heart had we known the outcome. Our hearts break. We would turn ourselves in to share the same fate as those in the caves."

"There would be no merit in that. No one could have known that the backlash would be so…"

Angelina sat on the bench, listening. The Father seemed at a loss for the word to describe what had happened in the cave outside Rome. She knew him to be a gentle man. He often said that one ought to render unto Caesar the things that were Caesar's, as Christ had commanded. He had complied with the civil authorities, but their demands had not seemed too hard.

He said, "My life here has been so easy. Even with the war and the occupation, the new rules, it has not been cumbersome here in San Placido. There is no one here of the Hebrew faith. We have not seen anyone exiled or interned. In my house, gentlemen, there are no secret compartments. Otherwise your day might have been spent in more comfort. I can offer no asylum."

He rubbed his palms against his cassock. "You three, and you Berto, found me. I suspect you are with the Bandiera Rossa, but it is better for me not to know. I know the story of Via Rasella, the round-up of prisoners, the slaughter of innocent people. You have told me and I, in my dark church, have listened.

"Gentlemen, were not those German soldiers also innocent men in need of salvation? And the Italians who were killed in the explosion? Were not their lives sacred to God himself?"

The men had no reply. Neither, in her conscience, did Angelina. It was for the ten that she felt remorse. Not for the one. She looked around at the partisans. They had likely each done worse than set off an explosion from a safe distance. Each one had German blood on his hands. Boys they had cut and eviscerated, seeking information, seeking to intimidate the other prisoners who cowered as witnesses to what they themselves would face. They said this to the Father by way of confession, Angelina hoped.

"Did you find, when you killed the German soldiers, that their blood was a different colour?"

They did not answer.

Father Paolo looked tired.

"Matters of war and vengeance are too great for me. You ask for my help. I give it freely."

They hid in the garden until dusk deepened to full starless night. Angelina held Berto's hands. He seemed resigned to her affection now that he was leaving. She hoped it comforted him. One of the men stood to say that it was time to go.

"The Americans are moving north. We hear that they are very close. We are hoping to meet up with some advance troops, to provide information and join the liberation of Italy. Father, you have done enough. *Signorina*, we thank you."

Angelina shook hands with each of the men and kissed Berto who grabbed her around the waist and tickled her.

"Don't dream too much about that man from Spoleto!"

She shoved him and would have laughed to see him trip and fall on his backside. She would not let him see what a pang he gave her when he mentioned Dante as a joke. She hoped there would be reason to joke. She hoped he was safe.

"Berto, *mio bambino, ti amo.* Be careful, all right?"

The men put on jackets and rubbed damp earth on their faces. Father Paolo said, "*Aspetta.* Please, wait."

He raised his hand. Right hand up, left on his breastbone. He looked at the men.

"May the Lord bless you and keep you. May the Lord make his face to shine upon you and give you peace.

In nomine Patris, et Filii, et Spiritus Sancti. Amen."

With this, the men, black-clad, silent, and dark, disappeared over the rise.

When she returned to the kitchen, Angelina saw that her father had put some of their belongings on the table. He gathered them into a cloth and tied it into a bundle. Soft echoes down the lane told Angelina that her neighbours were busy at the same task throughout the night watches. They would assemble a few pictures and pieces of silver, candles, spoons, one or two small garden implements, and wrap them in tablecloths or sacks. When she went outside, she saw several of her neighbours gathered in front of the church, wondering where Father Paolo was at such a critical time. They said their prayers outside that night and went home in the small hours of the morning to await the breaking sun.

In the morning, the clouds broke with the dawn. The first drops of rain pounded the clay roofs of the San Placido houses. The sound blasted around the deep stone walls and people rose from their chairs to look out the windows at the deluge. The heavy rain would make the switchbacks impassable.

Alfonso sipped his coffee in peace. "No heavy guns will find their way up the mountain on this morning."

As if they had been waiting for Alfonso's statement, as if they had heard it, the San Placido wives and daughters fired up their stoves. Angelina could see new smoke gusting out of chimneys against the hard rain. Breakfast was cooking up and down the street. In Angelina's kitchen, and, she suspected, in the kitchens of her neighbours, breakfast would be as lavish as the cupboards would allow.

By the time the rain eased and the kitchen door was opened to let in the fresh air, Angelina could hear her neighbours laughing, as though they had gotten themselves into new wine before breakfast. Outside, Questo leaped with young Carlo from massive puddle to puddle, the two of them slick with mud. Signor Martinelli sat on his balcony with a guitar and serenaded the young people in the village who had gone out to play in the rain.

At the end of the day, soldiers finally did arrive, but not from Visso. Angelina saw them come from the south, heard them speak strange English words. They handed out chocolates and kisses to the whiskered widows. The old ones stood at attention in the square and saluted. Alfonso spoke to a couple of the soldiers. Angelina leaned on the lintel, stunned to hear her father speaking English. She had never heard him do this before. How and when could he have learned this? She would ask him, but not now. Right past her kitchen, an invading force of Americans had come up the other side of the mountain. There would be no more Germans in San Placido.

Angelina unpacked the cloth and set her parents' home to rights. Her ancient *nonni* were set back on the mantel in their polished frames. The silver spoons that she knew had not been used in decades she left on the table to stir the next morning's espresso.

Dante and Angelina

Leaving Taranta, Dante began to work his way north. He took care not to get his legs blown out from under him. The Allied advance was in full swing, and travelling in secret for a man his age was risky. If either side found him, he would be shot, imprisoned, or conscripted, and then he would not be able to get to Angelina. And so it turned out: it took months, and included a stint in a makeshift American prison, but prison was nothing new to him. He waited them out. When the pitched battle moved, so did Dante. He escaped easily and avoided anything like a town until he got to Spoleto.

Before he returned to Angelina, Dante wanted to take Sabino's identity tags to the bereaved mother. That day in the truck, the fragments of bone and the paste of blood and brain had made the tags sticky and slick. He washed them in champagne. He had taken the letter from Sabino's breast pocket, the letter they had all written before that final battle. Sabino's said nothing more than, *My mother, I love you. All is well.* Dante had carried the letter on the train back to Spoleto.

The trains were still on time. Mussolini, he knew, had been moved to the north, protected by the Germans. Dante did not believe the war could last much longer. The artillery he had worked to embed at Pantelleria was failing. Dante read the papers, read between the lines. He knew that blazing headlines declaring the bravery of the gunners at Pantelleria meant that their hold on the island was slipping. The island, so embattled by the wind and the sea, would now be scarred and smouldering. Pantelleria had been grand. He had stolen the plane. He and Sabino. Flown like daredevils to fetch a few pounds of cherries. Now the papers called the Allied attack on the island "Operation Corkscrew." Strange words for him to try to pronounce, but the article translated it: Operazione Cavatappi. *Allora*, Dante thought, they will remove the cork in the bottle between Tunis and Sicily. There would have to be a massive artillery attack for the battlements there to fail. Thousands of sorties and tonnes of bombs. Dante imagined his work blown to bits. There would be nothing left that could strike back. He had left the island long ago, gone across the fifty-three sea miles to Tunis, and down the long highway of the Duce to join the North African front where it seemed that poor Signor Rommel still waited for reinforcements that would, without Pantelleria as a staging point, fail to arrive.

The Germans were losing the war. Dante was out of it.

Dante got off the train and walked into Spoleto. He walked past his own mother's house, up the narrow streets to the Via Monterozze, past his father's garden, his uncle's grapes, to the house of Sabino's mother and sisters. He gave them the letter. Accepted their embraces, their tears that darkened the wool of his old suit, their coffee and cake.

"He was brave," he said. How vapid his thin voice sounded in his own ears.

He tried again.

"Every time I turned around, there he was. He gave me courage."

The women praised Dante's kindness. That he would come to them and bring these things. Not some stranger from the war office. Not in the mail, but a true friend to bring them to the door. To tell them about Sabino.

Dante's legs twitched. He was ashamed. He sipped the coffee and surrendered to the nurture of the women. That day was with him always. He would give Sabino's family the best of it. Dante would have liked to explain to the mother and sisters that he and Sabino had been home free. They were getting out when almost no other Italian infantry were allowed to retreat. Everyone else had been ordered to fight to the last man.

He and Sabino, by good fortune and the avarice of the colonel, were getting out. They were nursing the truck along. It would make it to Tripoli for sure, Dante thought. They would make it. They had the champagne. Dante wanted to tell them how Sabino had hung on to the frame of the door and poured the fine wine into the grinding truck, small brooks of bubbles sparkling down the side. How Sabino did this easily, as though it were a service he always provided on dusty roads. Then Dante veered left and then right to avoid an artillery shell unexploded in the road. He almost laughed because Sabino fell over. Dante thought it was the sudden force of the shift. He wanted to tell them how Sabino turned to face the bullet. Such a small thing, to take a bit off the side of a man's head and send it yards away, opening a wound that would not heal in the centre of the one who loved him best on earth.

How everything stopped in him. Breath, blood, speech. How he buried his friend beneath the bold stars.

Dante wanted to tell them how Sabino was his brother, how he marked for Dante his own place in the world and how he had not been able to find it since Sabino died. How Sabino could conjure a fire and brew coffee anywhere on earth. He sang in a sandstorm. Fascist songs. Can you imagine?

In response to their praise, he said, "Your son, who was worth ten of me, is dead and I am alive. He has been buried at Bardia. He is in the heroes' cemetery." A cemetery with a single hero.

Dante answered their questions. "He did not suffer. No military hospital, not even a medic. It was over before he knew it."

They embraced him again at the front door. Dante was reluctant to leave, as he had been in Tunis. Now in Spoleto on the doorstep of Sabino's home, he stepped back across the threshold for a moment, delaying, as though with each departure he left his friend further behind. He finally said goodbye to them and promised to visit again.

He walked toward the Ponte once more and looked out across the divide. The sun was setting behind him and he could feel the warmth of it on his back, gentle and soothing. Not like the sun of the desert.

Dante turned away from the bridge. He would follow the road out of Spoleto in the morning. It was time to go to Angelina.

On a sunny morning, Signora Martinelli knocked on the door.

"We have had a phone call from Visso."

Angelina dried her hands. "*Si, signora*. Please come in."

Angelina poured a small demitasse of coffee for the *signora*. She waited while the woman stirred in the sugar.

"You know, I have always liked these cups your mother brought with her on her wedding day. They are so fine. Do you know if they came from Visso?"

She sipped her espresso.

"*Signora.*"

"Ah, *si*, Angelina. I'm sorry. The telephone call. Yes."

She stirred her coffee. Angelina let her fingers dance the tarantella on the table.

The *signora* smiled. "All right, my dear. I'm sorry. A young man is expected in the village today. Your friend, Dante from Spoleto."

Angelina dropped the towel. At the sink, right in front of Signora Martinelli, she washed her face with cold water. Without a word to her neighbour, she went to her room and unwound the crown of braids from her hair. She combed and combed it, braided it and wrapped it again. She put on her dark blue dress, the one she wore when she first met Dante. Her Rome dress, as she thought of it. When she came back downstairs, the *signora* was gone, the cup washed, and a posy of violets left behind on the table beside a piece of brown paper with the words, "For luck," written on it.

He came to San Placido finally in 1944. He rounded the last turn into the village and looked up to see Angelina waiting on the low wall before him. To his eyes she appeared cool and lovely. Hundreds of letters had joined them across air. Now here she was. Dante reached out his hand and she took it. She stood and embraced him. A kiss on both cheeks he gave her. She stepped back from him and then forward again into his arms. She gave him another pair of kisses and added a third of her own, in plain view of the clutch of neighbours behind her.

There was such a pain in her throat and her chest, as though she were instead receiving news of Dante's death. As though the man himself were not directly before her. He handed her a handkerchief for her tears. She moved away from him, let her eyes focus on the contours of his face, his unfixed face before her.

Dante seemed to have the same difficulty in recognizing Angelina. He ran his hand across her cheek.

"There you are, *carina*," he said. "There you are, *cara mia*."

"Here I am."

"*Si*, Dante," said Signor Martinelli. "You are there, she is here. *Adesso*, may we have some supper?"

"Always your stomach, my husband. Come on. We will find something for the starving man to eat."

The collected audience laughed and turned back to business.

He walked with Angelina up to the garden. He sat down with her and took her hand in both of his. He stroked the fingers and palm. Electric.

She thought, so that is what skin is for.

"It is a beautiful day."

Angelina thought, there will never be one like it again.

"*Si, tanto tanto gentile*." Very, very nice.

"Every man in my company envied me because of you."

"Because of me?"

"The mail would take months sometimes to find us, months of nothing, no news from home at all. And suddenly the quartermaster would arrive with something like thirty letters in the mail pack and twenty-five of them would be for me."

"I wore out a few pencils."

"You did. I'm sorry, but I could not keep them all. But I have here the first one, the first time where you signed your love. 'With love, Angelina.'"

"Well."

"This one kept me alive. It drew me back to you."

She could not bear much longer the nuzzling of his thumb against her palm.

"Would you marry me, Angelina?"

Finally. She did not wait. She did not need to think about what she should say. She kissed him on the lips, happy and brazen.

"*Si. Certo.*"

Dante stayed that night of the proposal with the Martinellis as there was not room for him at Angelina's father's house. Signora Martinelli had left the flowers for Angelina and then gone home to prepare a quick feast and invite her neighbours and the young couple to supper, in case they had something to celebrate. Signor Martinelli dug deep into his wine cellar and he and Alfonso sampled the vintages of several years' work. They drank late into the evening and even Angelina's mother, who had been carried down the lane in a soft chair, sipped the new-pressed grapes. She said it would be good for her stomach. Francesca came into the small kitchen with marinated peppers and eggplants. Father Paolo blessed the supper. Anselmina stomped past on her way to the cistern, waving away their invitation to drink a toast to the newly engaged couple.

"You will see what happens now," she said.

"Poor Anselmina," they said as a chorus might.

"It turns out that she is not as poisonous as she would seem to be after all," said Francesca.

"We could all be dead," said Signora Martinelli.

Dante looked around the table. Everyone was quiet.

"What has happened here?" he asked.

"It is such a long story," said Angelina. "I will tell it to you some rainy night."

How would she tell him? Angelina thought it would be best not to speak of things that no one could change. She looked at her betrothed, a man whose eyes turned down and echoed the corners of his mouth. Those shadows that fell, those were new since Rome, she thought. He had written to her, but she knew he did not tell her everything. God willing, there would be time for confidences, for telling sad stories beneath the comfort of warm sheets. She felt the quick blush in her cheek.

Again, the pall of quiet fell.

After a moment, Francesca looked up. "You know that mayor in Visso."

Alfonso bit his hand in disdain. "That Fascist! He did nothing for those poor people or their families."

Dante was once more confused. "Is this another long story?"

"It's part of the same one. He is a vile man, this mayor. You will just have to believe us for now."

"He cultivates honey, you know."

"Honey. Something sweet from that collaborator? I don't believe it."

"It's true. I heard from my cousin. He keeps bees."

Signora Martinelli replied, "Then I wish they would swarm and sting him. Put him in the hospital, if not in his grave."

"He is very miserly with that honey," said Francesca. "And it is so good for my heart. But he charges so much."

The old people around the table began to argue about the mayor and the health benefits of honey.

Dante looked at Angelina across the table. She met his gaze. A mayor with honey that he ought to surrender. A cloudless night outside.

"Do you know what I am thinking?" He spoke very quietly. She leaned toward him to listen. "Do you?"

She looked so pleased, as if she did. "I know that a Fascist, bee-keeping, collaborating mayor should be shown the error of his ways."

"I agree."

Late in the night when the moon had risen high, Angelina and

Dante stole away. They clasped hands like children and ran down the road with all its bends and turns. They ran until they were just outside Visso. Angelina knew the house. It was large, right on the outskirts of town, so that the mayor could promenade into his offices down the main street.

The garden was fenced. Dante lifted himself over and turned around.

Before he could help Angelina, she landed beside him. She made no noise, but she flashed deep dimples and then slipped away toward the back of the property. Well behind the house, beyond the lights that the mayor kept burning, they found the hives. Not far away, the mayor had built a storage shed for the honey. The door was padlocked, but the wood of the frame was rotten. It was easy work to wrench the whole door off the hinges and step inside. Angelina had brought with her a market bag that they filled with jars of honey.

The stable to the left of the shed housed one emaciated mule who seemed to regard their activities with patent sorrow.

Angelina said, "The mule."

"Poor thing. Look at him."

Dante turned and nodded.

"We will liberate him."

They untied the thin fellow and walked him out of the stable. Angelina produced from one of her pockets a sweet apple, which he crunched through in three bites. They tied the hives together with a rope, having first blocked the entrances. Then they tied the rope to the mule. It took two hours of slow going to walk back up to San Placido, dragging the hives behind them. The bag of honey jars clanked against the mule's flank, but none broke. Angelina tied the mule up at the side of the house to let it graze on the sweet grass there. Questo trotted over as though for inspection and, seeming to approve of the must-and-mud fragrance of the mule, sat down beside it, a guard over its safety.

Angelina said good night.

"Is the ground so interesting, Angelina? Look at me."

When she looked at him, it was to find those unhappy shadows lifted, at least for now. He kissed her, smiling against her lips and it made her laugh. Such a funny feeling. Her mouth went soft and Dante kissed her again without smiling, lips slipping and sleek, all sympathy and supple impulse.

She stumbled when Dante leaned back. She had been holding her breath.

"*Buona notte*, Angelina. I will see you tomorrow."

In the morning, Dante and Angelina went up and down the village street giving away jars of honey. There was in the village a sense of jubilee, of unexpected and rich release. Angelina's neighbours took the honey and pressed *lire* on the young couple, offering their good wishes with kisses on both cheeks and embraces all around. With the unexpected profit, Angelina went to Visso to buy new shoes for her wedding day.

Angelina stepped onto the train at the station at the bottom of the hill in Spoleto. She had been twice to Dante's mother's house to meet his parents and talk about the nuptials. She asked Maria Pia for permission to cook in her kitchen, to cook her own wedding lunch before the ceremony and to invite the guests back to the large garden behind the house and serve them. Maria Pia was shy with Angelina who stood so tall in her kitchen. Two days before the wedding, she came again to Spoleto. Dante met her at the station and escorted her to the market where she used some of the money she had earned working for her uncle to buy what she needed.

Angelina worked, tasting the eggplant, salty and savoury, layered with tomatoes and cheese. The chickens she roasted slowly, stuffed with unpeeled garlic and wild rosemary. Rubbed with butter and oil. She would not risk her own wedding feast in the hands of city people, good-hearted as most of them seemed. She spent the dawn in the quiet kitchen, preparing the broth, the vegetables, and the chickens. She had picked flowers for the table from the garden of Dante's mother, poppies and roses, and placed tumblers with flowers all around the house.

She would not carry a bouquet for herself. She did not want to think of herself as one flower among those picked as from a garden.

Angelina had decided her own future. She would go to Dante at the church. Following the letters she had written, now she herself would go to him.

She found lavender and hung it in the kitchen. She pressed some into her fingers. She smoothed her hands across the pressed towels in the *bagno*.

She cut the *pecorino*, prepared the *minestra*.

It pleased her so much to have her hands on the food, measuring and tasting. There was an hour of peace in Dante's garden shelling vivid green peas and dropping them into the red clay bowl. There was the sweet sun. She watched the boys in the street kick the football up and down and across. When she finished, she went up to the room they had given her. She washed herself and rubbed more lavender into her wrists. Angelina put on the cool dress and zipped it. It was the colour of new cream, not very practical. Tight at the bodice and flaring out from the hips. Stefania had made her parents buy it in Rome, a gift for Angelina who had helped them out so much. She put her feet into her new shoes. That mayor. If the theft of his honey were the worst that happened to him, he would be lucky.

She was reluctant to look in the mirror in case she did not recognize the person she saw. Everything was about to change. The new taffeta lining of her dress, stiff and whispering against her arms and back, made her take notice of her own body. It was strange enough, the new uses to which skin and lips could be put. There was alchemy in Dante's touch, how it changed her skin from some base and functional thing into slipping quicksilver. She shook her head to try to clear it. She could cook without forgetting to breathe, but to stand in a fine dress and think about her wedding, that forced the air out of her and she had to remind herself, it seemed, to force it back in.

She had lived her family's life on the mountain and now she would live her own. Nico was not coming home. He had been sent to die in Russia. Her own foolish brother. These were not good thoughts for a wedding day. She said a prayer for the soul of funny Nico. Her parents would look after themselves, with Berto's help.

She had asked her papa, "Do you like him?"

Her father said, "If you marry, it is for you to choose, Angelina. Not for me. It does not matter what I think. Only you must like him."

She did like him.

Angelina left the *bistecca* to stay warm in the pans. She took a last look around the kitchen before leaving. There must be more than enough food for everyone. Everyone must rise from the table, groaning, barely able to heave themselves from their chairs or they would complain that she had stinted on the meal. She must kill them with food this day.

They went to the church, *alla famiglia*. All together. They went to the Wedding Mass and took Holy Communion. Angelina bowed and rose and spoke all that was required of her. She came back across the threshold a married woman, holding on tight to Dante's arm.

Father Paolo had come down from the mountain, thinner than ever. With the permission of the priest in Spoleto, he performed the sacrament of marriage for Dante and Angelina. Dante listened to him with great respect. He had heard from Angelina what the Father had done for the partisans, the risks he had taken, the forgiveness he still wished to exercise in the face of the horrors he knew. The Father's voice was deep and breaking, as though he were a thirsty man.

The Father said, after the formal blessing of the mass, "Greater love hath no man than this, that a man lay down his life for his friends."

In his white and gold vestments, Father Paolo was magnificent. Dante stood before him, looking up. The Father wiped the cup, he made the sign of the cross and he smiled at Angelina, whom he had known for years.

Dante had not had a chance to tell him about Sabino. His friend had leaned out of the truck to keep the vehicle moving, to get them to safety. How did the Father know that Sabino had leaned out, laid down his life, and kept Dante alive?

The Father did not know. He was not speaking of Sabino.

The understanding came to Dante that Father Paolo meant marriage.

The Father said, "Marriage affords the most intimate opportunity to lay down one's life for the one who is to be the best, truest friend."

Angelina was beside him, to his left. There she was, calm and sure, and his longing for her kindled and flared as he stood next to her. She would be his intimate friend. Therefore, how could his chest be breaking? He was not a man to cry, but he felt all at once a dreadful joy and a dull, hollowing sorrow. Sabino was in the desert. What was left of him had been laid to final rest beneath dust to become dust. Dante here and now made his vows to Angelina. He would feast beneath green olive trees, *nespole* and blooming *mandorle* trees. He held her hand. Looked at her lovely face. Behind her, over her shoulder, he looked also into the empty space, hoping to be haunted by Sabino.

On the wedding trip to Marmore, to see the famous waterfall, Dante leaned across her to open the window, thinking she might be too warm. Then, worrying she might take a chill or that the wind might bother her, he leaned again to close it. He pointed out things he knew she could see perfectly well. The train shifted on rails, shifted his arm against hers. He could feel her beside him, and see her and speak with her. The train lurched, blessed and delightful train, pushing him against his new wife. He apologized for the thrill of apologizing to her for something. He bit back on his own smile. He felt himself on the verge of lunacy. Of cutting a caper down the aisle of the train. She was beside him, finally.

The window was dirty and the seat of the train was worn. They were sitting with their backs to the sun as it set and its rays, magnified by the glass, hit his shoulder. He could feel the radiance burn through to his skin, but it would not do him harm. There was a bright shine on his shoes. His fingers, hands, legs, all intact. All whole, as he regarded them. He had shaken the desert dust from his feet and crossed continents, all the while writing to Angelina of the banalities of war. There were blood friends not with him, not whole, nor in any way present in this earth. Behind him, he left the colonel, driven off the desert road on a fool's errand to find the treasure he had stored and hidden. Dante recalled the corona of smoke and dust as the colonel's transport drove away, east instead of west, and into harm. And poor Marseille, who had died so stupidly and whose one death seemed to reverse the current of fortune for the entire Axis force. Marseille, smashed and broken in the desert. Dante would not think about Sabino.

After the church and the lunch and the warm wine, they had left. The train moved. The waving family in bright wedding clothes on the station platform remained. Dante and Angelina would see the *cascadi*, the high tumbling water, and go to the small hotel and she would be his wife and he would be her husband.

Il mio marito.

La mia sposa.

Her hair was braided and wrapped in a shining brown coronet around her head. She sat straight and firm in the seat beside him.

When they arrived at the hotel, Dante offered to sit with her in the lounge. Perhaps she would like a drink? Some coffee? Or a liqueur?

She was not thirsty, she said.

They went up the stairs to the room.

"What do you think of the place, Angelina? *Ti piace?* Do you like it?"

"It is very clean."

"We could walk to the falls in the morning. We could take a picnic. Perhaps some cherries."

"I love cherries."

Dante looked out the window at the street below. He kept his hands in his trouser pockets, uncertain about how to proceed. She had become so timid.

Angelina found speech difficult. Her insides felt strange to her. Hens fighting under her flesh.

Now she was married.

Underneath her dress, she wore a new slip, given to her by Stefania, whose great-aunt had purchased it in Rome and then died on the way home before she had a chance to wear it. The fabric slid against her skin. Raised gooseflesh. Dante, who had forgotten to close the door behind him when they came in, moved now and sealed it, slow and quiet, as though he had come to the end of a long passage on a stormy sea and wished to close a door against the memory of it.

She gave him her hand when he came to her. They sat together on the bed. He stroked her skin, cool against his own. Her hand, her arm, her shoulder.

"How do you feel?"

"*Bene, grazie.*"

He laughed.

She felt well. Yes, she did.

"*Anche io.*"

"Angelina, I am going to kiss you, now."

"*Certo.*"

Angelina raised her face. She had been kissed on the mouth before by Dante. He smiled and she thought how difficult it is to kiss and smile at the same time. She waited. Dante touched his lips to hers, still holding her hand. He pressed and withdrew, looking at her eyes, which had remained open. He smiled again. His eyes were so dark. He kissed her again and she sighed.

"Shall we count our money?" she asked. The kiss, she would like to do that again, but she did not want to rush.

"*Come?*" Pardon?

"Shall we count the money from the wedding?"

Dante let go of her hand. She wanted to tally the gifts now. Very well. He would move as she wished. From the bed to the two chairs they moved and emptied her purse. As the lire notes fell out in their envelopes onto the small table, he watched while she counted the generosity of their family and friends. Enough to support a short wedding trip and set them up when they got back. Enough to buy Angelina a new dress.

"Would you like to go for a walk?"

"No, *signora*."

"Shall we have some supper?"

"It is very late for supper."

"There are still people outside, Look."

"Are you hungry? *Chai fame?* "

"*Allora*, I have an apple in my purse."

It had fallen out with the money. Dante picked it up for her. He withdrew his pocketknife and peeled it. He sliced thin half moons of apple and held them out for her. When she reached with her hand, he moved the slice above and toward her mouth.

"Usually the woman feeds the man," she said.

"There will be time enough for that. Come; sit with me on the bed."

"No, *grazie*, I am not tired yet."

Dante smiled. Patient.

"Would you," she began.

"*Si?*"

"Would you go to the café and see if they have, *qualcosa*, something, a pastry and perhaps some hot milk?"

"*Si*, Angelina, you are hungry. I will go but I won't be gone too long."

"*Mille grazie*, Dante."

He was out the door.

———

He had always confused her. Because of him, she had looked in the clouded mirror above the basin in the house in San Placido more often, trying to see what he saw. What would make him write letters to her every week without fail? Why would a man cross the street to speak with her? She knew she was not a laughing light girl. She used to think that she might pass her days caring for her mother and working alongside her father until both were gone and the old house was hers and she joined the ranks of the San Placido widows without ever becoming a wife. Though there were men, distant cousins of neighbours, who came to her father's kitchen, for whom she had occasionally cooked dinner. She gave them no thought. The German. He required thinking about. Not tonight. Not now. She decided. There had been no men. Not until Dante.

So, what would make this man climb the mountain? She opened her mouth around the apple and ate it. Rose, and went back to the bed. She stroked the sheets with her fingertips and wondered who would wash them in the morning. She unbraided her hair and let it fall to her waist. It was silky against her skin, rippling around her white shoulders. She unzipped her dress and climbed between the cold sheets, waiting. She lay in her slip, waiting to warm up.

The café must be further away than she remembered. Angelina's breathing deepened and she was, after her exertions of the day, asleep. She did not hear Dante's quiet knock at the door.

"Angelina…"

He waited, standing like a fool in the corridor, a paper bag balancing on a glass of hot milk.

"Angelina? Open the door, my love. It is pouring with rain outside."

"Angelina?"

Dante waited, dripping on the thin carpet outside the door of his bride. He could not force his hand to knock harder. He would not raise his voice. He would not ask the clerk for another key. He took himself off to the small garden courtyard. It was covered and in this weather, at this hour, abandoned. He composed himself to read a days-old newspaper.

The pages wrinkled, noisy in his hands. He still was not used to the span and smell of the newsprint. So many things were remarkable to him. He had been caught in the rain the week before the wedding, a sudden sun shower that startled him and he ran for cover. What was this, falling on his head? Water falling freely on his head. He would have laughed in the next instant and told Sabino the story.

Imagine to be so long in the desert that you forget the touch of rain.

Some creak of the stair, some wind driving rain against the glass near her head, woke Angelina. She was startled and sat up too quickly, bracing herself against swift vertigo. She could not quite get her bearings in the strange room whose floors and walls were suddenly and comically crooked. She braced her hands on the mattress and leaned her forehead against the window. "*Va bene, va bene.*"

There was no ugly, drunk German in the room with her, pressing on her. He was certainly gone to hell. She did not need to be afraid. She told her reflection, do not be afraid. It will be all right.

She was in the room, but where was Dante?

She remembered her timidity, her request for hot milk, for pastry, for anything that would give her a bit of distance and now that she had gained it, it was too much. She went to the door, but Dante was not waiting there. Had he left town? Had he left her? She saw the water pooled outside the door. He was gone. And she was an idiot. In flashes, she imagined heading back to her father's house in disgrace, a wife unhusbanded. She closed the door and turned back to the empty room. Her dress on the chair. Her hairbrush and pins on the small dresser. She saw Dante's suitcase. Perhaps he would come back? But where had he gone?

Angelina lay again on the bed, the thin coverlet over her feet, calming herself.

She still tasted wine on her lips from her wedding supper.

He had walked so long ago, following the switchbacks up the steep mountain path to be with her. He had coaxed her, smiling, questioning, accidentally brushing her hand or arm. She was quiet, still in his presence and certain that he would go back down the path, back to Rome or Spoleto or to war and in any case, not be seen again. He persisted. Her father said, like a bad cough. He was handsome. Though he used too many words, nevertheless his blue eyes wrinkled so kindly at the corners. His hands, in spite of all the hardship of war, things of which he would not speak, were not rough. He would not hurt her. She waited for her husband.

When she heard footsteps coming down the corridor, she rose and moved quickly to the door. She would have opened it, but standing in her slip and uncertain that the footsteps belonged to Dante, she merely waited with her hand on the knob. When it did not turn, when the steps moved past her door and farther down the hallway, her sore eyes dampened. She turned away when again she heard a steady pace coming toward her. This time, she flung the door open and cast herself on Dante and held on as though for dear life.

"*Calma, calma,* Angelina."

Dante caressed her back and neck and kissed her cheeks and eyes. Now conscious of the doors around them, one or two cracking open, he moved, still holding her, into their room. She held him tightly.

"*Signora,* my wife, I beg you, a man must breathe!"

When she stepped back, he pulled her close again.

"No man, in your presence, needs that much breath. *Vieni qui, mi amor.* My love, come to me."

He lay beside her, his arm across the silk of the white slip. He felt new beside her, made new. "*Senti carissima,* you are altogether beautiful. To look at you like this makes me lose all sense."

She looked back at him, her hand on his face, across his brow and on his mouth. Navigating territory newly claimed. Dante reached to turn out the light.

The outline of her thigh beneath the slip against a cotton bed sheet bleached to bright white. She waited for him. The long day dropped off him like loose clothing, the stiff suit and raw wine, then men's rough jokes, jokes he would have laughed at before about the fate of married men, uxorious, spineless, delirious.

Deep night had fallen, covering them, wrapping them and holding them. In the distance the water crashed and clapped down the cliffs of Marmore, resonant applause that rocked against the closed window of the room, misting the glass. Dante cupped his hand against the scar on Angelina's forehead, frowning. She smoothed her palm against his chest, as though soothing him. When she moved, he moved. She lay beneath him, beside him, above him, within him.

Acknowledgements

If I told the truth about Rico, no one would believe me. I'm indebted to him, first and always, for compiling a vast fund of research documents, newspaper articles, histories, videos, testimonials, and personal anecdotes from a variety of sources too numerous to attribute. For such success as I've achieved in rendering the contexts of war, I owe my thanks to the writers whose work provoked and challenged mine, and to my husband for finding them.

Thanks to my family, especially Carla, Paul, Bianca, Claire, and James.

For their good constant company, I'm grateful to my friends Cathy Fairchild, Krystine Mooney, Susan Wi-Afedzi, and Susan Morrison.

Thanks to the Canada Council for the Arts and the Ontario Arts Council for providing financial support for this book, as well as to the Banff Centre for providing time to write.

He moved against her skin, an unfamiliar cloth, neither coarse nor smooth, but alien. Woven by some alien hand. Frictive and enticing to one for whom enticement had been as distant as diamonds from Africa.